THE FATED MAGE

A CARTOGRAPHER'S WAR NOVEL

ALLISON ANDERSON

For Lizzie
Sorry, there aren't any frogs in this book.

TO THE
CONTINENT
The
TALARIA
Draco House
ELEUSION
Hermen
Barclay
ELEUSI.
Olyr

Mist
THE ISLES OF AIGEAN
PECULO
Speculo Hall
The Green Forest
OLYMPIA
Olympia's Royal Palace
Park
TAUROS
Donaldson Manor
CALYPSO
DELPHINE
Iatrus Castle
bia

PROLOGUE: AN UNEXPECTED PACKAGE

Paulo pressed his seal gently into the hot wax. The indigo wax curled up around the metal seal, hugging it tightly. Paulo sat back in his chair to wait for it to set, but his eyes didn't move from the small package. He touched his breast pocket where he had carried the weight with him for months.

He'd wanted to send it before they'd even put Laurel's body in the ground. Before she even had the chance to draw her last breath.

But that hadn't been in the lines of Fate.

He'd watched a hundred different packages be stolen, destroyed, lost, and even misplaced. In one of his visions, a cursed dog grabbed the package and ran off with it. The Goddess could be awfully callous when She wanted to, and it seemed She wanted Paulo to feel every bit of this pain. To leave the nightmares plaguing his sleep only to keep waking to this one.

The wax set, and he pulled the seal away with a *pop*. The twisted lines around the symbol of the sun in the center were slightly crooked, but he didn't care. Penny would know who it was from.

He took the already-sealed letter he'd written and set it on top of the palm-sized package. Digging around in his drawer, he found less than three inches of twine. *Curses.* He pushed himself away from his desk and stood, the crumpled up remains of his previous drafts crinkling under his boots. Jenkins would be a muttering mess when he saw the state of Paulo's room.

Though, maybe not.

The castle had been much quieter of late.

It wasn't the quiet of bated breath or the hush of isolation. No, it was the suffocating silence of heartbreak and mourning. Paulo wasn't the only one who faced every morning with an empty chest. He'd thought he knew what true heartbreak was after Father had died, but this... this devastation had not let up. Paulo understood now why Mater had never relinquished her full-mourning black even after so many years. Paulo likely wouldn't give up the color either if this package didn't make it into Penny's hands. If this one last spark of hope was finally put out.

He stepped into his study and found Mater shuffling through some papers. She looked up when he closed the door behind him.

"Were you able to finish?" she asked. She didn't know the chain of events that would begin to roll today, but she knew Paulo harbored that last spark, and that was enough for her.

Paulo crouched down next to her, pulling open the bottom drawer of his desk and grabbing a fresh roll of twine. "This is the last thing I need."

Mater ran a hand over his hair. She hadn't done that since he'd been a lad, when she'd actually been able to reach the top of his head. She gave him a whisper of a smile. No more words passed between them. None needed to.

He stood and marched back toward his room. The post would arrive in two short hours.

By the Goddess, if the border wasn't still closed, he would march all the way to Faerie on his own two feet. But he'd already gone to the border and not even his connection to Faerie's High Queen could gain him access to the magical land. To the place of impossible miracles and second chances.

So, he found a seat at the window in the front parlor and watched the driveway, doing his best to breathe life into that infinitesimal spark sitting where his heart used to be.

1

THE REBELLION

The branches clawed at Laurel's face. Their knobby fingers and sharp nails caught on the loose hairs sticking out from her bedraggled braid as she raced past the trees. The skin of her palm where it met the bow in her hand was slicked with sweat. Her lungs burned, screaming for air even as she kept her breathing steady. She had to keep it even, sure, calm. She'd learned the smallest noise could reveal her. The crunch of new growth under her boot. The sharp intake of a breath. The snap of a rippling cloak. Praise the Goddess, spring was already well under way, and she didn't need so many noisy layers.

The telltale feeling of eyes on the back of her neck had the hairs on her skin prickling all over her body.

When Laurel's lungs nearly burst, she slid to a stop at the base of one of the large oak trees. Her ears caught every sound, waiting for the thump of footsteps behind her, for the whistle of an arrow's fletching, but there was nothing. She tucked herself closer to the trunk and reached up toward the lowest branch. Careful not to make a sound, she climbed the wide oak tree. The mountains and magic fed the plant life on this isle. Even the forested places within the Continent's borders didn't boast such old foliage. Perhaps the Goddess really had walked these forests before She departed this world. Had these trees witnessed Her passing through?

Laurel shook her head. *Focus.* That feeling of being watched heightened, and she glanced below the tree before she reached up toward another branch.

An arrow sank into the wood next to her gloved hand.

Curses, she'd been so sure she hadn't left a trail. Laurel dropped to the branch she'd been balancing on and sprang toward the trunk, trying to put the tree between her and the arrows.

"Did I nick you, Laurel?"

Laurel checked her hand, and her lungs deflated. "Not this time."

Diana laughed. "I'll need to try harder then."

"Yes, you will." Laurel's mouth stretched into a fierce grin. She pushed away from the trunk, running down the length of the branch until it sagged under her weight.

"Are you insane?" Diana hollered, a laugh still in her throat.

Laurel reached the end of the branch and sprang into the open air. Her feet wheeled as she fell. She hit the branch she'd been aiming for on the next tree over with her gut.

"*Blast,*" she hissed. Her gloves saved her palms from the worst of the tree's rough bark.

"Oof. That had to hurt." Diana's voice rang up from right below.

Laurel gritted her teeth and swung her legs over the branch.

"You didn't break anything, did you? I don't know that my *darling* brother would appreciate me bringing you back in anything less than pristine condition."

Laurel's teeth nearly cracked with the tension in her jaw. It didn't matter one whit how Paulo felt. She was in this cursed mess because of him. Yes, he'd saved her— by the Goddess, she didn't even know how many times, but he had. His mage gift allowed him to see the future and for some Goddess-only-knew reason, he'd been plagued with visions of her for a good portion of his life. Laurel would feel bad for him if he wasn't such a scheming, two-faced, peacock of a man. Before they'd left Olympia's capital two months ago, before the palace had been taken, he'd tricked her into thinking he was nothing but a nobleman in pretty clothing.

She knew better now.

After all, he'd been the one who had puppeteered this entire rebellion. Because he hadn't told anyone about Adira Durant's plans or the fact that the youngest prince of Olympia would become High King of Faerie, he'd made it possible for Laurel to come to Olympia. To be trapped on this cursed isle by an unbreakable geas that would only be satisfied when she killed King Dion. But killing the king had flown out the window once Paulo got involved. She couldn't leave and he knew it.

It was exactly what he wanted.

On some level, she understood it. She understood why he'd allowed things to play out as they had. Why he hadn't let anyone know she'd come to Olympia to kill the king, but that didn't excuse what he'd allowed to happen because of it.

Aspen's screams in the royal sitting room plagued Laurel's days and nights. The glaring light of Luc's death at King Dion's hands flashed in her mind at random moments. How had everything gone so wrong? Aspen was the only family Laurel had left. It was them against the world. But Aspen had kept secrets about what she was doing in the palace, hiding that she was poisoning the queen by lifting her skirts high enough to get into King Dion's good graces and gain access to the royal couple. While the queen wasn't perfect, she hadn't deserved to nearly die. Not by Stellataen Arrow, a poison that tortured a body. It was reserved for the worst of people, not queens caught in the crossfire of a rebellion trying to see her husband dethroned. The queen's despair had been palpable in the cottage they'd gathered in after their escape. The poison had broken her somehow. Taken something from her.

Aspen knew better than to hurt innocents. Laurel had done her best to teach her not to. But the queen's poisoning was more than cruel. It was something Teagan would have certainly done. Something Adira Durant *had* done. It was like Laurel didn't know Aspen at all. Hadn't realized how far Teagan's claws had sunk into her.

Luc's betrayal had only made everything that much worse.

"Do you think Mater already had Cook ready breakfast?"

Diana's voice broke through Laurel's thoughts. Letting herself get sucked into the questions and hurt wouldn't help get her out of this tree. She shook her head, ducking closer to a thick group of branches. "You aren't going to lure me down there with promises of food."

Laurel had been trained better than that. Though, her stomach did grumble at the thought. It was a luxury for her to play guest at Iatrus Castle— not that she had much of a choice. There was nowhere else for her to go. She was no friend to either side of this war, and there were more than a few people in this kingdom that wanted her head on the end of a pike.

And last time she checked, Aspen was one of them.

Sweet Gaia, how had they gotten to this point?

Laurel searched for Diana's head of red hair below. Usually, she kept it concealed under her hood, the vibrant color an easy mark in the greens and browns of the forest.

But no one stood beneath the tree.

"Curses," Laurel hissed. She wiggled her way closer to the trunk, and Diana dropped down onto the limb right in front of her.

Laurel drew her dagger.

Diana only put a gloved finger to her freckled lips. Both MacGregor twins had more freckles dotting their skin than there were stars in the sky.

Laurel slid her dagger back into the sheath at her thigh and listened. After what had to have been a full minute, she finally heard it.

Voices.

"You think The Cartographer is going to let that mage boy keep his castle?" a gruff voice said. The man snorted and spit what sounded like quite the glob of phlegm from his throat.

"I'm not saying I don't know why they sent us to scout the castle," replied a higher pitched voice, a woman from the sound of it. "I just don't know why they didn't send out one of the new recruits. Anyone could do this job."

"Exactly," replied the man. "That's why they sent you."

The woman scoffed as they finally came into view. The pair wore dark-green cloaks matching the foliage around them. They stood at roughly the same height, though the man was much thicker around his middle. They continued bickering as they walked right under Laurel's feet and disappeared.

"Should we pursue them?" Diana asked.

Laurel crept down from the branch. "Yes."

While Laurel thought herself quiet, Diana was practically a ghost beside her. This was Diana's forest, her territory. Laurel had watched her run through these woods over the past several weeks. She knew every branch and every bramble. The first time Laurel had come with her, Diana had pointed out every burrow slumbering critters had been tucked away in for the winter. She'd brought Laurel out once in the middle of the night, and they sat at the banks of the thawing river within the forest until a family of otters emerged from their den. This was Diana's place, and the forest claimed her as one of its own.

However, the feeling of eyes on Laurel's neck remained. She checked over her shoulder and kept her ears both on the rebels ahead and the forest behind.

"How much longer do you think The Cartographer will want us to stay in Eleusia?" the woman asked. "Most of the rebellion has moved northward."

"Yes," the man grumbled, "but they need others to hold the ground we've claimed while The Cartographer takes Faerie."

Laurel bristled. The cursed rebellion. The one led by Adira Durant— The Cartographer. The woman who had sealed her blood with Laurel's on the geas blade that likely still lay in Teagan's desk drawer at Stellatus Hall. Adira Durant was a menace to not only this kingdom, but the one across the sea as well.

The rebels made it to the top of one of the hills, and Laurel knew what they would see. The top crenellations of Iatrus Castle peeked just above the trees. The pair of rebels climbed down the hill, but Diana stopped Laurel before they could go farther.

"We need to tell Paulo."

Laurel bit the inside of her cheek but didn't allow her words to cross over her lips. She could easily take out the rebels. Make sure those looking to scout out the castle knew it was fiercely protected.

But everything at Iatrus Castle had to get Paulo's shiny stamp of approval.

Because if it didn't, it could mess with the puppet master's schemes.

Every move I've made, every future I've altered, has been to save you.

Laurel shook the words from her mind, even as they sank their claws deeper still. She couldn't let his words get to her. Couldn't let them break down the walls she'd fortified between them.

With careful steps, she followed Diana back the way they'd come until they were well out of the rebels' sight. They circled back, headed toward the castle.

"How long do you think until the rebels make a move?" Laurel asked.

But Diana didn't answer. Instead, her head was tilted to the side, eyes narrow.

Laurel's steps slowed.

Before she could come to a complete stop, Diana spun, an arrow already nocked on her bow. Within the span of a heartbeat, she'd turned all the way around and the arrow flew from her fingers.

Laurel drew a dagger from her waist and faced the same way. The only thing she saw was a flash of white disappear into some brush.

"What was it?" Laurel asked, her grip on her dagger tightening.

"I don't know." Diana watched the trees around them. "We should get back to the castle."

Taking up a quicker jog, they raced back in the direction of the castle. It wouldn't do to be caught out in the forest when they knew the rebels were sniffing about.

Laurel checked over her shoulder as they ran.

The trees fell away into open fields and Iatrus Castle stood sentinel in the center of it all. It crowned the top of a tall hill, Lake Luna sparkling to the west of it. It wasn't the largest lake Laurel had ever seen, not as wide as the Black River though certainly not a pond, stretching to either side of the castle. Tall stone walls surrounded the entire castle, a gatehouse at the front and one at the back— which they were headed toward. The outer walls looked newer than the old castle, the stones not quite so gray with age, but Laurel hadn't looked much into the building's history yet to know if they were an addition or not. Olympia's Palace had undergone many renovations since the Faerie Wars, but Iatrus Castle, while still in good condition, was obviously older than the two-hundred-year-old kingdom. Ivy climbed up one of the three towers— one on the northwest side, one on the southwest, and one in the center. The gray stone looked dark in the early morning light, but it would be bright under the sunlight. It was a beautiful building. A tribute to the past and a beacon of the future.

"That's the third set of rebels I've seen this week."

Laurel's chest tightened. "Are you serious?"

Diana gave her that *stop asking stupid questions* look. "I thought they were poachers. I kept coming across tracks, but they never laid traps or left remains of animals behind. I finally stalked the first pair through the woods and found them returning to the river, where a boat waited for them."

Laurel scanned the edges of the forest. The trees lining the fields stood a good half a mile from the castle, curving around Lake Luna in an arc, but it was more than close enough for someone to watch the MacGregors' comings and goings. Close enough for anyone to keep an eye on who was at the castle.

Who else knew she was here?

Did Aspen?

"Come on," Diana said. "I'm sure Mater's already had the table set. If we don't head in, they'll send someone out after us."

Laurel followed her to the castle, her attention never fully leaving the line of trees.

2

AN UNEXPECTED GUEST

PAULO STOOD IN THE PARLOR, WATCHING THE SUN FINALLY CREST THE tops of the trees. It caught Diana's hair as she approached the east side of the castle, turning the reddish-orange golden. Laurel shadowed her, her dark hair soaking up the rays of sunshine. While Diana strode through the gates, Laurel glided in. She stood a few inches shorter than Diana, but Laurel's presence was thick with self-confidence that made her seem taller. Paulo felt his lips twitch upwards. He couldn't take his eyes off her.

"You know, if you keep smiling at her like that, people might start to talk."

Paulo turned to where Mater stood in the doorway. "What if I want them to talk?"

Mater chuckled. "Then you'd best sleep in a full suit of armor."

She was probably right. Laurel would have his head if speculation about them started flying around the castle. Of course, it already was. He hadn't been quiet about his feelings. Jenkins was just very good at keeping talk from Laurel's ears. Paulo would have to give his valet a raise— or perhaps some painting lessons. The man really did need another hobby besides fretting.

"Are you going to finally get over yourself and bridge this divide between you?" Mater asked.

Paulo stopped a sigh before it slipped between his lips. When they'd arrived at Iatrus Castle after the palace in the capital had been taken, Laurel had very quickly let him know she was still upset with how he'd handled things. While she may have said she trusted him, her actions said otherwise. Which was fair. He didn't exactly ooze dependability. Not when he was still trying to figure out how to keep her from dying. The first week after their arrival, she'd disappeared, running about the lower half of the kingdom, trying to figure out how to get back to the capital. Back to her sister. Back to her life.

However, Paulo had needed to intercede. The rebels had her on a list of people to kill on sight. With the Mist dividing Faerie from Olympia having fallen, Teagan had apparently been able to get word to his people. When Paulo told Laurel, she'd been furious.

Was still furious.

And she had every right to be. She just needed to stay out of trouble.

Not that she didn't try to cause enough for Paulo.

He glanced down at the waistcoat he wore. It had originally been a lovely yellow that someone had dyed a horrible shade of putrid green.

Paulo turned back to Mater. "I don't think now is the time." Especially not when Laurel wanted him to tell her things, and there were some things better left unsaid for now. Like the fact that Queen Carnation had lost her babe due to Aspen's poisoning. And the things happening on the Continent.

No. Now was not the time.

Mater huffed. "You can't let this go on for much longer."

A flash of magic passed over his consciousness.

A silver mask.

Laurel on her knees, her face twisted in rage as she was held down.

"You're probably right," he said.

The sitting room door opened, and Diana strode in. Her blue eyes blazed when they met his. Yes, she was still angry at him too. Still fuming that he had made her run from the fight in Olympia. Furious that he had forced her to flee like a scared child.

He was the bane of every woman in his household today.

"The rebels arrived right where you said they would," Diana

said, voice clipped. She was still furious at him for making her leave the palace before the rebels took it. For lording his title over her. He didn't regret it, not when she stood there breathing in front of him.

Diana flicked her braid back over her shoulder. "Not that it would have been difficult to know they were there with the way they jabbered at each other."

Paulo nodded. He'd seen the scouts a couple of days ago. They weren't the first to take a poke at Iatrus Castle's defenses and they most certainly wouldn't be the last.

Laurel slipped in behind Diana, closing the door behind her. Her brown eyes flicked over the room but never landed on Paulo. As if he didn't exist. As if she wouldn't even allow him one second of her attention.

Mater was absolutely right. They needed to talk. Paulo wouldn't stay sane much longer if he didn't have at least a hint of Laurel's regard. A morsel. He'd even settle for a speck.

"How long until they attack the castle do you think?" Diana asked, plopping herself down on the fainting couch across from Mater.

Paulo turned back toward the window, but he could still see Laurel out of the corner of his eye. She settled in a chair next to the bookshelf in a corner of the room. He pushed the longing he felt at the back of his throat deep down so his voice wouldn't betray his heart. "It's still muddled, but I suspect it won't be too much longer."

"Estimate."

Paulo turned at Laurel's voice, but her gaze was not on him. She'd taken up one of the books and was studiously staring at it. If he hadn't already been watching her, he might have questioned whether she spoke at all.

He ran a hand through his hair. "A month at the least. Two at most."

Mater sucked in a breath, the only sound in the room as his words settled over them. He hadn't told her his suspicions, but the day was drawing near. The rebels were coming for the castle. He'd set events in motion, and there was nothing he could do to stop them now.

"How long have you known?" Laurel asked.

Paulo turned back to the window, but his attention stayed riveted to her as it always did. "I don't *know*. I can only guess at the moment."

That got her to look at him. She scoffed but didn't reply. She didn't believe him, that much was obvious. There wasn't much he could get away with when she was paying attention— especially when she was angrier than the rams during breeding season. By the way her eyes narrowed, he wouldn't be surprised if she tried to bowl him over like they did when someone got too close to the ewes.

Mater cleared her throat. "It's a good thing the harsh winter let up early then. The flocks have had plenty of time to graze before we need to bring them into the castle walls."

Paulo's fingers twitched with the compulsion to run a hand through his hair again. There was much to do before the rebels arrived. Would they be able to keep everyone safe? What would be left behind after?

He leaned against the window frame. A small carriage crested the hill at the side of the castle, disappearing as it headed northward. "I've invited Peter and his family to come stay at the castle for a time. He's set to arrive at the end of next week, after Oliver gets back from his honeymoon." Honestly, what man in his right mind took his wife on a honeymoon while their kingdom was under attack? While they may have only gone to stay in one of the hunting lodges owned by the estate, it was still ridiculous.

"Wouldn't you want your *precious heir* far from this place?" Diana snapped. "I don't see the logic in having both of you here risking the sacred family line."

What Paulo wouldn't give to stop all the daggers glared in his direction. He shook his head, stepping away from the window. "Having my heir here is unavoidable since the rebels plan to raze all of Olympia to the ground. Best bring everyone together so we can pool our resources and work as a team."

Laurel coughed, but it was to hide whatever sound had been about to come out of her mouth. Likely a snort or an outrageous cackle. Paulo sighed. Fine, it wouldn't have been an outrageous cackle, but it definitely would have been in disagreement with what he said, whatever it was.

One step forward, one hundred steps back.

A small knock sounded on the door, and Hiatt stepped in. The butler looked about the room before finding Paulo at the window. "Breakfast is served, my lord."

Hiatt had served Iatrus Castle for as long as Paulo could remember. While the butler's hair had grown lighter with age, Paulo had never seen a single strand out of place or a button on his suit unpolished. He was the epitome of everything a butler should be, which was likely why Mater kept him around.

Paulo gave the very polished man a smile. "Excellent. Please let the kitchen know to set out one more plate."

Diana had already taken two steps toward the door but whipped around to stare at Paulo. "For whom?"

One of the footmen, Linus, materialized at Hiatt's shoulder. "Lady Barclay has arrived, my lord."

"Excellent." Paulo swept past Diana. "Have her brought to the dining room. She can break her fast with us."

But before he could make it to the door, the two servants had shuffled back, and a storm of brown skirts and flashing green eyes swept into the doorway.

Lady Dominique Barclay set her hands on her hips. "What nasty game have you been playing, Paulo?"

It had been years since the duchess had used his given name. Paulo paused. His brain couldn't wrap itself around the fact and words escaped him. "Pardon?" he ended up asking.

She pointed a stern finger that made him feel small even though she stood a head and a half shorter than him. "You know *exactly* what I'm talking about, young man. You sent my daughter to that blasted land without my knowledge or permission."

Mater set a hand on Paulo's arm and stepped around him. "Dominique, please come sit with us for breakfast. We've already let the kitchen know to set you a place."

"Don't try to distract me, Luciana," the duchess snapped at Mater. "Your son has caused me months of grief when he could have simply told me what was going on instead of allowing me to run about on a cursed will-o'-the-wisp chase."

Paulo grimaced. "I'm sorry, Your Grace—"

"I don't want your meager apologies. I want you to tell me exactly what on Gaia's blasted green earth is going on with my daughter."

Paulo blew out a breath. "We can speak in my study." He turned to Mater. "Will you have Cook send up two plates—"

"Three."

Paulo turned with everyone else to look at Laurel, who stood only a pace behind him. Her brown eyes met his with a challenge, as if daring him to contradict her.

Swallowing, he said, "Yes, three plates."

He led the two ladies down the hall to his study, the space between his shoulder blades itching. As if their sharp glares were using his spine for target practice.

The door to the study was unlocked, and he held it open so the ladies could pass through. Laurel settled down into the worn leather chair in the back corner. The fireplace slept against the wall to his right, a light breeze sweeping in from the two large windows across the room the servants had opened earlier that morning. The head of the fierce-looking bear Diana had bagged nearly five years ago hung on the wall between the windows, over a handful of bookshelves. Lady Barclay swept past the two red stag heads framing the doorway, one silently bugling above Laurel's head.

Lady Barclay settled in one of the two chairs situated opposite of Paulo's colossal desk.

Paulo shut the door and cleared his throat. "I'm sure breakfast will be up shortly."

One of Lady Barclay's immaculate eyebrows curved upward. "Stop trying to chit chat and sit down." Her eyes narrowed on the limp fern that sat on the corner of his desk. She reached out a single finger, which lit up with her green mage tell and tapped one of the leaves. The little fern sprang up, glowing with renewed health. Lady Barclay's narrowed gaze turned back to him.

Paulo gave a nervous laugh and scurried to his seat. "Your Grace, I know you probably have many questions—"

"No, I only have a very simple one," she said, brushing invisible lint from her skirt. "Why on this cursed planet did you think it was even remotely a good idea to put it into my daughter's head to go to Faerie?"

"While I appreciate your faith in my intelligence, Your Grace, I didn't put the idea in her head."

Lady Barclay flapped her hand at him. "Put away your flippant mask, Paulo. You and I both know you've been playing the game for a long time. I never questioned you about it because I believed you to have at least Penny's— if not the kingdom's— best interests at heart. This is the first instance where I'm questioning that possible lapse in my judgement."

Paulo stiffened. Just slightly. "I do have Penny's best interests at heart. All I've done is give her the best chance for success."

"What success?" Lady Barclay snapped. "You've taken her from her home, from her family. She's the Goddess-only-knows where, and she's completely alone."

"She's not alone."

Lady Barclay stilled. "Then who went with her?"

"The youngest prince's three-headed dog."

"You think a mutant dog is protection from the wiles of the fae across the border?" Lady Barclay blew out a breath from her nose. "You really might be an idiot."

From the corner of his eye, he saw Laurel shift, crossing one leg over the other and settling back further into the chair. She likely agreed with the duchess.

Paulo leaned forward, settling his elbows on his desk. "I can assure you that I only did what I thought would help Penny."

"Help Penny do what, exactly?" She stabbed a finger in his direction. "Don't think you can twist your words in a way that makes it seem like you didn't send her into danger."

His heart twisted. "You're right. I know I sent her into danger, but I know she's needed there. She needed to reach the prince— I mean the High King." He chuckled. "I still haven't gotten used to calling him that."

Lady Barclay leaned toward him. "Are you telling me that you sent my daughter after the Lord of the blasted Underworld? What would he need her for? They've never even met."

Paulo leaned back, straightening the small potted fern. "Are you sure about that? I seem to recall a young farm hand on your lands when I visited not too long ago. One with rather unique amber eyes."

Lady Barclay's mouth was open with a retort, but she froze before words slipped past her lips, her eyes looking beyond Paulo as she searched her mind. "By the Goddess, he was on my farm."

He nodded.

Her gaze sharpened back on him. "And you didn't see fit to tell me the Lord of the Underworld was masquerading as a farm hand in my lands for months? What was he even doing there? The rebellion wasn't even close to taking Eleusion at that point."

"I dare you to take a guess. What would a young prince be doing so far from home?"

She stood abruptly from her seat. "He came to seduce *my daughter?*"

"That's not what I was inferring." Not that her conclusion was completely wrong. The prince had had multiple possibilities pop up on his string of fate after he met young Penny at her debut ball. The man had been smitten from the beginning. But Lady Barclay didn't need to know that. It was probably better for Penny if Paulo tried to subvert this line of thinking. "I believe he arrived after Penny's kidnapping, which was a rebel endeavor if you recall. He likely wanted to question what she knew."

Lady Barclay began to pace behind her chair, her lips crushed into a firm line. "So, he came to woo Penny and take her from me. Did he plan on stealing her away to Faerie as well? Was this all some sort of plot to weaken my position? To tear apart my family?"

Well, Paulo had tried to get her off the crazy wagon. "Why would he try to take her from you?"

She stopped, her skirts twisting around her ankles. "Did you know I was under suspicion as a rebel? *Me?* As if I would join a bunch of morons who think they know how to run a kingdom."

"You mean you don't wish everyone had to listen to your commands and you didn't have to put up with politics?"

Her brows lowered dangerously. "What kind of imbecile do you take me for? If I'd wanted to run this blasted kingdom, I would have taken out all three cursed princes and their loathsome father ages ago. I wouldn't have started a rebellion and burned down my own house to do it."

Paulo raised his hands in innocence. "I would never suspect you to do anything of the sort."

"No, but you allowed everyone to believe it. Even my own child." Her chin lowered further, making her eyes darken. "You could have stopped them. You could have told Penny whatever suspicions that upstart of a prince whispered in her ear were false."

"You're right," Paulo said. "I could have, but what fun would that have been?"

Lady Barclay shot toward him, her hands blazing green with magic. The fern on the desk exploded, the leaves cascading over the top and shoving all of Paulo's ramshackle stacks of papers to the floor. Paulo jumped up from his chair, his magic activating, and time layered over the room a few seconds ahead.

The tumult stopped as quickly as it started.

A thin, silver blade sat just under Lady Barclay's chin.

Laurel came around the duchess, her brown eyes never moving from Lady Barclay's hands.

"Perhaps the upper bailey would be better suited to your temper, Your Grace." Her knife never moved from Lady Barclay's neck. "I hear the gardeners have had a blasted time trying to get the roses to bloom."

Lady Barclay's gaze didn't break from Laurel's, but she spoke to Paulo when she said, "I'll be returning to Eleusia in the coming days. I hope I'll have your support should I need to call on you for anything."

It was not a request.

Paulo came around the desk and laid a hand on Laurel's arm. She lowered the knife, but didn't slip it back into whatever hidden place it had come from.

He gave the duchess a nod. "Of course, Your Grace. I would do anything for you and Penny."

Lady Barclay's eyes still hadn't moved from Laurel. "We shall see, won't we?"

<h1 style="text-align:center">3
THE ABDUCTION</h1>

LAUREL LAID ON THE FLOOR OF THE OTHER SIDE OF THE SERVANTS' DOOR leading into Mater's private sitting room. The woman hadn't allowed Laurel to call her anything else. When Laurel first arrived at Iatrus Castle, she'd attempted to call her "my lady." Mater wouldn't even respond to the title— though if it was because she was unused to being called such or was just to force Laurel to call her by the silly moniker, Laurel couldn't say.

"Luciana," Lady Barclay's voice hissed under the door, "I don't know what to do. I've tried to cross the border to find her, but even with the Mist gone, I can't get past the cursed rebels, and no one will help me. Not Lady Delmar, not the king, and certainly not your little brat."

Laurel bristled. It may have been a bit overkill to have threatened the duchess with a knife to her throat earlier, but something about Lady Barclay attacking Paulo made Laurel want to stab something. If anyone was going to take a chunk of flesh out of him, it was going to be Laurel. Everyone else could get in line behind her.

"I'm sure Paulo did it with the best intentions," Mater soothed. "You know he wouldn't hurt Penny or let anything happen to either of you."

"Oh yes. He looked very concerned when that girl held a knife to my throat."

Laurel grinned.

"Laurel is very protective of Paulo."

"I haven't seen her here before."

"You wouldn't have." A few seconds stretched between them. Mater was likely trying to figure out how much she could tell Lady Barclay about Laurel.

Laurel pressed closer to the door.

"She came with Paulo from the capital," Mater finally answered. "They were there when the palace was taken."

"When I saw him last, His Majesty revealed that Paulo had been paramount to his escape, but he didn't mention the girl."

The king was wise, Laurel would give him that. He wouldn't want anyone knowing one of the very assassins who had helped the rebellion also helped him escape certain death. It also probably wasn't wise to share that she had been out to kill him. She still would be if she thought she could get away with it, but that ship had long sailed into the wild blue yonder.

"She worked in the palace kitchens," Mater said quite diplomatically. Paulo likely inherited his twisty words from her, though Laurel couldn't imagine Mater using them in the same way he did.

"And he brought her here with him?" Lady Barclay asked.

Mater sighed. "I'm just waiting for the two of them to realize how ridiculous they're being and just kiss already."

Laurel's good mood evaporated.

"Oh? It's of that sort, is it?" Lady Barclay's tone turned a bit lighter. "I didn't know what kind of woman he was ever going to convince to look past his ridiculousness long enough to see him as an actual man."

Laurel's fists clenched. It wasn't like that *at all*. Yes, he'd admitted feelings for her, but did she reciprocate those feelings?

Not a chance in this world.

As if summoned by her denial, the kiss they'd shared in the palace all those months ago flashed into her mind.

She shoved the memory down.

Deep down.

"The two of them have been tiptoeing around one another since they got here," Mater said. "It's only a matter of time before one of them capitulates."

Laurel pushed herself up, leaving Mater to fend off any attacks from Lady Barclay that might arise on her own. Not that there likely would be. It seemed the old marchioness knew how to divert a conversation. She was as wily as her children.

The servants' passages in Iatrus Castle weren't nearly as vast as those in Olympia's Royal Palace. Laurel crept through them quickly, jumping into the main hallways every so often. She strode past the door to her room, located just down the hall from Diana's empty one. Diana had taken to sleeping in the menagerie of late. Her anger with her twin was still palpable.

Laurel almost wished she'd taken her up on her offer to bunk out there.

The kitchen was silent when she arrived.

She hadn't known where her feet would take her, but it made sense it would be here. Whenever she was in a foul mood, she usually resorted to tucking herself away in a kitchen. She touched the lead weight hanging from the leather cord wrapped around her wrist. Father had always hidden in their kitchen when he was distressed. Usually because of his greedy, unfaithful wife.

Laurel sighed and sneaked into the pantry, snagging an apron off one of the hooks. The cook at Iatrus Castle wasn't as heavy handed as Cook had been in the palace. Laurel didn't feel the need to ask permission to raid the larder and cook up a storm, though she always cleaned up after herself.

She collected the ingredients for a *karydopita*— oranges, walnuts, breadcrumbs, all of it— and deposited them on the long counter stretching across the room. The cake would be thick and could probably feed most of the servants for breakfast if the castle's cook allowed them to indulge in it. Once everything looked well mixed, she grabbed her last bowl and whipped up the egg whites until they formed stiff peaks, then mixed that into the rest of the batter.

She turned to the warm oven and nearly dumped the bowl onto the floor.

Paulo leaned against the wall next to the oven. His frilled neckcloth from earlier had disappeared and the top two buttons of his shirt were undone, exposing the freckled skin at the base of his throat. He still wore his dark-green waistcoat from supper that night, the little embroidered sheep she knew existed all over the fabric hidden in the shadows. The chain of his pocket watch glittered in the light from the oven.

"How..." She shook her head. Really, she shouldn't be surprised. He'd sneaked up on her before.

His lips tipped up the slightest bit. "What are you whipping up tonight?"

"*Karydopita.*" She pulled a wooden spoon from a bouquet of kitchen utensils sitting next to the stove. He must not have been in the room long. She could usually feel those blue eyes on her. From afar, they looked just like his twin's, that forget-me-not blue. But up close, there seemed to be a shimmer behind the color, like blue tourmalines. She'd seen the gems once, on the ring of a warlord she'd done a job for when she was fifteen.

Using the spoon, she scraped the mixture into the pan, trying not to twitch under his stare. It wasn't so much that it made her uncomfortable. More that she wanted to hide from the depth she often found in his gaze. Like he was a man on the brink of death, and she was the antidote to the poison running through his veins.

He glided from his post near the wall and came up beside her. When she set the bowl down, he ran a finger around the rim, swiping some of the batter still clinging to the edge.

Laurel cringed as he licked the batter off his finger. Slimy, cold cake batter? She could think of a thousand better things to eat— like the cake that came from the batter.

"What?" he asked.

Words sat on her tongue, but she clicked her mouth shut. She didn't need to explain herself to him. He didn't deserve the teasing she wanted to give him. Not when he'd just turn it around on her. This wasn't the palace. He wasn't the masked man, and she wasn't the undercook. She couldn't let herself fall into that trap again.

Those moments died the night Aspen took the palace.

When the queen had finally recovered enough to travel from the cabin in the mountains, she and the king headed southwest, toward the Hermen Family lands closer to Eleusion. Laurel had fled with Paulo south, straight to Iatrus Castle. It had taken them ten days on foot. Ten days of Paulo trying to prove to Laurel why she could trust him. Ten days of her realizing more and more that she really shouldn't. Not when all he'd ever done was play with everyone else's lives. Not when he'd strummed the strings of fate in his favor over and over again.

He was dangerous and he couldn't be trusted. Not with her loyalty and certainly not with her heart.

Which did a little skip when his blue eyes turned to her.

He sighed. "Still a bit angry, are you?"

She grabbed the pan. "I'm not angry."

"That's what women say when they *are* angry."

The fire in the oven had truly sprung to life. She set the pan inside and shut the little door. "I don't have anything to be angry about," she said, wiping her hands on her borrowed apron.

"You have plenty to be angry about." He picked up the bowl and walked it over to the sink.

She ignored his prodding and folded her arms. "I can do my own dishes."

He waved her off, rolling up his shirtsleeves. The faucet wasn't enchanted like the one in the palace, so he had to pump the water in from outside. After a few pumps of the handle, water trickled into the basin. Laurel's mouth went a bit dry at the sight of his toned forearms as he worked. She turned back to the counter and gathered the rest of the bowls before he could catch her gawking. By the Goddess, they were just forearms.

Laurel set the smaller bowls next to the larger one. "I really can do these."

"I know you can." He grabbed a rag from the basket on the counter next to him. "But I got the bowl first, so I get to do them this time."

She sidled up next to him, grabbing another rag. "Well, you can't have everything you want."

Before she could dip it into the soapy water, he snatched it away. "Says who?"

She stole it back. "Says me."

"I don't know that you can claim to be the queen of this kitchen— though we can change that if you want."

"Oh? And how would I acquire such a crown?"

Paulo's lips curved with a smirk. "Considering this is my castle, I'm king. It wouldn't be too difficult to make you queen."

The bowl nearly slipped from Laurel's fingers, but she caught it. Her cheeks heated, and while she couldn't bring herself to meet his eye, she tried to appear nonplussed. "Don't be ridiculous. I could just as easily wage war and take it for myself. A coup is perfectly within my abilities."

She expected him to laugh. He usually did when they went back and forth like this.

But he didn't.

Finally, she looked up at him.

His eyes shone with a miasma of color.

The hairs on the back of her neck rose.

One moment, Paulo was staring past the bubbles in the sink. The next, he spun, throwing the bowl in his hand across the room. It shattered against the wall, right where a shadow had stood.

The shadow turned, revealing a silver mask covering their face.

Laurel charged, sliding a knife out from where she had it strapped to her back. Her heart hammered against her ribcage.

Aspen?

But the schola stood straight, shorter than even Laurel.

By the Goddess...

Nightmare.

Laurel threw the knife and leapt over the table.

Mare ducked under the thrown knife but came up right in front of Laurel when she drew another blade. The schola had always been quicker than the rest of the order, as if even the very air made way for her movements.

Laurel crouched as Mare made a swipe at her face and slipped the knife she had tucked in her boot into her hand. She came up again, the knife angled at Mare's throat.

"Laurel!"

She turned at the sound of Paulo's voice and found him battling against two others. She hadn't even heard them come into the room, their entrance as silent as Mare's had been. They were there to kill her. Somehow, Teagan had turned her own sect against her. Had given her silent killers a reason to find her here and try to kill her.

But where—

Mare shoved Laurel and her lower back smacked against the table.

Before she could right herself, a cloth came around her face.

Curses. She didn't dare breathe in the drug coating the fabric. Holding her breath, she grabbed at the wrists pressing the cloth to her face and pulled the new attacker over her head.

Mare was right there with a right hook.

Her fist slammed into Laurel's jaw.

The last thing Laurel heard was Paulo roaring her name.

4

AN UNEXPECTED
AWAKENING

"*Wake up.*"

The voice tickled Paulo's ear.

He tried to rub at the side of his head with his shoulder, but he couldn't reach.

In fact, he could only wiggle the smallest bit.

"There you are."

He opened his eyes, but he could only make out the faintest outlines of lumps in the dark.

A bump sent his head smacking into something hard behind him.

He groaned. They were in a cursed cart. He could just make out the silhouettes of boxes around them. Canvas stretched taut a few inches above them, concealing the sky and whoever was driving the cart.

Laurel hissed, her breath at his neck. "Don't let them know we're awake yet."

Them. The scholae. He'd known they would arrive that evening. It was the reason he'd made sure to be in the kitchen with Laurel. He'd seen what would happen if he hadn't gone with her. What he'd seen too late was the knockout powder that made him feel like he'd been trampled by a herd of cattle.

He blinked, summoning his magic, but nothing happened. He tried again, blinking into the darkness. *Curses.* There must be charms on the cart or somewhere on his person. He tried to reach out to Laurel, but his hands were tied behind his back. So, he brushed his cheek against the top of her head. "Are you all right?"

She nodded against his cheek, but he could feel the way her heart raced against his chest. They were pressed so close together his bound feet were tangled with hers. Thank the Goddess she was wearing trousers rather than a skirt. They wouldn't have been able to move at all if she were.

Laurel wiggled against him, her shoulders sawing back and forth. If they weren't in the process of trying to escape from what was gearing up to be certain death, Paulo might have enjoyed the proximity... By the Goddess, who was he kidding? It might have been a bit deranged, but he did enjoy being so close to her.

A puff of satisfaction rustled the hairs next to Paulo's ear and Laurel brought her hands between them. She rubbed at her wrists. "Curses, that hurts."

Paulo tried not to move too much as she set to untying his arms. He nearly cursed when the blood made its way back into his hands. Pins and needles stabbed into the ends of every finger.

Laurel grabbed his shoulders. "It's going to be difficult to get our feet untied without them noticing our weight shifting about. I'm going to flip around and untie your feet if you can do the same for me."

He nodded, his cheek pressed against hers.

She released him and carefully twisted in the limited space they had until her boots were next to his chest. He fumbled in the dark, feeling for the knot that would release the rope. Not having his gifts readily available really chafed.

Laurel finished with his feet and patiently waited until he'd finally untied her before she manipulated herself back to where her face was close to his again. "What can you see?"

"Nothing," he whispered back. "Something is blocking my magic."

"Serene." Laurel cursed. "All right, we need to move slowly. If they catch us, we're probably dead."

That could be true. Paulo had seen enough of the scholae through the years to know the assassins could put both Laurel and him out of their misery before either of them even had a chance to plead their case. However, Paulo also knew them in ways Laurel didn't.

"I think we should talk to them."

Laurel flicked him in the forehead. "You're too pretty to be thinking. Just follow my lead and keep silent."

Paulo grinned even though she probably couldn't see it. "You think I'm pretty?"

He could practically feel her eye roll. "I think you're a moron," she mumbled.

Before he could settle on a witty retort— of which about a thousand crossed over his tongue— she squirmed and pulled him along with her. They moved toward the back of the cart, carefully maneuvering boxes out of the way. It would help redistribute the weight and give them a little more time before the scholae realized they'd escaped.

Laurel carefully slid her finger through the seam between the canvas and the back of the cart, allowing a ray of light to stream in. She quickly closed it again.

"What is it?" Paulo whispered.

A knife split the canvas right next to Paulo's cheek. He ducked down as the knife slashed the fabric apart. Laurel reached out through the tear, quick as a viper, and snatched the knife. She pushed through the slit in the canvas, throwing herself toward whoever was on the other side. The cart came to a sudden halt, sending Paulo smashing into the crates at the front of the cart. Curses, he was going to be horribly sore tomorrow.

The clash of steel rang out on the other side of the canvas, and Paulo pushed himself up, tearing the fabric from its hooks. Magic roared back to his senses, layering over his vision.

Chaos met him.

Laurel was surrounded, three masked shadows circling her. She was a blur of movement, the short knife in her hand her only defense against her attackers.

Paulo jumped from the back of the cart, ready to tear them all to shreds with his bare hands.

Two of the scholae materialized in front of him, their steps silent. One was shorter than the other by two heads, but he could see the ferocity in the set of their shoulders. The honed killers within.

Paulo grinned.

They brought up their swords, but Paulo had already moved. He ducked to the right, blocking the shorter of the two fighters from view. Dodging a slice from the tall one, he got close enough to see the intricate carvings of their mask. Silver lips curled to expose large fangs, sharp as daggers, over the mouthpiece. Imprints of scales glittered across the entire thing. They'd gone with the visage of a dragon. Ironic, being from a land that hadn't seen dragons in what had to be centuries.

Paulo saw the schola take a step back. He hooked his foot around the assassin's ankle. The schola easily evaded being tripped, but Paulo was banking on it. The shorter assassin behind them got in the way.

These particular assassins weren't used to working as a group.

They both stumbled over the other, and it only took Paulo's well-timed boot to send them sprawling.

He stood over them, a grin stretching across his face.

Laurel yelped.

He spun toward her and saw one of the schola get her to her knees. Another was holding a knife to her throat.

Paulo's magic surged through his mind as he raced in their direction.

A schola popped out of nowhere, their blade pointed at his gut.

"Mare!" Laurel yelled. "Don't!"

Paulo avoided the blade, slipping right through *Mare's* guard.

But Mare moved in a way he'd never seen anyone move.

She twisted forward, kicking one leg up in the air and with a speed only some of the greatest mages displayed, she was turned around. And completely within Paulo's guard.

A knife grazed his arm, drawing blood.

"I'll kill you!" Laurel screamed, the sword at her throat drawing blood, "I'll kill *all of you!*"

Paulo threw himself out of the way of the coming stab, but he knew it was only stalling the inevitable. They were outnumbered and Laurel was in their hands.

He fell to the dirt, rolling himself up to his feet.

But Mare didn't engage him. She stood, watching Laurel, her head tilted slightly to the side.

The schola that held Laurel also looked down at her, his plain mask hiding whatever he was thinking.

The smallest schola materialized again in front of Paulo, though they kept their distance. "What kind of spell have you cast on her?" The voice was high, almost musical even muffled by the mask. Another female assassin, then.

Paulo's heart beat in his ears as he watched the blade at Laurel's neck. "What? Spell?"

"He didn't cast a spell on me, you idiots!" Laurel snapped.

The shorter schola took a step closer to him. "A person under enchantment would say such a thing. What kind of magic has turned her against us?"

Paulo's hands dropped. "*You're* the ones who attacked *us*."

The tiny schola grabbed a pouch out from under her cloak. An entire belt of pouches wrapped around her tiny waist. She tossed it to the beast of an assassin holding the blade to Laurel's neck. They deftly caught it, dumping the contents onto Laurel's head.

Laurel held her breath, but another of the scholae, a giant of a man, stepped forward and punched her hard enough in the gut to make her gasp, inhaling whatever was in the powder.

"Laurel!" Paulo dodged the other assassins, racing in her direction. He grabbed the man holding her down, using his gifts and the fire burning in his blood to pull him away from her. Paulo had his arms around the schola's neck in seconds, holding him down as the rest of the scholae crept in his direction.

He would need to move quickly. Whatever was working its way through Laurel's system might kill her before he could get through all of them.

"Paulo, quit it! It's not poison."

He stilled, not breaking his hold on the schola even as the man beat into his side. His fist felt like a cursed hammer.

Laurel shook out her hair, sending white powder flying in all directions. She stomped over to him, grabbing his arms and ripping them off the schola's neck. "You can't kill Declan. Not yet at least."

The schola, Declan, rolled away from them, coughing as he tried to suck air into his lungs.

Paulo pushed himself to his feet, grabbing Laurel's arm and pulling her behind him.

She shoved at him. "Knock it off! I don't need you to protect me from them."

He held firm. "The powder in your hair and the blood at your throat says otherwise."

Laurel finally broke away from him, prodding at the trail of blood down her neck as if she hadn't realized it was there. "The cut is shallow. If they wanted to kill me, they would have. You're the one in danger here."

All five scholae stood in a line in front of him. Even though they all wore silver masks and dark clothing, they couldn't be more different from one another. Tall, short, broad, wiry, men, women. All contrasts. All deadly.

The short one stepped forward. "You've been holding Master Schola captive." Her head tilted in Laurel's direction. "The powder is made of rowan shavings, salt, and other things. It dispels most enchantment the moment it's inhaled, but whatever you've cast is far stronger than most enchantments. She's still delusionally trying to protect you."

So they thought *she* was delusional? Well, that would be very easily remedied. Paulo's mouth ticked up. "I do hear true love is the greatest magic of all."

Laurel shoved him, making him stumble a bit. "Shut that mouth of yours, or I'll kill you myself."

"My lady, my tormentor." Paulo grabbed one of her hands and laid it over his heart. "You know your constant death threats only make me yearn for you more."

He could feel the shock radiate from the scholae still watching them.

Laurel glared at him. "Stop being a moron," she hissed, yanking her hand out of his grasp.

"Master?" The tiny schola had taken a step toward them. "You're not under an enchantment?"

"Sweet Gaia, no," Laurel said.

Paulo threw a charming smile on his face. "If anyone is doing any enchanting, it's this ravishing woman right here." He reached for Laurel again but stopped at her glare. If she had a blade, it likely would be pointed at him.

Her jaw ticked, but she turned back to the assassins before she could give him the verbal lashing his ridiculousness warranted. "We need to get a few things straight. Are you all here to try to kill me?"

The four quieter ones remained still and silent, but the smallest answered, "No."

"Did Teagan take control of the sect and order you to come for me?"

The assassin jerked back. "No. We follow your orders."

Laurel's shoulders sagged with relief. "Then, what are you doing here?"

This time, the brute that had been holding her down— Deagan? Derek?— stepped forward.

"We've come, because Stellatus Hall has been taken."

5
THE HALL

Laurel stared at Declan for a few moments before finding the right words, fiddling with the lead weight tied around her neck so it wouldn't rub against the shallow cut on her throat. "What do you mean 'taken?'"

Serene practically bounced on her toes. "The warlords from the south— Palus and Argilla— came a few weeks ago. They took the entire Hall."

Laurel's stomach dropped to her toes. "How? Where were the guards?"

Stellatus Hall, while full of assassins, also boasted a fine security system. There were men and women trained to protect the hall, to guard the talents of those within. They were usually those that hadn't been able to become assassins for some reason. Often it was the loss of limbs or the lack of ability. It was either serve or die with the secrets they'd learned. Most chose the former. Those that chose the latter often didn't have a choice in the first place.

"They overpowered us," Conley said, stepping forward. As her second, it was only right he give her the full report. "Teagan took half the guard with him on his cursed Faerie hunt and left the rest to die. The assassins that could get out simply fled, not willing to fight for our home— especially after the warlords killed all the masters. I don't know if any other scholae were able to get out. The five of us barely escaped before they locked the gates."

"No one tried to scrounge up a group to take it back? Not even the provocationists?"

Conley gave one firm shake of his head. "No, they didn't. We tried to find everyone who had made it out, but they were in the wind."

"How many did you account for?"

"Three dozen."

Laurel nearly tripped in her pacing. "There were nearly two hundred assassins in the hall at any given time."

"Yes, but with Teagan here on the isle with a host of them and the rest out on assignments, the hall was left with only a hundred or so, excluding the children."

Teagan had brought a host over with him? Were they still in Faerie then? She shook her head. *One problem at a time.*

There were two dozen scholae sworn into their sect. Laurel was the only one who knew each of them by name, what their skillsets were, and kept detailed files of each mission they completed. Most of that knowledge was stored in her head, but she'd created a secret system that Conley knew about in case anything happened to her. When she'd left for Olympia, half of them had been out with orders. Three of them were permanently stationed in a few key households on the Continent. Hopefully, none of them had been discovered. Hopefully, the others had made it out and were in hiding.

Laurel took a step toward them. "The children?"

Serene's head hung, her charm-riddled mask shadowed. "There was a massacre, though we don't know everything. We were outside the hall for training when it happened and were able to get out of the compound because of it. But the ones we cut down showed no mercy."

The scholae had an intense training regimen the previous master had instigated that Laurel had kept alive after he'd passed the mastery on to her. They trained for every situation, every weather, every hour. But not for this. Laurel could scream. They were an order of mercenaries. Every man worked alone most of the time and only for himself. None of them would have been able to band together to fend off an attack. Not like what Serene was saying. They would have been sitting ducks.

"What's happening now? Did enough of them get out to rally and take back the Hall?" Laurel brushed past an uncharacteristically quiet Paulo. "Why are you here and not there?"

"You forget what kind of people lived in that place," a soft voice added.

Laurel looked past Conley and Serene to find Cal, arms folded over his chest. The tall schola stared her down, his words echoing in her head. She hadn't forgotten what kind of monsters dwelled in those halls. They would leave their own mothers behind to be slaughtered if their lives or even fortunes were threatened.

She pinched the bridge of her nose. "So, what was your plan?"

"We came to find *you*," Serene chirped. "Though I will say, it's been quite the ordeal to track you down."

Conley folded his arms over his chest. "We arrived last night."

Serene gave a little giggle. "We followed a couple of rebel scouts, listening in for information on the castle when we saw you."

Laurel stilled, remembering the flash of white she'd seen. She glanced at Mare. "You were in the forest."

"Xander nearly took out the MacGregor lass when she shot at you," Conley said.

Paulo tensed next to Laurel, his blue eyes taking on that pearlescent sheen that told her he was searching the future for his twin. His expression didn't waver, so she couldn't decipher whether what he saw was good or not.

"But you didn't reach out until tonight?" Laurel asked.

Serene shook her head. "You were never alone. A captive in the marquess's castle. Mare shadowed you nearly the entirety of today, and it wasn't until you made your way to the kitchen that we even dared approach you."

"Then, you attacked Nightmare," Conley said.

Laurel rubbed a hand down her face. "I thought she was there to kill me."

"Why?" Serene's voice was laced with indignant shock.

Laurel opened her mouth, but Paulo cut her off.

"You know, we really ought to make camp." His face was turned toward the trees on the south side of the road. "We don't want to be caught out here."

Laurel closed her mouth tightly. Paulo obviously didn't trust her scholae enough to tell them Teagan wanted her dead or about what happened at the palace. Not that she even could. The geas kept her from revealing anything about her mission to anyone who didn't know. Her fingers tapped at her leg. She'd have to ask either Paulo or Diana to help her tell the scholae about her time at the palace.

Conley stepped forward. Laurel could feel his gaze sweeping over the marquess. "We're only fifteen or so miles from the castle. We can return there before morning even thinks about breaking."

Fifteen miles? Whatever Serene had used to knock them out must have lasted hours. Was there a charm for such a thing? There certainly wasn't a poison that could do that without some rather uncomfortable side effects.

Paulo's eyes didn't leave Laurel's, even as they transformed with his magic. His mask of indifference slipped for a moment, only fast enough for Laurel to see the line of worry between his brows.

"No, I really think we should camp."

Of course. No one could say no to the puppet master. Laurel sighed. "Grab whatever supplies we have. We'll make camp in the trees and start back for Iatrus Castle in the morning."

While everyone else scurried to grab supplies, Conley remained where he was, his attention fixed on Paulo.

With his mask back in place, Paulo turned toward Laurel's second. "Yes?"

Conley spread his feet slightly. "Who are you to command Master Schola?"

"Me?" A maniacal grin spread across his face. "I'm the madman who's made it his sole purpose in life to earn the high esteem of your illustrious leader."

Laurel snorted, but Conley remained where he was. His chin tilted down slightly.

"Well," he said in his low timbre, "it seems I'll need to keep an eye on you."

"Oh, please," Laurel grumbled.

Paulo's eyes brightened.

Conley remained stoic, but Laurel caught the words he said under his breath.

"Perhaps both eyes."

Paulo grinned. "I like him."

"We'll see how much you like him when he sticks a sword between your ribs." She grabbed Conley's arm and pulled him toward the cart. She needed more information. To know what they'd seen before they arrived in Paulo's march.

"What can you tell me about the border?" she asked. She didn't dare ask about Aspen. Not yet.

Conley glanced behind them, likely checking where Paulo was. "We never made it that far, but we heard enough about it. The rebels are moving en masse toward Faerie. When we arrived, the capital was all but occupied by The Cartographer's men. There were wagons of fair folk coming in and out of the palace all hours of the day, so the rebellion has obviously made it quite far into the kingdom north of us."

Teagan's plans for the fae had already begun. Laurel's stomach twisted as she remembered the little fae boy lying at her feet when she'd helped the rebels attack the watchtowers in Olympia. How many other fae children had been ripped from their families? From their land?

She yanked herself out of her thoughts. "What about rebel occupation farther south?"

Conley gave a quick shake of his head. "The farther you go from the capital, the less there is until you hit Eleusion across the river. The Cartographer's compass is all over Eleusia and the outlying towns. They've got the entire waterway locked down as well. It was a blasted time getting past the Aigeans in the water."

He continued until they reached the cart, painting an ugly picture of the city southwest of them. Laurel almost couldn't reconcile what he was telling her with what she remembered. Eleusia had been a bustling river town, rich with trade and people. The streets had been so crowded at times, Laurel was sure she would get swept away. It had reminded her of Vale, the city closest to Stellatus Hall. There were always people.

But based on how Conley described it, that liveliness and color had been sucked out of the city of Eleusia. The rebels had set up prisons for slaves— mage and fae alike. Instead of farming tools, the blacksmiths' anvils hammered out iron chains. The rebels patrolled the city and the waters. The men and women who ran the town allowed their comrades free reign. There were just as many horrors in the light of day as there were in the deep shadows of night.

Laurel had to keep her face blank as Conley described the atrocities. When he finished the report, she asked, "If we made a play for Eleusia, what do you think the best course of action would be?"

"Declan would be the one to ask." Conley reached under his hood and wiped his gloved hand over the back of his neck. "Why? Are we planning to fight them?"

She shrugged. "Perhaps." If she got the chance to free those slaves, to free those like that little boy...

Conley grabbed her arm. "It would be a suicide mission. We don't have the manpower or the authority. The people being suppressed by the rebels there would just as soon turn on us as they would work with us. You would need someone they respect."

Someone they respect? Laurel straightened. Lady Barclay likely still roamed about Iatrus Castle. Would she be able to help them?

Laurel reached into the cart and pulled one of the packs toward the edge. It held a few bundles of wool. She dropped it back into the cart and grabbed another, finding some rope and a few sacks of beans.

"Where on earth did you get all this stuff?" she asked no one in particular.

Paulo jumped into the back of the cart and shuffled about. "They stole it from my barn."

Laurel dropped the lid of the crate she'd been looking in. "Oh..." Any words she might have come up with fizzled on her tongue. Of course, she shouldn't need any words. She didn't need to justify anyone's actions. It was an assassin's life— stealing when one needed to and doing whatever it took to get a job done. Yet, her gut sat uncomfortably in her abdomen. She grabbed another sack.

Paulo peeked into one of the boxes. "Aha!" He threw the lid off and pulled out an armful of blankets, a hunk of dried meat, and what looked like a bag of—

"Are those biscuits?"

Paulo jumped down from the wagon with his bundle. "Of course they are. Did you really think I would let us get kidnapped without proper provisions?"

The sack fell from her hand. "You knew about all of this?"

That smarmy, silky grin spread over his mouth as his pearlescent eyes glittered again. "Of course I did. Why do you think I was in the kitchen with you?"

She pulled back the sack in her hands and hurled it at him.

Too bad it was full of wool. All it did was bounce off his broad shoulders.

Paulo laughed as he swaggered over to the others.

Laurel grabbed another sack to throw but set it back in the cart as the others turned in their direction.

One of these days, I really might kill him.

6

AN UNEXPECTED RETURN

If Laurel wasn't staring daggers at the back of Paulo's head, he might have thought the morning just perfect.

His plans to gain her trust were working.

Well, his plan to gain the trust of her comrades was going particularly well. Especially after giving them meat. People always said the way to an assassin's heart was through their stomach... or something like that.

At least they'd avoided the rebel scouts spotting them on the road last night. That would have gotten particularly messy, especially in regard to said plans. He couldn't risk the scholaes' delicate trust.

Paulo threw the last crate back into the cart and turned to Xander— at least, he was pretty sure it was Xander— standing next to him. His silver mask was very dramatized, the mouthpiece pulled up into a manic smile that created wrinkles below his eyes that looked like sideways half-moons. There were thick furrows on the forehead as well as a long, slightly pointed nose. It would probably be terrifying if Xander popped out from around a shadowy corner, but in the full light of day, it was comical.

"Isn't your mask terribly uncomfortable?" Paulo asked, checking his pocket watch. It was nearly nine o'clock. The weather had started to warm weeks ago. While the morning might be cool enough, he couldn't imagine having a metal mask plastered to his face in the afternoon.

Xander shrugged. "I'm used to it now."

Laurel came up beside them and dropped one of the crates they'd used as seating around the fire the night before in the back of the wagon. "Give it up. They aren't going to take their masks off for you."

"Why not? Aren't they a bit over the top?"

Her brown eyes, dark as earth and hard as stone, met his. "They don't trust you."

Paulo didn't allow himself to frown. Maybe his plans weren't going as well as he thought they were. "Yet?" he said with what he hoped sounded like puppy-like optimism.

Laurel's brow curved up. "That's entirely up to you."

"Oh? Is there some secret code I need to learn? Some kind of trial I have to pass?"

"Yes, it's called actually acting like a decent human being and not puppeteering everyone to get what you want."

Paulo sighed. "Laurel..."

"*Paulo...*" She walked to the other side of the cart, giving Paulo a glimpse of the thin scab along her neck that she'd received the night before. Declan was lucky Paulo hadn't stabbed him.

"You know you can trust me."

Laurel huffed a sardonic laugh, grabbing one of the blankets he'd brought from the castle. "Can I?"

He circled the wagon, following her to the other side as he scratched at the bandage wrapped around his forearm. "I didn't think me being prepared for the chill of the night would warrant such complaint."

"That's not what I'm complaining about."

"I would hope not, especially after how you snuggled close to me last night."

While her expression remained impassive, the lightest tinge of pink stole across her cheeks. "I was not *snuggling.*"

Paulo grinned. She had absolutely been snuggling, and they both knew it. He'd woken early that morning to Laurel pressed tightly against his back. His heart had nearly burst out of his chest at the contact. While they'd all slept somewhat close that evening, they hadn't been touching when they settled for the night. Not until she'd gravitated toward him. Or him to her. However it happened, she'd ended up right behind him, her nose practically tucked into the crook of his shoulder. He didn't know what he would have done— turned around and wrapped his arms around her, pressed a kiss to her soft hair, moved away— if he hadn't caught the glint of Conley's mask next to the fire. The schola hadn't been joking when he said he'd be watching. Instead, Paulo remained where he was and had dozed off and on until dawn. Laurel had woken and nearly leaped over a sleeping Nightmare in her haste to put distance between them.

She narrowed her eyes. "Stop smiling like that."

His grin only deepened, and she spun away with a huff. At least she wasn't as unaffected as she pretended to be. Just one step closer to "weaseling his way into her heart" as Diana would say. He'd never thought that euphemism as derogatory as others did. Had they seen weasels? They were adorable with their wispy little whiskers and tiny ears. Father had given Diana a brown and white one when they were younger, and Paulo had spent just as much time as she did with it wrapped around his shoulders. The little beasts could burrow themselves into his heart any time they wanted to.

Maybe Laurel wouldn't mind a weasel. Paulo pushed his magic forward, looking through the future of that decision.

Laurel will hold the white weasel by its scruff, her nose crinkled. She will look to Paulo, asking what she's supposed to do with it.

Paulo blinked his magic away. No, a weasel wouldn't do. *Pity.*

He continued to trail Laurel as she rounded up her men and the last of their supplies from the ground. They all convened at the back of the cart, and Laurel looked over them with a critical eye.

"With only the cart and two horses, we'll have to do rotations, so no one gets too tired, especially after the fight last night." Her gaze stopped on Nightmare. "Mare, you and Cal take first turns in the wagon. Conley, you and I will take front. Declan, you drive." Conley took a step forward, but Laurel raised a hand. "He was the one who took the hardest beating last night."

That was apparently all the explanation the second in

command needed. Paulo glanced over at Declan, who stood stoically by the wagon. He looked unruffled, but there were sure to be bruises from the fight he'd had with Laurel.

Next, Laurel turned to Paulo. "You'll sit up with him."

Paulo shook his head. "I'm more than capable of walking on my own two feet."

"Those fancy boots of yours say otherwise."

Paulo looked down and noticed his now-scuffed black boots. The mouth of the boot was made of supple brown leather, which stopped just below his knee and covered the top of his calf before meeting the polished black leather of the rest of the boot. Jenkins was going to be quite cross when he saw the state they were in. Paulo had gotten them a couple days ago.

She was right. They would blister his feet miserably. He pushed his gift out, looking for all the ways his walking would go wrong.

He will trip and gouge his knees.

Blisters will blossom all along his heels, taking an entire week to finally heal enough for him not to wince every time he slipped his feet into shoes.

His foot will be run over by the wagon when he's not paying attention.

He hadn't expected all the ways it would go *right.*

A silver mask unbuckling from a hood.

A smile tugged at the corner of his mouth as he released his magic. "I couldn't allow myself to ride, not when the others have traveled so far. It wouldn't be right after all the lounging I've done around the castle the last few months."

A couple of silver faces tilted to the side. He could feel their curiosity. After all, what marquess thought about anyone else's comfort? Not that Paulo had much choice when it came to thinking about everyone else. All he ever did was think of others. Sweet Gaia, even now he was preparing for the wearying day ahead of him, but he would enjoy this morning as much as he could.

Laurel gave him a shrewd look, like she knew exactly what his game was but couldn't call him out on it without looking a little crazy. And she would. These assassins hadn't been exposed to the full scope of magic like she had. While they would believe their leader, it would still be odd for her to tell them he was trying to play them. Well, she could, and it might turn their loyalty back to her, but they might not be happy to walk the entire trip.

Paulo folded his arms over his chest. "I'm sure I can walk a handful of miles without too much cause for concern."

Laurel shook her head in exasperation. "Fine. Serene, you walk with him in back, and Conley and I will take the front. Xander, you sit up with Declan. We're fifteen miles out which won't take us more than four or five hours to get back. We can switch at the hour mark, so we aren't all worn out by the time we get to the castle."

The scholae followed Laurel's direction without hesitation. While Conley might have been ready to challenge her order, he was quick to follow Laurel's command and get into position.

Laurel took her place at the front, standing beside Conley. The scholae hadn't had much of a chance to speak the night before apart from getting the broadest information about what happened to Stellatus Hall. Laurel was likely trying to gather as much information as she could before they arrived back at the castle.

The wagon started rolling forward, the wheels creaking their objections like the joints of an old man. Paulo sauntered behind, doing his best to make his steps as comfortable as possible. It probably wouldn't keep him from getting blisters, but it might lessen the severity of them. Hopefully.

"You really ought to have ridden in the wagon, my lord."

Paulo turned to the sprite of a girl walking next to him. "Just Paulo, if you don't mind. And why is that?"

"Because now everyone is going to be watching you to see if you falter. They're measuring you."

Paulo chuckled. "I didn't know walking would warrant such attention."

She looked up at him and he caught a flash of her eyes behind her mask. They were such a dark brown they almost looked black. "You challenged Master Schola."

"By walking?"

"By not doing as she ordered."

He looked up to where Laurel still grilled Conley, who was nodding sharply at everything she said.

"Conley was going to challenge her," he pointed out.

"Conley's her second. He's supposed to challenge her, especially when he knew she was going to walk to give Declan, who would have been fine to walk, the chance to rest. He did it out of deference to her. You, however, did it out of stubbornness."

Paulo shrugged. "Stubbornness is one of my best qualities."

Serene walked several paces beside him in silence. He couldn't tell if their conversation had simply come to an end or if she was mulling over his words. Either way, he didn't do well in silence, at least, not with silence he hadn't manufactured.

He kicked a stone ahead of them on the path, hitting the back wheel. When he looked up, he saw two silver masks pointed in his direction. There was something about being scrutinized by a person who knew how to kill you in a hundred different ways that made the hairs on his arms stand up. He waved at Nightmare and Cal.

"How are you not dead yet?" Serene asked, though he couldn't tell if it was actually directed at him.

He answered anyway. "I have an uncanny knack for getting out of potentially life-threatening situations."

She looked him up and down. "Obviously you have some kind of magic. Even if I hadn't seen you fight, your eyes give it away."

"Ah, yes, my tell." He often cursed the pearlescent sheen his eyes took when his magic was in effect. He hadn't been able to get away with simply watching the future play out in front of him instead of listening to his tutors, and they often thought he was cheating on his tests.

But Serene shook her head. "Not just that. All mages have very vibrant eye colors. The fae claim such bright coloring in their genetics, but mages all have it too. It's how you can see through a glamour. The eyes say it all."

Paulo opened his mouth, then shut it. She was right. All the mages he knew did have strikingly bright eyes, like gems. "How did you learn that?"

She straightened the thick belt around her waist, which hung heavy with baubles and pouches. "My parents were Sireadh. Any good trader could spot a mage a mile away— though I've only ever seen a handful of you on the Continent. Most of your kind remain here on the isle. The magic doesn't work as well across the sea. Something dulls the magic or connection to the Goddess or something."

Hadn't Paulo felt the same? His magic wasn't as strong in the capital as it was when he was home, away from everything else. It was especially strong near Barclay Manor, where the Barclays had continuously poured magic into the ground.

"You're quite the well of knowledge," he said. "Laurel is lucky to have you, and I can't imagine how invaluable you'll be while you're here. Sweet Gaia, you probably know more than I do. I hope we can all come to a place where we trust one another and can work together."

Serene's attention returned to the cart in front of them. Had he pushed her too far? He allowed his magic to surface, looking ahead a few moments. Fragments of the future flashed in front of him.

Serene, ignoring him for the rest of the walk.

Laughing in his face.

Slapping him with a charm that would make his magic go haywire.

Unclipping her hood from her mask.

The girl was mulling over his words. Paulo bit back a smile and let the magic fade. He pulled at the collar of his shirt. "My, it's awfully warm out here. While the sun is good for the plants, I don't imagine it will be too much longer before we'll all be sweltering."

Serene's gloved fingers twitched. "Is the heat normal for this time of year?"

"I'd say this is mild. Come summer solstice, my sister and I will often gravitate to the cold room in the castle kitchens just to escape the oppressive temperature." Paulo rolled up his sleeves. "Luckily, the castle gets enough of a breeze that you can often shed some layers."

"Not much of a breeze here." Serene tugged the gloves from her fingers. Paulo tried not to stare at the long dark hands covered in thin, pale scars. The whole tip of her right ring finger was missing and ended in a nub at her first knuckle. She tucked the gloves into her belt, wiping her palms on her dark pants.

Paulo pulled his watch out from his waistcoat. "If Laurel's predictions are correct, we should hit a stream in three hours. She's a smart woman, your master."

Serene stared up at him, her fathomless eyes taking him in. "You're actually in love with her, aren't you?"

"I am."

"Oh, curses. There's no point in wearing this blasted thing if you can see the future and your heart is set on her." She reached up and the hood fell back, revealing black, kinky hair that seemed to have a life of its own as it sprang up from Serene's scalp. The silver mask pulled away to reveal a woman with a wide nose and round cheeks. Her plump lips pulled wide in a smile, flashing the charming gap between her two front teeth.

She groaned. "By the Goddess, that mask was suffocating!"

Paulo tried to push at least a little sliver of surprise onto his face, even if there actually wasn't even a speck of it in his body.

He'd seen Serene's face before.

His magic slammed into him.

Serene's charm-covered mask, bobbing through a maze of trees, eyes set on flickering torches. She walks past a tree and comes to a stop. A man stands under one of the large oaks, a black seal skin wrapped around his waist.

Paulo blinked the vision from his sight and pulled a lazy smile onto his face. "It's a pleasure to finally meet you." He held out his hand. "I'm Paulo."

Serene giggled when she placed her hand in his, and he pressed a light kiss to the back of her knuckles.

"And I'm Serene."

He released her hand without dropping his grin.

Yes, he'd seen Serene's face before.

He'd seen all their faces before.

7

AN UNEXPECTED HOMECOMING

A line of silver masks march down the road. Six faces turned away from the castle burning at their back.

Paulo nearly sighed when Iatrus Castle finally came into view. The afternoon sun hung high above the towers, making the scene almost picturesque. A scene from a dream. If he didn't know what was waiting for him behind those gates, he might have even sung. But that might have been his feet talking. The sores around his heels and on the tops of his feet burned from being ruptured five miles back. He'd likely have to burn his socks and hide his boots in the back of his closet. He didn't want to look at them again.

The blisters almost were enough to overpower the throbbing in his head.

After seeing Serene meet with Caspian in the forest, he'd searched the other fates of the scholae.

And every single one of them were much the same.

Mare stabbing one of Iatrus Castle's guards in the neck and racing out of the castle gate.

Declan taking a shell from the hand of Caspian Delrio.

Conley swinging a case full of weapons onto his shoulder and abandoning Laurel bleeding out on the carpet of Iatrus Castle's sitting room.

Xander with the fletching of an arrow at his cheek as he aimed at Laurel's chest.

Cal watching Paulo's family foam at the mouth over their breakfast plates through a cracked door.

Each and every one of them had the potential to betray them. To leave Laurel behind or outright kill them all.

And all of it rested on the fact that Laurel hadn't earned their trust.

Laurel will stand in front of her silver-faced scholae, awaiting their judgment as Diana tells the tale of her failure to kill the king.

Conley will ask her to give the scholae time to deliberate.

A blade sinks into Laurel's throat.

Paulo kneaded his fingers into his temples. He needed to get to the castle. He needed to sit in the cave and let the magic show him what he could do. Needed to take off these blasted boots.

Laurel fell back from the front of the wagon, her brows still pulled together in a frown whenever she saw Serene's exposed face. The petite assassin had been bounding about the wagon all day, talking the ear off anyone who would listen. At the moment, she walked beside Mare, who silently listened as Serene kept up a steady stream of words.

Paulo sidled up next to Laurel once he caught up to her, trying to keep his voice quiet as he said, "There's more than enough room in the back of that wagon for you."

She glared at him. "I'm not going to sit up there like a porcelain doll while the rest of my sect walk. Besides, I need to talk to you."

He pulled on a flirtatious mask to cover up his wince as he stepped on a rock wrong. "Missed me, did you?"

"Yes, like I miss the pox." She grabbed his arm. "Listen, I've been speaking with Declan, and I think if we play our cards right, we could get Lady Barclay to take back Eleusia."

His chest tightened as magic tried to bloom behind his eyes. He pushed it down. "What do you mean? We can't send Lady Barclay on a suicide mission."

"Obviously we would help her come up with some kind of strategy or at least lead her in the right direction. Declan is a provocationist. He can help her come up with a plan."

Paulo hummed, staring at the back of Declan's head. "Like Luc?"

"Yes, like Luc. They were actually from the same town even." She seemed to shudder. Would that make him more motivated to betray her? Would he be the most dangerous out of the bunch? Paulo's magic stirred again, but he would wait until they returned to the castle.

"Anyway," Laurel continued, "he could help her take back her city while she waits for Lady Penny. If all goes well, she would be able to dismantle the hold the rebels have this far south, and they would be spread out. It would make it harder for them to turn on Delphine."

Paulo finally allowed his magic to surface.

Lady Barclay, huddled in a room with thick curtains, measuring out small seeds and placing them in envelopes scattered all over the floor.

Long vines shooting out between cobblestones, wrapping around a man wielding an iron ax.

He blinked the magic away. "I think giving Lady Barclay a nudge in that direction would be wise."

Laurel pinched her lips together. The answer was vague, but she wouldn't press him on it. Not right there. Not with the scholae sniffing at him. He was counting on it. He'd need to study the fate lines out more. Talk it over with Lady Barclay. He wouldn't send her into danger. He wouldn't do that to Penny.

As if feeling Paulo's need for an easy escape, Serene skipped up to them, nearly tripping on her unlaced boots. "How mad do you think your guards will be when we show up? I'm sure they were fretting over where you went. I'm surprised we didn't even see any search parties on our way out."

"Why would we have seen search parties?" Laurel asked from where she walked beside him. She hadn't allowed him to walk with anyone else. Her obstinance even forced Paulo to take a turn in the wagon simply to make sure she got some rest. Stubborn, untrustworthy woman. It wasn't like he was plotting against her.

Well, perhaps he was working against her sometimes, but it was for her own good and they both knew it. She just wanted to keep being muleheaded about it.

Serene spun back toward them, continuing her skipping but backward. "We abducted their marquess right from the castle. Someone should have noticed."

Laurel's eyes snapped to his face. "You didn't tell her?" She looked at Serene. "He didn't tell you?"

"Tell me what?"

"About my magic." Paulo smothered a dark chuckle. "I can see the future."

Serene froze mid-skip, her foot hovering off the ground. "The future? As in what's going to happen? You saw us arrive? You saw all of this?"

He shrugged. "The most important bits." *And everything else.*

But he wouldn't say that. Some people couldn't wrap their heads around Paulo's gift. Sometimes, it was easier to let others draw their own conclusions instead of trying to explain how it worked.

Especially those with possible intents to betray the master of their sect.

A curse slipped from Serene's tongue, her floating foot joining its partner on the ground. "You mean we could have avoided all the cloak and dagger and simply walked in, and you would have let us?"

"Would you have just walked in without thinking it was a trap? I thought you all believed I was using sorcery on your master." Was that what had brought on the vision? He would have thought the scholae understanding the relationship between him and Laurel would have eased fears and brought them to their side.

She lifted a defensive finger but paused. "Conley certainly wouldn't have. He would have thought it was a trap."

He leaned in as he passed by her. "I know."

She gasped. "You mean you knew Conley would think it was a trap? But that's not what happened!"

Laurel sighed. "He can see possible futures as well. But trust me, it's not as mighty as you think it is, so don't get any ideas about Paulo being some great mage or anything."

Serene caught back up to them. "But he can see the future!"

Paulo's chest tightened as he thought about all the destruction his gift had wrought. About how one of his best friends now found herself in the middle of a war in a kingdom that would scorn her for her magic. How he hadn't been able to keep Queen Carnation from harm. By the Goddess, he really needed to talk with Laurel about what Aspen had done. How he hadn't been able to save the queen's child.

But his other best friend now waited for him within the castle walls. Perhaps now wasn't the best time.

He shook his head, pulling a smile onto his face that felt as frail as porcelain. "Laurel's absolutely right. It's not as amazing as it sounds."

When they were only a little way from the gates, they opened without Paulo calling for the guards. The thick wooden doors swung inward, and Paulo found himself face to face with Mater.

Her brown eyes passed over him and looked over the party at his back. "Is this everyone then?"

He pressed a kiss to her cheek as he passed by her. "Yes, Mater."

"Excellent. I've had the rooms readied and baths drawn. Jenkins is waiting for you in your rooms, and Dominique has requested an audience before she heads out tomorrow morning."

"Thank you, Mater. Did our other visitor arrive?"

Mater's eyes pinched at the corners. "Yes, I left him in the drawing room and had his servants head to the kitchens to get sorted."

Paulo blew out a breath. "I'll see him first."

"Come along," she called to the scholae, as if gathering chicks rather than a crew of deadly assassins. "I've had Cook prepare a light lunch, so you all don't have to starve until supper. If anyone needs to see the infirmary, we can head there after we eat."

Paulo could hear Serene's voice behind him as he left.

"And you said his magic wasn't mighty."

He almost didn't hear Laurel's reply.

"I never said there weren't perks."

He smiled as he walked up the front steps.

The front door opened just before he could reach it. A pair of blue, bloodshot eyes met Paulo's under a curtain of limp, brown hair.

"Hello, Donnie."

Donnie had never looked so severe in the entire time Paulo had known him. His pallor was pale, the golden hue of his skin sickly with stress. The cut of his clothes fit loosely on his shoulders, not to mention the dust that covered most of him. The man looked like he'd been rolling around a forest, which he had in some ways. It was a two-day ride from Donaldson Manor.

Donnie's expression grew darker as he took a step forward. "Did you know?"

Paulo closed his eyes, keeping his magic at bay and clenching his hands by his side. "Yes, I knew."

The punch to Paulo's jaw came fast and quick. He fell back, staggering on the steps behind him. His vision blacked out for a second, but he did his best to keep his feet. Someone grabbed his arm, keeping him from toppling into a heap. He blinked the spots in his vision away and found Laurel there, her eyes fixed on Donnie.

"How could you not *tell me*?" Donnie cried. "How could you not warn me that they would take *everything* I've worked for? I thought I was your friend!" He took another step forward.

Before Paulo could open his mouth, Laurel was between them, her hand still gently wrapped around his arm.

"You got in one lucky shot," she said, "but that will be your last."

Donnie's jaw tightened, but he took a step back. If it had been anyone else but Laurel, he might have fought his way for another piece of Paulo. But Donnie held a noble respect for women, and he would never harm one intentionally— no matter how seething mad he was.

He pointed a sharp finger at Paulo. "You are a liar, Paulo MacGregor. You're a liar and a blackguard."

"I'm sorry, Donnie."

Donnie let out a bark of a laugh, hurt and pain rippling through it and stabbing Paulo straight in the chest. "No, you don't get to say sorry. You don't get to brush away the fact that you didn't at least let me know the rebels were coming for Tauros. People, good people, *died* on my vineyards. Hundreds of years of carefully grown vines burned to the ground. Everything I've worked for my entire life, gone."

With a whisper of skirts, Mater came up next to Donnie. "What's happened to your home is awful. I'm so sorry for all that you've lost." She wrapped an arm around him, turning him toward the door. "Come, let's get you inside. You deserve a rest, and Paulo's face will look much more satisfying in a few hours when the bruise has finally purpled."

Paulo held back a groan. Only Mater could make something so gruesome sound so comforting.

But Donnie nodded and allowed her to pull him back inside.

The scholae remained on the front step, their masks shadowed by their hoods.

Laurel turned to face him. "Are you expecting anyone else to come looking to attack you in your own home, or have we finally reached a quota?"

He rubbed at his jaw, doing his best not to look at the silver faces behind her. "I'm sure there will be more."

"Sounds about right."

His feet and head still ached even after a hot bath and a liberating amount of salve slathered over every inch of his skin, but he wouldn't keep the duchess waiting. He kept his steps sure as he strode over the carpets of the castle hall toward his study. Praise the Goddess it was only around the corner. If he wasn't on a mission to figure out what each of the scholae was up to, he would have ordered his dinner brought to him there. The temptation picked at his resolve until he turned the corner.

Laurel leaned against the wall outside his study, her hair braided back away from her face and a clean shirt hanging down over a pair of leather breeches. Sometimes, he didn't know whether to thank Diana or curse her for exposing Laurel to that particular article of clothing.

Her dark eyes looked up at him. "Even with that nasty bruise marring your face, you clean up nicely," she said. Her eyes widened, realizing what she'd said out loud.

"Do I?" Paulo preened, straightening his lapels and flashing her a smile— though his face hurt enough that it probably was only half as bright as he wished it to be. "I'm glad you think so. I was starting to believe I was going to have to try something else to garner your attention."

She pushed away from the wall with a huff. "Don't let it go to your head or anything."

He chuckled. "Too late."

Before she could come up with another retort, he opened the door to his study.

Lady Barclay sat behind his desk, a ledger settled in her lap and a cup of tea steaming in front of her. Paulo didn't even flinch at the fact that the duchess had made herself very at home in his study. He took a seat in one of the chairs across the desk, sticking his feet out in front of him and slouching into the back of the chair. His feet protested the movement, but the pain settled after he did.

He waited for Laurel to take her spot by the door once more, but she didn't even look at it as she strode across the room and slid into the chair next to him.

It was to be a dual attack on the duchess then.

Lady Barclay closed the ledger and set it on the desk. "The blacksmith within the village is overcharging you for horseshoes." She didn't mention the bruise still darkening on Paulo's face, but he did see her eyebrow twitch up just a fraction at it.

Paulo settled his hands over his stomach and rested his head on the back of the chair. "Yes, but I'll happily pay him for those horseshoes and the information he passes along with them."

Lady Barclay's lips turned up. "It's good to see you aren't solely relying on those powers of yours, my lord."

"I can't see everything all the time. It's best to delegate where I can."

Lady Barclay hummed her agreement and took a sip of her tea. Her jade eyes shifted over to Laurel. "And what has he delegated to you?"

"Me? Why, I'm the court jester, of course."

Paulo choked on a laugh.

Lady Barclay looked at him with raised brows. "Clearly, you're very good at your job."

"Laurel's humor is an acquired taste." Paulo cleared his throat. "However, her quick mind also benefits us in other ways."

"Us?" Lady Barclay asked.

"Indeed. I think she's helped come up with something that will be mutually beneficial."

Lady Barclay set down her teacup. "And what would that be?"

Laurel leaned toward her. "The way you're going to take back Eleusia from the rebellion."

The duchess's keen eyes sharpened. "I'm listening."

Paulo sat up straighter in his chair, withholding a wince. "Laurel and I left the castle to collect a friend of ours. He's someone who specializes in physical and mental warfare— especially to ignite unrest within highly populated areas."

"A provocationist," Lady Barclay cut in. "Yes, I know what you're talking about."

Laurel's head tilted slightly. Lady Barclay must have read the question there. "It's only been five years since the Tyrant King was finally deposed by his sons, but many of us lived under his reign for most of our lives. Before King Dion even dreamed about wiping his father's existence from this earth, there were those of us preparing to do whatever it took to get rid of him. We reached out across the sea, knowing there were those on the Continent who would make the Tyrant King disappear."

"Why didn't you do it then?" Laurel asked.

"Unfortunately, we didn't know about Adira Durant. She had already established a relationship with the assassins of Stellatus Hall. We were discovered and many of us died because of it." She looked to Paulo. "It was your father that saved me. He and I were the only ones who weren't found out, and it was because Lord MacGregor saw that we would be discovered. He was able to warn me in time, but our comrades fell. The former Lord Abrams, Duke Speculo's younger brother Lord Samos, and Lord Nikitas all were killed."

"I'm sorry to hear it," Paulo said.

Lady Barclay shrugged. "We all knew it was a risk, but we

were given a responsibility along with our titles to protect our people. All of us saw the doom the Tyrant King was leading us to. We did what we could at the time."

"But my father saw the princes rise up," Paulo pointed out. "Why not just wait?"

"He hadn't had that vision yet, as King Dion was only a boy of fifteen when we started. Your father had the first vision of the princes' coup the next year, which was the only reason we waited so long afterward."

"And why not just take the throne for yourself before the princes had a chance?" Laurel asked.

Lady Barclay pursed her lips. "While I'll admit that I don't think three boys who can't control their vices should have any command over a kingdom, I know the Goddess had better plans for this kingdom than I could have ever helped Her attain."

"Why do you say that?" Paulo asked.

"Look at where we are." She gestured to the room, but Paulo had a feeling that wasn't really what she was referring to. "We have a king who can strike fear into the hearts of many yet chooses peace at every turn. Because of his brothers, we have—well we *had*— peace between three kingdoms that have regularly been at war for hundreds of years. By the Goddess, I'm sure the princes' births wouldn't have even been a thought without the Goddess's hand in all of it. It wasn't until the Tyrant King that the other kingdoms even looked our way, and their attention only increased after Prince Evan then the youngest prince were born. The borders that separated us were thin even when the Mist was up, and now that's even gone. The Goddess's children have never been closer than we are now, and it's because those princes were born."

Paulo allowed the duchess's words to sink in. King Dion was a man of peace. The last five years of his rule had been riddled with strife, but nowhere in any history books that Paulo had read were there so many instances of the kingdoms interacting with one another. Not since the Isles of Aigean split away from Faerie, and that had been nearly a thousand years ago. The Faerie Wars had only further separated them. Hate and prejudice had wormed its way into the hearts of all those that lived on these isles.

And the Tyrant King had changed that.

Maybe he was good for *something*.

"While the history lesson is enlightening," Laurel interrupted, "we're in the house of an oracle. We should be looking to the future, and that future includes you taking your duchy back from the hands of the rebels."

Lady Barclay nodded. "You're right. Fetch your man. I'm eager to hear what he has to say."

Laurel stood and glided from the room. Paulo allowed his magic to come forward, watching as she strode through the castle and found Declan huddled with the other scholae in her rooms.

Lady Barclay's voice distracted him from the vision. "You know, I'm surprised by you."

Paulo pushed his magic away. "Your Grace?"

She pointed toward the door. "That girl is obviously far more than she appears. I imagine it won't be long until I hear tales of assassins running amok in our kingdom— Sweet Gaia, at least on our side of things."

"And you're surprised she's here with us?"

Lady Barclay snorted a very Penny-like snort. "No, I'm surprised you think your peacock mask has any sway with her." She pointed at his pinstriped jacket and floral waistcoat.

He chuckled. "It doesn't. At least, not in the way it does with other ladies."

Her expression remained unimpressed. "Then why are you giving her any reason to think you aren't worth her time?"

Paulo tilted his head.

"Don't play the stupid fop now." She leaned toward him. "We are at war, Paulo. A war that my daughter, the princes, you, and that girl are all playing a role in."

He gripped the arms of his chair. "I'm well aware."

"Then take off the mask and prove you can be trusted with the responsibilities of your title and gifts." Her green eyes flashed. "Do it soon, or you're going to find yourself on the other side of this war with a battered soul and more bruises than the one on your face."

8

THE MASTER

The grinning fool's mask of silver will stop at the edge of Lake Luna, the shine of the moon on the water casting wild shapes onto the mask. From his pocket, the schola will draw out a small pouch and slip it into the water. When the moonlight finally disappears behind the trees, a black shadow will break from the water. The selkie's two, obsidian eyes will blink up and narrow, but the creature will slip back into the water for a moment. Not two minutes later, the selkie will reappear, a white shell balanced on the tip of its nose.

LADY BARCLAY LEFT TWO DAYS AFTER LAUREL HAD BROUGHT THE SCHOLAE back to the castle, taking the plans Declan had proposed to reclaim her lands with her. Laurel had poured over every detail with her, knowing she couldn't prepare the duchess for everything, but could give her some direction. Hopefully, Lady Barclay could make the best of all of it.

Laurel tied off her boots and stood from where she'd been sitting at the vanity in her rather expansive rooms. Even her quarters back in Stellatus Hall hadn't been so luxurious as the ones here. The servants' rooms were even nicer at Iatrus Castle than they were back at the palace, though it was probably due to the fact that Iatrus Castle boasted half the staff the palace needed. And the lord of the castle could also see any future problems and keep on top of maintenance. How no one could really see past Paulo's fake exterior, she would never understand.

Grabbing her jacket from her bed, she strode out of her rooms. Her fingers tapped the weapons attached to her body; three daggers strapped to the outside of her right thigh. A long dagger on her left, a garrote wire in the seam of her trousers, and her jacket had one tiny dagger tucked into the back. There wasn't a cloud in the sky when she walked outside, which would be perfect for the events she had planned for the afternoon. She rounded the corner, pausing outside Paulo's study. The door was closed, though she could only guess if he sat on the other side or if he was running around the castle. She never knew where he would be at any time. The man ran about on a schedule that she wasn't sure even he understood.

She shook her head and continued walking. Hopefully, he was far from the castle. She had too much to do without worrying about him popping up and ruining her plans. Perhaps she should pray he was gone for the whole day.

When she finally reached the training yard, thoughts of Paulo had almost faded from the front of her mind. The ring of steel drew her to the sparring area, and she watched as Mare knocked her opponent to the ground.

One very blue-eyed, red-headed opponent.

"What are you doing in the ring, Diana?" Laurel asked, stopping at the edge of the circle.

Diana rolled to her feet, as if she hadn't just been dumped on the ground by a woman half her size. "Training of course." She dusted off her trousers and drew closer to Laurel. "Isn't that what training areas are for?"

Laurel rolled her eyes. "You know what I mean."

Conley stepped out of the shed situated against the house, arms heavy with weapons. It looked like it had once been a gardener's toolshed but had been converted into a pseudo armory for the training area.

He dumped the weapons on the ground. "These need to go."

Diana squawked, descending on the pile like an insulted seagull. "What do you mean they need to go?"

Conley toed the edge of one of the short swords. "None of these weapons are worth practicing with, let alone having the honor of severing a soul from a body." He went back to the shed, Diana chasing after him as she strapped her quiver to her back. The weapons expert was in for a treat if Diana decided to actually fight for the contents of the shed.

Cal sprinted from the direction of the front of the castle, arms laden with heavy sacks. He'd probably found them in the stables. He ran all the way around the training area and turned the corner on the other side of the castle.

Declan arrived a few seconds later in much the same situation, though he only had two bags on his shoulders where Cal had four.

"He's right around the corner, Dec!" Serene called. Laurel looked and found the woman sitting on a bench near the archery targets. She was still the only one maskless. It was unbelievable that she'd let Paulo trick her into taking her mask off. Though, Laurel really shouldn't be surprised. When Paulo wanted something, he knew how to get it.

"Where's Xander?" she asked.

An arrow sank into the grass between her feet.

She glanced toward the tree line and barely made out where Xander sat in a thick oak. The shot must have been close to five hundred feet or so, but she'd seen him make a shot nearly a thousand feet with accuracy.

Mare glided past Laurel and slid onto the bench next to Serene. A slim notebook and wood shavings sat between Serene's loosely tied boots. She never tied them as tightly as she should.

Having the scholae at Iatrus Castle was like watching two worlds collide. Laurel could feel the tug in her bones as she tried to fit herself back into the mold of the person she was before leaving Stellatus Hall all those months ago. But she no longer fit, and she didn't know how she would be Master Schola and this new Laurel she was still trying to come to terms with. The one who had failed her mission and left her sister behind. The one who had followed a man she wasn't sure she could trust.

Laurel came around the other side of Serene but didn't sit. "What new charm are you working on now?"

Serene nudged the notebook with her toe but didn't look up from the carving in her hands. "I'm wondering about blocking someone from seeing the charm holder's future."

The revelation of Paulo's gift had obviously done a number on her. Hopefully, the Sireadh blood she boasted about did hold some of that discerning power her people were known for—whether it was good or bad for Paulo.

Dozens of scribbled runes covered the page Serene used as a reference. The largest one, which looked the closest to what Serene was whittling out of the block in her hand, was an intricate mess of knots. It would be complicated to get just right for the charm to work, but if anyone could pull it off, it would be Serene.

Cal's form came around the castle once again.

Laurel stepped away from Serene. "All right, gather up."

Without hesitation, every single one of the scholae dropped what they were doing and lined up in the middle of the arena. Even Declan arrived a moment later, his heavy cargo falling from his shoulders onto the ground. Diana joined the lineup, grinning like a madwoman. A quiver of arrows peeked up above her shoulder and a bow dangled from her fingers.

Laurel stood before them, feet wide and hands behind her back. She met the eyes of each schola. Studied each of their masks. None said a word or moved an inch. Not even Diana. The only movement Laurel made was the flick of her eyes. She felt their appraisal just as much as they likely did hers.

She clenched her fingers tightly behind her and took a step back. "Diana."

The scholae didn't move, though she felt surprise ripple through them as Diana broke rank.

Diana turned to face them, mimicking the stance Laurel had just eased out of. "Your master has asked me to speak on her behalf this afternoon. There's something you all don't know and I'm the only one who can tell you."

That certainly got their attention. Laurel refrained from rolling her eyes at the trademark MacGregor dramatics. Their gaze flicked back and forth now, and a line formed between Serene's brows though Laurel was sure a few of them frowned at her behind their masks.

"Get on with it," Laurel ground out.

Diana set the tip of her bow in the dirt. "All right, Laurel isn't able to talk to all of you about the cursed luck she's had in our beautiful kingdom because she's under a geas."

Laurel rolled her eyes. "They already know that." It was a regular practice in Stellatus Hall. She knew each of them had entered into a geas at least once since she'd taken over.

"Can't even revel in the dramatics," Diana huffed. "This particular geas was made with Adira Durant, leader of the rebellion in this kingdom. She made a deal with your assassin boss man for a bunch of slaves in exchange for Laurel killing our now king before he got his crown."

Diana retold Laurel's story— in much Diana fashion. From the moment Laurel arrived in the city of Eleusia to the time she jumped through the portal with Paulo. Diana skimmed over the details of nearly everything and told the basics, holding back the small details Laurel had asked her to keep out of the telling. Like the part where Laurel got Luc killed. That particular fact still sat like a rock in her stomach, one she wasn't quite ready to pull out and look at yet.

Four silver faces flashed in the light as they leveled on Laurel. Serene's eyes were as wide as the others.

"You failed," Declan said.

Laurel gritted her teeth. "Yes."

And failure in the scholae was unacceptable. Especially from a master. Masters were supposed to be above reproach. She was an elite assassin, one who had never come back from a mission without having completed it. It was the main reason she'd wanted to gather them together today. She wished to lay her failures before them. Give them the chance to decide what they wanted to do. She couldn't return with them to the Continent. She couldn't rejoin the rebels and take the rest of the isle. She couldn't kill the king.

"Not that she had much of a choice." Paulo sauntered out of a shadow next to the castle wall.

Sweet Gaia, she really should have prayed he was away from the castle. The scholae all set their hands to whatever hidden weapons they had on their persons. Paulo's words might have been light, but even Laurel had heard the threat in them. This wasn't Preening Paulo but Predatory Paulo. It was another mask, but it wasn't something to be taken lightly. She knew that for certain.

Paulo cut right through the middle of them, a smirk playing on his lips. "Don't mind me."

"We never do," Diana retorted.

Cal stepped out of the line. "What do you mean when she didn't have a choice not to fail?"

Conley's head whipped in his direction, ready to put him back in place.

"It's fine, Conley." Laurel raised a hand, stalling his reprimand. The disrespect wasn't the worst she expected to come from her confession— though it was surprising it came from Cal. The man often kept his words more to himself.

Paulo straightened the lapels of his jacket and puffed out his chest. "I'm so glad you asked. Laurel here has the great misfortune of being the sole subject of my devoted attention and found herself in quite a bind when I didn't allow her to kill my monarch."

Laurel sighed. "You couldn't have said it any other way?"

Paulo grabbed her hand and held it to his heart. "I'm just speaking the truth."

Laurel yanked her hand away. By the Goddess, the man was incorrigible.

A chuff sounded from the lineup. "You mean to say *you* actually foiled our master's plans?" Declan asked.

Paulo grinned. Laurel knew that grin now. It was a taunt of a thing as much as it was an expression of absolute delight. It was dangerous.

She clapped her hands together. "Enough. Yes, Paulo was a part of why I was unable to complete my mission, but it's more complicated than that. Once I figured out what Adira Durant had planned, I realized I couldn't go through with it."

Cal scratched at his neck. "So you went against orders."

Laurel nodded. "I did, and I don't regret it, even if it's made it impossible for me to leave this isle."

"This is a lot to take in," Xander said.

"I understand." Laurel bowed her head. "I don't expect you to follow in my footsteps and abandon our order. However, I hope you'll take the time to consider my actions. I truly believe what I've done is for the best."

The scholae stood quietly, their stares a weight on her shoulders. She couldn't expect them to understand. Couldn't expect them to simply forgive her. She'd broken promises. She'd failed. Their judgment was justified.

Another clap echoed off the castle wall, this time from Conley. "We all need time to digest, and we're not out here to stand about. Xander. Nightmare. Grab some swords and set up in the ring."

Conley's words broke the spell and the scholae quickly found other things to occupy themselves. But Laurel knew it was only a matter of time before they made a decision. What it would be, she could only guess. They could leave her behind and join the rebels with Teagan. They could attempt to take her as they had earlier and chance the consequences. They could kill her.

"Is her name actually Nightmare?" Paulo asked, practically out of the blue.

The question jolted her out of her ruminating. Her attention strayed to Mare in the sparring ring. "It's the only name I've ever heard her called."

"Were her parents so cruel?"

Laurel glanced up at him. His brows were low with concern. She would have laughed if her stomach wasn't still in knots. "I don't think she ever knew her parents. There are quite a few who make it to Stellatus Hall on their own."

"Not like you."

"No," she said. "Not like me."

Mare had arrived years before Laurel did. If the rumors around the hall were true, she'd suddenly materialized inside the compound. They found her in the kitchens one night. The entire hall took turns helping the cooks prepare meals, and the head cook thought some of the younger assassins had been stealing.

Many of the assassins ended up being reprimanded even though they all pled innocent. It took the masters three weeks to catch Mare. She'd been sleeping in one of the crates in the larder.

A light breeze ruffled the open collar of Paulo's shirt. "How did she become a schola?"

Laurel pushed a stray hair from her cheek, tucking it back behind her ear. "You saw the way she can move. She can fit through any size hole. Can squeeze into the tightest of spaces. They call her Nightmare because she can appear like an apparition and leave just as quickly. She's known for being the best thief on the Continent."

Paulo wiped a bit of sweat off his neck. Some of it glistened on his brow as well. "I thought Stellatus Hall only focused on assassinations and murder plots."

"She's the only one who can get away with saying no to Teagan. I was there the very last time he attempted to give her an assassination contract. I was eleven. She disappeared for six months, but somehow, every day, Teagan would discover a letter on his desk. Her refusal, over and over again, until he finally gave the contract to someone else. That was when the previous Master Schola invited her to join our sect."

"Was the previous Master Schola better than Teagan?"

Laurel snorted. "Great Goddess, he was probably worse, but not in the way you think. He was difficult and borderline psychotic."

"What does that mean?"

She tried to figure out how to explain what the previous master had been like. Perfection to him had never been a matter of if but *when*. He drilled the scholae every hour of every day. If they didn't do it the way he wanted, they continued to drill until they could do it perfectly a hundred times in a row. And when one of them challenged him, he would show them exactly what perfection looked like himself and make the challenger do things two hundred times. But because he held them to such a high standard, they wanted to do it.

"He made us believe we could be better than we were," she said, "and when we gained whatever scraps of his approval we could get, it felt like being blessed by the Goddess Herself. It was worth every single bloody knuckle and broken bone— at least to me it was."

Paulo didn't look away from her as she spoke, and she had to turn away before a blush could spread up her neck. By the Goddess, she couldn't look at him when he stared at her like that.

But he wouldn't let the topic drop. "Why did he leave?"

Laurel shrugged. "He didn't tell me. I woke up one morning to find him in the middle of the training room, alone. He challenged me to a duel."

"And you won?" he cut in.

"Absolutely not. Fighting him was like fighting the elements of nature. He nearly killed me. At the end, I thought he would. I thought I'd done something to earn his ire and would meet my end. Instead, he stopped fighting and told me the scholae were mine to lead. Said he no longer belonged at Stellatus Hall and simply vanished. He left me everything he had— his rooms, his things, even his money. He's one of the reasons why I'd been able to save up so quickly for mine and Aspen's contracts."

"I bet Teagan wasn't happy about that."

"He wasn't." In fact, he had expected to be put in charge of the scholae, even though he wasn't one. When he found out, he punched a hole through a wall. It was one of the only times Laurel had ever seen him lose his composure. Had seen that cool mask of his slip to reveal the vile creature she knew lived beneath.

"Why didn't he just take the sect from you?" Paulo asked.

"And risk the wrath of the scholae?" She shook her head. "He knew better. No one but the master knows every identity of the scholae, so he couldn't even be sure who he would be up against, though I know he had his suspicions. Instead, he just made me his plaything. With his hold on my contract, he could make the scholae his own personal minions. We guarded him while he was at the hall, and I had to fight tooth and nail for him not to send them on missions that weren't within the confines of our oaths."

"And what about the others? Are all of you under Teagan's thumb?"

A chuckle that sounded a bit more self-deprecating than she would have liked hummed from her chest. "That particular honor extends only to me and Xander."

"Then why do they all stay?" he asked.

"Actually, you are looking at five of the most elite scholae, which is likely why they were able to escape and make it to us."

She introduced each of the scholae in front of them, starting with Conley, her second. He was the oldest of the group and was one of few assassins in Stellatus Hall that had joined as an adult. He'd been a warlord's general for years before that. He could name and knew how to build or buy every weapon Laurel had ever read about. His expertise with weapons made him a critical part of their group as he could equip any member of the sect with specialized weaponry.

The next most senior was Declan, who was the sect's provocationist. The man had singlehandedly started and ended three different wars in the last ten years on the Continent. Laurel had to quiet her voice as she spoke about how quickly his mind could work, how he could dissect how exactly a group would fight. Though he had no mage gifts, it was like he could see exactly where each move would take them.

Then Serene, the enchantment expert. Her role was the most obvious as her mask was absolutely riddled with charms. She'd been one of the only ones in Stellatus Hall with any knack for magic. She'd been known to have a few charms do the exact opposite of what her contractors had said. It was one reason the previous master had recruited her. Her moral compass, while skewed, had given him reason to believe she would thrive with a little more structure.

Xander was the sharpshooter. Laurel had seen him shoot wings off a bee at a hundred paces. He was cool confidence and humor bundled into one handsome package. When she'd met him, she hadn't understood why he'd chosen the mask of a fool, but as she'd gotten to know him, she'd realized it just fit him so well. He was transparent and quick with a quip.

"Then there's Cal," Laurel said, "the poisoner."

Paulo frowned. "I thought you would have been the poisoner."

"Cal is actually known as the best in Stellatus Hall. While I can give him a run for his money, the man has created concoctions that will melt skin off bones and kill a man in seconds. His mentor was the one who discovered the poisonous properties of Stellataen Arrow. Cal's only a couple of years older than I am, but he was the one who taught Aspen and me when we were starting with poisons."

"So, they already had a poisoner when you were inducted in?"

"At first, I thought it was my propensity for poisons that had caught Master Schola's attention, but he told me why a few months after."

"Are you going to make me guess?"

"I figured it wasn't too hard." She smirked.

A light chuckle rumbled from him, and he tapped the side of his head. "Your mind."

"Yes. I'm the only person in Stellatus Hall that can memorize everything I've ever read or look at a map once and know every detail drawn on the page. I'm practically a walking library, which Master Schola believed was being wasted on the missions Teagan sent me out on."

"He saw your brilliance and decided you needed to be a part of what he was doing. But that still doesn't answer the question of why the others stick around."

Laurel sighed. "Each of us has our reasons for doing what we do. I can only guess at the others' motivations, but I can't imagine better or more talented people to work with. Each of us comes with a certain set of skills that sets us apart from the rest of the assassins, makes us both an idol and a threat. There's protection in what the scholae offer and sometimes that's enough."

"Is it enough for you?"

Laurel opened her mouth to answer, but no words came. A year ago, before she had arrived in Olympia, she would have said no. She would have said that she wanted to be free of all the chains that leashed her to Stellatus Hall. She'd had every intention of passing off the mantel of Master to Conley. He was a natural leader with the men and women they worked with.

But looking at the last few scholae she had, knowing the lengths they'd gone to seek her out, she didn't know if she could give them up so easily.

Declan sauntered toward them, his hand around the handle of a rather wicked-looking ax. His gaze was trained on Paulo. "I find it hard to believe you're the one who stopped our master from completing her mission. All I see is a fancy buffoon in a castle. I think there's more to this story you all aren't telling us."

Conley stood from his crouch next to a pile of weapons, gaze flicking between Declan and Laurel.

Laurel's heart skipped in her chest. She wasn't ready to talk about Aspen or Luc. She wasn't ready to bare her soul. Not yet.

Paulo brushed at the silk of his bright-pink waistcoat. "I may be a fancy buffoon with a castle, but I'm a fancy buffoon who also knows how to beat every single one of you in that ring."

An eye roll threatened to break, and Laurel had to tamp it down. "By the goddess."

Declan's knuckles went white around the ax handle. "As if you'd risk getting that pretty jacket dirty."

Paulo's mouth stretched into a wicked smirk. "I distinctly remember a certain someone taking a few nasty hits the other night. Would you care for another demonstration?"

"And we're done here." Laurel grabbed Paulo by the sleeve of said pretty jacket. She would have grabbed his collar and shook him like a naughty pup, but she knew he wouldn't have even budged. He fit in right alongside Conley and Declan in breadth—which was already a bad combination. The two of them fought like bulls. Throwing Paulo in the mix would likely end up with internal bleeding.

"Ah, see?" Paulo drawled, "She doesn't think she can take me either."

"Shut up, you idiot," she muttered.

Conley stepped forward, coming to Declan's side. "You would have us question our master's abilities?"

Paulo tapped the stranglehold she had on his sleeve. "I think we really ought to give them a demonstration."

Laurel yanked him forward, back in the direction he'd come in. "I think we really ought not to." What did he think was going to happen? That he would prove his mettle to her assassins? That he would win them over that way? If that was what he thought would impress the scholae, he was delusional.

Before she could take another step, he slipped from her grasp.

She spun. "What are you doing?"

His hand came up, brandishing a knife like the ones she had strapped to the outside of her thigh. She reached down and counted two. There had been three.

"Give it back." She held a palm out.

He dangled it in front of her. "Come take it."

Laurel glanced over at the scholae. Six sets of eyes were trained on her again, their practices put to a full stop. Serene and Cal stood on either side of Declan now. This wasn't how this afternoon was supposed to go. She was supposed to bare her sins to them but keep up a show of strength. To prove she was still the same master as when she'd left them, but make sure they knew she respected them. Was it Paulo's sole purpose in life to humiliate her? To not just make her feel like a failure but show the rest of the world that she was one? What would it take for him to finally give up this game?

Laurel dropped her hand. "I'm not going to fight you, Paulo."

"I didn't say anything about a fight." He flipped the knife over his shoulder. It sank into the dirt behind him. Xander and Mare had left the ring, joining the others around Declan. "You can get the knife whenever you want."

Her eyes narrowed. Everything was a game to him. A way to show that he knew better than everyone else.

She nearly turned around, but Conley shifted his weight, drawing her eye.

"You really shouldn't leave that blade in the ground like that," he said.

Which Laurel immediately interpreted as *please show this preening peacock what fighting a scholae looks like.*

She blew a breath out her nose. "Fine."

Paulo grinned as she shucked her jacket and stepped into the ring.

"I really don't want to do this." She drew two more blades from the sheaths on her legs and twirled them in her fingers, feeling the balance of the blades she recently had crafted. Conley was absolutely right in saying the practice weapons in the shed were paltry, though not the worst she'd ever fought with.

"I know," Paulo said. His hands dangled loosely at his sides, but the magic in his eyes swirled. He was ready even if he didn't look it. If she watched, would she be able to get a glimpse of whatever he was seeing? How would it feel to have the future at her fingertips? No, she couldn't even fathom it, and she didn't really want to. She was looking at the product of such a gift— a man who played with people's lives and pretended to be someone he wasn't.

Diana gestured for the scholae to join her on the benches situated around the ring— as if preparing for a good show. "Show him what a master looks like!" she cheered.

Laurel took a deep breath and leaped forward.

But Paulo was already gone.

She twirled, following the flash of his dark purple jacket. He hadn't even taken it off for the fight. Her dagger followed him, going in for a slice where the buttons glimmered.

But her blade only met air.

"Really?" Paulo whispered in her ear. "Going for the buttons is a low blow even for you."

Laurel spun the dagger in her other hand and stabbed behind her.

He was already gone.

She whirled. "What are you playing at, Paulo?"

He stood a few paces away, still between her and the dagger sticking out of the dirt. "Who said I'm playing at anything?"

She gritted her teeth and feinted left before striking right.

But of course, he saw it.

He grabbed her wrist, using her momentum to spin her around until she was fully in his arms. He plucked the dagger from her hand and sent it into the dirt next to the other one.

"Keep the rest of my daggers out of this," she said, elbowing him to get him to back off. He did and she faced him once again. "I already know I'm not going to win this fight."

He dodged one jab, then the next. "Perhaps this little display isn't for you."

She glanced over at the silver masks lining the ring. "They already know you can beat them in a fight. You can quit playing with me now."

The playful Paulo fell from his face. Laurel nearly flinched as he charged her.

She leapt to the side, but he saw that coming too.

He grabbed her, spinning with her as they both fell to the ground.

She wrapped her arms around him.

But he already had a blade to her throat.

The very blade that had been in her hand.

In the next heartbeat, he flicked the blade to the side, and it sank into the ground right next to its siblings.

He stood up, offering his hand to her.

Her chest heaved, fire building up in her throat, but she took his hand.

He didn't let go as he turned to the scholae. "I know you're used to being the best, but this war is about to teach you the expertise you claim on the Continent means little to those who can snap their fingers and command the earth to swallow you or can walk through fire."

"Says the man who probably hasn't had to fight for anything in his life," Declan said.

Paulo ignored the jab as seamlessly as he had the ones Laurel had made with her daggers. "This isn't a mission to sneak into a house and slay a warlord in his sleep or stir up unrest in a quaint little mining town in the mountains. This isn't a skirmish between two greedy merchants looking to take out the competition." Paulo hauled Laurel behind him, his grip on her hand unrelenting even if it wasn't painful. She could feel the magic radiating off him.

Paulo stopped right in front of Declan, standing only a few inches taller than the other man, but he made it look like a foot with his stare. "You've walked into a war, one that will decide destinies and see those you love ripped from you in the blink of an eye in unimaginable ways. I suggest you take whatever ego you think you have, lock it in a box, and bury it even deeper than whatever issues you've been suppressing because you'll find out very quickly that no one here cares about you or your shiny little mask. That there are bigger monsters on this isle than the ones you whisper about to scare your naughty little ones on the Continent into being good."

Declan's chest rose and fell evenly, but anger practically poured off him.

"By the Goddess," Laurel wiggled her hand free and shoved both of them. "Enough. The rest of us came out here to stretch our muscles, not judge a posturing contest. Both of you, get back to doing something productive before I give you something to do."

Paulo broke away from said posturing, but it certainly wasn't because he felt outdone. Declan's eyes narrowed behind his mask as Xander came and pulled him in the other direction.

Laurel folded her arms over her chest. "Are you going to tell me what that was all about?"

Paulo leaned down until his lips were nearly touching her ear.

"I wanted to make it very clear to the scholae who plan on betraying you that they know their hours on this planet are numbered."

9
AN UNEXPECTED INTERVENTION

Paulo sat at the breakfast table, staring down at the plate in front of him. The egg remained unbroken in its little cup and the sausages on his plate had grown cold. Even the toast had sagged a bit against his plate. But he couldn't pick up his fork.

A hand settled on his arm, and he looked up to see Mater next to him. It was only the two of them in the breakfast room that morning. Donnie was still sleeping off whatever he'd imbibed last night. Diana was still avoiding Paulo at all costs. The scholae had already come and gone an hour ago as he'd seen last night.

So it was just him and Mater.

She gave him a single quirk of her brow, but he just shook his head.

His magic flashed.

A stack of envelopes, carried on Hiatt's favorite silver platter.

"Is it good?" Mater asked.

Paulo blinked the magic away. "Depends on your definition."

The door opened almost exactly two minutes later. Hiatt strolled in, silver platter aloft. Paulo let out a long breath as the butler reverently set the stack of thin envelopes on the table beside his untouched plate.

"Thank you, Hiatt."

The butler disappeared, but Paulo didn't touch the envelopes. He already knew what each of them said. Had watched them be penned the moment he'd seen his messenger walk away from Iatrus Castle nearly a month ago.

"I see the duke's seal on that envelope," Mater said coyly.

Paulo sighed. "Have at them. I can't find the appetite for food or rejection today."

Mater snatched up the first envelope. "Lady Nikitas does have the loveliest handwriting." She used her butter knife to slice open the edge of the envelope. She never had been able to open letters like a normal person and break the seal. The cream-colored paper slipped out and Mater unfolded it. As she read the letter, her brows slowly drew together.

"She won't send any men to aid us?"

Paulo gestured to the rest of the pile. "You'll find much the same from everyone else. I believe Lord Discordia's letter will be the most interesting read, but the rest of them are quite short."

There would be no help coming to Iatrus Castle.

The rest of Olympia was under fire just as much as he was, but he'd sent the letters anyway. Praying one of them might help, he'd written two dozen letters to the highest members of nobility, the ones seated on the king's royal council. He'd also written to several of the lesser nobleman who had large estates in northern Olympia but not much political weight. Everyone was under fire from The Cartographer's rebel horde. All of them.

The only person he didn't write was Lord Hermen. The man had enough on his plate as it was and wouldn't be able to help Paulo now. He'd taken on caring for the king and queen after their flight from the capital, which was no small thing. Not that he wouldn't be playing some key roles in the coming fight later, but the Hermens needed to focus on the queen. Needed to help her come to a better place after what happened to her babe.

Paulo took a sip of his orange juice as Mater ripped through every single envelope, her frown deepening with each letter.

When she finally set Duke Speculo's down, she looked up at him. "Not a single house will help us?"

"Not a single one."

He'd been completely right. The only house he had at his disposal was Stellatus Hall. Now, he just needed to convince all the scholae to rid themselves of their traitorous tendencies and help him win this war.

Totally doable.

Paulo sat in the sitting room, staring at the ceiling above him. Mater had a decorative paper put up when Paulo had been a boy, and he'd spent countless hours staring up at it. Tiny bunches of blue flowers peeked through long leaves, turning the ceiling into a flowerbed of forget-me-nots. There were three hundred and fifty-seven of the little flowers and five hundred and twenty-one leaves. He'd stared at this ceiling enough to know. It was certainly a style choice; one he'd seen popularized by the nobility over the years. He wouldn't be surprised to find it was the Barclays who had made it such a trend. The iconic Lady Barclay could be blamed for many of the latest fashions. Like the empire silhouette now decorating so many of the ball gowns he'd seen in the past two years.

Night had fallen already, but he knew tonight wouldn't end anytime soon. He just prayed Laurel had fallen asleep quickly so he wouldn't have to wait forever.

Not when he had traitors to deal with.

After Laurel's decision to confess to her scholae, the possibilities for betrayal had only expanded. Each one seemed worse than the last.

Mare disappearing from the castle without a word, pale hands caked in blood.

Xander meeting Caspian at the edges of Lake Luna and taking the shell.

Serene with the selkie in the woods outside Iatrus Castle on the outskirts of a rebel encampment.

Conley taking control of the scholae and abandoning a bleeding Laurel just before a battle.

Cal poisoning Laurel in her sleep, leaving her there for Mater to find.

Declan attacking Laurel on the castle wall and hanging her body from the castle's central tower.

The visions whirled in his mind, playing over and over again with only the slightest variants. Dinner had been a near disaster as he was nearly so distracted he almost dumped his wine glass all over Donnie's soup across the table. Donnie's perpetual frown had let up for one second when he had stared at Paulo in incredulity. The frown returned in full force only moments after.

But the visions didn't abate no matter how Donnie scowled at him.

He scrubbed at his face with his hands. Maybe he should get rid of the scholae. Send them away. Kill them all. Whatever it took to keep Laurel safe, he would do.

But that also meant he had to keep them here.

Because if he didn't, the rebels would come.

The castle would fall.

And she would die protecting Paulo's family.

He couldn't let that happen either. If he didn't want Iatrus Castle to fall into rebel hands, he would need the expertise of the scholae. He would need them to trust him. To trust their master. To turn away from their mercenary hearts and find a reason to fight for a kingdom they had no allegiance to.

Talk about a miracle. Paulo was already trying to get Laurel to trust him, and she'd known him for a year. How would he get these assassins to turn away from what they believe to be a life they chose and that chose them? He saw the path a hundred different ways as well, but which one was the correct path? It should be so simple to convince six people with proclivities for violence to fight a bunch of rebels in a war.

But the Goddess wasn't ready to give him that information for whatever incomprehensible reason. Sometimes, he really believed She wanted Laurel's death and just tortured him with all the ways She could bring it to pass. Sometimes, he thought it was punishment for having this magic, from somehow taking more than he should or something. Or that She knew he would be the liar and the cheat that he was. That She knew what havoc he would wreak, and She had to get started on his recompense early.

The air around him shifted, growing heavy. The hairs on the

back of his neck prickled. It was time. There were no footsteps to announce their presence, but he knew he was no longer alone in the sitting room.

With an inward groan, he tilted his head, not getting up from his lounging position on the fainting couch. Lined up in a perfect row in front of the fireplace were five shining silver masks. He'd figured out which scholae went with which mask.

The dragon faced mask with the fangs over the mouthpiece and scaled silver was Conley. The man probably could breathe fire if someone was foolish enough to get under his skin. His betrayal of Laurel would certainly hurt them the worst if he ended up convincing all the assassins to leave Iatrus Castle behind.

Next to him stood Xander in his fool's mask. Honestly, the silver face drawn up in a wild grin looked more suited to a stage than an assassin's face, but that was likely the point. Xander seemed the least likely to betray Laurel, laid back as he was. Paulo was concerned about his allegiances, but if the other scholae gave their loyalties to Laurel, he probably would to.

Mare was third, her mask a study of constellations. It was beautiful, though not as pretty as Laurel's with the filigree design. But Paulo might have just been biased. It didn't have a mouthpiece like Conley's or Xander's which also matched Laurel's. Mare's gaze on him was the most unsettling, the light from the window behind him turning her blue eyes pale.

Serene stood next to her, her mask still removed, but her expression was as hard and unreadable as the silver would have been.

Then came Declan and his completely blank mask, as if he couldn't have been bothered with the task of coming up with a design. It didn't look any less fierce though. It made it that much more mysterious because it didn't let anyone get a read on him. He was a blank slate with a blade. Dangerous indeed.

Cal stood at the end of the line, his mask made up of a patchwork of silver rectangles and squares all held together by small round studs. It was probably the heaviest mask in the group, but the man was built like a bear, so he could probably... *bear* it. Paulo nearly chuckled to himself.

Whoever the mask maker was, they certainly had a flare for design.

"Good evening," Paulo greeted. "Are you all gathering for some secret scholae meeting? Do I need to find another ceiling to stare at?"

Conley stepped forward. "We've come to speak with you."

"Oh?" Paulo pushed himself up, stretching his arms overhead. "What can I help you with?"

"Why would our master align herself with the likes of you?" Declan asked.

"You mean someone devilishly handsome with an abundance of wealth and a wardrobe that makes even kings jealous? I've even got a castle. Why wouldn't she align herself with the likes of me?" Paulo gave them a wide grin.

"This is ridiculous," Cal said.

Paulo leaned back, spreading his arms over the back of the couch. "Laurel really enjoys saying that word. It must be a poisoner thing, am I right?"

Declan folded his arms over his chest. "I think it's a *you* thing."

Paulo feigned an expression of thoughtfulness. "I don't use that word half as much."

His comment was rewarded with a huff. *Good.* He needed all of them in a state of some imbalance if he wanted to figure out which one of them would betray Laurel first. He needed them to make mistakes. To show their hands early.

"Don't listen to them." Serene bounced over to him, sitting on the chair next to him. "A few of us have some concerns that I think you'd be the best person to address."

"Concerns?" he asked, raising a brow. "I hope the staff has been being kind. And I know you aren't used to such food, being from the unruly lands of the Continent. I've heard your culture revolves around warlords. Horrible business, war."

Conley's shoulders stiffened. Paulo kept the languid expression on his face, though it took quite an effort. Conley was a loyalist through and through. Hopefully, his loyalty was honorable enough that he could give his allegiance to Laurel rather than only his sect.

"Our thoughts as well," Xander said, taking another chair. The schola's long, gloved fingers steepled in front of him. His movements were sure, not a twitch or a shake to any of them. Being a sharpshooter, the man had the grace of a cat. The memory of Mr. Hart Carys flitted across Paulo's mind, but he batted the thought and the twist in his gut away before they could take hold.

As if Xander's position were a kind of cue, the rest of them settled as well. Mare perched herself on the arm of Serene's chair, legs crossed under her. Cal sank into the chair furthest from him, the quiet poisoner tucking the shadows around him. Conley took the couch directly across from Paulo and Declan remained standing next to the fireplace.

Will they realize I moved the furniture around so the chairs all faced this way?

Conley leaned forward, resting his elbows on his knees. "There are a select few of us that think this entire situation is a waste of time. We've come to speak with you to understand what it is you're trying to accomplish and why we shouldn't simply steal Master Schola away until this is all over."

Yes, that line of thinking fit Conley very well.

Paulo tilted his head slightly. "Why would you wish to leave?"

"This isn't our fight," Declan said, straightening and coming to stand next to Conley's sofa. "We have an entire hall's worth of people across the ocean who need us. If we don't focus on that, we won't have anything to return to after this little skirmish you lot are dealing with is over."

Paulo mirrored Conley's pose. "But as Diana so helpfully explained earlier, Laurel can't leave."

"That doesn't mean we can't get her out of harm's way," Cal said. "We can wait out this war until it's over and figure out how to get the geas removed. Teagan has done it before."

Serene scoffed. "For his cronies. You know he won't do it for Master Schola. Not when he views her as such a threat to his stranglehold on Stellatus Hall."

"There isn't a single schola he would do it for," Xander said.

"Then we get the master to the cursed king and help her kill him," Declan snapped. "Whatever it is, whatever Master Schola decides, we aren't army grunts who will fight for a kingdom we don't even belong to."

Paulo smirked. "Not even for a contract?"

Declan's sharp, gray eyes narrowed behind his mask. "There isn't enough money in this entire kingdom to tempt me to be part of this war."

Conley sighed, reaching up to rub his eyes, but his mask made it cumbersome.

Paulo's smirk pulled wide.

With a curse, Conley unbuckled the mask from his hood and tossed it onto the sofa next to him. The magelight gleamed on the bald skin of his head as he scratched the dark goatee around his mouth.

"Conley," Declan hissed.

"Just shut your trap, Declan." Conley rubbed the bridge of his nose. "Master obviously trusts him to some degree, or we all wouldn't be here. If she's willing to fight for this man, then I can at least trust him enough with my cursed face."

Paulo looked over each of them. "Conley, Serene, and Xander are on the *stay at the castle* team and Declan and Cal are on team *run for the hills*." He turned to Mare. "Which side are you playing for?"

She stretched her legs out and padded silently across the room, stopping where Declan stood by Conley.

"Ah, an even split then," Paulo said. Would one of the three that wanted to leave become bitter and that would drive them to betrayal? He didn't let his magic surface, though it was tempting. He'd have to look at the lines of fate when he didn't have six pairs of deadly eyes on him. Instead, he tucked his hands behind his head. "What does Laurel have to say about all this?"

Serene was the only one to meet his eye. "We haven't discussed it with her."

"Mutiny then?" Paulo asked, quirking a brow. "Color me intrigued."

Conley shook his head. "We wouldn't go behind her back if we didn't think it was for the best. We know if we tell her we want to leave, she'll stay and be on her guard with us. Best to come to a conclusion now."

"And you don't think I would tell her?" he asked.

Cal folded his arms over his chest. "Not if you want what's best for her."

Paulo could only agree with him. If it was for the best, he would allow them to sneak Laurel out and hide her away. He'd thought about it more than once already, but it never worked out. The Goddess always found a way to take her.

He slapped his hands on his thighs. "Well, how can I help mend the rift between all of you?"

Cal shifted in his chair. "Some of us just want some answers."

Paulo spread his arms wide. "I'm an open book. Ask away."

"Why should we think this is the best place for us to be?" Declan asked first. "We can make it out there on our own. We don't need to get swept into all of this."

Paulo allowed the question to hang between them, allowed them to think he was pondering even though he had each answer on his tongue, could tell them their questions before they passed their lips. But that would make him look like a tyrant. He needed not only their concerns dissolved but to gain whatever crumbs of their trust they would give him. It was one step closer to saving Laurel.

"You have no friends in this kingdom besides my family," he finally answered. "You likely know better than I that the rebels are looking for Laurel, that they have a bounty on her head after she betrayed them by helping the king escape. You'll have absolutely no other support out there. I have a castle, a guard, and a giant wall standing between you and the rebels. If you don't wish to fight, I won't make you, but I don't think you'd have a better chance out there than you would here."

Especially because Laurel couldn't leave. Eventually, they would run out of places to hide and either return to the castle or be caught. And Paulo wouldn't let Laurel go anywhere if it was up to him. He couldn't imagine going back to watching her through his visions. Couldn't imagine not being able to walk through the halls knowing he could brush his fingers over her cheek when he passed her— even if he would get punched in the eye for it.

Declan stepped forward. "But Master Schola doesn't really

trust you, does she? I see how she watches you out of the corner of her eye. Like she's waiting for a trap to spring."

Paulo pushed out what he prayed sounded like a genuine laugh even as his heart squeezed in his chest. "Does Laurel really trust anyone? And after what happened with Aspen, I can't imagine she would be ready and willing to jump back on the trust wagon again— though, I'll still do everything in my power to earn whatever confidence she'll give me. It means that much to me."

Declan's shoulders bunched up. "I think she's simply confused. She's latched onto you because you helped her, but now we're here. She doesn't need you anymore. I don't understand why she's deluding herself."

Conley jumped to his feet, whirling on the other schola. "You do not get to question our master's motives or her capacity to make choices, whether they be for herself or the rest of us."

Declan's hands clenched at his sides. "And you can't speak for her either. She didn't tell us we had to stay, but you assume we should simply because she does. She's made her choice, but that doesn't mean I have to turn my back on our people with her."

"Do you truly think that's what she's doing?" Paulo asked.

Each of their faces turned back to him.

"Yes," Declan snapped. "She betrayed our order, betrayed her contract, and even betrayed her sister. She's turned her back on our kingdom and left us to rot. Why shouldn't we do the same?"

Paulo shook his head. "If that's what you think, then you might be the delusional one." He finally stood, folding his hands behind his back so he didn't shake the man. He took up pacing instead. "Do you know why Teagan Obscuritas is here in the first place?"

"He came for slaves," Xander answered. "I'm sure he has some masterful plan to create a fancy empire just so he can sit on a faerie glass throne across the sea."

"He came for *fae* slaves," Paulo corrected. "He came for magic. His plan is to take the fae back to the Continent and hire them out for their gifts. With a whole boatful of fae slaves, where do you think he's going to keep them?"

"Wouldn't he sell them?" Serene asked.

Paulo stilled his feet. "Perhaps some. Maybe those with less impressive powers, but do you think a man like Teagan would sell all of them? Would give control of some of the deadliest beings on the planet to his enemies?"

"He wouldn't," Conley answered sharply.

Paulo settled back in his seat. "And with a force like that, where does that leave the rest of you? Especially those who don't come when he whistles for you like dogs?"

Xander sighed. "He would either kill them or put them on the street. Likely the former."

"You all know him better than I," Paulo said. "I imagine this is something he's been thinking about for a while."

He could see the gears behind their masks spinning. Could see them connecting dots and drawing conclusions. Mare's eyes were the first to spark with the conclusion they were all smart enough to reach. She glided over to Serene, setting her hand on the head of the other woman.

Serene looked up and met her eyes, reading the same thing Paulo had.

"Oh," she said, straightening. "*Oh!* That blackguard. He knew. He knew the warlords were banding up against us somehow. That they would come for the hall, and we'd be overpowered. He left us all there to die."

"Taking only his most loyal with him," Conley finished. "By the Goddess, this has all been his plan from the start."

Paulo settled back into his more languid position, stretching comfortably across the fainting couch. "That's the reason Laurel stays. Because she's seen what a snake your leader is, and this is the first time she's been able to figure out how to bite back." Though, it hadn't come about in the way she likely hoped. Her brown eyes still held the shadows Aspen's betrayal had born. Of Luc's death.

Not that Paulo had any regrets about that particular man's demise. *Backstabbing idiot.*

"We knew he was a snake from the beginning," Declan said. "We're mercenaries. As long as the money's good, we don't care what blood it's drenched in."

Paulo picked invisible lint off his bright-green trousers. "But what good is it to fight for someone you know is doing everything he can *not* to pay you? Not to give you jobs? With the fae, he can order them to do what he wants. It won't take him long to break them and turn them into mindless killers."

Conley shook his head. "There's no honor in that."

No, there wasn't. If Paulo ever got the chance, he would personally love to rip out the blackened heart of the cursed man.

"So, we fight him instead?" Cal asked. He started shaking his head. "He'll kill us."

"Then you should fight with Laurel— with me," Paulo said. "We can work together. I have magic enough to counteract what Teagan has. Help me keep him and his friends from taking my home, and I can help you take back yours afterward. We can keep Teagan from returning to Stellatus Hall with his new toys and leaving you all to rot. Do the honorable thing by fighting for your home and for your order. Do it here, before you have to go back and fight for it without help."

"But Teagan isn't even here," Cal argued. "He's all the way across the isle."

Paulo met his eye. "Who's to say he's going to stay there?"

Declan took a step toward him. "What do you know?"

"I know there's a particular girl sitting in a palace on this isle that he probably wouldn't wish to leave without."

"Aspen," Serene breathed. "He wouldn't want to leave without his golden girl. He's too twisted for that."

Conley studied Paulo. "You've seen it."

"In a hundred different ways," he replied.

"Does Laurel know?" Xander asked.

"You're not the only ones willing to hide things from your master because you want what's best for her."

"So, we wait," Declan said. "We strike when he comes for Aspen. We figure out how to keep the two of them apart or take them both on when he comes back over here."

Paulo allowed a real smile to stretch across his face. "Now you're getting it."

"Why not go get the girl now and stay one step ahead of him?" Serene asked.

Paulo stood once more. "If we take Aspen now, we would be fighting a battle on two fronts instead of one. I haven't seen when Teagan has planned to come for her, but that means she's safely holed up in the palace until then. We need to sweep his allies out from under him first. Take out the rebellion here at Iatrus Castle then rally to take the capital back." The plans were still unformed, still out of reach for even Paulo's sight. There was something missing and he couldn't see what it was. Just like he couldn't see exactly when each scholae would stab them in the back. The future was so unclear, and it made Paulo want to throw something.

"You expect us to just sit on our heels?" Declan asked.

"No, I want you to go to war with me, to fight not only for the lives of my people, but for your freedom. For your own future." He stood in the middle of them, meeting each of their eyes. "What do you say?"

Mare was the first to step forward. She reached up and unclipped her mask, tossing it to the floor at his feet. She let down her hood, revealing the pale skin of her face and pulling a long, white braid out from under the collar. Her blue eyes met his and she gave a short bow.

Xander followed after, a crooked grin stretching across his mouth under a mop of sandy brown hair. He nodded his head, pulling his hair back into a bun on top of his head, and dropped his mask on top of Mare's. He scratched at the scruff on his cheeks. "Sweet Gaia, I'm glad I don't have to wear that all the time now."

Conley lifted his mask from where it sat on the sofa and tossed it onto the pile.

Declan muttered what had to be a dictionary of curses, but he unclipped his mask. Paulo couldn't help taking in the head of silver hair, almost the same color as the mask in his hand. The short hairs did not match the youthfulness of his face. His gray eyes sparked with mistrust and his mouth was turned down into a frown, but he added his to the pile.

Slowly, Cal stood and came toward them, anxiety turning his brown eyes bright. "I still don't think this is a good idea, but if anyone can get us through this, it's our master and a seer." He dropped his mask.

A vision hit Paulo like a charging bull.

Cal laying in a coffin as the scholae surround him, their faces streaked with blood and dust.

Well, Cal definitely wouldn't be betraying them after all.

10

THE MASKS

The dark of night will be thick and quiet. Laurel will stand at the western wall of the castle, her eyes focused on the lake ahead of her. Behind her, a mask of silver, flat and plain with no decorations besides the eyes and mouthpiece. A garrote wire will come up around Laurel's throat.

THERE WERE SHEEP IN THE TRAINING AREA.

They'd been sheared recently, their wool shorn for the heat of the summer that was swiftly making its arrival in the southern part of Olympia. Laurel set her hands on her hips. Looking about, she noticed the benches and equipment missing. Likely moved to accommodate the sheep. The scholae were supposed to practice in five minutes and none of them were in the training area.

She blew out a breath. The day before had not gone as planned. Paulo's little show had derailed her objective. She'd been gone from Stellatus Hall for over a year. She needed to show the scholae she was still the same master. Needed to prove they could trust her. This war they were all walking into would be so much easier if she could convince the scholae to stay and work together. Then, when all of this was over, she could offer them a new life. She hadn't dreamed about bringing the scholae with her when she left Stellatus Hall behind, but she also hadn't imagined anything besides getting Aspen away from Teagan and the hall.

But dreams evolved. The future with her sister remained murky, but Laurel could still help the scholae. She was their master and would remain their master until her death or until she passed the title on to the next master. Probably Conley, if he wanted the job.

"But before you all decide to abandon me to this isle," she mumbled, trying to piece together what she would say to all of them, "perhaps helping me find my new mission— no that's not it."

One of the sheep bumped into her leg. She nudged the little beast with the toe of her boot. It bleated its objections, staring at her with one big, creepy eye.

Why were their eyes so unsettling?

"Laurel!" Diana called.

Laurel whipped around to see Diana hustling in her direction. She pointed at the flock taking over the training yard. "Are we to start training the sheep for battle now?"

Diana barked a laugh. "Ah, no. They're much better suited to being landing cushions than warriors."

One of the sheep nibbled on the edge of Laurel's jacket. She batted it away. "I'm guessing this was your brother's idea?"

"They've been bringing the flocks in closer to the castle. Paulo saw something a couple nights ago and started prepping."

More visions. It was always more visions. Did the marquess ever sleep? Likely not, considering how many times he somehow continued to run a fully functioning estate on top of harassing Laurel.

Maybe harassing was a strong word for it.

Pestering maybe.

Laurel shook her head. "Well, we can't train this lot, but now we don't have anywhere else to work." And if the fight was coming, they would need all the practice they could get.

"That's why I came to get you," Diana said. She gestured for Laurel to follow and headed back toward the castle. "We're set up in the ballroom. Paulo had the equipment moved already."

Laurel frowned, falling into step with Diana. "Why didn't he say anything?"

"He probably wanted it to be a surprise or something." Diana shrugged. "He has a skewed sense of what kind of surprises women actually enjoy."

A grin stretched across Laurel's face as they stepped back into the castle. "Doesn't he know all it takes is a bouquet of new throwing knives and a velvet box of rare poisons to weasel his way into a girl's heart?"

"Exactly!" Diana agreed. "You'd think after all the years I've helped him practice he would have it figured out by now."

The grin on Laurel's face didn't fade as they jogged up the grand staircase leading to the ballroom from the grand hall. Having Diana around had been a boon Laurel hadn't realized she would need. The fiery woman understood Laurel on a level not many did. They were both utilitarians, almost to a fault. From the clothing they wore to the way they did their hair, no one could say that either of them was frivolous. While Diana allowed emotions to rule her more than Laurel did, the fierce woman's mind was quick and critical. Not unlike Paulo's. She was so similar to her twin, yet so different. Side by side, they were exact opposites, but when someone got to know them well enough, it almost seemed like they shared a brain.

However, Diana was an open book.

And Paulo wasn't.

They reached the double doors to the ballroom and Diana pushed one open. The clang of swords had been muffled by the closed door but hit them in full force as they walked through the doorway.

As did the sight.

Laurel had come to the ballroom before, in the first few weeks of her stay at Iatrus Castle. It had been at night, with only a mage-light to light her way. The ballroom was positioned in the middle of the castle, not allowing for any windows to stand sentry against the walls.

But the roof was made of glass.

It would likely become an oven by the end of the afternoon, but some of the panes had been opened above them and a slight breeze blew through. She squinted a bit and saw there were moveable shutters decorated to match the wall. So maybe they could avoid the worst of the heat. The sun shone down, lighting every inch of the room— and all the training equipment that had been brought in with it. Targets, weapons, dummies all lined the walls, looking out of place under the gilded sconces and marble pillars.

Laurel froze in the entry, her gaze flicking from one schola to the next. Not a silver mask in sight. Her fingers tapped at the long dagger strapped to her left thigh.

"Ah, Diana, you found her." Paulo sat on one of the benches lining the edges of the room, his bright hair disheveled, though not a thread was out of place on his brown striped jacket. It was one of his less flamboyant jackets, even if the stripes were comically large.

At Paulo's words, the scholae stopped whatever they were doing and came together in a uniformed line.

Laurel marched forward, her steps growing firmer and firmer with every clip. "Scholae, where are your masks?"

Conley stepped forward, as he was supposed to. The rigidness of his spine spoke volumes about how the rest of them were interpreting her tone. *Good.* They still held respect for her, even if she had failed in her mission and they were questioning her abilities.

"Master," he said, voice stiff, "we've set our masks aside in a show of trust to those of House MacGregor."

"You would put your identities, your sect, your lives in the hands of these people?" Laurel raised her chin, pulling all the height she could into her spine. She walked down the line, doing her best to not tap her fingers. "I know Serene is quicker to trust, but the rest of you?"

"We wish to follow your example," Conley said, his deep voice echoing in the cavernous ballroom.

She narrowed her eyes, walking down the line the other way. What had persuaded them to do this? She had to keep herself from glancing over at Paulo. He had to have done something. This had his magic little fingerprints all over it. But what? Had he confronted them about betraying them? Laurel had been watching all the scholae up until she spoke with them yesterday, and Paulo had said they would betray her. But how? He'd kept quiet about that bit, and now he'd gotten them to shed their masks.

She paused in front of Xander, meeting his eye. "Why?"

Xander met her gaze unflinchingly. "Why not, Master? If you trust him, why wouldn't we?"

She almost snorted. "Are you so sure I trust him?"

"See?" Declan muttered under his breath.

"You wound me," Paulo said dramatically.

She spun, flicking a blade in his direction. It sank into the wood of the bench next to him, but he hadn't even flinched, those pearlescent eyes of his whirling with magic and mirth. Blasted man had seen it coming. One of these days she would surprise him, and he wouldn't look so smug about it afterward.

She moved along the line, passing Serene and pausing in front of Declan. "I'm most surprised by your acquiescence. You're not usually one to bend to peer pressure."

He bobbed his head, his silver hair catching the light coming from the ceiling above them. "We can't abandon a fight here, knowing that we would be abandoning our master as well."

"And you would fight for a kingdom you have no loyalties to? To a place that would likely kill you just because of what you are and what that represents? The Order of Stellatus is not looked upon favorably on this isle, especially because of what they've done to aid Adira Durant. I wouldn't blame you if you decided to walk away."

"We'll see this through, whatever the outcome, and we'll return to our home stronger for it."

Laurel stopped in front of Cal. "Does he speak for the rest of you?"

Cal gave a sharp nod.

She watched him, seeing the swirl of anxiety in his eyes, slightly shadowed by the curtain of dark-blond hair that perpetually lay over his forehead. Cal had always been the quietest of the group, even when there had been dozens of them. He was also the youngest before her, his work with poisons making him a prodigy.

He was also the most likely to back out of a fight.

If anyone was going to have concerns about all of this, it was going to be him.

But he met her eye, his unease obvious, but fortitude was there as well. He would be willing to see this through for whatever reason. He'd made up his mind somehow.

Great Goddess, they all had.

Laurel turned, seeking out the man she knew played a hand in it.

Paulo gave a flirtatious wave of his fingers.

Cursed man. She turned away from him, going back to her prowl in front of her scholae. "I had woken this morning fully intending to convince you to help the MacGregor's, but I see my work was done for me. I'm glad to know each of you will be beside me as we face the challenges likely to come. I wouldn't wish to have anyone but the strongest with me for what we're about to take on, and I can only thank the Goddess I got the maddest, genius, most ruthless of the scholae."

She tapped the corner of her eye, the side of her nose, the quirk of her lips.

I am watchful.

I am focused.

I am silent.

Xander gave a little howl and Laurel had to keep herself from smiling.

She paused when she reached Serene, who was standing in the middle. "Will you go to war with me?"

Serene looked over to Xander and took up a howl as well.

One by one, the others joined, raising their heads and sending a bone-chilling shudder through Laurel, even as her heart swelled with their voices.

Their song sounded like a promise.

A pact.

A geas of their own making.

Laurel looked to Mare, the only one who didn't howl.

But the gleam of excitement in her blue eyes was loud enough.

Laurel drew the blades from the sheaths at her sides and twirled them in her hands.

It was time to get to work.

11

AN UNEXPECTED PLAN

Laurel's eyes flashed with warning. A dare. A cursed dare that Paulo has to answer. He reaches for her. He kisses her. Her hair will be like silk in his fingers, her lips soft against his. He won't be able to stop himself from pulling her tightly against him. From drawing her as close to him as he possibly can. Her lips press more firmly against his. The smoldering between them finally catches flame. But only for an instant. A cough from beside them will break the spell. She will draw back, her eyes wide when she realizes what she's allowed herself to do. She will slug him in the gut and walk away, taking his breath and his heart with her all over again.

PAULO ROLLED HIS RIGHT SHOULDER, ATTEMPTING TO RELEASE THE tension that had taken root between his neck and shoulder blade. The muscles practically burned. He'd have to get Jenkins to draw him a hot bath after supper tonight.

He stepped out of the study and caught his first glimpse of the world since he'd stepped into his study that afternoon to meet with Peter and Oliver. There had been some difficult decisions made over the course of the day. While they did their best to protect what they loved, the siege would still take much from them. They'd have to kill off flocks, burn down crops, and evacuate homes to keep everyone safe. It also didn't hurt that it would keep valuable resources out of rebel hands.

With a sigh, he rubbed at his temples. It should have broadcasted a sky full of color, or at least the first hints of evening's approach. Instead, stars glittered in the velvet night. The moon hung high in the sky, shedding its light on the clouds of wool clustered about the grounds below. It was quiet, almost deathly so. Only a few scant magelights lit the hallway.

He took out his watch and stepped over to the window. It read only four o'clock. He pressed the device to his ear and heard the ticking. *Not broken.* The night had gotten *very* far away from him. There wouldn't be dinner or a bath at this hour.

A sigh slipped between his lips, and he leaned his forehead against the window. The cool summer night had already chilled the glass. Hopefully, the few tenants that had arrived at the castle found good lodgings on the grounds. Mater had been collecting tents since the fall, saintly woman that she was. *There should be enough for everyone.* Hopefully. If everything went according to plan.

His magic flared behind his eyes slightly.

Brown eyes, deep and dark as the earth beneath them.

He straightened, a smile growing on his face as he turned around.

Laurel leaned against the wall near the closed door of his study. She wore those cursed trousers again, but a dark jacket hung down to just above her knees. The open collar of her brown tunic exposed the tanned skin of her throat, but little else. Not like that dress she'd worn at the solstice ball had.

Sweet Gaia, he really ought to have gone to bed earlier. Though he couldn't begrudge it. The conversation with Peter hadn't been a light one. The preparations for the flocks would be miserable— especially because they'd have to cull a large portion of the sheep. He rubbed at his brow.

Laurel folded her arms over her chest. "I thought marquesses only stayed up this late when there is a constant stream of good wine and pretty women."

Paulo leaned against the windowsill and mirrored her stance. "Who says I haven't been enjoying such debauchery?"

She pointed her chin at his folded arms. "Those ink-stained fingers for one. Also, the complete lack of giggling I would expect from any ladies that made your particular acquaintance."

He looked at the offending appendages. There really was ink all over his fingers. The black spots blended into the brown freckles all over the back of his hand.

Laurel gave him a knowing look, and he tucked his hand back into the crook of his elbow.

"Well, I can't say I haven't enjoyed a generous helping of wine or the company of a beautiful woman, so my evening isn't completely lost."

Her eyes rolled upward as if pleading to the Goddess for deliverance from him. "Why do you have to say things like that?"

He pushed himself away from the window. "Like what?"

"You know what. That you think I'm... you know."

"Beautiful?"

Her eyes narrowed. "Yes. *That.* You're well aware such flattery isn't going to be the thing that gets you into my good graces."

He sighed dramatically. "A shame. I really was banking on you finally let that prickly wall down by simple words alone. I don't know what I'll do now."

"I know you can do far better than that, *my lord.*" Laurel looked up at him, her gaze challenging him to break down her wall. To make her believe he meant it when he told her she was beautiful.

A tingle started up in his fingers, and he had to stop himself from twitching. He took a step toward her. Then another. Until they stood toe to toe.

She looked up at him, her expression daring him to try.

He lifted his hand, brushing the very tips of his fingers against her forehead, tucking the few wispy strands there off her brow.

By the way her breath hitched, she wasn't as unaffected as she wished to appear.

It sparked something deep inside him.

He leaned down. Sometimes, he appreciated how tall she was, but in this moment, he really enjoyed how tall she made him feel. He still had to bend over slightly for his mouth to level with hers. She froze in front of him, but she didn't look away.

He drew close.

Her lashes fluttered slightly.

His mouth stopped a hairsbreadth from her ear.

"Good night, Laurel."

He whirled away from her, taking long enough steps to escape her intoxicating presence fast enough not to be reeled back in but praying he masked his hurry to get away as quickly as he could. He needed to sleep off the wine. And her. By the Goddess, he probably wouldn't even be able to breathe properly again for days.

Laurel stirred behind him. "Is that all you've got?"

Paulo threw back his head and laughed.

But he didn't turn around. Instead, he rounded the corner and side stepped just enough to keep Donnie from running into him.

Donnie looked up from staring down at his feet. "We need to talk."

"Of course." Paulo took a step back, gesturing down the hall toward the study. "After you."

Donnie rolled his eyes, the first semblance of his true friend that Paulo had seen in days. He swept past, his shoulders rolling back as if readying for battle.

Glancing down the hallway, Paulo didn't see Laurel, but she likely hadn't gone far. His magic surfaced and he saw her appearing at the other end of the hall before gliding away. Probably a good ten minutes from now when she realized Donnie wasn't going to throw any more punches.

Paulo's lips twitched. Honestly, she tried to act like she didn't like him, but her tendency to be overly protective was telling. Too bad she wouldn't just marry him and save them both the trouble of all this tiptoeing around.

But maybe having a wedding right before a siege wasn't the *best* idea. Especially after watching Oliver's wife ghost around the castle with red-rimmed eyes. Honestly, the girl was beyond weepy. *A perfect fit for Oliver.*

"I can practically hear all your scattered thoughts," Donnie said, opening the door to the study. Paulo had left it unlocked. Donnie strode toward the table set against the opposite side of the room. He removed the vase of fresh flowers— likely Mater's doing— then opened the top of the table to reveal a tray of crystal decanters and glasses. One of Grandfather's hiding places.

Grandmother had not appreciated Grandfather's heavy drinking habits, which seemed to be a MacGregor House specialty. The liquor dulled the mind enough for the visions not to come so fast. Or at least made processing the visions a little less intense. The headaches from the hangovers were never as bad as some they got from the worst of the visions. Father had been a little more frugal with his consumption, but Paulo had seen him down a glass of wine every so often when it had been especially hard.

Paulo shut the door behind him. "What did you want to talk about?"

"As if you don't already know." Donnie poured blood-red liquid into one of the glasses.

It probably was a better idea to make sure this conversation was on equal ground. Paulo gravitated toward the two chairs in front of his desk instead of the one behind it.

Donnie returned with two full glasses of wine and one glass with likely three or four fingers of brandy, probably for himself. He sat down in the chair and held out one of the wine glasses. Paulo took it, though the ache in his head warned him against the drink.

"I want to talk to you about Tauros." Donnie set his wine glass down on the edge of the desk and twirled the brandy in his hands. He threw back the brandy, draining the entire thing in a few gulps. He hissed as he set the empty glass next to the wine. "Where on Gaia's green earth do you get that stuff? It's strong enough to put down a horse."

Paulo leaned back in his chair, fiddling with the stem of his glass. "I'll give you the woman's contact information. But what is it you really want to talk about, Donnie?"

Donnie stared across the room, looking out the windows at the dark sky. He didn't say anything for several minutes, not even glancing at the wine next to him. Magic stirred at the back of Paulo's mind, but he kept it as suppressed as he could. He already knew his magic wasn't the answer. If he allowed his magic in this moment, it would only come between them more. Donnie didn't need someone to tell him exactly what he wanted to hear. He needed his friend just to listen to him.

He finally looked away from the window and met Paulo's gaze. His bloodshot eyes were tired but clear. He set his shoulders back and finally picked up the glass of wine, but didn't drink any of it.

"I was helping Mater with inventory today. Do you really think there's going to be a siege?"

Paulo took a sip of his wine. "I know there is. They're already on their way."

Blowing out a breath, Donnie lifted the glass up, admiring the red liquid before he took his own sip. "Barclay pomegranates really do make the best wine. Besides mine, of course. It really is a shame the rebels hit those orchards. Generations of trees burned to a crisp." He eyed Paulo. "Could you have stopped it?"

The words beat against the inside of Paulo's lips, but he didn't let them out. Instead, he kept quiet, leaning forward and resting his arms on his knees. He kept Donnie's gaze though.

"Of course you could have. I bet you could have stopped this rebellion from ever happening. You were always too smart about everything, no matter how you paraded around like a parrot."

Paulo allowed the corners of his lips to curl up. "I think you mean peacock."

"You talk too much for a peacock." Donnie drained half his glass. "Parrot fits much better."

"Have you heard a peacock? Diana has two in her menagerie and they're worse than roosters in the morning."

Donnie flapped a hand at him. The brandy must have started hitting his system, as his shoulders had softened a bit and his blue eyes weren't as serious. "I'm not going to fight about birds with you. Mater told me not to let you sidetrack me."

Ah, Mater. Everyone accused Paulo of being meddlesome, but Mater was the master meddler. He just hadn't figured out how she was able to do it without anyone noticing.

"I've been away from Donaldson Manor for two weeks and I still can't wrap my head around the fact that it's gone. They burned everything." It was as if Donnie could see the flames even now, his eyes distant. "*Everything*, Paulo. The vineyards. The house. The distillery. All of it. They didn't even go through and steal anything. Just razed it to the ground. Why? Why would they do that?"

Paulo settled back in his chair. "I only see the future, not the past. I can't tell you what drives a man to do evil, only what that evil will bring about."

"And what will this evil reap? What besides destruction or heartache can this bring about?"

"Rebirth," Paulo said. "New beginnings. Reunited families. Answers to questions long asked. It will tear down walls keeping people apart and bring others together that would have never had the opportunity to find one another."

"Are you talking about you and Laurel?"

Paulo shrugged. "Among others." Both Adam Cyrus and Prince Evan were trapped on the Isles of Aigean for the foreseeable future. Their fates were still being written. Still being decided. But the end of this war could put them on a path they wouldn't have been able to walk if it wasn't for their capture.

Donnie slid down in his chair until his chin rested on his chest. "Why didn't you tell me, Paulo? Why didn't you at least give me some warning?"

Paulo swirled the wine in his glass. "If I had told you, what would it have changed?"

"I wouldn't feel like kicking you in the face right now," Donnie grumbled.

"I'd rather you alive and wanting to break my nose than dead in a ditch back in Tauros."

"Would it really have come to that?"

"It may have. That or burned in your own house. Or stuck on the end of a pike. Or—"

"All right, all right." He sat up. "I get it. You did what you thought was best. You still love me in that blackened lump of a heart in your chest."

"You'll forgive me?"

Donnie rolled his eyes but nodded. "Still blasted hurts though. I don't like the idea of having this between us, but I know it's going to take me a little longer to come to terms with. Especially because I don't know what to do now. Don't know where to go."

Paulo set his glass on the desk. "You'll always have a place here. As long as me or Mater or Diana draw breath, you have a place here. Sweet Gaia, even Peter would keep you I daresay."

Donnie snorted. "That's real comforting until you remember your castle is about to be put under siege."

"I have no plans to allow Iatrus Castle to fall into the hands of rebels."

Donnie drained the rest of his glass. "I just hope you're ready to pay the price of those plans, my friend."

Paulo walked down the dirt path at the front of the castle. Diana's menagerie was located outside the walls. Mater had insisted, knowing Diana's tendency to bring home any creature she felt needed help. The day she'd brought home the jackal, Father had already had the builders halfway through setting up the enclosures.

His magic buzzed at him, but he was so tired of watching Laurel die by the hands of her friends that he kept pushing it away. He would let it out once he faced Diana. He would need it in case she decided to stab him or something.

The menagerie stood on the southside of the castle, butting up against the outer wall. It looked like a glorified barn, with its white paint and golden accents. The cupola at the top held aloft a weathervane in the shape of a crescent moon. Diana had been in her twelve-year-old rebel phase and had wanted the exact opposite of the family crest.

When Paulo finally reached the small side door on the northeast side, he couldn't help but press a hand to the white paint for a moment. But this conversation was inevitable. He grabbed the handle and pulled it open.

Father had the building charmed when built, and it did a fair job of keeping the worst of the noise to a minimum. It didn't stop the animals from making a ruckus when they were outside, however.

But there was little cacophony now as he entered.

He walked down the aisles of enclosures, all empty except one. The white hart scratched his antlers against the post of his enclosure. Paulo looked about as he walked. Perhaps some of the animals were in the outside parts of their enclosures. He didn't even see the peacocks. When Paulo got close, the hart looked up, his ears flicking.

"I can't get enough of you at the castle, so now you have to invade the menagerie?"

Paulo followed the sound of Diana's voice and found her climbing down a set of stairs against the wall. She carried a box under one arm and a sack slung over her shoulder.

"The hart's leg looks well healed." The creature had been caught in a poacher trap the previous autumn, and Diana had nursed him back to health.

All the animals had been nursed by Diana. She'd rescued the peacocks from an abusive owner in the capital. The alpacas she'd saved from death when an ambitious man had brought them from the Continent, thinking to start a lucrative textile business. The herd had cut from a hundred alpacas to only a dozen, which Diana had made Paulo pay the previous owner an exorbitant price for, then rebuild their enclosure so they would be comfortable here in the varying climates Olympia boasted. Most of the enclosures had been home to one animal or another, starting with that blasted jackal. There had been otters, bears, snakes, swans, anything she felt she needed to rescue. It seemed silly, considering she was such an avid hunter, but she was a protector of the beasts as much as she was a predator of them.

Diana plopped the box down on the bottom stair. "I'd been planning to release him in a few weeks. His herd just returned from the coast."

"Do you think they'll accept him back?"

She stretched her back, not meeting his gaze. "He'll definitely have to work for it. I'm sure whatever siblings he has will want to pummel him for being an idiot."

It seemed they weren't just speaking about deer anymore.

"How many creatures do you have in here right now?" he asked.

Diana left her pile at the bottom of the stairs and walked past the large mound of hay at the back of the building to stop near the farthest enclosures from the entrance. "The alpacas are in their enclosure outside with a few of the shepherds who are helping out today. The hart. I have a raven in the loft upstairs that has a busted beak. But that's all."

Paulo looked around. "What happened to the falcon? The fox? I thought you had a marten in here too."

She didn't answer, instead turning around and climbing back up the stairs.

Paulo followed after her, taking the stairs two at a time. "Diana, I came because I—"

"I know *exactly* why you came." Her voice barked out from the open door at the top of the stairs. When Paulo hit the top, Diana strode out, a cage with a large black bird sitting stoically on a perch. She thrust the cage into Paulo's hands. He fumbled with it, much to the raven's annoyance. He gave a very distinct squawk then said "Idiot!" in a very practiced voice.

Diana kept talking. "I was poking through your office last week when I saw it. The plans to dismantle the menagerie all written up with your girly signature next to the line waiting for Peter's. I nearly ripped it to shreds."

The loft above the menagerie was a study in sophistication and barbarianism. The ceiling had been painted sky blue and decorated with gold foil animals. Like a child's mobile above a crib. Diana had always been Father's favorite child. A large window at the back of the room gave a lovely view of the forest to the south of them. A quaint writing desk had been pushed up against it, covered in arrow fletching pieces and jars of arrow-heads. Instead of a chair, there was an old wooden stool next to it. The bed was a giant pile of furs on a mattress and there was a brown bear rug laid out on the floor. The walls were painted white, but someone had painted them to look like birch bark, making the whole space feel like a winter forest. Bows, buck knives, strings, axes, and a few wicked-looking carving knives hung from pegs on the wall, though most of the pegs were empty. There was also an entire section of the wall taken up by thick oakwood shelves that housed jars of tinctures and different remedies safe for animals. There were leg splints of every size and an entire box full of linen. A taxidermized squirrel sat on a tiny log next to the box.

Paulo blinked. "My signature isn't girly."

He hadn't been doing a good job keeping up with Diana's fate. The scholae and the rebels held all his attention as of late.

Diana scoffed, throwing a black tunic into a bag. "It's girlier than Penny's and she has multiple loops. Yours looks like the doodles of a lovesick schoolgirl. I'm surprised you don't frame it with little hearts."

"Hey now, at least mine is legible. Not the chicken scratch you pass off as handwriting."

"But of course, you didn't even ask me if it was all right if you could come in and dismantle my entire menagerie. No, instead you waited until Peter was here to sign the cursed thing, *then* you came to face me and order me to pack up and leave. I'm just another woman in a man's cursed world. My every choice is dictated for me and not even the things I care about are taken into consideration."

"Of course they are," Paulo argued. He considered Diana's wants and desires very carefully.

She scoffed. "Did you even think about the animals? How was I supposed to get them to safety? Where was I supposed to put them?" She tied off the bag she'd stuffed the last of her clothing in and picked up the small trunk off the end of the bed.

He looked back down the stairs. "Where *did* you put them?"

She stomped past him. "I let them go."

Paulo followed her back down. "You let them go?"

"By the Goddess, Paulo, it's like you can't even come up with your own blasted sentences." She stuck the little trunk on top of the box and grabbed the other bag. "Yes, I let them all go."

Paulo couldn't even follow her out as she kicked the large double doors at the end of the menagerie. They swung open and one of the footmen stood there, several bows and a few empty quivers hanging from his arms. A maid came up alongside him, taking the sacks from Diana and hoisting them over her own shoulders.

How had Paulo not seen them when he arrived?

Diana returned, grabbing the boxes from the stairs. She stopped at the hart's enclosure, popping open the gate and clipping the lead onto his halter. He eagerly followed behind Diana like a puppy instead of a wild animal. "Are you going to help or are you going to just stand there like an idiot?"

The raven in Paulo's arms shook out his feathers and gave a very jolly "Idiot!" back to Diana.

Paulo scrambled after her. "I can have the servants come get the rest of your things. We can move them into your rooms until we rebuild. I have Father's blueprints in my study."

"We aren't going to rebuild, Paulo," Diana said.

He followed her out the door, where she set down her things and unbuckled the halter from around the hart's neck and slapped him on the rump. The creature bounced a bit, but took off toward the trees, his leg much improved.

"Why wouldn't we rebuild?" asked Paulo.

She walked over to where her favorite bow and an arrow tipped with cloth sat against the wall. She pulled a flint from her pocket and held the arrow between her knees as she lit the end. When the sparks touched the cloth, it burst into flames.

Paulo's magic flooded his sight and all he saw was fire.

He clutched the raven's cage to his chest. "Diana, what are you doing?"

She nocked the arrow, pulled back the string, and let the flames fly.

They hit the pile of hay at the far end of the menagerie.

It didn't take long for the fire to eat away at the dried grasses.

"We aren't going to rebuild because if we do, someone, somewhere, will simply find another reason to tear it down again." Diana slung her bow over her shoulder and picked up her boxes as the flames spread. She carefully took the cage from Paulo's hand. "See you back at the castle."

She walked away.

But Paulo couldn't.

He stayed right where he was until he couldn't take the heat of the fire any longer.

12

THE ARRIVAL

Laurel took a sip of the hot tea in her cup as she looked out over the castle grounds through the sitting room window. The smoke from the fire of the great sheep slaughter still trailed lazily in the air, but it was finished. The rest of the sheep had been collected already, mingling with the residents of the closest village as well as the men and women who had come with the militia to withstand the siege with Iatrus Castle.

With their marquess.

"It's quite a sight," Mater said from beside her. "I do hope we're able to get everyone ready before we have to lock the gates."

"We will." While the words were sure, the tea sloshing uncomfortably in her gut told her otherwise. Mater glanced at her out of the corner of her eye, though she didn't call her bluff. And Laurel had thought Paulo was perceptive. It seemed he hadn't only inherited gifts from his father.

Mater glided over to one of the many sofas scattered about. The sitting room had become something of a command center. A large buffet table had been brought in, now covered in maps and missives from the few militia leaders under Paulo's command. They'd also brought in more seating to give a place for their entire group to sit about as they strategized. The preparations hadn't ceased since Paulo had announced the rebels would attack.

Soon.

But of course, he'd gone and disappeared on her before she could corner him about it. After their... whatever it was in the hall outside his study the week before, it was like he'd become a ghost. She should have punched him in the gut. Or kissed him.

No. Not that. She wouldn't kiss him again. It did weird things to her brain. She couldn't think. Couldn't remember anything but the feel of him under her fingers. Pressed against her lips.

"Cursed man," Laurel muttered.

"Pardon?" Mater asked.

Laurel shook her head and stepped back from the window. "Are we expecting any other meetings today?"

Mater pursed her lips as she thought. "No, I don't think so. I have Donnie keeping me company in the attic today. We're trying to find an old map of the lake I'm sure the twins' grandfather stuck up there somewhere. Diana and Xander should be back from scouting any time now."

"Then I'll let you have a moment to drink your tea without someone breathing down your neck." Laurel set down her cup. The Goddess knew she could use such a moment, if it ever came.

"I truly don't mind your company, Laurel. You're more than welcome to stay if you wish to take a moment."

There was that MacGregor perceptiveness again.

"Thank you, but I can't." She didn't need Mater seeing too far into her soul. Not after what happened with Paulo in the hallway.

Without another word, Laurel stepped toward the door. There was enough to do to keep her distracted. She had scheduled to meet with Declan and the guard captains in an hour. They needed to come up with a definitive defense strategy for when the rebels attacked the walls. Needed to get everyone in position. Needed to convince the scholae this was the right thing to do.

As she stepped out of the hallway, she paused.

Footfalls.

She turned and found Diana and Xander, followed quickly by Conley and Declan, racing toward her. Xander wheezed. The two of them had obviously sprinted from wherever they'd been, their faces red with the exertion and chests heaving.

Xander stopped before her. "They're coming."

Laurel stiffened. "When?"

"Before nightfall," Diana panted from beside him.

How had they gotten so close so quickly? The host had been closer to the Black River than they were to the castle when Laurel had been on patrol the day before. Moving so many men took time and effort, much more than it would with a small group. There should have been at least two or three more days to prepare.

"Where's Paulo?" Laurel asked.

"I'm coming!"

Laurel turned to look down the other end of the hall and found Paulo nearly running toward them. Both Lord Peter and Lord Oliver jogged behind him. The family resemblance struck fiercely with the furrow of their brows and straight set of their shoulders. Paulo likely would resemble Lord Peter in his later years and if it wasn't for Lord Oliver's darker coloring and slighter shoulders, he and Paulo made for more believable twins than Paulo and Diana. Laurel couldn't even blame herself for getting the two of them confused at the palace before she'd discovered Paulo's identity.

Paulo breezed up to her, not making eye contact. Words formed at the back of her throat, a snip about him disappearing all the time, but his finger brushed against hers. Barely a whisper of a touch. The words died in her throat, and he disappeared into the sitting room, Lord Peter right behind him.

Lord Oliver stopped before he could follow after his father, the furrow in his brow deepening when Laurel's eyes met his. "I know you."

No, you really don't.

Laurel gave a short nod and left him to gawk after her as she returned to the sitting room. She had to wind her way to the table. Paulo had already taken a seat, legs thrown over the arm of a chair as he tossed a letter opener in the air and caught it, his face turned down not even watching the sharp blade.

Declan stood at the table, staring at a map of the castle, Lord Peter at one elbow and Captain Isaac at the other with Conley across from them. The captain's finger trailed the lines of the wall leading to the upper bailey on the west side of the castle.

"This will be our weakest point," he said.

Declan tapped the map, right where the edges the lake near the castle barely bled onto the page. "This would normally make that side of the castle the least accessible."

"But we're dealing with water folk," Paulo added in.

Laurel stepped up next to Declan. "Can we drain the lake?"

Lord Peter shook his head. "We don't have the time."

Diana sidled up to the table and pulled a notebook from a pouch attached to her belt. "I counted five hundred rebels and six possible Aigeans in the first wave, but there are more behind them." She handed the notebook to Captain Isaac.

"What kind of soldiers are we looking at?" Captain Isaac asked. As captain of Iatrus Castle's guard, Captain Isaac had been appointed lead on the walls. He knew the men best and set patrols for guard rotations as well as helped the militia captains get their men in the best positions to defend the castle. "Are they all on foot? Are there bowmen? Any on horseback?"

Xander shifted papers around until the full map of Delphine was visible. "They have most of the men on foot, but there are a hundred or so carts. They aren't hauling any siege engines that I could see at that distance, but it doesn't mean they don't have any."

"There's enough wood around the castle to just build them," Declan said.

The steady beat of Paulo tossing the letter opener in the air punctuated each second they took talking.

Laurel tried to glance at every page on the table, memorizing every detail they had. The two most vulnerable spots were the west wall and the front gate. While there wasn't much room to attack from the west side, that didn't matter much if they had enough water folk to use the water against them and push the advantage. Luckily, the lake lay a ways off from the castle, so it wouldn't be a simple thing to get the water up the hill and drown out the castle. It would also give them time to see if an attack from the lake was coming. The front gate was also a problem, considering its build but also the fact that there was more than enough room for an entire legion of rebels to spread out along the wall because of the fields. It would be difficult to get enough men to cover the gate to fend them off.

"Pardon me," said someone behind Laurel.

Paulo gave a long sigh. Served him right. He deserved to be annoyed by someone else every once in a while.

Lord Oliver stood a few paces away, his eyes flicking from one face to another. "Paulo, who are all these people?" He glanced at Laurel. "And why is one of the royal palace's kitchen girls armed?"

Paulo flapped a graceless hand over his shoulder in the direction of the table before catching the letter opener again. "These are the professionals who are going to help keep my castle mostly intact."

Lord Oliver scuttled around the table, stopping next to his father. "Professionals? Professional what? I thought she was a cook."

Laurel couldn't help herself. "I am a cook."

Lord Oliver's puzzled expression grew even more confused. His father must have realized he needed help and looked up from the paper in his hands. "They're assassins, son."

"*Assassins?*" Lord Oliver spluttered. "Paulo, you purchased assassins to defend against the rebels?"

Declan bristled next to Laurel. "We have not been *purchased* like a bunch of circus monkeys. We're here at the will of our master and answer only to her." He nodded to Laurel.

Lord Oliver's eyes went even wider, and he leaned forward to see Paulo around Conley's thick frame. "Have you gone raving mad?"

"When are you going to realize I've always been a bit mad?" Paulo said, not even looking at his cousin.

"Father?" Lord Oliver looked to Lord Peter, as if the older nobleman would make everything make sense.

But Lord Peter only shrugged. "They're here to help. I'm not going to ask questions when we so obviously need it and neither should you."

That finally put the gentleman in his place. His eyes narrowed at them and Declan answered with his own glare.

Laurel refrained from rolling her eyes. "What mages do we

have?" she asked, diverting the conversation to something more productive. Hopefully.

Captain Isaac pulled a sheet of paper from a stack and handed it to her. A short list of mages and their powers filled half the page. She stepped away from the table, snatching the letter opener from the open air before Paulo could catch it again. She set it on the table next to his feet and looked at the list in her hands. There were three mages who could manipulate light, five with animal affinities, a stone worker, one who could rid metal of tarnishes, one weather mage, and two that had gifts with water.

"And bronties?" she asked. "Who do we have that can be on the walls? What about a force to meet them outside the gates?"

"We have a hundred and fifty trained as castle guard," Captain Isaac said, "and another three hundred from the militia. There's two hundred able bodies in the upper bailey as backup, but they've no combat training."

"That won't be enough to stop them," she said to Paulo, putting the paper in his lap. "We can't risk any of them outside the wall. We'll likely be facing three times that many from the rebels."

Paulo finally glanced up at her and she realized that he'd been hiding his face from her.

The swirl of pearlescent magic was red-rimmed.

"I know."

Laurel settled herself against the side of the guard tower. There were five towers placed around the outer wall of the castle, one on each corner— excluding the southeastern corner that housed the bastion— and one facing the lake. She stood on the northeastern tower facing the forest to the east, where she and Diana had seen the rebels only two weeks before.

How had everything fallen apart so quickly?

She watched the edges of the trees. The sun turned the leaves gold with its waning light. The day was ending, but the long night was just beginning.

Laurel didn't move from her position even as she felt a presence approach at her back.

"Report," she said.

Mare's pale fingers materialized in front of Laurel's nose, a slip of paper between them. Laurel plucked it from the schola's loose grip and unfolded it. The swirl of Serene's handwriting covered the entire paper. Not that Laurel should expect anything different. Mare only ever played messenger for Serene.

Laurel read over the short note quickly, counting the number of fighters on the west wall. They'd allocated most of their forces to that side to account for the Aigean threat, but there hadn't been anything more than a ripple on the water all day. From the report, there had been glimpses of rebels on the other side of the lake for hours, but no sign of the main host until a few minutes ago.

"The Aigeans will wait until the moon sets behind the trees, when we won't be able to see the water move, but I imagine it won't be long until we have rebels knocking on the door." Laurel ripped the paper to shreds and tossed it from the wall. She turned to the west, just glimpsing the moon over the tallest tower of the castle. A little less than a quarter of the glowing face was now in shadow, the full moon having come only three days before. Laurel could see almost every nook and cranny of the castle wall around her, the tower before her silhouetted against the light. The moon would disappear from view before midnight, taking its glow with it.

They had three, maybe four, hours before Lake Luna spelled their doom unless they could get the rebels to retreat.

A light bobbed along the inner wall, flickering in and out of view as it passed the openings through the crenellations. The wall was hundreds of feet away, but Laurel could swear she saw a flash of red hair.

"Wait here," she ordered Mare, already charging for the stairs. The guard towers were large enough to allow five guards at the top and five more in the room below with enough space to maneuver weapons and escape any projectiles aiming for their comrades. Laurel passed by the five men below, a mixture of militia and Paulo's guard. Iatrus Castle boasted a plentiful guard, but it wasn't an army. They had just enough guards to man the towers and leave a small fighting force for one of the walls. The militia filled in some of the gaps, but not all. Laurel prayed it would be enough.

Her boots hit the walkway of the north wall, and she raced past the men stationed there, keeping her gaze on the sinking moon.

13
AN UNEXPECTED PARLAY

PAULO'S MAGIC FLASHED IN FRONT OF HIS EYES, MOVING STRINGS ABOUT as he sprinted along the inner wall, his fingers clenched around the ring of his swinging lantern. The glow of the magelight brought the shadows around him to life, and he nearly jumped at every disembodied specter. His rapidly beating heart had his magic rushing through him.

He hadn't wanted to be outside tonight. In fact, he'd been happy to sit in the sitting room with Donnie and a rather large glass of Abrams's best wine. It had been part of his plan to get the scholae to think him a bit off. He wanted to show them he was confident in their abilities to keep the castle from falling on the first night. That he wasn't worried about them stabbing him in the back or throwing him under a speeding wagon.

However, the magic wouldn't be silent. Not tonight. It raged behind his eyes like a cyclone, flashing with possibilities.

A hand grabbed his arm, and he swung the lantern around.

Laurel barely avoided getting smacked in the face. "Watch it with that thing."

"Sorry." He continued forward, not even shrugging his arm out of her grasp. He didn't have time to stop. He never had enough cursed time.

"Where are you headed?" she asked, pulling up next to him.

"Where I'm needed," he retorted. It came out a little shorter than he would have preferred, given that he was still trying to worm his way into her heart, but she didn't even blink at his tone.

Laurel did let her hand drop, quickly tapping each knife strapped to her body. "I thought we discussed you holing up in the castle."

"We certainly discussed it, but that doesn't mean it was the overall plan." He grabbed her hand, pulling her along with him.

Her brows furrowed, but she said nothing, keeping up with his pace as they rounded the wall around Mater's beloved olive tree. His magic attached to the branches, and he watched the leaves shift back and forth with an invisible sun. It took effort to rip his gaze away. His head pounded enough already.

The only connection the outer wall made to the inner wall was the sixty feet of wall next to the great hall. Paulo's legs started protesting the sprint as he raced across it. The windows of the great hall watched them with soulless eyes, the lights within completely dimmed. The hold he had on Laurel's hand tightened. He'd ordered every light in the castle put out except those at the wall. He didn't need any of the rebels targeting one part of the castle. He needed them as focused on the walls as he could make them.

But the castle looked dead before the battle even started.

A mixture of guards and militia greeted them on the other side. Paulo only employed fifty men to guard the castle and another hundred to serve with the shepherds. The local militia had another three hundred men, and the castle guard regularly sent out training regiments throughout the march for those who wished to hone those skills in case of something like tonight. While Paulo couldn't be sure any of the villagers actually did the training, he was hopeful at least some of them would be able to learn quickly.

Laurel let go of Paulo's hand and darted through the armed men, dodging fumbled weapons and wary looks. She swept through the door to the first guard tower and took the stairs two at a time.

Paulo shadowed her every move. If he admired Laurel as she ran, well...

They stopped at the top and Paulo strode toward where the petite, hooded shadow stood at the edge of the tower.

Serene turned before he reached her. The silver face of her mask tilted in Laurel's direction. "Did you not get my note?"

"I did," Laurel said, pointing a thumb at Paulo, "but his most honorableness here decided to go off script."

Paulo grabbed her thumb between his fingers, pulling her hand into his. "Is it going off script if the playwright is the one doing the changing?"

Laurel did her best to disentangle her hand from his. "It is when it's a war and there are lives at stake."

War. This was a war, wasn't it? A war of his making. Of his choosing. His stomach twisted and he finally released her hand. "I had to. They're coming."

Serene snorted. "Of course they're coming. They've *been* coming all night."

Paulo pointed toward the lake. "No, I mean they're coming to the gate."

Laurel strode toward the edge of the wall, and Paulo stepped up right behind her. Lights flickered along the other side of the water, torches raised high over heads and fires burning in baskets at their feet— probably for archers. He knew Diana was somewhere on the bastion on the east side of the outer wall with a similar setup.

His eyes trailed the line of light until he watched two bob away from the host.

With those lights came their demands of surrender.

Ones that would not be met.

Paulo stayed standing at Laurel's back as those lights drew closer. Until he could make out the shapes of three men. Three. One held a banner of a crudely painted compass and the other two held the torches. They had to circle around to the road, the abatis Paulo had made around a good portion of the castle cutting off a more direct route. Though, he wouldn't have been upset if the men decided to fall into the ditches or spear themselves on the pikes above the hole.

Laurel flicked her fingers at Serene, sending her some kind of silent code— much like what Prince Evan used to communicate

— and stepped away from the wall. "They'll come to the gate first."

With a nod, Paulo took the lead. He could feel the men around him shift that way as the rebel torches drew closer. Every man on the wall was attuned to the rebels as they reached the edge of the lake and started toward the gate.

Paulo's eyes never wavered from them. He and Laurel reached the gate first, stopping on the walkway above it. He'd stood on this walkway many times as a boy. He'd sit on the edge, waiting for Father's carriage to return from the capital. Count the fluffy heads of sheep as they bounded over the fields. Watch the walls of rain from autumn storms sweep across the grass before they would hit the castle.

But there was no joy found in standing on that walkway now.

The rebels finally started hiking up the curvy road at the front of the castle. Paulo took a step back, allowing some of the men to stand in front of him, as if shielding him from what was to come.

If only they could.

Sooner than Paulo would have liked, the rebels stopped at the closed gate. The shortest of the three men, one holding a torch, stepped forward. He pulled a wide sheet of yellowed parchment from the satchel at his waist, raising it so everyone could see it in the light of his companions' torches.

"We have come to negotiate surrender terms to Iatrus Castle and the mage Paulo MacGregor!"

Paulo took in a deep breath and stepped forward once more.

"Oh, excellent! I'm *Lord* MacGregor," he said, stopping at the crenellation and hopping up on top of it. Laurel hissed at him, but he ignored whatever grumblings about ridiculous marquesses she was making. He set his fists on his hands and puffed out his chest like he'd seen some of the heroes do in drawings inside the few books he'd bought Penny over the years. He was sure the pose looked utterly ridiculous to anyone with actual sense, but he couldn't help smiling at the rebels' widening eyes.

He gave a magnanimous bow of his head. "I accept your surrender."

The rebels startled slightly. The speaker shook his head. "No, we're here to accept your surrender."

Paulo straightened from his bow, pouting his lip out slightly. "But you have the terms of your surrender right there."

The rebel frowned. "No, I have the terms we have for *your* surrender on this page."

Paulo turned his back to the rebels, looking over the men until he recognized one of the captains of the militia. "Greg, did you send the terms to these ruffians? You scoundrel. I told you that was for my battle with cook, not these..." He waved a flippant hand back at the rebels but paused. "I'm sorry, who are you again?"

The leader's face grew dark. Finally. "We are followers of The Cartographer, the future ruler of Olympia!"

The rebels with him cheered. When one of them raised their banner, the rebels on the far side of the lake joined in the cry.

Good to know they're paying attention. Paulo gave a little spin and plopped down, so his feet dangled over the edge of the wall. "Oh! I see now. You're apprentices then. I didn't realize mapmakers had begun replacing measuring tools. I guess I'll need to get rid of the yard sticks used by the tutors throughout my march. We don't want to be teaching our young people the wrong methods of measurement."

"No, you buffoon!" the rebel snarled. Oh, he was really mad now. "We're here to secure your surrender of your castle!"

"Wait, wait, wait," Paulo said, raising his hands to quiet the man. "So, you're not mapmakers?"

"No!" the rebel hollered, indignant.

"Well then." Paulo swept his legs back over the wall. "I guess I really will accept your surrender."

"That's not—" The rebel took a deep breath. He held up the paper once more. "If you do not agree to our terms, we will rain fire down on this castle. We will show you the might of the true rulers of Olympia and purge those with the stain of magic from these lands. We will—"

"But I didn't put on my lucky surrendering jacket. I was saving it for my parlay with Cook. I can't surrender if I'm not dressed for it."

With a roar, the rebel drew a hidden crossbow from under his long cloak.

A knife sank into his eye socket before he could take aim.

He fell to the gravel road beneath him.

The two others jumped back, pulling blades from their waists.

Paulo looked to where Laurel stood, halfway down the short set of steps with another knife in her hand.

He leaned back down over the wall. "Oh dear, he got blood on the terms. I guess you lot can't surrender after all."

It didn't take the remaining pair of rebels long to reach their comrades.

And the moon went with them.

Paulo meandered back to the western wall, meeting the eye of every man he passed. Giving them a firm nod of confidence even as his insides slowly rotted. He stopped once more at the guard tower on the western side. Laurel had disappeared again, but Serene gave him a silent greeting at the top. Even he could feel the air thicken around them. If it got any thicker, they'd have to swim in it.

He took up a spot facing the lake, watching the fires on the other side of the water gnash their teeth at him, waiting to be unleashed on his castle. On his people.

The low bellow of horns moaned in the woods.

They weren't the conventional horns of Olympian royal trumpets, with their straight necks and golden visages. These horns snaked above the rebels' heads like beasts, their faces painted in wicked visages made only more grotesque by the dancing flames below them. Their low song sent shivers up Paulo's spine.

It was the song of war.

Of destruction.

Of death.

And it was coming across the lake.

Ice spread over Lake Luna, white and stiff as the rebels marched toward the wall. It was certainly a power move. The lake would have been quite the defense if the castle had been facing a regular human war.

But this was Olympia.

Paulo expected there to be shouting. Of his men to be racing about the walls with fear in their eyes and prayers on their lips. He expected it to be so loud he couldn't think. He expected fire and rain and everything in between. But it was silent, as if the song of those horns had done the heavy work and stolen the souls of those around him. Only Paulo's soul was left, cursed as it was.

The first line of rebels made it across the lake.

And Paulo sensed the shift around him.

Heard the creak of taut bowstrings behind him.

Felt the whisper of arrows above his head.

Watched as they hit their marks.

Then it was loud.

The men around him roared at the first taste of blood.

But Paulo didn't roar.

He said nothing as a single tear ran down his cheek.

Said nothing as he allowed his magic to sweep him forward.

Always forward.

14

THE SIEGE

Caspian Delrio will race out of the forest, two spears strapped to his back. His eyes will be drawn to the flash of red on the wall of the castle. He'll slow, waiting until Diana turns in his direction. With her eyes on him, he'll charge to the front gate.

LAUREL BARED HER TEETH AS SHE SLICED ANOTHER ROPE DANGLING OFF the ring of a humongous iron hook. The beastly things sank into the ash-stained walls, but the rope fell uselessly down to the ground below.

Another hook sailed through the air.

This time, however, it caught on one of the men standing beside her, helping another man dump hot oil down the side from one of the many vats.

With a yank, he was torn from the wall.

She didn't watch to see when he hit the bottom.

The militia captain behind her barked orders, but before she could even process what he was saying, she threw herself to the ground as a ray of hot, white light cut through the air. The smell of burning blood soured her stomach, but she stood as soon as the light was gone. No one around her had lost their heads, but a line of black now streaked the wall of the castle behind them.

It was a good thing stone didn't burn so easily.

Declan met her eye from where he lay a few feet away. His gray eyes were narrowed, his face screwed up in disgust.

The very tips of his silver hair smoked.

Perhaps she shouldn't have insisted he stay with her at the front gate. He might have served better at the bastion or even along the western wall.

A group of rebels had come north around the lake, the host splitting off to attack the western and northern walls first. Not that it would remain that way. They were already spreading, like a swarm of black-eyed beetles, over the lands all the way around the castle.

"There!" the captain shouted. "That's the fae!"

Laurel shot up from the ground. A tall, willowy specter stood in the middle of the field, their hair shining white with the light that poured out of their hands.

"Xander!" Laurel shouted.

The fae sagged to the ground a moment later.

A white-fletched arrow stuck out from his chest and a black-fletched one from his eye.

Xander wouldn't be caught dead with white fletching.

She glanced down the wall. A crudely made ladder stuck up over the edge— right next to Diana. Laurel watched as Diana drew another arrow, nocked it, and shot one of the rebels that was attempting to climb up the ladder.

Diana, who was supposed to be on the bastion.

Laurel jumped over the limp form of a man and raced to Diana's side. She grabbed her by the arm and yanked her away from the wall. Why couldn't either MacGregor sibling stick to the blasted plan? Laurel punched the rebel who climbed up next, and he fell backward, taking a few of his comrades on lower rungs of the ladder with him.

Diana jumped in next to her, grabbing the top of the ladder. "Help me!"

Her plea summoned the other fighters around them. Laurel took hold of the top rung. It took five of them to push the ladder away from the wall. The weight of the rebels didn't allow for it to fall backward, but it slid down the gray stone and crashed onto the heads of the rebels beneath them.

Laurel whirled on Diana. "You're supposed to be on the bastion."

Diana shrugged. "You know I never do as I'm told."

"You—"

A crash cut off her words. Laurel looked back down at the gate. The rebels had gotten a battering ram into place. Apparently, they *had* brought a siege weapon on those blasted carts. The rebels inside drew back the thick trunk of wood and drove the sharpened end into the tall wooden gate.

"Come on!" Diana hollered, taking off in the direction of the gate.

Laurel could only follow.

Another swing of the battering ram shook the stones under her feet.

The boom of Conley's voice rang out over the men. "Get that blasted ram *down!*" he hollered.

A line of archers stepped forward and let their arrows fly. Several of the arrows met the flesh of the men below, but when one man fell away from the battering ram, another took their place.

Cal's mask glinted on the opposite edge of the walkway, hunched over a bucket. The golden liquid within looked suspiciously like the very strong brandy that Paulo kept in a crystal decanter on the sideboard in his study. Though, the smell of pine told her it wasn't strictly brandy. Laurel stopped next to him, looking up at the clouds hanging just over their heads, pregnant with rain. The weather mage had been busy. "I give you two minutes," she said.

A quick nod was his only response.

He dipped a long strip of linen into a bucket. It came out dripping in the firelight around them. Grabbing the handle of the bucket, he swung it around to the other side of the wall and threw the entire thing over the edge. Laurel watched as the liquid splashed over the battering ram and its rebels. The still-soaked linen dripped from his fingers, which he carefully kept away from any flame.

Conley's scowl deepened as he glanced around. "Where the curses is Xander?"

But Laurel pushed Diana forward, plucking one of the arrows from her quiver and snatching the linen out of Cal's hand. She wrapped it around the tip of the arrow and held it out to Diana.

"Set the tip in the torch," Cal said, "and shoot the wettest spot on that log."

Diana didn't even hesitate. Within moments, she had the arrow strung, lit, and soaring over the heads of the rebels below.

It sank into the wood of the battering ram.

The entire thing burst into flames.

The couple of men that hadn't thought to step far enough away from the battering ram after being splashed with Cal's concoction went up in flames with the log.

Screams rent the air.

And at the very back of the ram stood Caspian Delrio, the selkie Laurel had seen in the capital. The Aigean that had befriended Diana. He looked up at the wall, his face turned in Diana's direction.

Laurel looked over and saw Diana's face go pale, then green. She ran to the side of the wall, losing her stomach.

Grabbing her arm once she finished, Laurel hauled her away. Diana allowed it, stumbling behind her. The fighting grew thinner the farther south they went, the battle staying closer to the lake. As the bastion came into view, fat raindrops started to fall. The mages were beginning their part of the siege then.

Diana finally ripped her arm from Laurel's grip. "You don't have to escort me all the way back. Besides, I'll just head back to the real fight after you leave."

"This isn't a game, Diana. This is a war."

"Isn't war just a game to those that start them?"

Truer words had never been spoken.

But Laurel wasn't about to give Diana one inch of slack. She spun around, making Diana stop in her tracks. "This is *not* the time to flaunt whatever entitlement you think you might have. It's time to shut your mouth, listen to your superiors, and do as you're blasted told."

Diana rolled her eyes, though her face remained pale. "Sweet Gaia, Laurel, you sound like Paulo."

"At least your brother listens to reason." As far as Laurel knew, Paulo hadn't even moved from his spot on the western wall. They'd decided he would be best situated there, his magic more useful against the Aigeans that would attack from that side rather than at the front gate where most of the humans were.

Diana threw her hands up. "Paulo is the one who made the assignments. He put himself on the front lines and stuck me back in the bastion."

"This is his castle."

Her expression darkened, her jaw tight and eyes shadowed. She stomped forward, smacking her shoulder against Laurel's as she passed. "You say that as if I haven't woken up every day with that knowledge shoved down my throat. Believe me, I understand my place perfectly."

Laurel took a single step after her but didn't take a second. She turned around instead and jogged in the direction of the gate. Her legs protested the exercise, but she ignored the sensation. The rebels would soon fall back to regroup. The sun wasn't far from the horizon, though the weeping clouds over the castle hid any indication.

Diana was headstrong, but she wasn't truly foolish. At least, she had a good head on her shoulders. She wasn't usually one to jump into dangerous situations, even if she wasn't necessarily one who ran away from them. By the Goddess, it was usually Paulo who made such impulsive decisions. She was honestly surprised she hadn't seen more of him running about and getting into trouble. She had kept her eye out as the hours dragged on.

So why was Diana the one at the gate?

15

AN UNEXPECTED FRIENDSHIP

PAULO COULD SEE THE LINES OF HEAT WRITHING ABOVE THE STONES OF the outer wall as he stared at the west wall out the window. Rebels and their fae captives toiled in the steaming mud left by Iatrus Castle's weather mage. They'd been digging up the ground on the other side of the abatis Paulo had built before the rebels arrived, placing what looked like plates under the dirt. There were others chopping down trees and they had started digging pits for large fires. Maybe Xander could be stationed at the bastion later and pick some of them off. It wouldn't do to let them get too comfortable.

They certainly hadn't made his people in the castle comfortable in the week since this cursed battle started.

"We've taken minimal losses on the west wall," Captain Isaac said, "but we're still holding."

Paulo could feel the frustration in the rumble of Laurel's unsatisfied growl through the floorboards.

"Their attacks have felt more like a test run," she said. "They've only targeted our front gate and the western wall. Seeing how strong our most vulnerable sides are. I imagine this isn't the worst of what they have in store."

And you would be correct. But Paulo didn't want to make the sentiment aloud. There were still too many ways the next battle could go. There were too many decisions to be made to pinpoint one fate.

Xander joined Paulo at the window. He pinched the bridge of his nose, likely trying to rub away the exhaustion gathering under his eyes. He'd been one of the last to come back inside the castle after the battle. Paulo hadn't seen him much through the long hours during the first week of the siege, but he'd seen enough of his black arrows. The man had a speed to rival Diana's.

A sigh built in Paulo's chest, and he refrained from turning to look at where his twin sat in the corner of the room. What was he going to do with her? He'd seen her at the west wall this morning, an arrow nocked in her bow. She'd shot it out into the lake and Paulo had made himself walk down to where Mater was helping serve food to the soldiers off patrol out in the upper bailey.

Laurel had told him of Diana's abandonment of the bastion the first night of the battle. Told him about what had happened. Diana's countenance hadn't lightened all week. She'd hardly touched her breakfast— though, most of their group hadn't done more than pick at their plates besides Declan. How the man could eat after the things they'd seen, Paulo could only guess. Maybe one had to be a bit soulless to be a provocationist. Luc had been Paulo's only other point of reference, and it was very likely that man had slept like a baby every night, not even caring what shadows marred his soul.

Lucky him.

Well, maybe not that lucky. He'd been zapped so hard by King Dion's magic he'd been nothing but a smear of ash on the floorboards at the end.

"How are you holding up, your lordship?" Xander asked.

"Just Paulo, please." Paulo shrugged. "Not as good as I would like but probably better than I should be."

Xander chuckled. "I imagine that's true for all of us. Well, maybe everyone besides your darling mother. It seems nothing phases that woman."

A smile tugged at the edges of Paulo's lips. Mater had done remarkably over the night. She hadn't left the confines of the castle, instead settling everyone who remained inside and making sure people were where they needed to be. She'd stayed in this very room the first night, collecting reports, but had finished off the rest of the week assembling crews to repair any damages to the outer wall and treating injured soldiers. A second wave of rebels had brought in a miniature onager and had barraged the outer wall on the west side, but they hadn't broken through. The stone mage from the village had already set to work making sure the repairs were sturdy enough to take another beating.

There were certainly more beatings to come.

His magic flickered, catching on Diana's fate.

She will kneel on the rubble-strewn ground, hands bloodied, roaring at the sky.

How many times would he see this future? How could he save them all from this fate while also allowing things to happen that would push them toward the future they all needed?

He couldn't and he knew it.

"By the Goddess," Xander whispered. "I didn't realize how much your eyes changed with the magic. They're so..." He snorted. "I was going to say *magical*, but that's a little too on the nose, eh? But there are so many colors."

Paulo couldn't help but smirk, smoothing a hand over his tangerine-colored waistcoat. "Why do you think I have such a varied wardrobe?"

Xander's teeth flashed with his grin. "You've got to have the colors to complement it. What's the point in having a magical tell like that if you can't have the getup to match?"

"Exactly! It would be a travesty."

"Indeed," Xander agreed. He unbuttoned the row of dark buttons on his jacket, opening it up to reveal the silver silk lining underneath. "All I get is silver accenting for the gear. I can't complain too much, considering how the color really does go with everything, but it grows old. I'll take the silk over the sturdier fabrics though. I'd rather die a bloody death wrapped in silk than the scratchy wool everyone else uses— no offense to your sheep."

"None taken. May I?" Paulo asked. At Xander's nod, Paulo trailed a finger over the fine fabric. "I'm jealous. You likely have access to all kinds of silks being on the Continent." They had a wide silk trade across the sea. Many of Paulo's favorite articles of clothing were made with fabrics from the boats sailing from the Continent's shores.

"Why do you think I had to find such a lucrative career?" He laughed, rebuttoning the jacket.

Paulo turned back to the room. "Laurel, why didn't you bring Xander with you from the beginning? He understands me."

She looked up from the map on the table for less than a second before returning to her notes. "I knew very well how dangerous it would be if you ever did get the chance to get to know each other."

Xander, mask back in place, set a hand to his chest in mock offense. "You would have kept us apart?"

Paulo could see the eye roll she refrained from using.

"No one person should be half as ridiculous as either of you," she said. "I don't know if it's a miracle or a tragedy that I know both of you in this life."

"A miracle," both of them said.

Laurel shook her head. "One I'll probably regret ever being part of."

"Probably," Xander agreed.

Conley stood at Laurel's right; his arms folded tightly over his chest as he gave an exasperated shake of his head. It was growing easier to read all of them, even when they had their masks on. Except Mare. But Paulo didn't expect anyone to be able to get a good read on the phantom woman, besides perhaps Serene who seemed to be able to speak telepathically with her.

"Enough chatting," Declan said. "We need to come up with a plan for when the Aigeans make their move."

Paulo sighed and walked over to the table. "Do we have numbers on how many there are?"

Laurel plucked a sheet of paper from the edge of the table. "This says six were spotted along the lake last night, trying to stop the rain."

Six to fight against the one weather mage and two water mages in Paulo's employ. The weather mage was formidable, but the water folks' control over water was nothing to scoff at. It would take many water manipulators to battle against the will of someone who could actually control the clouds above them with more skill. It was like wolves going up against a bull elk. The elk was swifter, larger, in its element. It had horns larger than a wolf's fangs. But get a pack of wolves together and there was nothing the elk could do, no matter how mighty his horns.

"There will likely be more than six," Laurel said. "If not presently, then later on. They're probably in communication with the isles. It wouldn't be too much effort to get more water folk here, especially with the castle's accessibility to both the Black River and the sea."

Declan looked up at Paulo. "You would think the family of oracles would have thought about how easy it would be for an enemy force to attack."

"The thrill for danger must be genetic then." Paulo threw himself onto a fainting couch, only a few feet from where Diana still sat, her eyes cast down at the floor between her feet.

Before Declan could respond, Laurel set her hands on her hips and turned to face him, her brown eyes narrowed. "Why aren't you over here helping?"

Paulo wriggled deeper into the couch. "I would just be in your way."

"This is your castle," she said. "Don't you want to see what we're doing?"

"Yes, but I get a much better view from right here." He let his gaze track over her, from the silk of her dark hair pulled back into a braid all the way down to the soles of her boots.

A dark growl rumbled from where Conley stood, but Laurel only allowed that suppressed eyeroll to emerge. They returned to the maps and notes strewn all over the desk. Paulo closed his eyes, counting his breaths, trying to look like he was completely relaxed even as his heartbeat increased with every second. He really should be at that table. He should be helping Laurel look for weaknesses in their defenses, come up with ways to take the fight to the rebels.

And he would.

Later.

Xander finally stepped away from the window, joining the other scholae around the table.

None of them noticed when Diana crept from the room.

And no one called after Paulo when he followed her out.

Paulo and Diana had played this game many times in their youth. He would trail her through the castle, woods, even the village. Diana's senses were those of a hunter, her eyes keen and instincts sharp. He wouldn't be surprised to find out that she truly was gifted by the Goddess, and it was just that her tell was so small it didn't even register. If he hadn't watched her train, watched her dedicate her life to becoming one of the greatest hunters in Olympia, he might have truly considered taking her to a mage who could see magic just to check. There was no other way she would have been able to beat him in this game otherwise. He'd have his magic before him, waiting to see when she would finally catch him. He'd gotten good over the years, but she almost always caught him. It wasn't until the last couple of years that he'd really been able to play without getting caught, though each instance had been a close call. As he'd grown into his gift, she'd only grown more into her skills.

The fact that today's hunt wasn't a game had his palms sweating.

Diana glanced back over her shoulder, but Paulo was already out of sight, ducking down beside one of the bushes in Mater's lavender garden. If his heart wasn't pounding in his ears, the smell of the purple flowers would have made him groggy.

When she turned back down the path, Paulo peeked over the top of the bush.

Diana stopped over a grate, looking down into the tunnel below. She just stared, hands on hips.

Paulo didn't move an inch.

This was her choice. Her fate. He wouldn't influence this decision any more than he already had.

As if waking from a trance, she crouched down and used the butt of her dagger to loosen the lock on the grate.

Paulo carefully tiptoed away. Once he was far enough, he ran. He burst through the front door, through the great hall, out the other side into the small courtyard in the middle of the castle, and into the west wing. He stopped at a nondescript door, pulled the key from his pocket, and grabbed the doorknob.

It was already unlocked.

He stilled for only a second before pushing forward. This door was never unlocked. He had the only key. Shaking his head, he locked the door behind him. The room could be described as a miniature study, perhaps built for a steward or a visiting lord. Neither was true. It was as much a façade as Paulo's wardrobe was.

He stopped at the quaint fireplace positioned against the middle of the right wall. The mechanism for the door wasn't anything fancy. Just a push of one of the bricks and the wall panels next to the fireplace popped open.

Panels that were already opened.

Magic surged through Paulo. He blinked as the visage of a ghost passed out through the door.

With a huff that he couldn't decide was out of exasperation or mirth, he pulled the hidden door open.

Mare didn't even pause in her ascension of the steep stone steps leading down into the ground. She only rose one white eyebrow and swept past him.

Diana had never found it, not in all the years even Father had been coming down here.

But the moment he invited Laurel into his life, he knew his secrets would eventually come out.

How had Mare found it? How long had she known about it? How many times had she been down there?

Mare shut the study door behind her, but Paulo didn't have the time to race after her with questions. Instead, he bolted down the steps, allowing the hidden door to click shut on its own. The stone steps were worn under his boots, the middles smoothed by the feet of his ancestors and perhaps even those that came before them. It wouldn't have been surprising to find out if the Goddess Herself had walked these steps. There was a certain thrum of magic resonated in this place. One Paulo had never found a reason for.

He hit the bottom of the stairs running, not bothering to light the magelights scattered about, though he grabbed one off a shelf. The room was as familiar to him as his own face. Water splashed under his boots as he walked straight into the small spring taking up about a quarter of the room. He didn't have to go far before he found the overflow lever with the toe of his boot. Crouching down, he reached for the lever, twisting it. With a gurgle, the water around his boots started to lower.

He'd used the lever before, when the rains came in late fall and the spring would swell. The lever opened a door under the water, pushing it through into the simple drainage system Grandfather had built when he'd been Lord MacGregor. The tunnels ran under the castle and let out on the west side, right into the lake.

When the water slowed its flow out of the door, Paulo lightly squeezed the magelight he'd grabbed and stuck his head through.

Not a sound.

With a prayer that this wouldn't irreparably ruin his jacket, he retreated back through. His shoulders were too broad to fit, so he stretched his arms over his head to wriggle himself through.

Only to get caught at his chest.

"Blast," he cursed. He pulled himself back through and shucked out of his now sopping jacket. Tossing it at the bottom of the steps, he once again attempted to push through the small door.

Again, he couldn't quite squeeze his chest through.

His cravat and waistcoat went next, joining the jacket at the base of the stairs.

He shoved himself through, his back scraping against the gritty silt coating the edges of the door. The button right under his clavicle broke. Blast, he should have just pulled the shirt off along with the rest of his clothing. Gritting his teeth, he dug his elbows into the wall on either side of the door, trying to push himself through.

Nothing. He was trapped.

Last year he'd been able to fit through. Or had that been two years ago? Surely, he couldn't have grown that much. Sweet Gaia, he really should have checked this path before he bolted down here, but he'd been too preoccupied with Diana.

He pulled on his magic.

But something kicked his boot.

He jolted, cutting off a yelp. He didn't need to alert Diana to his presence in the tunnels. Scrambling back through the opening, he summoned his magic once again.

Wide, brown eyes.

Pulling a grin on his face, he finally pulled himself back through.

Laurel stood a few feet away, a magelight in hand.

Those brown eyes trailed down his torso and they got wider the farther down they went.

"I suppose Mare revealed my little secret to you?" he asked, getting to his feet.

She blinked, a brush of pink staining her cheeks. "Uh, no. I mean yes. Yes. Mare told me."

Paulo took a step toward her. "Well, perhaps this is a boon from the Goddess herself."

Laurel's throat bobbed slightly. "Perhaps," she said, though Paulo didn't know if she had meant the words to slip out. Her eyes kept flicking to his open shirt.

At least this burning between them wasn't as one sided as she wanted him to believe. He allowed his magic to play out the next several minutes, following several strands of possibilities. Each one more enticing than the next. A slow grin spread across his face.

She met his gaze again. "What are you smiling about?"

"Oh, nothing." He took another step, slowly untucking his shirt from his trousers. "Would you be willing to help me?"

Her eyes followed the path his hands took. She cleared her throat. "What do you need help with?"

16

THE HUNTER

No, he was wedged into a trapdoor.

Shirtless.

By the Goddess, there were *so many freckles.*

When Mare had reported Paulo's whereabouts, Laurel hadn't really known what to expect. She'd known there had been some kind of hidden area where Paulo disappeared to. She'd tried to find it early in her residence of the castle, but sniffing out secret doors and false walls wasn't one of her strengths. Laurel had only tasked Mare with finding the room and securing it the day before. Laurel really shouldn't have been surprised. It was Mare after all.

One of Paulo's soggy boots rose in the air, bringing her attention back to the task at hand. She grabbed that boot, then the other, wrapping her hands around the gritty bottoms.

Both of them would be a mess after this.

When he straightened his legs, she pushed.

He finally popped out the other side.

She dropped his wriggling feet, and he pulled himself the rest of the way through. Crouching down, she unhooked the mage-light from her belt and held it out in front of her.

Paulo sat in the stream of running water on the other side, his chest red but not bloodied. He'd probably have some scabs later, but they'd be minimal. With a breath, he jumped to his feet, plucking his own magelight from the water trickling over the tops of his boots. It was a good thing the tunnels were only moderately cool. They wouldn't freeze down here from the cold water.

Laurel pushed herself through the doorway.

"What are you doing?" Paulo whispered, his deep voice still echoing off the stone walls of the tunnel even as he tried to be quiet.

"I'm coming with you," she said matter-of-factly. If he was going to ask her to push him through a hole, she was going to find out what all the excitement was about.

"This is a solo mission."

"Great," she said, coming to her feet. "Then you can tell me where I'm going, and I'll leave you here as a lookout."

He rolled his eyes, the magic tell taking over the blue of his irises. "Fine, but I take lead."

She gave a short little bow. "After you, your honorableness."

"Cheeky," he muttered under his breath as he turned. The rest of his words were stolen by the babble of water around them.

She followed him through the tunnel, stopping right behind him when he paused to listen or what she suspected was actually a chance for his magic to play out. The tunnels were more advanced than any water system on the Continent she'd ever seen. The sewage system in Vale, the city below the mountain where Stellatus Hall stood, was said to be one of the best, but it relied on cesspools, and more often than not, the sewage leaked down into the waterways.

These tunnels likely hadn't seen any sewage. Besides the smell of algae and earthy waste, she didn't smell anything foul. More than once, a bat flew over their heads, making Laurel jump. She'd have to tell Cal about them. He had a fascination with bats.

Paulo kept the pace quick, but his steps were as silent as hers through the water. How did a marquess know how to make his footfalls so quiet?

Paulo froze a step ahead of her. This was obviously a vision. She could tell by the way the muscles in his shoulders grew more tense as the seconds ticked on. As quickly as it came, he broke away from his frozen state, spinning and grabbing her hand before pulling her back the way they'd come and ducking down one of the offshoot tunnels. The map in Laurel's head told her they were under the residential wing of the castle, on the west side of the structure. She could probably find the water lines that drained into these tunnels from the sink of her washroom if she looked.

Except there was a bare chest pressed up against her, keeping her from seeing anything but freckles.

Paulo reached down and wrapped his hand around hers. His eyes met hers, their pearlescent swirl flaring as he went very still. The color faded, leaving only a deep, hungry blue in its wake. With a careful squeeze of his fingers around hers, the light went out, casting them into darkness.

His hungry expression was burned on the backs of her eyelids.

She couldn't breathe.

Why couldn't she breathe?

He didn't let go of her hand, but he did lean forward, pressing his forehead to hers.

By the Goddess, was he going to kiss her?

She set a hand to his chest. Her fingers met skin and nearly burned at the contact. He flinched, and she ripped her hand away.

That had been a *terrible* idea.

She could feel him shake.

Was he laughing at her?

He huffed a small breath.

Oh, he was most certainly laughing at her.

She smacked that ridiculously freckled chest of his.

The vibrations of his laughter stopped, but he still didn't let go of her hand around the magelight. They stayed in that position for what could have only been another minute before the tunnel around them lightened.

Laurel pulled Paulo closer, not caring if he smothered her with his bare chest if it would keep them from getting caught.

At the other end of the tunnel, Diana passed by, a magelight in one hand and a dagger in the other.

She didn't even look their way before disappearing.

Laurel didn't move, didn't let go of Paulo when he tried to pull away slightly until she knew Diana wouldn't be able to hear them. She kept her breathing even, allowing the trickle of the water around them to hopefully mask the sound of her pounding heart.

When she was sure Diana was out of sight and sound, she squeezed the magelight in her hand.

Paulo's face was turned toward the end of the tunnel, pearlescent eyes narrowed.

The huntress had become the hunted.

Without a word, he stepped away from Laurel. The magelight in her hand cast light over his back, bringing shadows out along the lines of muscle.

In all the weeks of quips, silks, and preening, she'd forgotten. His mask was always so fixed in place, so carefree. She'd forgotten for a second that under the finery there was a man who could prowl through a castle after a highly trained assassin as silently as a shadow. Who could adapt to a situation before the person he had made his mark even knew what they were doing next.

This was the opposite side of Paulo's coin.

Not the preening marquess.

The flippant business tycoon.

The off-key musician.

The idiot.

He didn't look for markings of Diana's trail, which Laurel knew wouldn't exist even if she looked. He didn't check around corners or stop to listen for any sign of her. His silent steps were sure as he walked through the tunnels, the glow of Laurel's magelight at his back. There was no worry in the set of his shoulders. His hands didn't shake with the adrenaline of a chase. He didn't even flinch when a snake slithered out of the dark.

No, this was the man under the mask.

The oracle.

The strategist.

The hunter.

If he'd ever wanted to, he would be the single most terrifying predator in the world. If he wanted to be. If he ever chose to be.

And no one really knew. Not like she did.

If the King of Olympia or his brothers truly understood what Paulo was, they would have done everything in their power to make sure he was eradicated and that no one else could come into this kind of power.

But even then, that knowledge wouldn't serve them.

Because Paulo would know.

Laurel watched his long fingers clench at his sides. His steps slowed as they approached the opening of another tunnel. Faint light streamed out from the mouth of it and the hiss of whispered words slid past Laurel as she crept behind Paulo.

He crouched low, signaling for her to stay at the mouth of the tunnel as he glided over to the other side.

Laurel finally peeked around the corner.

Diana huddled down at the mouth of an iron grate.

Caspian Delrio, the cursed selkie, stood on the other side. He didn't touch the bars, but he leaned forward, his eyes wide with pleading.

"Please, Diana. I don't want to fight with you."

Diana scoffed. "You made that very clear by attacking *my home.*"

"Did you really summon me here to argue?"

"No, I asked you to meet me here because I was certain my friend would have a logical reason for attacking my family and siding with the blasted rebels."

"I am your friend," Caspian insisted. "You know I would never do this if I didn't have to. I don't have a choice. My queen has made a bargain with the rebels. I can't outright disregard her orders without sealing my fate as a traitor, but I can help you. We can come up with a plan to make sure no one gets hurt."

"A betrayer of friends is still a traitor, Cas." She grasped the bars. "The only plans I'll be making with you are for your surrender, or I'm going to walk out of here and tell my brother and his band of assassins that you need to be taken out."

Caspian sighed, running a hand through his unruly hair. "Am I always going to be in your bad graces, Diana? I want this to end just as much as you do. I came so you and I could come up with a plan to end this without any more bloodshed. We don't need to involve anyone else, especially your brother."

Diana pulled back from the bars slightly. "And why not let Paulo help?"

"You know how he is. He does not do anything he does not want to. He always has to be the hero." He tilted his head to the side. "And you know it's true. You would have told him you had reached out to me if you did not."

Laurel looked across the opening to where Paulo crouched. His eyes were closed, brows drawn up as if the words physically pained him.

"I didn't tell him because I can handle sending you packing myself." Her hands dropped from the bars. "You need to go, Caspian. You need to leave our lands and tell your queen to shove her trident into someone else's business."

He lunged forward, touching the bars before hissing and pulling his hands back. The bars had to be pure iron to get such a reaction out of him. "We are friends, Diana. And friends trust each other. Haven't I proven my worthiness? You and I are the same. We want the same thing."

"And what is that?" Diana spat.

"Freedom," he said. "We want the freedom to do whatever we want, whenever we want. To be more than what others tell us we are. To not have to sacrifice everything we want for everyone else. To be just as important as the ones pushing us down and telling us we're not worthy of the greatness we know we're capable of."

"At what cost?"

"If we work together, we can figure it out. We can put an end to this war, Diana. I know you don't have enough men in that castle of yours to fight this. We can work together to help your people. To be heroes on both sides. I know it's hard to trust me. I have not made it easy, but I have also never lied to you. Not like your brother has." The drip of water counted the seconds as Caspian let his words settle. As if he was trying to figure out how to hit Diana in just the right spot. "I saw the remains of the menagerie on the wall. It's horrible what your brother has taken from you. What everyone has made you sacrifice for their own desires. Why should you have to fight in this war that your brother has decided to wage? Why can you not carve your own path?"

Laurel's heart sank along with Diana's shoulders, and she laid her fingers on the blade at her hip.

Don't do it, you foolish girl.

"What do you actually want me to do?"

Laurel had her knife halfway out of its sheath before Paulo's hands were at her waist, and he lifted her up as if she was made of nothing but feathers. If it were anyone else, she would have bit their ear off, but she allowed him to haul her back a few feet before he set her down. Without a word, he grabbed her hand and pulled her back through the tunnels.

His fingers trembled in hers.

When they reached the opening to his secret cave, she pulled him to a stop. "I had a clear shot. I could have taken out one of the blasted Trident that's threatening this castle. We could have gotten information. *Something.*"

He fell backward, his shoulders hitting the wall behind him before he slid down the soggy stones. His head hung, and he brought his knees close so he could rest his grime covered arms on top of them.

"And you accuse my scholae of being traitors when your blasted sister is literally making plans with a known enemy." Laurel let the quiet huffs of their breath fill the space between them for only a moment. "What was that, Paulo? What on Gaia's green earth was she doing with him?"

"That," he said in a hushed whisper, "was the true beginning of the siege."

17

AN UNEXPECTED SHAKE

PAULO PULLED THE BLACK RAM BY THE LEAD ROPE AROUND HIS NECK INTO Grandmother's lily garden. If Paulo remembered right, Grandfather had ordered it planted for his wife in celebration of Father's and Uncle Oliver's birth. Twins ran in the family.

The ewes and younger rams followed behind, chased by the dogs up the steps. Their cloven feet slipped on the stone walkways of the lovely garden. He passed by the one bench sitting under an awning. He'd spent many an afternoon hiding from Diana under that bench as a young lad, concealed by Grandmother's voluminous skirts. Grandmother had a mind for propriety, which she liked to thrust on Diana at any given moment. While Paulo had grown not to agree with everything she'd said, he hadn't hesitated using her as a shield when he could.

If only he could still tuck himself under that bench and hide under Grandmother's skirts. But not even the fiery woman could have prevented this from coming, even if she were still alive. Though, she likely would have had many words to impart on Paulo. She definitely would have had something to say about allowing sheep into the castle gardens.

Men and women bustled around him, moving water troughs and sacks of grain. With only two hundred of the priceless sheep left, they had to make sure every need was met while they had no access to the fields outside the castle walls. By the Goddess, Paulo would let them tear into the manicured lawns within the upper bailey and ravage the stock of grain in the castle stores if it kept these few sheep alive. His family needed to salvage something for themselves after this.

Once the entire flock was inside the hastily made gate, he untied the rope from around the ram's neck. The sheep quickly made themselves at home, their fluffy rears bobbing as they made their way toward the water troughs.

One of the younger shepherds carried a bag of grain on his small shoulders.

Paulo stepped forward. "I can help with that, lad."

The boy looked up, his short flash of relief quickly taken over with shock. "I can't let you do that, my lord."

"Nonsense. You can help grab that ewe trying to knock over the fence over there."

The young shepherd spun, nearly dropping the bag in his haste to look back at the sheep tangled up in the ropes making up a portion of the fence. The boy slid the bag from his shoulders, allowing it to fall into Paulo's waiting hands. "I'll take care of her, my lord."

Paulo chuckled as the boy scrambled to help the sheep.

The levity in his chest died as the ground shook under his boots.

The sheep around him bleated their displeasure at the sensation, shuffling together under one of the tall windows of the castle beside them.

Paulo raced to throw the bag of feed into the newly built storage shed at the far end of the pen. He passed by the boy as he left the pen, giving him a smile he didn't feel reach past his lips. It certainly didn't touch his heart.

When he was finally out of sight, he sprinted toward the closest entrance to the castle. This particular door led him into the residential wing, and he had to race through the courtyard in the middle to get to the command center— or the sitting room as Mater still insisted on calling it. They hadn't had a pleasant afternoon tea in weeks, but her stubbornness was one of her best qualities.

He skidded to a stop right in the open doorway of the sitting room. Serene, Declan, and Xander stood around the table, quickly flipping through papers.

"Where is it?" Serene growled.

The two men sifted through the papers quickly, but their brows only furrowed further as they came up empty handed.

"What's happened?" Paulo asked.

"It seems someone's misplaced the patrol route sheet," Xander explained, heaving a sigh as he set aside another stack of papers.

Magic sparked behind Paulo's eyes as he searched for where the page could have gone. But he couldn't track the fate of a piece of paper. Only the people Gaia tied Her strings around. The lines of fate flicked through his mind, but he couldn't see anything that would tie the paper to someone's fate. At least, not at this point in time.

Declan threw his hands in the air. "Who cares if we don't have it? We're going to have to reroute them to the front gate anyway."

Paulo made it to the table. "That's not what I was asking. What was the rumbling?"

"They brought in a mangonel," Serene answered. "The first launch landed harmlessly in front of the outer wall, but they're recalibrating. We need the patrol sheets so we can account for what men are where."

"We can have Captain Isaac get us another copy," Paulo said. "What are we doing to stop the trebuchet?"

"We've finished our own trebuchet already," Xander reported. "But Laurel and Conley both agreed to keep it on the other side of the castle in case moving it encouraged the rebels to attack first."

Serene rolled her eyes. "The archers have tried setting the thing on fire, but the rebels have an Aigean on it and they keep putting out the fires."

Paulo picked up a weapons supply list Conley had written up. "Is there anything we *can* use to put a stop to their machine?"

"We aren't here looking for a fix," Declan finally answered. "We're looking for a distraction."

Paulo stilled, his magic flashing across his mind's eye.

Laurel, running through a field of blood and fire, Mare's ghostly visage right on her heels. Blades in her hand. An explosion on the field.

Paulo shook his head from the vision. "Where's Laurel now?"

Declan's brows lowered, but Serene grinned. "She's at the bastion."

The bastion was completely full of fighters. Paulo pushed himself through the crowd, his teeth gritted. When he finally reached the middle of the crowd, he found Mare and Laurel sitting in the center, two cups sitting on the floor between them. Their gazes were locked on one another, Laurel's expression as emotionless as the mask that covered Mare's face.

Mare raised her hand, fingers flicking sharply.

The men around them whispered, coins exchanging hands.

Laurel grinned, lifting the cup.

Three dice sat underneath. A five, seven, and three.

The men around them all hollered, either in curses of anger or yips of elation.

Something dark took root in Paulo's gut.

These men sat about, making bets and playing games, as their wives and children trembled within the walls of Iatrus Castle. While rebels who would slit their throats gathered at the gates and threw huge stones at the very walls that kept their families safe.

When Donnie stepped out of the crowd with a handful of pages and one of Paulo's best hats used to collect the bets, his control snapped. His vision split with magic. He would hang Donnie over the side of the wall then report Laurel and Mare to Conley and make him run drills for them until the sun came up tomorrow morning. Then, Captain Isaac would put every man here on double duty patrols for an entire week.

Yes, that was what he would do.

Before he could even twitch in Donnie's direction, thin but strong fingers wrapped around his wrist. Mare slipped through the crowd, pulling him behind her. Why he followed, he couldn't actually say, but the cool fingers on his skin chilled some of the boiling in his blood. He trailed her all the way out of the bastion, and she stopped right outside the entrance connected to the west wall.

It wasn't far enough.

"Who's up next?" Laurel's voice boomed over the crowd.

Paulo turned back to the bastion, fists clenched at his sides.

Mare simply grabbed the collar of his jacket and yanked him backward.

His magic sparked again, and he whirled on her.

"You can release the angry dog."

Paulo deflated at the sound of Laurel's voice. He turned to find her leaning against the opening to the bastion. Mare let go of his jacket and he strode toward her.

"What is the meaning of this?" he said, gesturing to the crowd behind her. Two guards had taken the center, cups in hand.

He should rip the MacGregor crest from their sleeves.

Laurel set a hand on his chest, as if reading his thoughts and hoping her touch would keep him from ripping apart the closest guard. "This is battle strategy."

He whipped his head back in her direction. "What?"

Her hand dropped from his chest only to take his hand and tug him down the walkway. They passed the crenels of the south wall until they reached the guard tower. Laurel led him halfway up the tower until they found Conley, squatting near one of the thin arrow slits in the tower. A spy glass sat against his mask as he mumbled numbers to the young guard sitting on the stairs near his feet. He pulled away from the window, removing the device from his face to turn to them.

"You were right," he said, speaking to Laurel. "They're amassing on this side."

"Excellent," she said, holding out her hand. Conley set the spyglass in her open palm and swapped her places. She set the device to her eye. "How many have arrived?"

"Only two hundred, but Cal reported another hundred or so coming from the lake."

"That should do it." She brought the spy glass back down. "Tell Serene to meet me on the northwestern guard tower."

"Yes, Master." Conley handed the spyglass to his guard companion and jogged down the steps.

Paulo blinked over at Laurel. "You're setting them up."

The bastion was a trap. She'd collected as many of the men on the walls as she could, drawing them in one place to tempt the rebellion into thinking they were gathering over on that side for a reason.

She grinned, practically skipping down the steps. "Of course. I need them distracted while Mare and I take care of the mangonel."

Paulo chased her down the stairs. "How did you know it would work?"

"What is the one thing all the rebels can agree on?"

Thought seemed to stutter and cyclone in his brain all at once. "I don't know," he admitted.

"Righteous justice," she said. "All of them are trying to prove that their way of thinking is the only way. They're zealots, looking to convert and anyone who gets in their way is an obstacle that either needs to be brought to their side or annihilated. Your men have clearly signaled they will not be swayed to the other side, so the rebels must crush them."

"The collection of so many men on our side is enough to pique their interest?"

She shrugged. "If it seems like we're up to something, it will draw them like flies to dung. They won't be able to help it."

They reached the bottom of the steps. "Wait," he said, grabbing her arm. "I can't let you go down there. They've put something in the ground."

"Yes, we saw them. It's plates."

"They're enchanted plates."

Laurel rolled her eyes. "What are they going to do? Jump up from the ground and do a dance number? We can get past them."

"Not if they can blow you to pieces. They're infused with light magic. From the way my vision looked, if you step on the plates you die." The scene played out in Paulo's head again. Laurel stepping on the soft ground. A flash of light. The enchantment wasn't anywhere as powerful as King Dion's lightning, but it was effective.

Her lips thinned and her brows puckered. A wisp of hair swept across her cheek, and Paulo couldn't stop himself from carefully tucking it behind her ear.

Laurel glared, but didn't bite his fingers off. He could have crowed with success, but then she really would have bit him. He'd take progress where he could get it. Only a few months ago, she wouldn't have let him even stand this close let alone touch her.

"You said I died?" she asked.

He nodded. "It was enough to take out both you and Mare."

Her face went still, but not emotionless. It was her deep-thinking face. It never revealed her thoughts, but it was different than her blank mask. There was a soul behind her eyes.

She spun, striding back toward the tower.

"Where are you going?" he asked.

"To find Cal," she said.

18

THE POISONER

LAUREL HAD TO TREK ALL THE WAY OUT INTO THE VILLAGER TENTS BEFORE she found Cal. He sat near a quaint fire, five children gathered around the flames— the unnaturally red flames.

With a flick of his wrist, he tossed a small paper pouch into the fire. The heat devoured the paper, but only moments later the flames turned from red to purple.

The children around the fire cheered as they watched the lilac flames ripple and dance atop the logs. The flames stayed purple for only a few moments before fading to a more natural orange. He tossed another packet in, this time turning the flames green. As the other children cheered, one little girl plucked a dandelion from the grass at her feet and offered it to him. He took it with a slight nod of thanks before tucking it into the breast pocket of his jacket.

Paulo passed by Laurel, a grin of delight playing on his lips. "What are all of you little rascals doing out here?" he said in an exaggeratedly gruff voice. "I thought you lot were supposed to be chasing brownies out of my castle."

The children all turned as one, each of their expressions brightening as Paulo stepped closer.

"My lord! Did you see the fire?" one of the boys asked, pointing in Cal's direction. "He has magic that makes it change color!"

"I most certainly did," Paulo said, plopping himself onto one of the shortest logs around the fire. The little girl he sat next to beamed up at him, her brown curls bouncing as she scooted to make more room for Paulo on the bench.

The little boy turned to Cal. "What kind of magic makes the fire change colors?"

Laurel stepped forward to attempt an answer. She wasn't as well versed in chemical makeup as Cal, but she could get by.

She hadn't expected Cal to beat her to it.

"It's not magic. It's science." He pulled another pouch from his jacket. "There are powders in here that contain chemicals that when combined with fire, can change the color of the flame."

He tossed the pouch in, and the flames turned bright yellow.

"Isn't magic just science unexplained?" Paulo said, taking a stick and drawing lines in the dirt.

Cal shrugged. "Perhaps, but I don't know how science can explain the way some people can move water with a flick of their wrist or command a storm with only a thought."

Laurel peered over Paulo's shoulder. In the dirt between his feet, he'd drawn a sheep. He turned to the little girl and let out a very convincing *baa*. The girl giggled and took up a stick of her own. Laurel couldn't take her eyes off the two of them. The fact that a marquess would sit beside a commoner child next to a fire would make anyone do a double take, but Paulo looked as natural sitting on a log, his knees nearly at his ears, as he did lounging in a velvet chaise. Which was the real Paulo MacGregor?

It was exhausting trying to guess. She didn't know if she should trust the boy who could doodle in the dirt with a little girl or a man who could turn the tides of this war with the bat of an eye. He'd told her, probably more than she would like, that he'd only done what he did to save her. That he sacrificed so much to get her on this isle. To save her from a fate none of them wanted. But to what end? Was this little girl's happiness worth risking because this war had to happen? Were any of these children's futures worth sacrificing? How much of what Paulo had done was for his own benefit and not the benefit of these people?

Could Laurel live with his sacrifices if she knew they were for her?

"Master?"

Cal's call finally drew her eyes away from the two on the log and their quickly growing flock of dirt sheep. His gaze was fixed on her face, his silver mask giving nothing away. Had he seen the storm that seemed to grow every time she looked at the cursed marquess?

He shifted uncomfortably on his stool. "Was there something you needed?"

"Yes. Perhaps we can speak in private." She glanced down at Paulo, but he made no objections. He must not have been as nervous about Cal as he was some of the others. She swore she couldn't be in a room with Declan for more than two minutes without him showing up.

Cal nodded and stood, much to the disappointment of the children.

"Will you come back, sir?" one of the boys asked.

"Can I try to make the flames change colors?" asked another.

Cal shook his head and stood. The children's faces fell. This had probably been a much-needed reprieve among the group. Laurel had no idea where their parents were. This fire pit sat in the middle of the tent city that had been put up in the castle's upper bailey to protect them from the worst of the fighting, but it had obviously become the children's play area. Wooden swords and fabric dolls were strewn about. Blankets lay in rumpled piles and crude structures had been crafted using sticks and rope. The children had created a haven in the midst of a battle. A standing testament to their resilience.

Laurel couldn't be more impressed.

Paulo stood, his stick poised as if it were a sword. "I think you lot need challenged to a game!"

The children all cheered, quickly forgetting their woes. Laurel watched them gather into a horde as Paulo laid out the rules of the game. Had he known that they needed someone to distract them?

When Laurel met Paulo's gaze, he winked.

Oh, he certainly had. The meddler.

Laurel turned away from the fire and led Cal through the tents. They passed through the gate as well, leaving the tent village behind and marching out into the outer bailey where the adults that hadn't taken up a sword wielded hammers and spoons. Some kept steady watch at the cook fires speckled through the wide space while others slammed hammers into anvils.

"Please tell me you have something for me," Laurel said.

Cal looked around them, checking for open ears or eager eyes. "I figured out how to solve the mangonel problem." He tilted his head to the side, directing them toward the northern wall. A guard tower sat against the wall and the guards at the base all gave Cal a nod and even a few called out to him.

"Been over here much, have you?" Laurel asked.

He shrugged but didn't deny it. They walked through the door at the bottom, but instead of going up the stairs to the top of the tower, he led Laurel down into the storage area that all the towers had been built with. From what Mater had told her, they'd been used for a multitude of things over the years— old weaponry, sheep supplies, and the like— though many of them were now relegated to furniture storage so they could keep their food stores safe from harm inside the castle just in case the outer wall fell and they had to retreat to the upper bailey.

When Laurel finally reached the bottom, she had to stop in the doorway. The furniture and other crates had been shoved up against one side, haphazard piles of chairs with legs akimbo and chests piled in crooked towers reaching toward the low ceiling. But it wasn't the storage that Cal walked toward. On the other side of the room stood tables in neat rows, magelights and candles scattered between vials and copper pots. A decorative bird cage hung next to one of the tables, but no bird sang from its perches.

"You've certainly been busy," she said, lifting one of the vials off a table. Bright yellow liquid sloshed in the glass. It looked like linseed oil, but Laurel didn't dare open it. She'd made that mistake with Cal's ingredients before. "How long did it take you to convince the guards to let you put up shop down here?"

"Actually, they were very willing. I think your marquess had already spoken to them as they'd practically had everything I would need."

"He's not my marquess," she said automatically.

Cal looked over his shoulder, a single, unbelieving brow quirked.

She narrowed her eyes but left it at that. It wouldn't do for the scholae to think she had any attachments to Paulo other than what they saw— a marquess and an assassin, working toward the same goal. Nothing more.

"What are you working on?" Laurel asked, setting the vial in her hand back in its spot on the table.

He pointed at the cage. "I resumed the work I'd started back home."

Laurel walked over and looked in the cage again. It wasn't empty. Two balls of black hung from the very top of the cage, membranous wings tucked around fuzzy bodies.

"I remember you liking bats." It was why she'd told him about the little creatures in the tunnels under the castle. "I just didn't realize it had become such an obsession that you had moved your experiments onto animals and not just chemicals."

Cal gave a soft snort. "It's not the beasts I'm interested in but what they leave at the bottom of their cage."

Laurel's attention flicked down to the tray lining the bottom of the cage. "I'm not exactly following."

"It doesn't matter. That's not what we're down here for." He reached across the table and picked up a jar Laurel recognized as one of Cal's smoke screen bombs. She knew if she threw it into a fire, it would create a thick cloud of smoke for her to hide in. He then picked up a waterskin and handed it to her. "This is what we'll need to take down the mangonel."

Laurel plucked it from his hands. "What is it?"

"Fire paint. You just need to open the lid and throw it in the trebuchet's counterweight basket. It'll do the work on its own."

She gingerly hung the waterskin over her shoulder. "Do you have any more of it?"

He shook his head. "I had hoped to make more, but I don't have enough of the materials I need. This impromptu workshop isn't nearly as well put together as the one back at Stellatus Hall."

Laurel bit the inside of her cheek. "I'm sure what you have

here is fine. We just need to show these rebels who they're messing with."

Cal's chest deflated. "Is this really our fight, Master? Should we even be concerning ourselves with these people when our own are being scattered? I know Paulo has this crazy gift that he says will lead us to the future we need, but are we so sure he doesn't have his own agenda?"

Oh, how his words reflected Laurel's heart. She didn't know. She didn't have an answer for Cal. All she knew was that she couldn't escape this place no matter how hard she tried.

And for some strange reason, she hadn't wanted to.

"I appreciate your candid words, Cal, but I agreed to offer my help. You and the others are free to leave if you truly want to." It would likely ruin any chance Iatrus Castle had to get through this siege, but she wouldn't keep any of the scholae there if they didn't wish to stay. It was better to let them go rather than fight beside them knowing they hated her for making them stay.

Cal blew out a breath. "No. If for nothing else, we'll follow you because you are Master Schola. You're our leader for a reason, and we have taken oaths to follow your command, even if it comes in the form of your example."

Warmth spread through Laurel's chest. "Thank you, Cal. We will get through this battle and figure out a way for all of us to return to Stellatus Hall."

The corner of his mouth tilted up in a smile that said he doubted her word, but he didn't say otherwise. Instead, he plucked the jar from her hands.

"You should be able to take out the mangonel without too much effort."

Laurel sighed. "Can't say the same for getting to the cursed thing. Paulo told me about the magic in the border the rebels have dug. There's light magic buried under the dirt that will blast us to pieces if we step on one."

"I thought Paulo could see into the future."

"Yes, and he saw me and Mare get torn to shreds."

Cal tilted his head. "Don't you think a man who can see the future could tell you where to step in order to avoid getting hurt?"

19

AN UNEXPECTED ATTACK

> *The rebels will gather around a small fire. The Aigean*
> *accompanying them— a man with thick strands of gray*
> *hair and needle-like teeth— will stand up and walk away,*
> *heading back to the camp within the trees. The rebels will*
> *watch him go with relief in their shoulders.*

THE ROPE HOLDING PAULO ALOFT WENT SLACK. HE FELL, HIS HEART skipping two beats in his chest before it went taut once more. His shoulder smacked into the stone bricks, and he had to clench his teeth together to keep from yelling obscenities up toward the top of the wall. He shook out his stinging hands. The leather gloves he wore protected him from the worst of the burn.

"If you drop me, Diana, I swear," he hissed under his breath. He had made the mistake of trusting her with his line, not particularly liking the way Declan eyed him while they were preparing to scale the wall.

He really should have known better.

Looking down, he eyed the piles of debris collected from the rebel attacks on the wall. This side didn't have any abatis— they hadn't had enough time— and the rebels had taken full advantage of that. There were broken ladders, weapons, and large stones dropped from the top of the wall. No bodies littered the ground, having been collected by their comrades, but the stench of death still wafted up from the earth.

His beautiful castle, relegated to a graveyard.

Magic doubled over his vision. He saw himself make it to the bottom of the wall.

But he also saw himself fall and break his leg.

He hastened his climb, hurrying down the wall before Diana had the chance to drop him further. When the toe of his boot touched the ground, he felt his rope go taut and he was yanked up a few inches, just enough to dislodge him and smash him into the wall.

Again.

"Blasted twin sisters," he cursed. His hands fumbled over the knots wrapped around his torso.

"Let me," Laurel said, practically materializing out of thin air beside him. Her nimble fingers made quick work of the knots around his waist. He kept himself turned toward the wall to make sure no one could see them.

Praise the Goddess for good camouflage.

While Serene couldn't technically enchant items with magic, there were some things she could do with the charms she created. She couldn't craft a complete illusion like the fae could, but she could draw a charm that would make cloth shift like the color-changing lizard Paulo had seen in a market once. Father had taken him and Diana into town for market day when they'd been eight or nine. One of the traveling merchants from the Continent had brought the creature, with its three-toed feet and magic skin. Diana had found a book in Iatrus Castle's library that named the little reptile, but he couldn't remember what it was.

The rope finally fell away. The moment it hit the ground, it was yanked back over the top of the wall. Paulo took a deep breath and turned toward the wide-open field.

The plan was simple.

Get through the field without being shot at with arrows.

Sneak across the field of magic without getting blown to bits.

Throw the jar in Laurel's pack into a fire surrounded by rebels to create a smoke cover.

Toss Cal's very-not-magical potion into the counterweight basket.

Run back across the dangerous enchanted dirt.

Climb up the wall without getting mortally wounded.

Simple.

The swish of the grass around them concealed any sounds they made as they raced through the dark. It had been weeks since the sheep had been on this side of the wall and the foliage had grown green and full with the influx of water brought by the Aigean fighters. While Laurel didn't seem to have a problem ducking down in the grass, Paulo had to crouch uncomfortably low. More than once, he lost sight of Laurel and had to use his magic to keep up with her.

The grass ended at a patch of tilled earth, and he had to stop to stretch his back. Crouching low, he twisted back and forth. There was probably fifty feet between them and the next patch of tall grass, but it was that fifty feet that he dared not cross carelessly. The rebels had learned their lesson from the castle's early reinforcements, and Paulo had seen the enchantments simmering under the ground.

"Old age getting to you?" Laurel whispered, her brown eyes glittering in the moonlight.

He grinned. "Absolutely. You'd best marry me quick so you can take all my riches when I wither away and die."

"Sweet Gaia." She rolled her eyes and got to her feet. "There won't be any riches left for me if we don't get across this field and take out that mangonel."

Paulo straightened next to her. "Good to know you're at least considering the prospect."

"Paulo."

"All right. All right." He let his magic off its leash.

Step left.

Dead.

Step forward.

Dead.

Step right.

Live.

He took the steps as quickly as he could, doing his best to

leave obvious footprints for Laurel to step into. The moonlight above them stained the ground blue, drawing out shadows from behind rocks and weaving beams through the tall grass. Tiptoeing through the field was almost as strenuous as playing puddle jump with Diana when they'd been younger. Except instead of avoiding Mater's scolding for muddy socks, they were avoiding death and dismemberment. Paulo's head twinged when they hit the three-quarter point, but he didn't let up on his magic.

The vision hit him quickly, a flash of possibility more than a glaring beam of fate.

An owl diving for a mouse. A flash of light only a few feet away. Laurel, turning at the screech of the burning owl.

Paulo spun and grabbed Laurel's hand before she could take another step. He pulled her into his arms and leapt the last few feet to the border of the field.

Scorching light erupted only a dozen feet away.

Paulo kept his arms wrapped around Laurel as they tumbled into the grass. *Looks like the owl really couldn't resist the temptation.* With his magic still flaring behind his eyes, he stopped their momentum, tucking Laurel under him and covering her mouth.

She squirmed for a moment but stilled when she heard the voices.

"What do you think it was?" a woman called over the grass.

"I saw an owl make a dive," responded a man, much closer to them than felt at all comfortable.

The grass rustled ahead of them.

Laurel tapped his fingers on her mouth, and he carefully removed them but didn't move much more than to set his elbow beside her head and lift himself up the slightest bit to give her some breathing room. She wriggled underneath him, but it wasn't in an attempt to escape. She carefully flipped over until her back was pressed to his chest and she had a dagger in her hand. Paulo carefully crawled off her and settled beside her, reaching for his own dagger at his hip.

The snap of steps in thick grass sounded only a few feet away before it stopped.

Laurel tucked her feet up, ready to launch at a moment's notice.

"I don't see anything now."

Paulo nearly sagged in relief as the crunch of steps faded back in the direction of the mangonel.

As silent as death, Laurel got to her feet, staying low in the grass. Paulo pulled himself up behind her, his gaze drawn to their next target. From the top of the castle walls, the siege engine looked like a plaything. Up close, it was a behemoth with solid beams and thick rope. It would take ages to cut through any of the lines no matter how sharp the knife was.

A few torches flickered around the base of the machine, casting a glow around them. The steady hush of voices rustled in the grass, carried on the wind and straight to Paulo.

"... cursed water folk like we need babysitters." Whoever spoke gave a harsh cough. "The Cartographer must have been siren-spelled to make such a deal."

Paulo grinned. Their timing was perfect.

"Makes me wish the siren had come out with us instead of the merrow. I wouldn't mind being spelled myself if the one doing it looked like Lady Delmar."

Paulo's ears perked at the name. The last time he'd seen Amarissa Delmar was when she'd reported on the rebellion at a council meeting in the palace. The siren was certainly something else, an Aigean turned Olympian spy. He'd been watching her line of fate closely over the last couple of weeks. He needed to send her a letter... after he took care of this cursed siege of course and could actually send it.

Laurel stopped just shy of the firelight, putting the mangonel between them and the rebels. The entire group sat at the front of the machine, torches all over the place. They certainly expected to be attacked, but they obviously had never gone up against a schola.

Paulo straightened the waterskin slung around his shoulders. When Laurel had brought it to him, he'd insisted he carry it. The rusty-looking paint on the inside was as dangerous as the field they'd just crossed.

Laurel signaled for Paulo to stay put as she crept around the side of the siege engine, knife tucked against her arm. Paulo's heart lodged in his throat when some of the men laughed, though he saw it several seconds before it happened. The twinge in his head had grown into a full throb, but it wasn't anything he hadn't dealt with before. What he wasn't used to was watching the woman who held his heart put herself at major risk, a jar of magic dirt in her hand.

The seconds dragged on for an eternity, both in real time and with his magic. He watched a thousand possibilities play out— a few good, but most not.

Paulo had to loosen his hold on the waterskin in his hands.

A crash of shattering clay had his pulse spiking. Voices went up, confusion quickly morphing into alarm.

But Paulo shut down his magic to only see what was in front of him and raced forward to the front of the mangonel.

Black smoke billowed out from the fire, quickly consuming the trebuchet and Paulo with it. He pulled up the loose fabric around his neck he'd worn just for this and kept as close to the machine as he could, watching his fate for rocks or even people as he reached the counterweight basket. When he saw someone jump out of the smoke near him, he tucked himself close to the front wheel until they disappeared once again.

The smoke thickened the longer he stayed there, filling his lungs and making his chest ache for the want of fresh air.

He unplugged the water skin, careful not to get any of the liquid on his hands. He certainly didn't need to lose any fingers. As gently as he could, he tucked the waterskin tightly in between the boulders sitting in the basket as Cal had directed.

The moment his fingers released the waterskin, his magic flared again.

He whipped around as a hand grabbed for his leg.

Fingers met empty air.

Paulo jumped aside as the rebel made another grab for him, and he smashed his boot into the man's nose.

The rebel staggered back, giving Paulo room to jump down from the mangonel.

Blood oozed from the man's forehead where the tip of Paulo's boot had broken skin. The rebel bared his teeth and lunged.

But like an angel of death, Laurel appeared behind him. She stuck a dagger straight into his back.

The man fell forward.

And Paulo's dagger found its way into the rebel's chest.

He shoved the man aside to grab Laurel's hand. With the paint stuck in the rocks, they disappeared through the smoke.

20

THE MANGONEL

LAUREL SAT ON THE WALL, DARING THOSE AT THE MANGONEL TO MAKE A move. Barrels had been rolled in this morning and set next to the cursed thing, likely full of oil ready to be lit. The entire crowd that she'd drawn to the other side of the castle the day before had dispersed, preparing for the next barrage of bloodshed.

Movement out of the corner of her eye drew her attention. Xander strode down the wall, looking about as if he lost something.

"Xander?"

He glanced up at her, the worry on his face evaporating as he gave her a smile. "Yes?"

"Are you looking for something?"

"It seems I lost a bauble last night, but it's not a big deal. I'm sure it'll pop up somewhere." He sauntered toward her and took a seat at her side, kicking his legs against the wall and making the heels of his boots tap on the stones. "You know, I'm growing rather fond of this place."

Laurel turned to study his face. Xander had always had an easy way about him. He leaned back on his hands, the breeze rustling the wisps of brown hair escaping the knot on top of his head. His eyes met hers and a crooked smile spread across his cheeks.

"I think you're growing fond of it too," he added.

Laurel tilted her head. "What makes you say that?"

His brown eyes flicked up and she turned to find Paulo striding toward them, his eyes directly on them.

"Have I missed anything?" he asked, coming to stop next to her. He stood close enough for her to smell the musky scent of his shaving soap. It was woody, like cedar, but also held a warm note. Vanilla if she had to guess. She leaned forward slightly. Yes, it was definitely vanilla. The scent had probably been expensive, and it only just hid the earthy smell that soaked into him from his secret oracle cave. She hadn't recognized it until she'd gone down there.

"Nothing much," Xander said, leaning away slightly from Laurel. "They brought in oil barrels but have yet to put anything on the trebuchet."

Paulo gave a disgruntled hum. "They're waiting for the rest of their men to be in place. They don't want to smash a hole in the wall without people to go through it."

"How much longer?" Laurel asked.

He pointed toward the lake, where a mob of rebels crept out of the woods.

"You know," Xander said, "you lot keep life real interesting. I find it very fascinating that you're able to know when an army moves, yet you weren't able to keep the army from forming in the first place."

Laurel could feel Paulo stiffen, becoming very still.

"There are some things the Goddess allows me to see, others She does not, and most that She gives me reason not to toy with."

Xander tilted his head. "And which category would you say this war falls into?"

Paulo was quiet for several heartbeats. When Laurel looked up into his face, all she saw was grief and regret.

"All three," Paulo admitted quietly. His eyes were his normal blue, but they were dark with the things of the past instead of pearlescent with the future as he stared at the ground below them.

Every move I've made, every future I've altered, has been to save you.

Even now, months after they'd left the mountain cabin overlooking the capital, those words still lived in her head. She'd watched Paulo after that, waiting for him to let go of that blasted mask he always wore, as he had that night. She'd seen glimpses behind it, seen moments of what she believed to be the true Paulo, but nothing like that night.

If he wanted her to trust him, she would need more than glimpses.

He met her gaze. The blue darkened further, but it wasn't with regret any longer.

Xander leaned in toward her ear. "Like I said, you're growing fond of this place."

She shoved him away, breaking the stillness of the moment. He snickered but didn't say anything else. Leave it to Xander to ruin a perfectly acceptable moment of staring at someone.

Not that she had been staring.

Paulo leaned forward. "They're moving."

Laurel straightened, looking out toward the mangonel. A pair of men lugged one of the barrels onto the platform at the base of the trebuchet, wrapping the heavy cask in the leather sling.

The men on the wall around them started calling orders, preparing for yet another attack.

"Come on," Laurel muttered. Cal's plan had to work. The castle couldn't take a hit like that. While the barrel wasn't a boulder that could tear through the outer wall, it could still hit the tents in the village and destroy their shelters. Could still kill people.

"Is that going to hit?" Xander asked Paulo.

But Paulo didn't answer. His eyes were already swirling with magic, and that mask was back in place.

Laurel pulled her feet up and crouched on top of the crenel she stood in.

A cheer went up around the mangonel as a torch bobbed through the group. It disappeared under the counterweight basket, but not a moment later, the barrel at the base lit.

The men on the walls went quiet, though a few whispered prayers fluttered on the breeze. Nothing like a war to bring people close to their maker.

The mangonel moved.

The arm pulled the barrel out from under it.

But before it could bring it up, the counterweight basket exploded.

A red cloud bloomed over the machine.

Rocks flew in every direction.

And the flaming barrel flew straight up in the air.

"Get down!" Paulo shouted. He grabbed Laurel from off the top of the wall and tucked her underneath him.

Another *boom* sounded and stones under their feet shook. Debris rained down on their heads, clattering on the walkway. Laurel reached up to protect Paulo's head with her arms, though it probably did little else than bring his face further into her shoulder.

She might have imagined the light press of his lips to her neck.

The world around them quieted, but all she could feel was him wrapped around her.

Until a roar rattled the ground under her knees.

Every man on the wall thrust their swords into the air with victory.

Paulo released her, and she hurriedly shot to her feet.

Nothing but a flaming pile of debris was left of the mangonel.

A smile bloomed on Laurel's face, and she turned to Paulo.

But he wasn't there.

It took her a second to find him.

He stood on the other side of the wall, staring down into the outer bailey below.

Laurel strode toward him and slapped him on the shoulder. "We did it."

But he didn't look up at her. He only looked below them, eyes whirling with magic.

"We need to get inside the castle."

Laurel leaned forward to look below them, knowing she wouldn't see whatever played out before his eyes.

"What is it?"

He snatched her hand. "We need to get in the castle now!"

Laurel didn't resist as he pulled her forward. She knew better at this point. Her feet kept pace with his long strides as he sprinted toward the closest guard towers and down the steps.

They met Serene and Mare at the bottom.

"What's the hurry?" Serene asked.

"We have to get everyone to higher ground," Paulo said, rushing past them and out to the open ground of the outer bailey.

Serene and Mare followed closely behind.

Laurel wiggled her fingers, but Paulo didn't relinquish her hand. She had a sneaking suspicion his hold on her was more about keeping himself grounded while his brain worked through the possibilities rather than for any sort of romantic scheme.

The two scholae fell into step beside them. "Almost everyone is on the walls," Serene stated.

Paulo shook his head, turning toward the tent village. "I'm not talking about the fighters. I'm talking about the villagers."

He wanted to evacuate the villagers in the outer bailey. But why? Laurel turned to Serene. "Start rounding up the children," she said. "Get them onto the upper bailey walls."

Serene broke away, heading to the center of the tents. Mare went to follow, but Laurel grabbed her arm. "I need you to get to Conley and Mater and have them start getting people out of the castle. The quicker, the better."

Mare spun around and raced back in the other direction.

Laurel pulled Paulo to a stop, finally yanking her hand out of his grip.

"What is it?" she asked.

He ran a hand through his hair. "Caspian is finally going to make his move."

That was all she needed to know. For now. She gave Paulo a sharp nod and sprinted away, running toward the opposite end of the tents rather than in the direction she'd seen Serene go. The first villagers she came across were a group of women hanging clothing.

"Drop everything and get to the walls!" she shouted, pointing at the upper bailey. "Marquess's orders!"

At the sound of Paulo's title, they abandoned their chore and raced toward the castle.

Laurel zig-zagged through the maze that was the outer bailey work tents, assigning help to those that couldn't get to the walls quickly on their own. One old woman wouldn't leave her tent full of junk she'd brought with her from her home. Laurel had had to throw the old woman in a handcart kicking and screaming. Afterward, she recruited some of the younger women to race through the work areas with Paulo's order.

It was when she made her way back up toward the castle that she realized what Paulo had been afraid of.

The pond that sat a little way up the hill was spilling over. Water trailed down, swallowing up the grass.

"*Move!*" Laurel hollered. She grabbed a little boy whose mother already had her hands full of her three other children. "We need to get to the upper bailey walls *now!*"

They ran for the castle, water starting to rush around their ankles as it ran down the hill.

Laurel passed the little boy off to someone as they made it to the upper bailey, but the water around her ankles was quickening. Her eyes flicked over faces, looking for freckles.

She grabbed one of the guards running an armful of supplies. "Where's the marquess?"

He shook his head. "I don't know, my lady."

Laurel let him go, sprinting through the water back toward the gate.

A crowd had gathered, directing people onto the walls and carrying the smaller children through the flowing water.

Laurel paused at the gate leading to the outer bailey.

Paulo sprinted toward her, an elderly man slung over his shoulder. His face was creased with exhaustion when he looked up and met her eye.

"Get to the courtyard!" he shouted.

Oh, how much he probably reveled in bossing her around. She didn't argue though, even as she wished to smack him or hug him or something. Instead, she did as he said and ran for the courtyard at the center of the castle.

She was halfway to the castle when a huge spray of water shot into the sky.

Water rushed out the front doors, cascading down the stone steps bringing debris with it. Laurel had to grab the frame of the door in order to pull herself through the hip high water. When she made it through the door, she could wade quicker through the flow of it.

Serene came crashing down the stairs of the great hall. "Master! They're in the courtyard."

Laurel didn't even want to ask who.

Once they were through the great hall, she found the opening out into the courtyard.

And the six water folk waiting there.

Laurel crept to the opening, staying out of sight as much as she could. Her eyes scanned the shadows around them until she saw a flicker of silver. Cal stood in one corner of the courtyard, almost completely hidden behind one of the statues of the Goddess lining the perimeter. The others were likely within the courtyard as well. They all would have seen the water.

Caspian stood in the middle of the group, a head taller than the others. Laurel recognized his selkie friend, Kai, from their time in the palace. The other four were new. A sea hag, stringy hair dripping into her green-hued face, skuttled about, her crooked back and twiggy legs a contrast to the quick movements. Slitted eyes flicked about, and a blackened tongue ran along sharklike teeth. A merrow stood in the center, his sharp-nailed fingers clawed. A shudder ran down Laurel's spine just looking at him. He could be considered beautiful at first glance, but the stringiness of his white hair and the gray pallor of his skin looked morbid. A merman hovered in a bubble next to him, a trident in hand. The last new arrival was the siren, her looks absolutely devastating. The tattoo along Laurel's back burned as she stared and a little of the siren's beautiful glow faded. Caspian hadn't been wrong when he'd said Lady Delmar had been the most beautiful of the sirens, but this siren wasn't anything to scoff at.

"How much longer, Strider?" Caspian asked, turning to the merrow.

Water bubbled up from the grate in the middle of the courtyard, coming in from the underground tunnels.

Where Diana had met with Caspian.

The merrow's hairless eyebrows furrowed, his gaze never straying from the water. "I've just reached the outer wall. It'll be about ten more minutes for the water to spread all the way around."

The countdown started in Laurel's head.

Kai took a step toward him. "We don't have *ten minutes*. Thanks to your water show, we likely don't even have ten seconds."

"Kai, instead of berating our team, why don't you help out?" Caspian asked.

The other selkie bared his teeth.

Laurel had seen enough. She drew the long dagger from her hip and with a signal to Cal to stay put, pulled back. This wasn't a battle to jump into when she was knee deep in water that could be magically manipulated. She needed to find a way to split them up.

Nine minutes.

Carefully, she waded through the water up the stairs. There were windows on the second floor she could use. When she got higher than the water line, her boots squelched with every racing step she took up the stairs. If they were going to continue to fight with water folk, she may need to talk with any cobblers from the village about different footwear for everyone.

When she reached the second story, she found Conley and Declan on either end of a hallway, crossbows in hand.

Declan stood closest and Laurel paused next to him first. "Target?"

His eyes narrowed. "The big brute in the middle."

"You ought to leave him to Xander. The selkie's aim might be off, but he makes up for it with speed." The competition he'd held with Diana at the palace was fresh in her mind. His spears had stuck inches into the stone wall behind his targets.

Declan growled. "Xander told me to take him so he could take the merrow. He's the one doing the magic."

Laurel frowned but didn't argue. Likely every one of those water folk had some magic over water. But she wouldn't argue. Xander knew how to pick a mark. "Where is Xander?"

"Roof."

She bent her knees slightly so she could see the tiled roof above the courtyard. The very tip of Xander's hood peeked over the top.

"What's the signal?" she asked.

He tilted his head slightly in Conley's direction.

Six minutes.

Laurel left him to his post and crept past the tall windows facing the courtyard. Conley held his crossbow a little lower than Declan, both eyes focused on the group.

"What are you waiting for?" Laurel asked.

"Mare."

As he said her name, the schola came around the corner, a fuming Diana following behind her. Diana's right eye was swollen, and blood smeared along her chin. A quiver of arrows poked over her shoulder and her knuckles were white where she gripped the bow in her hand. Her entire expression went frantic when she met Laurel's gaze. "I swear, I was trying to save us."

Laurel took a deep breath, sheathing her blades to free her hands. She'd been in that tunnel when Diana had spoken with Caspian. Knew how easy it was to believe in those that had earned her trust. How easy that trust could be broken. The guilt that came when that person betrayed you.

"I know." She turned to Conley. "Now."

Conley gave the signal, which just happened to be an arrow in the merman's throat.

Before the Aigean could even fall, Declan and Xander's arrows promptly followed. Declan's went wide, only grazing Caspian's arm.

Xander's was caught in a shield of ice.

Conley cursed.

If only his sharp words could pierce the thick shell. The merrow now stood beneath a shell of frosted ice, concealing his entire body.

Four minutes.

Laurel unlocked the window and swung out, the others following on her heels. The colonnade on the west side of the courtyard stretched the entire length of the wall, a pair of staircases on either end and a set in the middle. Laurel raced for the middle while Mare broke off and followed Declan down the left side.

A shard of ice flew at Laurel's head.

She ducked and the ice shattered on the stairs behind her. With a flick of her wrist, she sent two of her throwing knives at the hag who had thrown the ice. A shield formed in front of the Aigean, and the blades sank into the ice.

Laurel took advantage of the hag's distraction and hurdled over the railing of the stairs, tucking herself out of view. She crept down the length of them until she was crouched against the last few steps.

"This is not your war, scholae," a voice boomed. Caspian from the sounds of it. "Our fight is not with you."

Laurel rolled her eyes as he continued to drone on about how they could all walk away from this peacefully. As if. She had two more throwing knives left, her pair of long daggers and two other regular ones on her at the moment. The boot dagger would be useless if she was being quick, so she pulled that one out, replacing her long dagger with it. She could draw one of those at a moment's notice since they rested against her thighs.

None of the other scholae answered Caspian's plea for surrender. They all knew what false promises looked like.

Laurel peered around one of the pillars holding up the railing. Five water folk slowly crept through the water, not even making a splash as they glided across the courtyard. The merrow remained at the opening, pulling more of the water through. The water now reached Laurel's calves. It would certainly put her scholae on uneven footing against the Aigeans. If Xander and Conley remained above, they might be able to pick off the water folk below them.

With a roar, Caspian sent a gush of water onto the rooftop where Xander had shot at the merman from. Xander's dark shadow leapt out of the way, but a second wave of water knocked him from the roof.

"Curses," Laurel hissed. She watched for several seconds to see if Xander would reappear, but he didn't. That left Conley with a crossbow and the four on the ground against the five water folk.

An arrow shot from above her. It sank into Caspian's upper arm. He yelped with the pain of it and broke the white fletching from the top half.

Laurel looked up and saw a flash of red disappear from a window just before a flurry of ice shards smashed through the panes.

Two minutes.

Kai crept closest to her, his eyes scanning the area as he moved in her direction.

His mistake.

Laurel once again hurdled over the railing, though this time she used it to propel herself out into the open. Her boots met Kai's sternum, and she used him as a springboard to land in the water a few steps away. She twisted as she landed, sliding a bit as the water shoved her back.

A splash sounded. She'd expected to see Kai on his rear, but instead he had wrapped thick cords of water around his arms, holding him up. He sent a sharp glare her way and raised his hand, the water coming with it. A whip of water lashed out toward her, and she had to dive sideways to avoid it.

Kai took a step in her direction. "Do I know you from somewhere?"

Laurel ignored him and leapt forward, her dagger slashing at his throat.

He dodged, bringing up a fist of water that he threw at her side.

Leaping back to avoid the blow, Laurel grabbed one of the longer blades at her side. Kai had a greater reach with the water, but it did slow him down. She would have to be quick to get under his defenses and make it count before he could smash his magic into her.

A screech rang out over the courtyard. Laurel took a split second to look over and saw the merrow with the point of a sword sticking out between his ribs. Declan stood behind him, his silver mask glinting under his hood. The merrow's mouth gaped open, and he exploded, his body disintegrating into sea foam.

Well, that's disgusting.

Kai growled, summoning a wave and shooting it in Declan's direction. Declan slammed into a wall, going limp.

Laurel took advantage of the selkie's distraction and leapt on him. She wrapped her legs around his torso and sank both her blades into his shoulders.

He roared this time, reaching up to grab her.

She twisted the blades, and he screamed, going down to his knees.

Water shot up and grabbed hold of her head, shoving her back and making her lose her grip on the daggers. Her shoulder hit the hard stone of the colonnade stairs. Sound became muffled and all she could see was the distorted colors of the courtyard through the water. She clawed at the bubble around her head, accidentally sucking in a lungful of water. Her chest rejected the liquid, trying to cough it out, but more water poured into her mouth. Drowning. She was drowning in open air.

As fast as it came, the bubble disappeared. She gagged, turning onto her side as her lungs heaved the water out of them.

Blinking the black spots from her vision, she looked over and saw Kai on his back, Paulo raining blows down on him. How had he gotten into the courtyard so quickly? Laurel shook her head. That was a stupid question. Paulo's eyes swirled with color as he dodged Kai's magically infused hits, the selkie's aim wide as he grew frantic. Paulo leaned back to avoid a wild spray of water and retaliated with a direct hit to Kai's face.

The selkie staggered back, but before he could recover, Laurel shoved herself to her feet. She grabbed the long dagger she saw lying on the ground and stabbed him in the back of the neck. He crumpled to the ground, revealing a grim-faced Paulo.

"Thanks," she said, voice raspy.

Paulo shook out his bloodied hand and stood. "No problem."

Without another word, she stepped over the dead selkie and raced toward the grate.

21

AN UNEXPECTED FLOOD

Cal will race in the direction of the outer bailey, right on Laurel's heels. Paulo will yell for him to stop. Will tell him to catch Diana. They will both be too late. Diana will shoot Caspian in the back. He will turn around and find Laurel right behind him. He will stab at her with his trident. She will dodge it, but he will use the water around them to yank her to the ground. He will bring his trident down on her chest.

PAULO WATCHED LAUREL SPRINT TOWARD WHERE CASPIAN STOOD. THE hag and the siren stood on either side of the grate, spraying water and magic at anyone who got too close. Mare sidestepped a rather large icicle hurtling toward her face. The hag was the only one who had power over ice it seemed.

Magic ran rampant through Paulo's mind, playing out scenarios in quick succession and muddling his thoughts. There were too many variables. Too many decisions.

All of it came to a halt when the siren met his eye.

Her flaxen hair shone, droplets of water on her dewy skin glistening with the light from the sun above them. Or was it just the natural glow of her skin? Her full lips pulled wide in a smile, and she beckoned him closer.

His feet moved of their own accord, but he didn't mind one bit. He wanted to be closer to her. Wanted to bask in her beauty.

"Come here you little sack of pond scum," she cooed. Her words sent a thrill through him. She was speaking to him and only him. How had he gotten so lucky?

Somehow, he'd moved across the entire courtyard in what felt like a second. He was before her and she touched his face, cupping his chin with her hand. He shuddered, the touch like nothing else he'd ever felt. His eyelids were heavy, but he saw her lips part in a beautiful smile. Beautiful wasn't even the right word. Glorious. Exquisite. Divine.

She opened her mouth as words formed on her tongue. He couldn't look away. Nothing else existed for him but her.

He didn't even blink when he saw the blade protruding from her throat.

Her hand fell away from his face, and she reached up at the blade, eyes wide. She slumped to the side and revealed Laurel standing there with a bloodied dagger. Her face was stoic as she watched the siren writhe on the ground.

At the sight of Laurel, the siren's enchantment broke. Paulo's magic flooded him, sending needles of pain into his head.

Caspian, sending a tidal wave to crush them against the wall of the courtyard.

Diana, falling from a third-story window.

Laurel, hanging limp from the tip of a spike of ice.

He blinked the magic away and stepped toward Laurel.

"Thank you," he said.

She shrugged. "No problem."

With a nod, he grabbed her hand and pulled her toward one of the doors on the ground floor. "We need to get to Diana."

Laurel yanked her hand from his. "You grab Diana, I'll finish taking care of the water problem."

He glanced back over his shoulder and saw a wall of ice around the grate. The hag had built a shield all the way around them, and Caspian was pushing water out of the top.

Paulo reached for her again, but she was already running

toward the wall of ice. He cupped his hands around his mouth. "Avoid the ice spikes!"

Laurel didn't respond, but she did slow a bit, turning to stand next to Serene who had joined the fight as well. Serene used blood from a wound on her arm to draw marks on the ice. The ice seemed to grow thicker as she did, slowing the flow of water.

Whatever they were doing at least disrupted the Aigeans' plans. Paulo spun around and raced back into the castle. Water sloshed against his legs as he pushed toward the stairs. The first two steps were completely submerged, and he gritted his teeth. The magic flooding his system directed him up until he stopped on the third floor. He raced down the hallway and turned a corner to find Diana there with an arrow at her cheek and her blue eyes narrowed.

Paulo raced toward her. "Diana! Move!"

His arms wrapped around her torso just as a tentacle of water smashed through the glass. The twang of her bowstring sounded, but Paulo didn't know if the arrow met its mark. They landed in a heap on the ground as the water quickly retreated back out the window.

Diana pushed him aside. "I can handle this," she snapped.

Paulo bit back his own sharp words and jumped to his feet. "We need you down below. Caspian's about to realize he's cornered, and they're going to retreat."

Diana drew another arrow from her quiver. "Then we need to stop them."

Paulo grabbed her arm. "Listen to me—"

She ripped her arm from his grasp. "No, *you* listen to *me*! That cursed selkie is going to get what's coming to him, and I'm going to be the one who delivers it." Shoving past him, she raced for the stairs.

Following quickly on her heels, he tried to reason with her. "Diana, people are going to die if you don't stop."

"People are going to die whether I stop or not, but if I do stop then he gets away."

She reached the bottom of the stairs.

"Diana! Stop!"

She flew out the door and into the courtyard.

He tried to reach for her, but right as he stepped out of the castle, the Aigeans' shield exploded, raining chunks of ice down on everyone's heads. Serene leapt away, huddling over a now unconscious Mare who was laying prone on the ground. Laurel and Cal were thrown back.

Caspian, now in his black seal form, bobbed through the water toward the west side of the courtyard. A crossbow bolt from Conley zipped through the air and stuck into the thick flesh of Caspian's tail. The selkie roared and the water around him grew into a bubble.

The hag was on her feet next to him, making a run for the short walkway that would lead to the upper bailey.

Laurel, followed closely by Cal, sprinted after them. They disappeared through the gate.

"Come on!" Diana hollered. She pulled her bowstring back and let the arrow fly. Without even waiting for the first arrow to hit its mark, she drew another and ran through the gate.

Paulo sprinted after her, his magic hammering nails into his skull one vision at a time. He finally overtook her, grabbing her arm and hauling her to the side.

"Diana, you have to stop. You can't take Caspian out this time."

She shoved him hard enough that his back smacked into the stone wall. "Stop playing games, Paulo. I can take him this time with or without your magic eyeballs helping me."

Before he could do more than open his mouth to answer, the ground shuddered beneath them. Paulo ran the rest of the way out of the tunnel and made it into the upper bailey. From where he stood, he could see the entire west part of the castle. The water had reached a good foot up the upper bailey wall. It rushed through the gates and headed out to the outer bailey, which was now completely submerged in water. The length between the inner and outer walls on this side of the castle was shorter than anywhere else and created a funnel for the water. Tent canvas bobbed with the currents, dragged down to the gates where the water tried to escape. A few of the village dogs paddled through the water and some of the men were standing on top of the walls trying to salvage whatever they could that rushed by them. Their comrades stood on the other side, fighting off the rebels trying to open the gates. The flood of water out of the gates would take everything out with it.

Paulo tried to ignore the few bodies floating in the water.

A tower of ice had shot up near the outer wall. The sea hag stood on the top, shooting icicles down below. Caspian, now in his human form, ran for the tower as blood dripped down his left leg. Laurel and Cal followed quickly on Caspian's heels even as the hag barraged them with ice. Conley appeared behind them, throwing his crossbow into Mater's favorite rhododendron bush before drawing the sword at his waist.

Laurel drew close to Caspian, a long dagger in each hand.

A black-fletched arrow whizzed through the air, hitting him in the shoulder.

Xander.

Caspian roared and whirled, right as Laurel closed in on him. His trident swung out, nearly stabbing Laurel in the chest.

She twisted out of the way, but Cal was right behind her.

The trident sank into his stomach.

Laurel's eyes went wide as Cal roared, ripping the weapon from Caspian's hands.

Caspian didn't even try to fight it. He dropped his grip on the weapon and ran.

Diana was the one who caught Cal as he fell.

The trident tumbled into the water beside him with a splash. Laurel grabbed it and hoisted it on her shoulder, the tips red with Cal's blood. The trident looked massive in her hands, but she held it as if she'd practiced with such a weapon every day. Her eyes narrowed as she watched Caspian run, but they flicked up at the last second and she launched the trident not at the selkie, but at the hag standing on the top of the ice.

With a screech, the hag fell, and her tower went with her.

The column of ice tumbled down. The men on the outer wall scrambled out of the way as it fell. The top half crashed into the stone wall, tearing through it and leaving a gaping hole.

And the water rushed to fill it.

Laurel ran toward the opening, and Paulo followed quickly behind. Caspian tore the arrow from his shoulder and limped toward the hole. Dodging the bits of debris rushing through the opening sapped Paulo's strength. Laurel flew through the water almost as fast as the selkie did, but he reached the wall before them.

With one hand, Caspian summoned a tall wave that crashed into the ice, breaking it away from the wall and freeing the opening. His selkie pelt whipped through the air and the black shadow of his seal form disappeared through the wall.

He'd escaped, just as Paulo knew he would.

Laurel went to charge after him through the gaping hole in the wall, but Paulo grabbed her arm. "You can't. You'll walk right into the rebels' hands."

"*You coward!*" Diana screamed. "*Get back here and fight!*" She charged toward the opening, but guards were already sending swarms of arrows after the selkie. The rebels on the other side were already gathering, preparing for another attack now that they had an opening.

"Diana!" Paulo snapped. "We need to get out of here. Now!"

She turned back at him, her eyes wide with a crazed frenzy. But she did stop. She looked down at her hands, now caked with Cal's blood, then back at the crushed wall. She fell to her knees, into the muddy ruins of the wall and roared at the sky.

Just as Paulo had seen.

22

THE GRAVE

WAR WAS A BEAST NO LOGICAL PERSON COULD WRAP THEIR HEADS around. Yes, fighting was natural. The need to protect what belonged to someone instinctual. The blood-soaked hands that reached for more and more until there was nothing left but their insatiable greed that ate them from the inside out somewhat explainable. Laurel could understand all that. She could understand the need to kill. She'd been raised to do it after all.

But she didn't understand war.

She couldn't understand why one minute they were fighting for their lives, but when the sun went down, each side came together to collect their dead. Watching from the top of the wall, she couldn't pick out which side was which. They were all just people hoping, wishing, praying their comrade, friend, lover wasn't a pile of bloody pulp out on that field. They were all on the same side.

Her fingers twisted the lead weight hanging from her wrist. Shouldn't that be enough? Shouldn't all of them take one good look at each other and realize this wasn't worth it? That greed or glory wouldn't actually fill that hole in their chest?

Conley stepped into her peripheral. "It's time."

Laurel gave a sharp nod and turned, not even meeting Conley's eye.

She didn't want to see the hole in his chest.

He'd been the closest to Cal out of all of them.

Turning, she saw the huge gap left from the ice tower's fall. The ice had melted in the warm summer sun, though not as fast as the rebels probably would have liked. The moment the wall had fallen, the rebels had scrambled for the opening, but even though Caspian had created a gap to escape through, the host of rebels had been bottlenecked. Cal had been dragged to the castle while the rest of them had pushed back the attackers. It had been a miracle the castle had been able to push them back long enough to get the holes sealed. There was a team even now watching the gaps as others pulled the ice chunks from the wall and replaced them with thick wooden beams. The Aigeans had made it harder for the rebels to maneuver near the castle, the thick mud making movement of any sort impossible. The castle would at least have a reprieve for a few days. Hopefully.

The climb down the stairs was too fast to come to terms with what she was about to do. She'd lost people during her time in Stellatus Hall. It was part of her job. But not a schola. Not someone she had sworn to lead. To protect.

Cal's body lay atop a stretcher. Someone had dressed him in clean cloths, but if Laurel blinked, she could still see the three gaping holes that had torn his stomach apart. He'd languished for two hours in the castle infirmary until his body had finally given up. Not even his vast knowledge could save him. It had not been a quick death as he'd deserved. It wasn't fair that someone with so much of their life left, with such promise, could be ripped from the world in a moment.

War really was a monster.

She stepped forward and grabbed one of the poles making the stretcher mobile. Conley, Declan, and Xander grabbed the other three. Declan's head was wrapped in a white bandage and one of Xander's arms was tucked into a sling. Mare walked at the front of the group, blades drawn, and Serene walked at the rear with puffy, red eyes.

Laurel was too broken to cry no matter how hard she wished for the tears to fall.

They took a path through the front gate and out toward the forest. Magelights bobbed through a small line of trees. An entire contingent of guards encircled the space, their backs facing the lines of headstones. The sound of a shovel drew Laurel's attention, and she found Paulo standing in a freshly dug hole. Dirt streaked across his freckled face and his shirt sleeves were rolled up to his elbows. He must have dug the entire hole himself as no other men stood around him except for Jenkins who held his master's jacket.

As they drew closer, Paulo looked up. His eyes met hers and he threw the last shovelful of dirt onto the mound he'd created. He climbed out of the hole and stabbed his shovel into the top of the pile.

"I've got a coffin just in there," he said, pointing to the small building on the outskirts of the graveyard.

As one, Laurel and the men set Cal's body next to the freshly dug grave.

Declan looked in the direction of the building. "You MacGregor's usually have prebuilt coffins lying around?"

Paulo licked his lips, glancing at Laurel with an indecipherable darkness in his eyes. "Comes with the territory."

"We need to hurry," Conley said. "We don't want the rebels getting any ideas about attacking us while we take our sweet time."

Serene sniffed. "You don't need to be callous."

"I'm not being callous," Conley snapped. "Just practical."

Laurel's limbs were heavy as she stepped toward Paulo. "Will you show me the coffin?" Her voice came out in a rasp. Nearly being drowned had definitely done something to her vocal cords.

He directed her to the building. She had to duck through the short door to get into the room, but once she was through, she nearly gasped. Leaning against the wall were two coffins, all hand carved with beautiful designs. The smallest was decorated with flowers of every kind, resembling the most beautiful garden Laurel had ever seen. It was layered in dust, though it looked well cared for. The one next to it was tall, covered with all kinds of carvings gilded with gold and silver. It looked newly made, the polish glistening in the magelight. There was a third coffin sitting on the table, a thick blanket of canvas thrown over the top.

Laurel turned to face him. "Who crafted these?"

"There's a woodcarver in the village. He had his own shop, but sometimes he liked coming here to work on projects. I've commissioned a few pieces from him over the years."

She looked back at the two coffins, her eyes drawn to the larger one. If she looked closer, she could see images of different elements, each melding into something new. There were Stellataen Arrow blossoms and razor-sharp swords. Even the edges were rimmed with round studs of silver. A mask, made of wood but decorated with silver, was carved into the lid.

It was a coffin for Cal.

Her heart lurched into her sore throat. "You knew."

With the detail on the wood, the dried polish, the cloth lining, it would have taken more than a single evening to craft. Whoever had built it had labored over it for days if not longer. And they'd been under siege for weeks. No one would dream of coming in here to work while a battle raged just outside the line of trees. The coffin would have been sitting here since before the rebels had made their move.

Which meant Paulo had been keeping it from her this entire time.

He didn't answer her for several seconds. It didn't even sound like he breathed until he let out a shaky exhale.

"Yes, I knew."

She whirled on him. "Why didn't you tell me?"

He remained where he was, his feet wide and expression stoic. "Because I knew we couldn't change it."

The backs of her eyes prickled. "But you could have told me. You could have let me know what we were all walking into." She jabbed a finger toward where Cal lay. "He didn't even want to fight. He didn't want to be part of this blasted war, and I didn't listen. If I'd known..." She took a deep breath and wiped her eyes. No crying. It wouldn't do any good now.

"I'm so sorry."

She raised a hand. "Don't apologize to me when you don't actually mean it, Paulo. Don't say you're sorry when all you're going to do is go back to lying and scheming and keeping everyone at arm's length."

"Laurel, please—"

"Everything all right in here?" Conley asked, his shadow filling up the open doorway.

Laurel pinched the bridge of her nose. "The coffin is here. Will you help me take it out?"

Conley stepped in and Paulo went to join him.

Laurel held out her arm, stopping him. "I think you've done enough."

Instead of stepping away, he set his hand over where hers lay on his chest. "I really am trying to help you."

She yanked her hand out of his grasp. Without another word, she joined Conley at the coffin and hoisted it onto her shoulder. The thing weighed enough to make her arms quiver, but she didn't ask Paulo for help. There were no more words for her to say. If Paulo wanted to keep playing these stupid games, he could play to his heart's content, but she was done. Her team wasn't made up of game pieces for him to move about as he pleased. They were people she had sworn to take care of. People she cared about.

And by the Goddess, she was so tired of losing people she cared about.

They returned to the graveside and set the coffin down beside Cal's body. Gently, Xander and Declan lifted him from the stretcher and laid him inside. Serene stepped forward, her cheeks wet. With careful fingers, she set his silver mask on his abdomen and moved his hands to hold it in place. Mare had gathered a few limp flowers from Mater's soggy gardens and placed them in the coffin around his head like a crown. Without any kind of ceremony, they pushed the lid into place. Conley hammered the nails in to the lid, each swing driving pain into Laurel's chest.

Swing.

Swing.

Swing.

Eight swings. Eight nails.

It took all the scholae to get the coffin into the grave without making a mull of it. When they finally settled Cal in the bottom, Declan took Paulo's shovel and started covering the coffin. Paulo emerged from somewhere with two more shovels and a few rakes in hand. Laurel took one without meeting his eye and joined

Declan. The only one who didn't help was Xander, who stood at the foot of the grave, his face pale and empty.

It was a warrior's funeral. There was no fanfare, no long eulogies or droning temple priests. It was just them and their silent prayers as they shoveled the dirt back into the hole.

Laurel remained at her post for two days. For two days, she watched the hole in the wall, keeping rebels from weaseling their way through while the builders finished their repairs. The castle guard had done their job and hadn't allowed the castle to fall into their hands. They'd been preparing for something like this, especially after the rebels had brought in their mangonel. The craftsmen had created a temporary wall out of wood. While it wouldn't hold off a heavy attack like the stone wall could, it gave them time to recoup and keep the rebels from trickling in. There were quite a few who attempted to attack the wall, but Laurel had made it her prerogative to make sure they were unsuccessful.

She wouldn't allow Cal's sacrifice to be in vain.

After dispatching a rather unruly set of pyromaniacs, she climbed back up the wall. At the top, she found Conley leaning against the edge of a crenel, his arms crossed over his chest and silver mask gleaming.

"What's the verdict?" she asked, taking a piece of cloth from her small cache she'd accumulated to wipe the blood off her blade.

"Verdict, Master?"

Sheathing her dagger, she said, "I assume you've come to tell me if the others have decided whether or not we ought to stay to see another battle."

It only made sense. They had come to her in the beginning to say they didn't wish to remain here. While they had been convinced to stay, Cal's death was a blow none of them expected. He had been their quiet giant. Their bookish madman. He should have never been on a real battlefield. Looking back now, none of them should be. They weren't warriors, they were assassins. They couldn't work as a team. Couldn't look out for one another the way a unit of warriors could.

"There's been no vote taken," Conley said, staring down at the stone between his feet.

That took her aback a bit. "You mean you all haven't been packing up your things to leave this cursed castle behind?" She pointed out toward the fires lining the edge of the forest. "I know all of you are more than aware Cal's death won't be the worst of it."

Conley sighed and turned toward her. "There's been no vote because our master has been out here trying to kill herself by fighting off every man across the lake who looks at this castle for longer than three seconds."

Doing her best to mimic Conley's stance, she settled her back against the wall. "You know my vote doesn't matter anymore. I can't leave this cursed place." Not until she got to Aspen. Not until she made sure Teagan was out of their lives for good.

"Come inside the castle, Master." He pushed away from the wall. "You can't avoid your little mage forever."

She opened her mouth to say he wasn't her mage, but she couldn't. The fire in her chest raged, snapping and crackling under her ribs.

"I can't even look at him," she said instead. "Why didn't he tell me?" But that wasn't the question she really wanted to ask. *Why doesn't he trust me?* Why did she have to find out after something horrible had happened that it would come? Paulo continued to push her about trusting him, but how could she? He'd proved over and over again he wasn't willing to give up any of his control. That he couldn't because then things would fall apart. It was hypocrisy in the highest form, and all it did was make the fire in Laurel's chest spit flames.

Conley straightened and moved to walk back toward the castle. "Maybe now is the time to start trusting. To look behind the masks and find the person underneath."

She looked up at him. "Whose trust are we talking about here? Mine or Paulo's?"

"Both."

23
AN UNEXPECTED CONFESSION

PAULO STOOD IN THE CENTER OF THE BALLROOM WITH A LONG WOODEN staff in his hands. One of the scholae— likely Serene— had put together a dummy on one of the many free-standing coatracks around the castle. At the top, a pillow had been strapped around the pole and a face that looked suspiciously seal-like had been painted on it.

The wooden staff smacked into the middle of the pole, the resounding *crack* echoing through the empty room. No one had been in the room when he entered, and no one had come in the two hours he'd been there. Since the first day he'd established the unorthodox training room there seemed to always be someone in it. The scholae regularly took shifts on the wall and when they weren't either on patrol, sleeping, or eating, they were in this room.

But he'd seen they wouldn't be here now.

Instead, they were gathered together in the sitting room, deciding whether they should help Iatrus Castle or leave it to rot.

He couldn't blame them. Not after what happened.

"Stupid," he murmured, hitting the pillow with a *thwack*. He shouldn't have let Laurel know that he'd seen Cal die. Not that he could have kept it from her. Eventually, it all would have had to come out.

Or I should have just told her from the beginning like she said, and we wouldn't be in this position at all.

But he really couldn't have. He'd seen how she'd tried to change things. How it would have been her who had taken a trident to the gut instead of Cal. How she would have fallen, and all of this would have been for naught.

Sweet Gaia, he hated being the puppet master. How was he supposed to earn Laurel's trust when the Goddess continued to meddle? He drove the staff into the pillow again, this time hard enough to send a few puffs of down shooting out the other side.

"I didn't realize we should be training to battle pillows now."

Paulo whirled and found Diana leaning against one of the pillars. Shadows concealed her face, but the rigid set of her shoulders spoke of her emotional state.

"I didn't think you were still up," he said. A stand for the taller weapons stood at the edge of the practice ring, and he marched toward it to put his staff away.

Diana made a noise that he supposed should have been a chuckle but sounded more like a wheeze of pain. "Donnie is drinking himself into a stupor in the kitchens, Mater is pacing the great hall waiting for word from the wall, and the scholae are gathered like vultures in the sitting room discussing if they're going to leave us for dead. You think I could sleep at a time like this?"

No, he didn't. And he couldn't exactly judge. There was a reason he wasn't sleeping either. He set the staff into its place and grabbed his jacket hanging from the rack.

"Why did you let him go, Paulo?" Diana asked.

He didn't need to know who she was referring to. A sigh slipped from his lips, but he couldn't turn to look at her. "Because he needed to escape."

Diana hissed. "That's not an answer. Why did he need to escape?"

"It's not time for him to die yet. He still has purpose."

"What purpose could he possibly have besides being stuck on the end of a pike for all the cursed world to see? He should be dead, not Cal. Why wouldn't you stop that from happening?"

He finally turned. "Hundreds of men are going to die for this war. Am I to be blamed for their deaths as well?"

"This is different."

"How is this any different? How is Cal's death different from the deaths of the fathers that fell from the walls today? From the grandmothers who were caught in the Aigeans' flood?"

"It's different because you could have stopped it. You could have told us all what Caspian was planning to do. It's your fault that he was able to get in."

A dark laugh bubbled up. "No, this time the blame does not fall to my feet."

Diana's expression grew tight. "What are you saying?"

"You know *exactly* what I'm saying. Do you think I didn't know about your little rendezvous with Caspian under the castle?"

All color drained from her face. "You did know. I assumed you would, but when you didn't say anything, when you didn't stop me..."

He shrugged, doing his best to mask the knots tangling in his stomach. "I couldn't stop you."

"Oh, you couldn't? Instead, you let me go in there and allowed Caspian to fool me into thinking he was trustworthy? Into believing he was going to use my directions to the grate to come help us? You could have done anything. Said anything to stop me."

He could have. He'd seen what Caspian planned to do with the information Diana shared with him, but he'd thought he'd have more time to prepare. But Caspian wouldn't be able to use that route again. Paulo had taken the stone mage down there after and the amount of iron alone would make any fae or water folk uncomfortable just walking through. The iron grate at the end of the tunnel had been ripped out from underneath, but it had been replaced as well, and there was now a constant guard under the castle just to make sure no one else used the tunnels to sneak in.

"If I'd tried to stop you, you would have found more dangerous ways to meet with him. You would have gotten your-self killed trying to go behind my back." He'd seen it a dozen times. Every which way he tried, someone died. Someone Paulo cared about found themselves on the end of a trident. Cal's death was the only one that served a purpose. Was the only one that sparked with any kind of hope of keeping Laurel alive.

Her voice grew quiet. "Why didn't you tell me? Why not give me a chance to rethink it?"

"I don't know if you remember a few days ago," he drawled, "but you barely spoke to me after what happened at the menagerie without trying to bite off my head. You've been stomping around the castle for months now. Do you think me saying anything to you would have gone over well? Do you think you wouldn't have tried to do something worse?"

"You didn't even *try* to talk to me about it. Instead, you let someone die."

"More people are going to die before the end. This is *war*, Diana."

"A war *you* could have stopped!" she snapped. "I know you could have stopped this all long before it started."

He gritted his teeth. "What is that supposed to mean?"

"It's exactly as I said. You could have stopped it. I've thought it bizarre for some time that Adira Durant made it out of Olympia alive. Honestly, I was shocked when you finally revealed the rebellion to Mater and me over a year ago. I didn't think anyone could have been left from the Tyrant King's inner circle. You helped the Lord of the Underworld track down so many of the traitors to King Dion's reign. I actually thought it impossible that one made it out. I watched as you moved about your little game pieces back then, putting the prince in contact with all the right people to form his little underworld of servants and spies. By the Goddess, I helped you do it. Yet, the biggest threat to the kingdom, a kingdom you claim to love, just walked away? Now, I know Adira Durant isn't *that* talented."

Paulo's entire body froze. He could try to deny it, could try to weave a lie that Diana would chew on for a time. But it wouldn't matter. In the end, Diana wouldn't let it go. She was a hound on a scent, and she always found her prey.

His magic niggled at him, but he pressed it down. He didn't want to know what chaos this moment would bring. He didn't want to know how much this would hurt all the work he'd done.

Her blue eyes went a bit wide, and a startled laugh burst from her chest. "I'm right. I knew you wouldn't admit it, but I expected you to try to at least come up with a good enough lie to make me question my suspicions."

He opened his hands, slipping his most frenzied mask over his expression to hide the flush he felt grow at the back of his neck. He stretched his lips back to show all of his teeth and widened his eyes to make sure Diana saw the darkness in them. Saw the death he lived with every day.

"What do you want from me?" he asked. "Do you want me to say that I'm a scheming blackguard who chooses when people die and when they don't? That I'm a lying monster who meddles in peoples' lives to get what I want?"

He laughed, a low, dark thing filled with every ounce of the anger and regret he felt in his gut. "All the things you think are my fault probably are, and you know what the worst part is? I don't care. I don't care that I let Adira Durant go. I don't care that Penny's house burned down or that the castle was taken. I don't even blasted care that our own home is under attack. All of this is because I took the path I wanted most, and I stuck with it."

He'd seen it all. He'd seen Adira Durant run from the palace. Seen her return to her house where her husband waited, railing at her about how she had let the princes ruin all their carefully laid plans. Seen when she stabbed Lord Nox Durant in the chest and left him bleeding on the ground as she gathered supplies. When she ran to Eleusia with curses on her lips and boarded a ship headed to the Continent. He'd seen every move she'd made as she wove the rebellion to life. Knew what she planned to do to their kingdom. And he knew what that future could bring him.

"I saw a future that I wanted, and I'm more than happy to make everyone else pay the price for it. Is that what you wanted to hear? Are you happy now?"

That drew Diana up short. Her mouth gaped open, shock, hurt, sorrow creasing the lines of her face. Her gaze flicked to the windows behind him, eyes growing wide.

He spun around and found Laurel standing just inside.

If Diana was the picture of hurt, Laurel was fury incarnate.

He took a step toward her. "Laurel—"

She cut him off with the raise of one hand. "You know, I came in here to figure out how I could trust you. To look for even one spark of reliability from you that would help me let go of the things that have happened." Her chest rose and fell in even breaths as she stalked toward him, her boots silent on the polished floor. She stopped several feet from him, but he could see the knowledge of his sins spin in her head as she processed everything he'd confessed.

His feet moved of their own volition toward her again.

The narrowness of her brown eyes stopped him in his tracks. "I knew it was bad, Paulo. I knew whatever truths you had tucked away would be earthshattering. That you had made some tough choices. What I didn't realize is that you didn't care about the lives you affected. That you really are just that selfish."

Before he could say anything, she spun around and slipped back out through the terrace doors.

"Laurel! Wait!" He ran after her, nearly ripping the door from its hinges when he opened it.

But she was already gone, and he knew whatever words he might say would only make things worse.

Diana's boots deliberately clicked on the floor behind him.

"At least now you can go to sleep knowing you're a sorry excuse for a human being just like the rest of us." She slammed the ballroom door closed behind her.

He buried his face in his hands.

Sweet Gaia, what had he done?

24
THE REGRET

Laurel's blades will fly in front of her, almost invisible as she charges. Declan will have to retreat, his eyes narrowing in concentration as Laurel continues to press him back. She'll slice at his abdomen and when he moves out of the way, she'll punch him in the face.

Sweat dripped down Laurel's back as she jabbed at the exposed abdomen in front of her.

Her opponent jumped back enough to dodge the blades coming at him and grabbed her wrist in a vice grip.

Laurel dropped the blade and caught it with her free hand before her opponent could try to rip it from her. She twirled the dagger in her fingers and aimed for the arm holding her.

He dropped his hold and took a step away from her.

She didn't let him gain any distance. Her feet met him step for step. Inch for inch. Breath for breath.

With a grunt, he held his ground and drew the short sword from the scabbard hanging at his waist.

Finally. An actual challenge.

The floor slid under Laurel's boot as she grabbed the other long dagger from her thigh. Her already quiet world went silent except for the music her daggers sang. All she could see was steel as it whirled in front of her. All she knew was the blades in her hands.

Jab.

Swing.

Dip.

Retreat.

Block.

Engage.

Slice.

Punch.

Bone cracked under her knuckles, though she couldn't tell if it was hers or not.

She blinked.

Her opponent staggered back, his silvering hair coming into focus. The furrow of his eyebrows over gray eyes deep.

The blades fell from Laurel's hands. "Sweet Gaia, Declan. I'm so sorry." She took a step toward him, but he held up a hand.

"I'm done. Can't fight you when you're as likely to stick one of those daggers in my side as the blasted rebels we're fighting against for no reason would be." He gingerly prodded at his left cheekbone and ran his tongue over his teeth. If she broke any of his teeth, Laurel would search all of Olympia for a mage who could fix them.

"Declan," she said, but he shook his head and turned away from her.

The air went out of her lungs as her shoulders sagged. Curses, her head wasn't on straight. Not for a practice bout. Not for any of this.

She really couldn't blame any of the scholae for betraying her now. Why wouldn't they? She had completely abandoned the oaths of their order. She had watched innocents die without protecting them. Had revealed her identity to someone she didn't have absolute trust in. Had not upheld her end of the geas and failed her mission. Even if they looked past all of that, the fact that she had listened to Paulo and allowed him to gain what little bit of trust she'd been willing to give— because even she couldn't deny there was some trust between them— should strip her of any of their regard. By the Goddess, even Xander or Serene would do a better job than she had with all of this.

Conley stood at the edge of the ring, wrapping a strap of leather around a thick wooden staff she'd broken at the beginning of practice. He cursed when the wrapping went crooked, and he had to undo nearly half of it.

She picked her daggers up off the floor and stuck them back in their sheaths with more force than necessary. Spinning on her heels, she nearly ran straight into Xander.

He passed by her with wide eyes. His arm was out of its sling, but he still had a large collection of stitches along his hairline.

"What?" she snapped. *Blast it.* She took a deep breath, summoning whatever dregs of pleasantness she had. "Is there something you need?"

"Not at present." Xander looked toward Conley then back to her. "Maybe there's something *you* need? Can I help you with anything?"

Shaking her head, Laurel turned away. "I'm going to go check on the wall."

"Mare and Serene are on the east side."

She gave a sharp nod and jogged out the large double doors of the ballroom.

But before she could even step three paces into the hallway, Paulo materialized in front of her.

"Don't," she said, quickly walking around him.

For four entire days, he'd dogged her every step. After his revelation about his role in Adira Durant's escape from this cursed kingdom, he'd tried to explain everything to her. Tried to tell her how it was to save people. How he was trying to save *her*. He explained how allowing the old spymaster to escape put the kingdom down a path the Goddess needed them to go down. That Laurel herself was meant to come to this kingdom and had a purpose. That this war happened for reasons she would under-stand if she just stopped for a second and let him explain.

Well, he could explain until he was blue in the face, but she wasn't going to listen to a single word of it. Not after what he'd said to Diana. She'd rather have died than let people go to war like this. She'd rather have fallen on her own sword than watch Cal die for something he didn't really believe in.

Paulo fell into step beside her, voice low. "We need to talk about the scholae and their possible betrayals."

"If you're looking for a two-faced idiot, there's a mirror right down the hall."

He huffed, though if it was in exasperation or amusement, she couldn't tell. She wouldn't look at him. Couldn't look at him.

"Tell me what to do, Laurel."

"Throw yourself off the bastion and see if you can track down the blasted selkie that killed my schola."

He didn't speak again until they made it out of the castle and onto the wall. "If we want to get revenge on Caspian for Cal's death, we need to figure out which of your scholae is speaking with him or is still thinking about speaking with him. I think Serene has been brought over to our side. Xander's been talking to himself a lot, but I don't see much else from him. Conley's still a concern—"

Laurel snapped.

Spinning, she grabbed the front of Paulo's ridiculous neck-cloth and shoved him back. He smacked against the wall, but his eyes were alight with magic.

The fact that he had very obviously let her grab him only made her blood boil hotter.

"I don't blasted care if I have the cursed Cartographer herself wearing a silver mask and running around this castle right this second. I trust any one of my scholae more than I trust you." She pointed out toward the outer wall. "Look at that, Paulo! Look at what you've done to your home. Your family. You expect me to trust you and put my team's lives in your hands when you won't even stop a war from coming to your door?"

"You know why I had to do it," he snapped. "If I hadn't, you'd be *dead*."

"Better dead than whatever the curses you are." She shoved off him. "Better bones in the ground than a lying blackguard who only cares about himself."

Paulo's chest rose with rapid breaths. "Do you understand what that means, Laurel? Can you actually grasp what your death would do? To me? To my family? To the scholae? To this kingdom? You think if you died none of this would have ever happened? That war wouldn't have come? There's a reason Adira was able to rally such a rebellion. If it hadn't been her, it would have been somebody."

"You can't know that!"

"*Of course I can!*" he thundered. "How on Gaia's cursed green earth do you think I know anything? I know *exactly* what would have happened if Adira had been caught, killed, tortured, all of it. I weighed the fates, combed through the timelines. I knew exactly what I was doing when I told the princes that I couldn't see Adira."

Laurel stared up at him, her own breathing ragged. She knew he could see that much. Knew his powers were so much deeper than anyone gave him credit for— apparently even herself.

Gritting her teeth, she took a step toward him. "Could you have saved Cal? Could you have prevented his death?"

The magic turning his eyes into a kaleidoscope of colors faded until only the vibrant blue was left. "Yes, I could have saved him. You know I could have."

Laurel breathed in through her nose, long and deep. While she'd known the truth, it still hit her like a punch to the gut.

"Why didn't you save him, Paulo? If you knew all of this would happen, that I would be angry, that Diana would lose faith in you, why did you let it happen? Why didn't we come up with a plan that could have prevented this?"

He stared down at her for a few moments before he spoke. "Because every other future led to your death or the complete betrayal from your scholae— which, if you couldn't guess, also led to your death and the death of the rest of your team."

"Are all of them still plotting to betray us? Has nothing we've done changed anything?"

His jaw flexed for a moment, his brows lowering. "I don't know. There are too many strings. Too many variables. If we can't figure out how to get Conley to stop thinking about turning everyone against you or Declan to stop figuring out how to kill everyone in the castle, or Mare from simply leaving, I don't know what else we can do. We need to figure out when they make the plans so they can be thwarted, but I don't know who to start with."

The frustration practically rippled from him. Well, it was about blasted time he got knocked down a peg. Laurel would have been happier if the lack of information wasn't so dangerous or if she actually trusted him. He could be lying to her now and she would have no idea.

Laurel folded her arms over her chest. "And if you had to take a guess?"

Paulo rubbed a hand down his face. "Honestly? Until I saw Cal's death, I thought it was going to be him who finally cracked and poisoned all of us in our sleep. He was the one most against you getting involved in this fight from the beginning."

"So, following that line of thinking, Declan or Mare would be the next choice." Declan had vocalized enough agitation with their stay at Iatrus Castle. His skills as a provocationist would lend toward the rebels' cause if they could. Mare would be the next best choice because she could get in and out of the castle without anyone knowing.

Paulo shook his head. "Mare is probably at the top of my list, but I have a hard time imagining her throwing her lot in with a group that would hurt any of you, so she's the least of a threat. Conley is suspicious too because he's in a position of power being your second and could easily just decide he's through and take everyone with him and they wouldn't take much convincing. Xander's a bit of a conundrum and his line is frazzled, as if split by two separate people. Serene is the only one I would take off the list completely because her fate is now dependent on the others'."

"She isn't going to die like Cal did, is she?" Laurel asked.

Paulo threw up his hands. "I don't know. I've seen her die a dozen different times, but they're all just possibilities. If you asked me which of their deaths I've seen, I'd say all because this is a war and the life expectancy of assassins during a war is drastically shortened."

Laurel's jaw ticked. "Don't get cheeky with me right now. I'm a split second away from making those magic eyes of yours black and blue for a few days."

"Sorry." He blew out a breath. "I just don't know what to do."

"If we interrogate them, it could drive them to betray us."

"I know. That's why I haven't started poking about. My hands are completely tied. I can't figure out which scholae are the most dangerous no matter how many times I search lines. And when I try to do something, it always blows up in my face. It's like they haven't decided. Like they're waiting for something to happen."

"Then why are you asking for my help now?"

He leaned back against the wall, the wind picking up and tousling his red hair over his forehead. "Because I don't know what to do. I don't know how I'm supposed to keep everything together. I don't know how to fix Diana or the scholae or you or any of it."

It was then that she saw the mask completely fall.

Somehow, he'd distracted her from the dark circles under his eyes. The stronger presence of his cheekbones. The starkness of his freckles on his drawn face. There was a slight tremor to his fingers as he brushed his hair back. She wasn't looking at a put together marquess, but an unraveling man.

Laurel couldn't keep the words from slipping out. "You can't *fix* anything if you aren't willing to fix yourself."

He stilled. "What is that supposed to mean?"

"Maybe if you could be trustworthy for once, neither of us would be in this position. You wouldn't be facing this alone."

His head thumped back against the stone bricks. "It's always been like this. I can't change it. The Goddess has made *that* very clear."

Her blood boiled. Of course. He was the perfect one. The oracle. The strategist. The puppet master. He wouldn't change. Not if he didn't want to.

The words fell from her tongue before she could think better of them.

"Maybe your Goddess finally realized She put Her faith in the wrong man."

She spun around before Paulo could respond, but he didn't follow after her to try to explain his reasoning. To try to bring her back to his side. To lie to her again.

Good.

She might have punched him right in the face if he did.

25

AN UNEXPECTED TURNABOUT

PAULO STOOD IN FRONT OF THE MIRROR IN HIS ROOM, THE HUM OF fighting outside vibrating through the closed window. The rebels had initiated another small attack on the broken section of the west wall only a few hours before, though the Aigeans had yet to be seen. Caspian was still licking his wounds last time Paulo checked with his magic. The pocket watch on Paulo's dressing table ticked away the minutes before he was set to meet everyone in the sitting room to go over the most recent reports. At least, he would be listening to them from the comfort of a sofa or something. It wouldn't be long until they would find themselves in the middle of another battle. Until he'd have to watch more people die.

Not that he wasn't constantly barraged with the death of every person in this castle on a daily basis. If he wasn't searching the scholae's fate lines all the time, he would simply ignore his cursed gift and avoid all of it.

A muttering Jenkins emerged from the closet. Paulo turned around and found him holding up two waistcoats, a canary yellow and lime green. Both would look ridiculous with the dark purple jacket Paulo had folded over the back of his chair.

"Which do you think, Jenkins?"

Jenkins blinked, but it was without any sort of feeling. "Does it really matter, my lord?"

Paulo shrugged. "I suppose not."

Taking up his muttering once again, Jenkins hung both hangers on a hook sticking out of the wall and began unbuttoning the lime.

Paulo returned to his own visage in the mirror. He'd lost a bit of weight in his middle and his shoulders were broader from all the sword practice. His white shirt stretched over his chest in a way that was almost uncomfortable. He wanted to rip the arms off and throw them out the window.

Instead, he stretched out his arms and allowed Jenkins to put the ridiculous waistcoat on him.

Maybe your Goddess finally realized She put Her faith in the wrong man.

Laurel's voice had been ringing in his head since the day before. He couldn't get the words out. They'd grown roots and thorns in his skull. Had Gaia finally decided to desert him? Was this a consequence of the path he'd chosen? Had he actually made the wrong choices?

With the waistcoat in place, Jenkins reached for the jacket laying over the side of the chair. There was a ripping sound as he lifted it.

"What was that?" Paulo asked.

Jenkins's muttering increased before he sighed. "Apologies, my lord. You won't be able to wear this jacket today." In the mirror, he showed the long tear along the inner panel of the jacket.

"It's fine. Just grab another one out of the closet." Paulo shook his head, tugging at the gold cufflinks at his wrists. The MacGregor seals were crooked. Was his wardrobe also to rebel against him?

But Jenkins didn't move. He stood in the same spot by the chair, his eyes staring down at the ripped jacket in his hands. The valet had never been so quiet or still.

"Are you all right?" Paulo turned away from the mirror. "Jenkins?"

"What are we doing, my lord?"

Paulo blinked. "What do you mean? I thought I was getting dressed so I could meet the others in the command center."

Jenkins tossed the jacket back on the chair. "Not right now. I mean at all. We're under siege, my lord."

"Yes, I'm well aware." Paulo crossed his arms over his chest and studied Jenkins. The man's gray-sprinkled hair that was always strangled into a perfect queue at the back of his neck seemed a little frazzled. The furrow between his brows was deep and his thick eyebrows sat low over his gray eyes. Jenkins had never *tossed* any article of Paulo's wardrobe. He was more meticulous than a surgeon, and in that moment, he looked like a tortured poet. It was easy to forget he was several years older than Paulo, his energy belying his years, but his age showed now. This was a tired man standing before him.

After what had to be a full minute of silence, Jenkins finally looked up. "I have always believed in you, my lord. From the time your father hired me as your valet, I've always known you were meant for greatness. I saw it in your eyes as a lad, and I caught glimpses of it every day as you grew. Not once in all those years did I ever doubt it. Until now."

The words didn't fully settle over Paulo for several seconds. "What?"

Jenkins pointed toward the window. "We have enemies at our gates. Our west wall is barely patched up. Lord Abrams's lands have been pillaged and destroyed. One of Lady Laurel's friends have fallen. And yet here you stand, in front of your mirror getting dressed up for no one and nothing. Now, I know more than most that you have your limits. That you've built up this caricature of what people expect you to be to protect yourself, but what is it protecting you from now? Your home is on the brink of destruction. Your people in danger. And we're here talking about waistcoats and jackets and every mundane thing we could possibly think of. It's enough to drive any sane man mad!"

"What?" No other words could break past Paulo's lips.

Jenkins growled.

He actually *growled*.

He'd never growled before, and Paulo's spine straightened at the noise.

"Was my faith so unfounded?" he demanded. "Are you not going to actually defend your people?"

Paulo finally found more words. "Of course I am! I'm doing my best to track down traitors in our midst and keep the rebels from getting past the outer wall."

"And what are we doing to rid ourselves of these rebels? Not once have our men attempted to go on the offensive."

"Where did you hear that?" Jenkins hadn't left the walls of the castle, had he? He'd been helping Mater and Hiatt for the most part.

"My brother."

Paulo stared at him, racking through his entire memory. Who was his brother?

As if seeing the question on Paulo's face, Jenkins huffed. "Isaac. The captain of your castle guard. The very man in charge of the safety of this castle?"

"Captain Isaac is your brother?" It was like Paulo didn't even know the man standing in front of him.

Jenkins's eyes went wide with incredulity. "We literally share the same last name."

"But we always call him Captain Isaac." Not once had Paulo ever heard the captain be called Jenkins in all the time he'd been the castle's Captain of the Guard. He pushed his mind back to even before he'd been captain, but he couldn't remember ever hearing differently.

"Because I was already working here when he got his position as guard, and your father called him Isaac to avoid confusion." Jenkins threw up his hands. "But my familial relations don't matter. What matters is the plan."

"Plan?" Paulo parroted.

Jenkins shook his head in disbelief. "Do you not actually have a plan to get us out of this mess? To defeat these miscreants and prove yourself to your people?"

Paulo's mouth opened then clicked shut. He had a plan. Of course he did. They were going to outlast the rebels and send them packing. The battles were but a moment in the whole of this war. They... they...

Sweet Gaia, I don't have a plan.

Waiting for the rebels to leave wasn't a plan.

All he'd been doing was planning for the next attack. Waiting to see which schola would attack Laurel first. Trying to keep everyone alive long enough for something to happen. For the Goddess to give him some unforeseen direction that would fix all of this. Of course, he knew the rebels would leave. It was inevitable. But what was he trying to do to move that along? What was he doing to really gain the scholaes' trust besides letting them run around his castle on their own?

Jenkins sagged back into the chair, right on top of Paulo's jacket as he hung his head. "My lord, we aren't going to win this battle just sitting on our haunches. Good people are dying on that wall even now. We can't afford to play games anymore. These people are trusting you with more than their lives, but their futures. Like me, they've served the MacGregor family with little more than faith and loyalty because we knew the MacGregors would always keep us from harm. That the future was safe in their hands. Until the flood, I had never once doubted you always had a plan. That you knew exactly what you were doing. Even your father saw how powerful you were— sweet Gaia it was why he gave a valet to an eight-year-old boy. He saw how much you could do with your gift. Knew you would need someone to help you. I believed him. I believed I was doing great things for this kingdom, standing behind you and doing my best to help wherever I could. Believed this was the most important work in the kingdom, as your father had said it was. But now, I don't know what to believe. Was he wrong? Was I wrong?"

Paulo tried to swallow back the lump sticking in his throat. "I..."

Was his father wrong? While he'd known Father had hired Jenkins before a boy should have had a valet, he didn't realize it came with such expectations. That Father had seen something, Paulo was positive, but what had it been? Had Father seen it all come to this? Seen Paulo walk farther and farther from the path Father had started paving? He'd always been a man of honor, of goodness. He'd helped the princes rid this world of the Tyrant King. Saved his friends from harm. Made choices to bring respect to the MacGregor name. Kept the legacy of his forefathers alive. He did everything he could to help this kingdom as if he were the sole one charged with its protection. As if he were the guardian of every soul in Olympia.

Every one of those people had had faith in him and his prophecies. Everyone had trusted him. Paulo pulled at his hair, staring at Jenkins. Those people still trusted him.

And what was Paulo doing to gain their trust?

He was picking out clothes.

Paulo looked down at the atrociously green waistcoat wrapped around his torso. From the first day he'd bought it, Diana had said he looked like one of the alpacas had spit their green cud on him and he hadn't been able to scrub it out. Even the embroidered stars were ridiculous. It made him look like one of the half-baked magicians that would walk the streets of Olympia tricking people out of their coin. When he'd seen the fabric in the shop in Olympia, he'd hated it and knew it would be perfect for his endeavors.

But it wouldn't help him now.

He grabbed the waistcoat, violently ripping it apart and sending the buttons flying.

Jenkins jumped to his feet, eyes wide with shock. "My lord?"

"There's no time for any of this. There's a thousand things to do and I won't have time for a jacket." He nearly gagged himself as he pulled the knot out of his neck cloth and threw it on top of his wash table.

Blasted clothing. He couldn't even get out of all of it without it rebelling. The mask he'd worn for so long trying to cling to him by whatever means possible. He needed to get out of it and see what was underneath. Would he even know? Would he find a man or just another mask? Was there even anything under all the silk and lace and buffoonery? He didn't know. But he would find out. He would leave this room and figure it all out. How to get rid of the rebels. How to gain Laurel's trust. How to fix things with Diana. How to save this kingdom. He would do what Father would have done from the beginning.

Before he could do any more damage, Jenkins helped him pull his waistcoat off.

"Do you need another waistcoat?"

"No." Paulo tore the cufflinks out of his sleeves and rolled them up to his elbows. He spun toward the door. "Throw that blasted jacket in the fire. Sweet Gaia, throw them all in the fire!"

"All of them?"

Paulo stopped just before he stepped into the hallway. "Maybe not all of them. Mater wouldn't care to have me running about in nothing but my underclothes."

Jenkins gave a small nod, the briefest curl to the corner of his lips. "Understood, my lord."

26

THE RECONCILIATION

LAUREL WAS PRETTY POSITIVE PAULO HAD HIT HIS HEAD SOMETIME IN THE night and had brain damage.

That was the only explanation for what stood in front of her.

Paulo sparred with Xander in only a pair of brown trousers and a white shirt, open at the collar with the sleeves rolled up. There were no frilly neckcloths or vibrant jackets. While his boots were polished within an inch of their life, he still looked undone. His regular smirk continued to flicker at the corners of his mouth, and he maintained that air of magic around him as he moved fluidly with the practice sword in hand, but the pompous marquess was cracking.

When he'd walked into the sitting room earlier, she'd chalked it up to him being in a hurry or simply doing it to cause a stir. She hadn't expected him to keep the look throughout the day. Not once had he gone to change into anything else. Even during the worst of the battles over the last month, he'd changed for every occurrence as if they weren't under attack and everything was normal. But now, he looked like a man on a mission. Like he couldn't be bothered with any of the frippery.

She wasn't sure if she liked it or not.

"If you keep staring at him, someone is going to notice, and then you'll have to admit you were staring."

Laurel turned to Serene, who stood on her right. "I wasn't staring."

Serene's dark eyes sparkled knowingly. "Of course not, Master. I would never suggest you might be distracted by a good-looking man. Even if you're still furious with him."

"I wasn't distracted. And I am furious."

"Then why has Declan been standing on your left without notice for over a minute?"

Laurel nearly jumped when she found Declan holding up a folded piece of paper between two fingers. Great Goddess, where had he come from? She plucked the paper from his grasp and opened it. The number of rebel attackers had dwindled throughout the morning. Even in the hour since the captain's report in the sitting room, the battle had slowed. She read over the numbers on the note. The attack had taken half a dozen men off the wall in total. Half a dozen fighters gone. If they continued on this road, there wouldn't be anyone left in the castle at the end of this cursed siege.

Declan stepped toward the sparring ring, where Diana and Mare sat. He and Conley had been on the wall all morning, though Laurel wouldn't be surprised if Conley came back into the castle soon as well. Now that the battle was waning, they would need to plan for the next one.

The knowledge that any one of these scholae could betray her beat like a drum at the back of her skull. She'd quietly been investigating each of the scholae since Paulo had spoken to her. He couldn't see if any of them had actually spoken to Caspian, but if there was evidence, Laurel would find it.

With the lot of them distracted with the battle, it had been easy to peruse their rooms and peek into the hidden spaces around the castle to see if they had any contact with the rebels. Serene and Mare's room had been a mess of notebooks and clothing. Serene had never been tidy and Mare put up with it. Conley had been sharing a room with Cal. Cal's stuff still sat in a trunk at the foot of the bed. She would have to go through it eventually, but she hadn't been able to do more than look through the contents to see if anyone had been using his stuff to hide any missives. There hadn't been anything in Cal's things or Conley's.

Declan and Xander's room was still unsearched. She hadn't had a moment to get in when one of them hadn't been sleeping. If she could be certain of Mare's loyalties, she would have had her do a bit of snooping. While it was seriously doubtful she had anything to do with it, Laurel wasn't going to risk spooking any of them.

She sighed. How much longer would this siege last? She nearly twitched with the desire to jump over the wall and run into the rebel encampment just to see how many she could take down before she was caught. It was stupid, but she needed to do *something*. She glanced about at the scholae, seeing the repressed fight in each of them as well. Even Lord Abrams who leaned against one of the pillars like some kind of shadow practically vibrated.

They needed to do something. They needed to become a team. To work together. Perhaps getting closer to one another would snuff out their traitorous hearts. Or simply bring it out faster. Either way, it would be finished.

But what could they do?

The thought circled her mind for over an hour as the sparring continued. Conley joined them, having been let off patrol as the last dregs of the rebels had slowly disbanded from the wall. Praise the Goddess. Conley sat next to Declan on the bench as they watched Mare go up against Xander in the ring. Paulo sat on the bench next to Diana, though she was doing her best not to look at him. Paulo's gaze flicked over to her every few minutes. Serene sat on the floor at the edge of the ring, her eyes studying Xander but not giving Mare any encouragement besides her presence.

A headache started to bloom above Laurel's eyebrows. Every person in this room was pitted against someone else. How were they to push past this?

Stellatus Hall had never been a place where camaraderie was encouraged. Any team training had been combative. Everything had been competitive, even down to mealtimes where you had to fight for food. That had been one of Teagan's favorite competitions. There had been multiple injuries over the cooks' *baklava*. No one was allowed to kill anyone at the hall, but bodily harm hadn't been off the table. Laurel hated it, which was why she'd had the kitchen built in her rooms the moment she'd gotten a space big enough to do so. Even the scholae had been kept separated, only meeting to spar or attend demonstrations Laurel put on to help sharpen skills she felt had been lacking. But not once had there been a time where those in Stellatus Hall had come together to work toward a combined goal. Which was probably why the hall had fallen to the warlords so easily. They didn't know how to work as a team.

So what could they do? She fiddled with the weight hanging from her wrist. How could she get a bunch of assassins, a broken hunter, and a future-seeing mage to work together? Her fingers stilled around the lead bead. Once, she and Aspen had viciously fought after Mother had come home only to scream at them for not having the house tidied before storming out again. Father had come in right in the heat of the fight and after a few minutes, decided to tie their hands together. He then had them clean the house as a team. He helped set the tiny house to rights and by the end of it, the heat of the fight had cooled, and they'd gone to bed happy that night.

She'd never forget what he'd told her when she later asked why he'd tied them together.

Always takes two sides to have an argument. More often than not, we're so blinded by the hurt we feel we forget the very people we're fighting against are hurting too. Sometimes, we need a reminder that we're on the same side, even when we feel like we're not.

Her gaze stayed on Diana and Paulo, sitting so close yet so far from each other. She'd known them for nearly a year and in all that time she'd never seen a rift like this between them.

She felt that very chasm in her own chest, stretching all the way to the capital.

If she could never solve things with Aspen, she could at least help the twins reconcile.

Well, she'd need to distract the mage first.

She glided through the room, stopping next to the sour nobleman who was scratching the patchy scruff that had grown along his jaw. "I need your help."

Donnie gave her a sideways glance. "What do you need my help for?"

"I need someone to push Diana's buttons. Enough to tick Paulo off that he'll come to her defense."

Donnie's mouth spread in a slow grin. "Say no more."

"Wait for my signal." She tapped her ear lobe twice. "Then, give me thirty seconds before you really poke the beast."

He nodded and stalked toward Diana, a wicked gleam in his eyes. Unceremoniously, he plopped down on the bench between the twins, garnering a sideways glance from both of them.

Without speaking to anyone, Laurel circled the room. The first person to notice her movement was Paulo, but she avoided his gaze, keeping her pace slow and watching the spar in the center of the room. She couldn't give him a reason to think she was planning something. When she reached the opposite side of the ring, she met Donnie's eye and tapped her ear.

Donnie's grin turned maniacal, and he slung an arm around Diana's shoulders.

One.

Two.

Three...

With a tap of her finger at her eye, her nose, then her mouth, Laurel had the scholaes' attention. None of them moved from their positions, but she could feel each of them turn their focus directly on her.

She had about twenty more seconds before—

Donnie knelt down on the ground, taking Diana's hand in his and setting it to his heart.

A protest jumped up Laurel's throat, making her gurgle, but before she could even move, Paulo was on Donnie. He grabbed the back of the nobleman's jacket and ripped him off Diana. Donnie fell to the ground on his rear.

"What on Gaia's green earth, *Donnie*?" Diana screeched.

Well, this was escalating quickly.

With a few sharp flicks of her hands, she motioned for the scholae to disperse through the room and conceal themselves. Each one of them slowly faded into the shadows.

Laurel crept toward the Olympians, pulling her belt from her waist.

Paulo stood over Donnie, his hands clenched into fists at his side and his entire focus trained on him.

"What the curses was that?" he demanded. "Are you *insane*?"

Donnie cackled like he was actually losing it. "I figure if I'm going to be stuck here, I might as well enjoy myself." He looked to Diana. "I would make you the happiest of women. Many come crawling for the honor of my lips on theirs."

Diana bared her teeth and lunged at him, passing right next to Paulo.

Laurel struck. She grabbed Diana's arm, yanking her wrist in beside Paulo's and wrapping the belt quickly around their arms.

"What—" Paulo started, but he stopped as Laurel buckled it tight and sprang toward Donnie. She grabbed him by the arm and hauled him to his feet. She sent him running out of the ballroom and spun around to face the two angry twins who were trying to unwind the strap of leather around their arms.

"I'd focus on defending yourselves," Laurel called, spinning around to face them as she backed out between the open doors, "instead of trying to unbind your arms."

Both of them stilled.

She shut the doors and bolted for the stairs. The furniture from the lower levels had been brought out to dry in the open hallways, so it was a bit of a maze to get through. There was another entrance on the balcony level, but she had to sprint up two flights of stairs to get there. She took the stairs two at a time and raced past a bewildered butler carrying a large rocking chair as she raced for the balcony door. Paulo's shout sounded through the open door as she came to it. Her boots slid slightly on the carpet as she stopped at the railing and looked down.

The scholae had understood her intent exactly.

All five of them surrounded the twins. Paulo had gotten his hands— well, *hand*— on a shield and Diana held a sword in her free hand. Both of their arms strained against the tight confines of Laurel's belt, but their attention was on the scholae surrounding them.

Laurel casually leaned against the railing. "I think it's about time all of us figure out how to stop going behind each other's backs and realize we're all on the same team. At least, when it really matters."

"What is this, Laurel?" Diana ground out.

"This is me being sick of watching people I care about die.

This is me trying my best to fix things before they break beyond repair."

Diana's head bowed.

"So, here's how this is going to go. Diana and Paulo will work together against the scholae. The spar will be to first blood. You'll have to defend each other. If one of you falls, so does the other."

Paulo's expression was grim as he looked to Diana.

Laurel turned toward the others. "And same goes for the scholae. If one member meets the blade and loses, so do the rest of you."

Xander barked a laugh, but it cut off short. "Oh, you're serious?"

"Very," Laurel replied. "The time for singlemindedness is over. If we're going to win this war, we have to do it together." A knot formed in her throat. "If Cal and I had trained to read each other, to work together, it might have saved him. If he had trusted me enough to follow my lead, he might not have walked straight into Caspian's attack."

Conley shook his head. "You can't know that for sure."

"Maybe not, but I won't risk it again. I want all of us to be able to work in tandem. To trust each other's instincts enough for our own reflexes to blend with our team. I really believe that is what's going to win us this fight. That we aren't going to be smaller threats, merely poking holes in the rebels' defenses, but an unstoppable force that rips those blackguards from this land."

She saw the words settle on them. The idea straightened their shoulders and lifted their chins.

Her lips split and she bared her teeth.

"Your fight starts now."

<h1 style="text-align:center">27
THE TWINS</h1>

Conley will swing his pack over his shoulder, not even making the bed behind him. He'll stare at Cal's trunk, still filled with his things. With a shake of his head, he will walk out into the hall. The rest of the scholae will be waiting for him there and he'll guide them out the front doors of Iatrus Castle.

THE SCHOLAE MOVED LIKE THE SECOND HAND ON A CLOCK. ONE SECOND, Declan. The next, Xander. They each took turns taking a stab at the twins, but Paulo and Diana were there every time. When Serene slashed at Diana's arm, Paulo moved his shield in place. When Paulo ducked down, Diana took a stab at Xander over his head. Even at odds, it was like the twins could meld their minds together. That they knew how well they moved as two people but as one whole as well.

Laurel had once gone to a bull fight in the city of Dei, the largest city on the Continent. There wasn't a capital like there was in Olympia, but if there was, it would be Dei. Every year, in the large arena in the center of the city, Dei would host a week's worth of festivities to celebrate the beginning of the harvest season. The bull fights at night were legendary.

She'd sneaked her way inside the arena and watched a giant

of a bull go up against a man with a stick of a blade. The bull had charged the man and sent him flying. He'd hit the wall of the arena with a sickening thud, and the fight had been over.

That was what Conley looked like as he charged Paulo.

But Paulo was ready for him. He spun, grabbing Diana in the twirl and sidestepped the raging Conley who tried reaching for both of them. As he passed, Diana used the flat of her sword to smack his rear.

Laurel nearly burst out laughing.

Conley stumbled to a stop, his face twisted in rage as he turned back toward Diana. The rest of the scholae took a step back to let him have a go. They didn't want to help him, but they also didn't want to get in his way.

Setting her fingers against her tongue, Laurel gave a shrill whistle and gained the attention of the fighters.

"Serene, why haven't five fully trained scholae warriors been able to make a single slice anywhere on two soft, upper-class snobs?"

"Hey!" Diana protested, but Paulo shook the arm attached to hers to silence her. He held his shield at the ready.

Smart man.

Serene's head swiveled back and forth, looking from the twins to Laurel. "Because of Lord MacGregor's magic?"

Laurel swung her legs up over the railing and sat on the wide handrail. "The man has an arm tied behind his back which is now attached to a whole other person. If that's not an advantage in your favor, I don't know what is."

Declan took a step forward. "It's because they work together."

"Yes. They work together."

"We're working together," Xander protested. "We did our best to stay out of the way of anyone else. To take an opportunity when it presented itself."

And right there was the very problem. They were looking for opportunities instead of making them. It wasn't that they weren't a sect, a group, a team. But were they a family? Did they know that even when they were at each other's throats, they were never a true threat to one another? That when one was threatened, the other would come to their defense?

Laurel blew out a breath. "If we're going to win this war, we're going to need to learn to trust one another. To look for ways to lift each other up instead of simply watching the one in front of us fall and taking their place. We aren't in Stellatus Hall anymore. I've seen one of the best strategists I know completely obliterated by someone who can summon lightning in his very hands. I've seen a woman on the very brink of death, poisoned by the poisons I was led to believe were a sure thing, be brought back to health within minutes. I know we saw many things back on the Continent, that we faced many different challenges on top of the mountain, but here? Here, we are facing an entirely different kind of enemy, and if we don't figure out how to become a weapon great enough to face it, we'll find ourselves in graves right alongside Cal."

Conley and Xander's heads dipped. Serene and Mare stared up at Laurel. Declan looked to the wall, his jaw clenched tight enough to make his teeth probably ache.

Laurel kicked her feet in front of her. "We're all mourning him, but we can't let his death be in vain. If we want to fight back, to take revenge on Caspian Delrio and his ilk, we need to be ready for that fight. We weren't, but I know we can be, we *will* be, if we can work together. If we can become a family."

Declan snorted. "Really, Master? You want us to get all mushy and hug each other all the time and sit around sipping tea like old chums?"

"Is that what you think a family does?" Diana snapped. "You think a family is all sunshine and daisies? Look at us!" She raised her trapped arm. "If I wasn't sure I wouldn't get yelled at for it, I would have ripped my brother's arm off and left already."

Paulo set the shield to his chest and looked skyward. "Not my favorite arm."

"Shut up, Paulo," Diana growled. She narrowed her eyes at Declan. "But no matter what, I know Paulo. He's my brother and I know he wouldn't actually do anything to hurt me. Is he an idiot and gets us into the worst situations? Absolutely. But have I ever thought for one second that he would wish me ill?"

"You're one of the lucky few," Xander said, "that can trust the people that have been put in their life."

Diana shrugged. "I know there are some messed up families out there, but you guys are lucky in that you get to choose to be a family. Look around. You get to decide whether or not you want to trust these people. I'm stuck with this moron for the rest of time whether I like it or not."

"You wound me," Paulo said, but Laurel could see the softened expression in his face, the looser set of his shoulders. Diana's words had eased something in him, and it was actually really good to see. Paulo acted like he didn't let even the good touch his heart, but that wasn't true. He was just usually good at hiding it.

"She's right," Laurel said. "If nothing else, you're all people who were chosen to join our sect not because of your ruthlessness or your bloodthirst. It was because a master saw something in you that no one in the rest of Stellatus Hall had."

"What was that?" Serene asked.

Laurel twisted her lips, trying to come up with the best way to say it. "I'd call it ambition, but our last master said it was hope. It was a desire to reach for more than what this life gave you. All of you could have settled for mediocrity in your skillsets. You could have even just settled for being one of the best and leave it at that. Instead, you sought to be *the* best. To not allow those in our order to bring you back down to their level. You didn't let Teagan tell you that you were making the other assassins look bad and rein in your passion. You didn't let anything come between you and what you wanted. You only expected excellence from yourself and from those you associated with."

Each of their faces turned distant in thought. She could almost see the words being absorbed, wriggling under their skin to find a place to fit. She just prayed the words found a way into their hearts. That they would understand what this meant.

"Call it hope," she continued, "or ambition or whatever you want, but it was something that scholae respected. It was what made it possible for a group of people to survive in those halls. We were all striving for the same thing, and in that, we became stronger. We can be watchful. We can be focused. We can be silent. Together."

"How?" Xander asked. "How are we supposed to accomplish something like that?"

Laurel leaned back so her hands strained on the handrail, but she didn't fall. "First, we're going to work in doubles. All eight of us. Every practice we run from now on, you'll be in groups, working together to fight against another group."

Her mind picked through each one of their skillsets and personalities. For this particular lesson, it wouldn't do to put two partners together who already clashed. They needed to see just enough to understand what it would feel like.

"Xander, partner with Conley. Declan with Mare. Serene, you come join me up here and help me guide them. Each one of us will be working together, figuring out how to work as a team in different scenarios."

The pairs came together, the twins against four. Serene set her elbows on the railing next to Laurel and leaned over the side. Laurel bit her lip, looking between each pair and slowly calculating who would be best where.

"Conley and Xander, attack Diana. Declan and Mare, Paulo."

"*What?*" the twins squawked in tandem.

But their attention was quickly taken up by the fight.

Declan and Conley both charged in at the same time, which Laurel had guessed would happen.

Mare followed slowly behind Declan, and Xander stayed back a bit, but he still followed.

The twins came together, their linked arms acting as an anchor that they hovered around as the scholae attacked.

Paulo shielded himself from Declan's rampage, knocking him in the shoulder with the edge of his shield.

Conley brought up his sword to take a swipe at Diana, but she was quick on her feet and was able to feint a slice to his abdomen and make him back off.

Mare attempted to take a stab at Paulo while he was turned around, but he saw it coming and put the shield between them.

Serene hummed from beside Laurel. "The issue is much clearer from up here."

Laurel nodded. "They're still taking turns, aren't they?"

"It's like a charm. There are different pieces, different elements tied together until they become one whole charm. No gaps. No spaces." She gave a little gasp. "Mare! Play shadow with Declan!"

Laurel leaned forward a bit more to get a good look at Mare. She hadn't heard of the game, but she could guess at the concept. Mare, not once second-guessing Serene's advice, took up the space right at Declan's back as he fought with Paulo. She jabbed when he jabbed. Dodged when he dodged. Soon enough, she became Declan's very shadow, even anticipating his moves before he made them.

Laurel barked a short laugh. "You're brilliant!"

Soon enough, Mare was shadowing Declan so well she was filling his empty spaces. It wasn't perfect, but when his guard opened, she was able to come in right before Paulo could make a blow. Xander even followed suit, trying to mimic Conley's movements and see where he would fall short or reach too far and be there to fill in the gaps. They were coming together. Seeing how it could work.

Laurel's chest squeezed.

It was when Declan had been able to knock the shield into Paulo's chin and make him stagger that Mare was able to strike.

A quick slice to his side.

"First blood!" Laurel called.

Paulo sagged to his knees.

Diana right behind him.

The scholae stood around them, their eyes wide and faces open. Then, as if the tension was so thick in the room he couldn't do anything else, Conley began to laugh. It wasn't a giggle or a laugh of relief, but big, heaving guffaws. Xander joined in, then Declan. Mare cracked the biggest smile Laurel had ever seen on her. Even the twins began to howl, falling onto their rears. Serene fell prey to the sound and her giggles turned into full-on chortles. Laurel couldn't help herself. She laughed all the way down the stairs and back into the ballroom.

Declan and Conley helped the twins to their feet. The laughs quieted, but the feeling of possibility still buzzed around them. Mare untied Paulo and Diana, handing the belt to Declan. Serene grabbed the sparse med kit from the edges of the sparring ring and brought it to Paulo.

"So, what now?" Declan asked, offering Laurel her belt. "What does this mean for us?"

Laurel took it from him. "It means starting today, we're going to stop waiting for someone else to make the first move. It means we're going to watch each other's backs and fight as one. It means we're going to bring the rebels to their knees and when they beg for mercy, all they'll get is the silver of our masks and the steel of our blades."

The coals in the stove still smoldered with heat even though the kitchen had likely gone to bed at least an hour ago. With a new log, Laurel had it roaring back to life in minutes.

She let the flames dance as she collected ingredients. There wasn't much in the pantry. They were lucky to have the sheep out in the upper bailey for cheese. The shepherds had done a good job making sure the villagers got the bulk of the sheep's milk, but there was plenty left for the castle itself. Between the live sheep and the dead ones, they were keeping the castle fed. For now. The grain stores had taken the biggest hit. While they'd been able to save some of it, a lot of the grain saved for the sheep had been ruined as well as several dozen sacks of wheat for the kitchen. Mater had already been rationing, but those rations would only increase until they were surviving on sheep cheese alone.

The recipe for *sfakianopita* didn't take much, and after having to clean everything after the flood, the servants would likely enjoy a treat. She gathered up a bottle of oil, a bucket of sifted flour, and a lemon. She'd been wrong. It would be sheep's cheese and citrus that would keep them alive, as the enchanted trees in the greenhouse would continue to provide food.

When she stepped out of the pantry, she found Conley seated on a stool next to the stove, arms folded over his chest and a frown puckering his brows.

Laurel set the ingredients on the table in the middle of the kitchen. He didn't look up or say anything, so she crossed the room to the liquor cabinet. Half the bottles were missing. Donnie had probably been plaguing the kitchen after he'd run out of options in the rest of the castle. Laurel closed the cabinet doors. If she were the cook, where would she hide things from a lord? Pursing her lips, she glided over to the barrel of clean linens and dug around. When her fingers grazed something cold near the bottom, she grabbed it and pulled it out.

"Aha," she quietly muttered.

A half-full bottle of brandy.

She added it to her pile of ingredients and grabbed the mixing bowls.

"What are you making this time?" Conley finally said, unfolding his arms to lean his elbows on his legs.

"*Sfakianopita.* It was the simplest recipe I could think of."

The stool creaked as he stood. "How do you make it?"

Laurel showed him, going step by step from combining the ingredients to kneading the dough to mixing in the clumps of cheese. He followed each step intently, remaining silent as she talked about how the bread would puff up a bit on the pan and the cinnamon and honey would make the sour flavors from the lemon and cheese tart and delicious.

Conley stood at the pan, flipping one of the flatbreads when he finally spoke.

"My wife used to make *sfakianopita.*"

Laurel paused flattening another mound of dough, wiping her wrist across her forehead. "I didn't know you were married."

"It was a long time ago. Before Stellatus Hall. She was a girl I'd grown up with. Someone I trusted."

Laurel turned, leaning her back against the counter so she could face him. "What was her name?"

"Gaylynn."

"Where is she now?"

Conley pulled the bread from the pan. "In a grave outside Palus's lands."

"He was the warlord you worked for before Stellatus." She didn't have to ask. She'd seen it in his old contract after she became Master Schola. He'd filled that contract the first year he'd been in the hall, but he hadn't been looking for quick coin or to pay someone off like so many of the assassins had been when they signed their lives away. He'd been looking for an escape.

"He was."

"Is he the reason she's dead?"

"No. I am."

Laurel let the words settle between them. Conley carrying scars wasn't a new idea to her, but the sharing of those scars was. He reached past her and grabbed one of the rolled-out rounds of dough. It sizzled when it hit the hot oil in the pan. Laurel took up her rolling pin again and Conley continued speaking.

"She died because I didn't like the things Palus was doing. I had worked for his brother, Old Palus. That man understood what being a warlord was. He could calculate when a house was on the brink and swoop in to take over. Could outwit any of the younger lords and when they came barking at him, he would send them running with their tails between their legs. His younger brother was not the same. When Old Palus died and his brother came into power, I made mistakes. I was too obvious in my disapproval, and Gaylynn was the one who paid the price."

Laurel didn't turn but kept flattening the dough. "Why are you telling me this?"

He flipped the bread again. "Because I want you to know that I was fully prepared to take the scholae from you when the moment presented itself. I had my bag packed this morning."

"I know," Laurel said, setting aside the rolled-out dough and grabbing another ball.

Conley stepped into her periphery. "You knew?"

She shrugged. "Paulo saw the possibility of it the first week you were here."

He cursed, turning back to the bread in the pan and removing it before grabbing another round. "I didn't even think about him seeing it or that he would tell you if he did."

Laurel snorted. "The things Paulo will lead you to think will astound you. He acts like an idiot, but he's actually a borderline genius."

"I've started to see that." He moved his full plate of bread to the table and grabbed an empty one. "Why didn't you confront me about the possibility?"

"Because it was one possibility of many, and I've decided that I'd rather give people the chance to choose their own fates instead of deciding what those fates should be. I've watched Paulo ruin people's lives with his meddling. This war came to this kingdom because he made it so. I'm not going to disrespect my people in the same way. If I want the chance to choose my own fate, I have to give all of you the same courtesy."

"All of you? You mean the others have thought about abandoning you as well?"

A smile tugged at her lips. "Among other things."

He cursed again and set the bread on the new plate. "And you would let us?"

She finished the last piece of dough and turned around to face him fully. "I have no reason to make any of you stay here. Do I want you to stay? Yes. Will Paulo let you actually leave? Debatable. I think we need you. All of you. But I'm not going to force you to stay. If you stay, it'll be because you want to be here—whether it be from a sense of justice or duty or depravity. I want us to become what Stellatus Hall never let us be."

"A family," he said.

"A family." She plopped another round on the pan. "And if you ask me, Iatrus Castle is the best place to learn how."

He met her eye. "Then Iatrus Castle is where I'll be."

28

AN UNEXPECTED CHANGE

Paulo rubbed at the knots in his shoulder. Fighting with one hand literally tied behind his back had left him sore and achy, especially because Diana had yanked him around like a rag doll. Praise the Goddess he'd been the one with the shield. It had kept him from the worst of the blows. Diana had been sporting a rather lovely black eye at breakfast that morning. The scholae hadn't held back any punches. Paulo was pretty sure the scholae were trying to take a piece out of them after everything they'd put the assassins through. He couldn't blame them. He even felt a bit better about all of it after getting the snot beat out of him. It had been a relief when Mare had finally sneaked in and sliced a hole into side of his shirt, drawing first blood.

Captain Isaac— Captain Isaac *Jenkins*— tapped his fingers on the map in front of them, pointing at the two towers on the west corners of the outer wall. "You're thinking one on each tower?"

Nodding, Conley smoothed out the wrinkled paper with a drawing of a couillard. "If we put two there and one on the bastion, it should give us enough long-range reach that the rebels will hesitate to come out of the trees."

The catapult looked very similar to a trebuchet but had a few distinct differences: it was much smaller and instead of having one large weight basket, it had two that swung on either side of the pole that held the arm of the catapult aloft. That way, the entire engine was easier to build on top of the towers.

"You might even use them on the forest itself," Declan added. "If you can topple some of the trees at the edge, it would make the terrain harder to work with for the rebels. If we can get the projectiles far enough, we might even be able to hit the edges of their encampment. Anything we can do to make them uncomfortable will help our cause."

Captain Isaac picked up Conley's drawing. "How far will it shoot?"

"We could stick a sixty-pound boulder on one of those and it'll fly four hundred yards. The precision isn't as good at that distance, but we could hit the edges of the lake with ease."

"It would definitely make their archers wary," Declan said. "If we have Xander on the springald we put up on the center of the wall, we'll really put pressure on the rebels. Level the playing field a bit."

Paulo stared at the blasted lake on the map. "The most concerning aspect is Lake Luna itself."

The rebels had a natural defense with the water, as Iatrus Castle had no way to keep the Aigeans from using it. While they'd taken Caspian's team out when they attacked the castle, there were more working in the rebels' camp. With Caspian's rank in the Trident, he likely had access to even more water folk if he needed them. If Paulo tried to send men around the lake, the Aigeans would simply wash them away. There wasn't a chance for a force to leave the castle and engage in a battle outside the walls.

"Yes," Captain Isaac said, "but if we can at least gain a little bit more ground through using long-distance weapons on the wall, we'll save lives and keep the castle from falling to the rebels. That's our main goal."

He was right of course, but it still rankled Paulo. Now that he was on a mission to get rid of the rebels, it felt as if there were a number of insurmountable obstacles. They couldn't even leave the blasted castle.

"What other ways could we attempt to bring the attack to the rebels?" He looked to Declan. "Surely there are other things we can do."

Declan stretched his arms over his head, relieving the stress from stooping over the table for the last hour. "There's always the mental warfare option. We could slaughter the rest of the sheep and throw the pieces over the wall on the rebels' heads. We could keep their dead and stick them on the ends of pikes. Could paint messages on the castle walls."

The captain frowned. "I hope to be the honorable party in this skirmish. Bending down to their level seems unwarranted."

"Sometimes it's being the more dishonorable sort that gives you the edge you need to overthrow an opponent," Paulo said, thinking of Diana for some reason. She could be barbaric at times, but because of her ferocity and her snubbing of societal regulations, she was more dangerous. "Besides, I'd rather save the people we have trapped in this castle than be known as the most agreeable castle under siege. It's time for us to act."

Conley folded his arms over his chest. "We'll be ready the next time they have a go at us. I've already got the smiths working on the couillards, and we have enough rubble to send hurtling over the walls."

"I'll get the men to move it to the guard towers," Captain Isaac said.

Paulo pulled an empty sheet of paper from one of the many piles scattered around the room. "Declan, if you could come up with a list of other possible methods of warfare we could use to gain the upper hand, I'd like to put them to everyone else when we meet again tonight."

Declan took the sheet of paper, his brows already low in thought.

Paulo grabbed the jacket he'd tossed over the back of one of the chairs, a dark blue with only gold buttons for embellishment, and headed for the door. Jenkins really had taken Paulo's words about getting rid of the wardrobe to heart. Only half a dozen hangers in Paulo's armoire held his leftover jackets and waistcoats. He still owned a black suit for balls, but there wasn't a spot of orange or lime green in the entire set. Most of them had been blues, browns, and modest greens. He would probably find himself matching Diana more often than not.

What he hadn't expected was finding the fabrics from his

wardrobe had been distributed throughout the rest of the castle. He'd seen a little girl with a bright yellow skirt that looked very similar to one of his old waistcoats and a young man wearing a striped, purple jacket that hung awkwardly on his lean shoulders. Each person he'd come across sporting an article of bright clothing had given him beaming smiles and grateful nods. Jenkins was clever, Paulo would give him that.

Paulo made his way to his study to find a minute to himself before his next meeting. Praise the Goddess the fight had finally taken a break. It felt as if the castle walls themselves sagged a bit with relief. They were safe for another day. They had a moment to breathe and fortify their defenses.

It was a terrible thing, how this had become a normal part of life in such a short amount of time. That the children within the walls had to go to bed at night, not knowing if they would wake again in the morning to a battle or not.

The door to his study was locked, so Paulo withdrew his key and slid it into the lock. He almost expected to find Mare on the other side, but no one waited for him in the room. He was so used to coming upon the scholae everywhere it was almost odd to be by himself. Even before he'd finally met Laurel, Diana or Donnie were regularly at his heels.

He stayed in the doorway for several moments, staring at the empty room. He almost felt like he should be looking for one of them, but each of them had their own assignments. Their own purposes. The war had created more work for every one of them. It felt like there wasn't a quiet moment to be found anywhere, but was that a good thing or a bad one?

"Paulo? Is everything all right?"

He spun and found Mater standing in the hall, her arms full with a tea tray.

"Of course. Here, let me take that." He pulled the tray from her hands. "I have a minute. Where are you headed with this?"

She brushed a loose tendril of gray hair from her brow. "I was actually heading here. Jenkins mentioned you were meeting with Peter and Oliver today. I figured since it's so close to luncheon, the three of you could use a little tea."

Paulo set the tray on his desk. "You didn't need to waste our tea rations on me."

"Oh, I wasn't doing it for you. It's for Oliver, of course."

He turned to give her a disbelieving look, but her lips were quirked with amusement, and he rolled his eyes. She stepped up next to him, taking up a plate and setting a small biscuit on top. The *amygdalota* was as simple as biscuits came, but Paulo's throat grew a bit tight at the sight of it. He shouldn't be eating sweets when their stores were diminishing.

Mater set the plate on his desk. "Now, I know that look. You don't need to feel one ounce of guilt about this. Cook and Laurel made a whole batch to share with the village children. I figured since you were also such a child, it was only fair that you get one as well."

A laugh burst out of Paulo's chest. "Oh, well, in that case..." It was good to hear Laurel had made her way to the kitchens. She hadn't had much time as of late to stretch her culinary muscles. Just the thought of her cooking made his mouth water.

Mater gave him a smile as she trailed out of the room. "Just make sure there's some left for Peter and Oliver as well. What kind of aunt would I be if I didn't save my nephew an *amygdalota* or two?" With a wink, she disappeared down the hall.

Paulo shook his head, pouring himself a cup of thin tea and picking up his biscuit. It was still warm as he bit into it. He moaned. The entire thing was gone in seconds, and it took all his self-control not to eat Peter and Oliver's as well.

He settled into the chair at his desk and let the warmth from the tea seep into his bones. He closed his eyes and laid his head back. It was the first moment of quiet he'd had in... Actually, he couldn't even remember how long it had been. Even his magic was quiet.

A knock sounded and Hiatt, in his very pristine butler ensemble, poked his head into the study. "Lord Peter and Lord Oliver to see you, my lord."

Peace and quiet could only last for so long. "Thank you, Hiatt. Send them in."

Hiatt slipped back through the door and Peter and Oliver

stepped through. Oliver stopped on the threshold, looking at Paulo with furrowed brows.

Paulo leaned back in his chair. "Cousin?"

Oliver shook his head and joined Peter, who was grinning. He pointed at Paulo's face. "That's a real shiner."

Paulo gingerly prodded at the large bruise he knew was growing along his jaw. Declan had got in quite a hit. "Yes, well, we all bear wounds during a battle."

Peter ignored the tea sitting on the desk and walked over to Grandfather's secret liquor table set against the wall.

Oliver frowned as he poured himself a cup of tea. "We've been under siege for nearly a month now and up until know, I had yet to see you sustain an injury."

"Then you haven't been looking very hard," Paulo quipped. He pinched the bridge of his nose. "My physical state isn't why I asked you here this morning."

"I would hope not," Peter said. He sauntered back to the desk, pulling out a folded stack of papers from within his jacket. "We've brought the latest report on the sheep. Seven ewes were lost in the flood. The water swept out one of the fences and took them with it. One of the rams was injured, but the shepherds assured me he'll be fine."

Paulo blew out a breath and took the papers when Peter stretched them over the desk. "I do appreciate you watching out for the flock. I couldn't imagine defending the castle and also trying to keep the little beasts alive, so we still have something left after it's over."

Peter gave a nod. "We're happy to do it, especially as it gives us something to focus on. I'm getting too old to wield a sword anyway."

"Father, you're barely over forty years," Oliver said.

"Even so, I'm a much better businessman than battle strategist. Phineas was always the better strategist— his magic aiding him that of course. I'm glad that particular set of talents passed from your father to you, Paulo."

Peter and Father had a close relationship growing up, which Paulo was more than grateful for. While Paulo and Peter were technically cousins, Peter's father, the elder Oliver MacGregor who had been Father's twin brother, had married at a young age and had four children before Paulo and Diana had been born. Father had been nearly thirty-five when he finally married Mater, who had been in her late twenties herself. It had also taken quite a few years for them to have Paulo and Diana, which was why Oliver the younger and Paulo were closer in age. Uncle Oliver had died in a horseback riding accident the same year Father had passed. Mater said it was the universe righting itself, as one twin couldn't live without the other.

"What measures do you think we need to take to keep the flock safe from further harm? Mater has already shared concern over bringing them into the castle proper, but I'll push for it if you think it's necessary."

"Beatrice has voiced the same concerns." Peter smirked at the mention of his wife. "I don't believe we're at that point yet."

"Actually, I had a proposition," Oliver piped in. He stood and walked over to the map of Iatrus Castle hanging on one of the walls. "As we're getting further into the summer months, we may want to consider planting some kind of crop for the sheep. We were able to get quite a few sacks of fava beans in the castle. What if we planted them?"

Paulo felt his left brow twitch. "Where would you suggest we plant them?"

"I know it sounds awful, but after the flood, the top of the hill in the outer bailey is practically emptied of most of the grass. We could use the cleared ground to get a crop in. With its open access to the sun and the walls to keep the worst of the wind at bay, we could have a pretty good harvest— that is, if we can keep the plants alive long enough for the beans to grow."

Paulo met Peter's eye. "What do you think?"

Peter shrugged. "The fava bean season ended a couple months ago, but we can plant them this fall for an early spring harvest next year. If we can get them to grow well, we would have a pretty good crop of them, which will certainly help, as our stores will be depleted through the winter and the fields outside the castle have been ravaged. We have no idea what anything really looks like between here and Actium Hall."

Rubbing at the unbruised side of his face, Paulo considered

Oliver again but could find no fault with his proposition. Maybe miracles really did still happen. Or perhaps Paulo wasn't the only one who had been affected by this battle.

"All right, Oliver. I see the wisdom of this plan. If your father here agrees, I'll put you in charge of execution. You'll need to work with the gardeners and staff here at the castle to get the job done."

Peter gave his son a smile. "Well done, son."

Oliver nearly sagged into his chair, his eyes wide in disbelief. "Thank you."

Peter turned back to Paulo. "Honestly, the best way we can keep them safe and get them back to thriving would be to end this siege."

"I'm working on that."

Peter pushed himself up from his chair, walking toward the study window on the wall behind Paulo. "How much longer are we going to be able to stretch supplies?"

"We've probably got a month more before we really start facing problems." Paulo sighed. "But I think the rebels would overpower us before then if we don't figure out how to get rid of the Aigean threat."

Oliver fidgeted in his chair. "I thought you and your friends got rid of them."

Friends. Paulo winced as his shoulder twinged. Who would call a group of assassins that would just as quickly kill him as they would save him friends? He nearly laughed. He would, of course. They were his friends. He had grown to care about them. All of them. It made the fact that any one of them could possibly still betray him that much worse.

He couldn't imagine how Laurel was handling it.

Magic flickered at the back of his eyes.

"We're fully at your disposal," Peter said. "Whatever you need, Paulo, we'll make it work."

Paulo blew out a breath, pushing the magic away. "Excellent. Then we can send Oliver off to give orders to the shepherds." He tapped the stack of orders Peter had just signed.

Oliver snatched them up, but he slowly got to his feet. "I'll be off then, I suppose."

It was difficult for Paulo not to point out the lack of enthusiasm.

Oliver stepped out of the study and the door clicked behind him.

"I assume there's something else?" Peter said.

Paulo took up his teacup and swirled the last few drops sitting at the bottom. "This battle is already making itself out to be a miasma of variables and loose possibilities. I need to make sure both of us are on the same page about the inheritance should anything... happen."

"Have you seen things that I should be made aware of?"

Paulo bit the inside of his cheek. He didn't need to tell Peter what he'd seen. The destruction. The heartache. The deaths.

No, it was better if his cousin didn't know.

Peter took his silence for enough of an answer and drained the rest of his glass in one large gulp. He stood. "I'm definitely going to need more wine."

Paulo pulled out the key he had tucked into his pocket and slid it into the keyhole on the bottom most drawer of his desk. "Yes, you will."

29
THE TRAITORS

LAUREL REMEMBERED HOW TEAGAN RANTED ABOUT HOW FOOLISH PEOPLE were that they believed the best time for assassinations was under the cover of late night, when even the moon was getting sleepy in the sky and the world was quiet.

It was one topic Laurel agreed with Teagan on.

There were certainly times when the night would be best suited. If the target was single and lived alone. If they were regularly found at a tavern bar late into the night. If the assassin was particularly memorable and needed a bit more cover to get a job done.

But there were situations where the light of day worked better for secret things.

If someone had a family they went home to every night, killing them on their walk to work in the morning would leave less witnesses. If the target worked alone in a fancy office that only had one guard that could easily be substituted. If poison was the best weapon for the job, the assassin couldn't stuff a poisoned pita in their mark's mouth in the middle of the night.

The good assassins could accomplish their missions any time of day in any circumstance.

Laurel had always thought she was a good assassin.

And she knew Xander and Declan were distracted outside the castle for at least the next hour.

She glided through the halls, her steps purposeful but unsuspecting. Looking like she had somewhere to be would keep anyone from stopping her, but she also had to remain calm so no one blinked twice at her. She was invisible in the way a white rabbit was undetectable in the snow until it jumped right across your path.

There were six doors along the right wall and four on the left. The lockpicks slipped from her sleeve into her palm. She stopped in front of the third door on the right and gently prodded the handle. It was locked of course. Her eyes flicked down each end of the hall before she crouched and stuck the picks into the keyhole. It took only a couple seconds of prodding before she had the door unlocked.

The picks slipped up her sleeve until they found the small loops that would keep them in place. Laurel drew a thin strip of paper from a pocket inside her coat, sliding it between the door and the jam. It caught three quarters of the way up. Carefully, she pushed the door open just enough for her fingers to slip through. A thin string had been attached to a hook nailed into the doorframe. She unhooked the string and pushed the door open the rest of the way. Looking up, she saw the sack of ink hanging above the door. If anyone came into the room without permission, they wouldn't be harmed, but Xander and Declan would know exactly who it was.

Good thing Laurel had told Paulo to warn the castle staff to leave the scholaes' rooms alone. She set the string back on the hook just in case she couldn't use the door to leave.

The room looked like Xander and Declan had made themselves right at home. Xander's things were sprawled all over his side of the room, clothes piled up near a bedpost and in front of the armoire, unstrung bows gracelessly thrown on the bed, and feather scraps for fletching sprinkled about. Declan's side looked like not a single soul had even touched the bed it was so well made.

Laurel started with Xander's side as it would take the longest. She knew better than to skew even one feather. Xander had always had a keen eye. He couldn't match Laurel's memory, but it was certainly nothing to scoff at. She gently shifted the bedding, looking for holes in the mattress. The bedframe held the bed a few inches from the ground. Underneath, lines of rope and leather held the mattress aloft. She ran her fingers along every piece, searching for anything. If Xander was plotting to betray her, there had to be something.

The bed yielded no clues, so she set to check the rest of Xander's things. Three out of the five bows on the bed had secret compartments. A couple held poisons while the last was stuffed with flammable arrow tips. The open trunk at the end of his bed also yielded nothing.

Whatever proof she was looking for, she wouldn't find it in his things.

She moved on to the room itself, looking for newly broken pieces of wainscotting or loose floorboards. There were no false bottoms on the drawers of the armoire nor messages stuck to the bottom of the writing desk. Not that there would be a stack of coded notes lying about. The scholae were too smart for that.

Counting down the minutes until the men would be released from their patrol rotations, she approached Declan's trunk. The latch on the front was locked tight, so she quickly unscrewed the hinges holding the lid on. It was always nice to find a trunk with outer hinges. Pocketing the small screws, she pushed the lid off the top. The lock in the front kept it from moving very far, but she could still investigate the contents. A pile of neatly folded clothes sat to one side and sheathes of daggers and throwing knives lay on the other. There were also a few well-worn books with slips of paper sticking out of them. Books on strategy. Luc had had similar volumes, though he'd hated reading them. She quickly thumbed through the pages, but besides a few notes in Declan's spidery handwriting, there was nothing.

The hum of deep voices echoed down the hall.

Blast.

Quickly, she closed the trunk and slid two of the four screws back into both hinges. She would finish putting them back in later.

The doorknob clicked with the key being inserted.

Laurel slipped under Declan's bed just in time to see a gloved hand pluck the string from the hook.

Xander's large brown boots came through the door first. "When do you think those couillards on the guard towers will be done?"

Declan shut the door. "Three days, four at the most. Conley has four different men on each for assembly. The one on the bastion is nearly done already."

Xander's boots stopped at the side of his bed and the bedframe creaked as he sat down. "It's too bad Conley won't let any of us near them. I'd love to take a shot on one of them. Imagine the damage it could do."

Declan stopped at his trunk and unlocked it. "You'll have plenty of fun on the springald, I'm sure."

Laurel waited with a knotted gut for the hinges to pop off, but the trunk held together as he dropped what sounded like a couple knives into the bottom. "I think you'll have to arm wrestle Serene for first crack at any of them. She's been moon-eyed since the bases went in."

Declan's black boots shifted as he walked to the side of the bed. Laurel pressed herself farther back until her hip met the wall. The side of the mattress dipped under Declan's massive weight. He would have certainly felt her underneath if she'd been any closer.

As his weight settled, the mattress sagged around the leather straps holding the bedframe together. Right under Declan, a small slit opened up in the sagging mattress.

A knock sounded on their door.

The mattress lifted back up as Declan marched across the room. He opened the door just a fraction.

"Paulo?"

Xander was on his feet next. "Ah, come to join the real party, have you?"

Paulo's warm chuckle filled the room. "Alas, not this time. I actually came to see if the two of you wouldn't mind helping Mater with a project."

Silence met his request for several seconds until Xander finally responded.

"She needs us?"

"Well, maybe not you two specifically, but I was hoping the reward of Cook's adoration would be enough to tempt you. I figure after the two of you were on the wall for the last little bit, you'd like to see what scraps of goods there were in the kitchens. I know there were fresh biscuits yesterday."

Both men followed Paulo out into the hallway, one of them stopping to secure the string to the hook and set the trap.

By the Goddess.

As quietly as she could, Laurel reached forward, wriggling her fingers between the leather and the mattress. Something smooth bumped against her skin, and she pulled it out.

A small white shell.

She twisted it in her fingers. Why was there a shell in Declan's bed? It was the size of her palm and pure white on the outside, but the inside was speckled with pink. She'd picked similar shells on the beach near her hometown with Aspen when they'd gone to the docks with Father. It was pretty, if not a bit out of place.

Another knock sounded on the door, and she froze.

"Laurel?" Paulo's voice came from the other side.

Her heart sank from her throat and back down into her chest, though it still beat too quickly. She tucked the shell back up into the mattress. It wasn't like she could take it with her. She slid out from underneath the bed and headed toward the door. She unhooked the string and opened it fully.

Paulo stood in the hall, his hands set on his hips.

"You found the shell."

Laurel pinched the bridge of her nose. Of course, he'd seen her. "Is there something special about it?"

"It's from Caspian."

She turned back into the room, kneeling down by Declan's bed. "What does it mean?" She grabbed the shell out and passed it to him.

Paulo tucked it against his ear and frowned. "There's nothing there."

She took it from him. "What do you mean?"

"The Aigeans can enchant shells as communication devices. I saw both Declan and Xander get one from Caspian, though I couldn't tell you if either of them actually met with the selkie to get them. I only saw the possibility of it. But if this shell was a communication device, we wouldn't hear the sound of the ocean inside. It would be different."

Laurel pressed the shell to her ear and found he was right. The quiet shush that one heard when listening inside a shell met her ear. She pulled it away. "This isn't proof."

"No, it isn't. He could have gotten it from anywhere."

She tucked the shell back into place so Declan wouldn't know she'd been snooping. "How long do we have until they come back?"

Paulo followed her in and shut the door behind her. "At least half an hour."

Pulling the small screws from her pocket, Laurel set them back into the hinges of Declan's trunk. "I don't understand it. Why was the shell under Declan's bed? And what does it even mean?"

"Perhaps we could confront both him and Xander?"

Laurel blew out a breath. "No. If anything, we start giving out misinformation and follow that trail. Except not even that would work because they're all smart enough to check with the others. If I was going to betray me, I'd be asking everyone else what they knew to make sure my information was correct before possibly passing it along to the enemy."

Paulo grinned, his magic sparking to life in his eyes. "That's because you're brilliant."

She pushed him back out the door. "Like you didn't already know." Once they were out of the room, she reset the trap and used her picks to lock the door.

But before she could walk away, Paulo snagged her sleeve. "I'm sorry, Laurel."

"For what?" She slipped her arm from his grasp, not particularly happy with the way her heart skipped at his nearness. How her attention flicked to his lips for half a second.

Those lips twisted to the side. "I'm sorry that trust is hard to come by these days." He raised a hand as if to touch her again, but it fell back to his side. "I really am going to try to fix that."

Laurel took another step back, putting a little more distance between them. Real Paulo was difficult to ignore. She shrugged. "Backstabbing comes with the territory."

His blue eyes darkened. "I swear to you, I am never going to stab you in the back."

She snorted. "Please—"

Now, he did touch her. A gentle brush of his fingers against her cheek.

"I'm serious, Laurel. I know I haven't given you much to trust me on, but it's my greatest desire to gain your faith in me. I want you to know that I'll always watch your back. For as long as you'll let me."

His fingertips set her skin ablaze, but she kept her nonchalant mask in place. She couldn't let him see how much he affected her, even after everything they'd been through.

The truth slipped out in her determination to keep her body from betraying her. "I want to trust you, but I don't believe that I can."

His hand finally fell away. "Well, then I'll just have to convince you."

30
AN UNEXPECTED FAILURE

PAULO'S VISION SWAM AS HE STARED UP AT THE CEILING OF THE CAVE. Only a couple hours separated him from dawn. From another battle. From another risk.

He sat up, rubbing at his skull. His ginger tea rations were all but completely gone. The ache in his head pounded like a drum. By the Goddess, it had been a while since he'd pushed himself so hard.

He still couldn't figure out if any of the scholae would betray Laurel.

There was no future where any of them met with Caspian again. At least, not in any futures Paulo could see. He had followed the lines of each of the scholae and had picked through every piece he saw. Each one of them went about doing suspicious things.

Serene writing charms in a book that she tore out and threw out a window.

Mare combing through the drawers of Paulo's desk in his study.

Conley passing coin over to one of the villagers in exchange for a bag of weapons.

Declan tucking something in his pocket when Laurel bursts into the room.

Xander combing through the papers in the sitting room before tucking them into his pockets.

Most of it came in flashes, Paulo's mind so full of the possible futures it was almost overwhelming. He was pretty positive Serene and Conley were on their side now. Serene never left the walls of the castle to speak with Caspian. There hadn't been any more visions of Conley taking the scholae from the hall, but Paulo couldn't risk being lax now.

He staggered to his feet, leaning against the rough wall. He just needed to get up the stairs. Then, he could pass out on one of the couches in the office up there. Mater would probably come looking for him a little before dawn. She knew where the entrance to the secret staircase was. His foot landed on the bottom step. Just one boot in front of the other. There were fifteen stairs. Fifteen steps to the nice, comfy sofa in the office that called his name.

Without any rails to hold onto, he set his hands to the walls and hauled himself up the stairs. It took way longer than it should have as he had to stop every few steps to blink the white spots from his vision. He needed sleep. Then water. Then wine. He sighed. No, not wine. Donnie had drained all the reserves in the entire house. He'd even found the hidden decanters in Paulo's personal sitting room. *Cursed drunkard.*

Paulo reached the top of the stairs and shoved the secret entrance open.

"Aha!"

Paulo jumped back, nearly falling back down the stairs. He caught himself on the wall and looked about.

Next to the window, Diana thrust a finger in his direction. "I *knew* it was in here."

Paulo sagged until he was sitting on the ground, feet splayed out in front of him and his hand on his chest. "By the Goddess, Diana! You almost put me in an early grave." His magic must have really been exhausted. It hadn't tried to warn him she was on the other side of the door as it had so many times before. He hadn't even been able to check without risking passing out in the cave.

She flicked her braid back over her shoulder. "That's what you get for sneaking around in hidden rooms and not sharing."

"Well, you finally caught me." Paulo rubbed a hand over his face. "What are you doing in here?"

Diana stalked toward him and plopped down onto the sofa, the very one he'd been daydreaming about only moments ago. She stared at the empty fireplace, her hands twisting awkwardly in her lap. Paulo couldn't help but stare at them. Diana hadn't had an awkward moment in her life. Not even when they'd been youth. Paulo had been all gangly limbs and squeaky voice for an entire year while Diana went from being a girl to a woman in a blink without an ounce of gracelessness. Whether that was due to her diligence in training and being very self-aware or simply complete self-confidence, Paulo couldn't be totally sure. Either way, watching her physically fidget was making his chest tighten.

He didn't move from his spot on the floor, but he did bring a knee up to rest his arm on. "Diana?"

She clenched her hands into fists on her lap and took a deep breath. "I came because I can't stand being stuck in this castle and feeling useless."

Paulo leaned his head back against the wall. "Mater made you come."

"Yes."

"Figures." A small chuckle reverberated in his ribs. Mater never did let them go too long without patching things up.

"Everyone's acting like I'm a victim in all of this."

Paulo shrugged. "Yes, but you admitted Caspian betrayed you."

"That doesn't mean I didn't know what I was doing. That I didn't understand the risks I was taking. Some part of me knew he was going to betray me, and I just ignored it. Call it pride or whatever you want, but I thought I could handle whatever happened. I thought that even if he did betray me, I could outsmart him. It still hurt like a punch to the face, but I wasn't surprised when he betrayed me."

"Then why did you do it?"

She shoved herself out of the sofa. "Because I was so tired of feeling trapped. Of feeling like I couldn't help. Of waiting around for you to do something and watching you sit on your hands and do nothing to help stop all of this. It feels like half the time you don't care about anything, and people applaud you for it while I have to practically kill myself to gain even one spark of respect.

I'm just as worthy to lead people as you are, and it drives me insane that no one sees it that way. That just because you have a title, you can sit around and wait for things to happen instead of trying to fix them yourself."

Again, his inaction caused more pain than not. What would have been the right choice? The question had been tapping at the front of his skull since Laurel confronted him on the castle wall after Cal's death. He hadn't had too many choices, not when he'd let himself get complacent, because he knew the rebels wouldn't stay here. There were bigger fights elsewhere. But he also didn't weigh the consequences for everyone else. He'd been willing to sacrifice lives so he didn't have to worry about it.

What kind of man did that make him?

Diana cleared her throat. "Did you seriously fall asleep?"

Paulo realized his eyes had closed and he shook himself. "No, I'm not asleep. I'm just trying to figure out the best way to respond."

Diana snorted. "Something along the lines of 'Oh, Diana, I really am just an empty-headed ninny. I should have been listening to you from the beginning about throwing my weight around instead of ignoring you.'"

"Still mad about me forcing you to come home from the palace before it got taken?"

She deflated. "No, not really. If I'm being honest, I told myself you wouldn't listen to me. That you'd just tell me you were the marquess and I had to do whatever you said."

The moment he'd ordered Diana to return home after he'd seen her die in a vision, he knew he'd pay for it. He'd seen Diana get her revenge on him a hundred different ways before she settled on reaching out to Caspian. It had just been her reaching out to him that had brought Caspian into the castle and possibly given Paulo a chance to figure if any of the scholae were working with him.

"I wish I could say I was sorry about ordering you home," he said, "but I'm still not. It saved you."

Diana rubbed a hand down her face, still pacing like an angry cat. "I swore I wasn't going to open this conversation with this. I came to that conclusion already, that you'd seen something you couldn't tell me or something bad would happen. I wish I would have come to it before I confided in Caspian, but here we are."

"Here we are," he echoed.

"I was so angry," she admitted. "I was hurt, and when you returned with Laurel, I felt as if I'd been replaced. Like you felt like you didn't need me anymore because you'd finally found her."

Paulo straightened. "What?"

She held up a hand. "Let me finish. I'd started to feel it at the palace but ignored it. I mean, it's *Laurel.* We've all been waiting for her for ages. But when you told me to go home, I felt like you didn't trust me. I realize that you probably *couldn't* trust me because I probably would have done something stupid, but I couldn't get over the fact that you were cutting me out. You'd never really done that before, and I couldn't wrap my head around it. I wanted to stay to help you, but you wanted to stay for Laurel. It shouldn't have hurt me because I know what she is for you, but it did."

Paulo's throat felt tight. "It was never because I didn't want you there. Honestly, I was terrified of you leaving me alone, but I was more terrified of what would happen if you stayed. I'm an anchorless boat without you."

A small smile played at her lips. "And I'm definitely a boatless anchor without you. After the duel with the scholae the other night, I realized I hated feeling like I couldn't trust you anymore. That all this boiling in my gut shouldn't really be directed at you or the scholae, but at Caspian." She took in a deep breath. "Don't get me wrong, I was angry at him and still blame him for his betrayal and for killing Cal, but I was turning the anger I felt with myself out on everyone else. It only got worse as I watched you and Laurel. I know it's natural for adults to grow apart, but maybe I wasn't ready for it yet. I felt like you were leaving me behind. It wasn't fair of me, though I still think you're a ninny."

Paulo gave a small snort but not much else. The pain in his skull shifted to a dull ache that made his eyes water, but he couldn't leave Diana like this. They needed to have this conversation. He'd missed her. He'd missed having his other half with him. He would need her there to keep him on the right path, as she always had.

The toe of Diana's boot dug into the floor. "When Laurel put us together for that fight, I thought I'd rather chew my own arm off than be that close to you, but when they came at us, I could think of nothing else but trying to keep you safe. I couldn't help it. You've always been there for me, and I realized that it was tearing me apart trying to keep you at arm's length. So, I've come to make amends. To say that I don't care if you want to sit on your hands or burn the castle to the ground. That if you ever want to run away with Laurel and leave the rest of us behind, I'll be right there to slap your horse on the rear and watch you fade into the sunset. I just want you to have every happiness, even if it is without me."

He studied the planes of her face, looking for any sense of falsehood but finding none in the open expression. "Are you serious?"

"Deadly." She crouched down next to him. "I know you as well as I know the freckles on my hands. Even though you're a selfish blackguard, you've still been someone I always knew I could trust. Things just got murky for a minute."

He grabbed her and pulled her into a hug, his arms tight around her shoulders even though he was still slumped on the ground. "Thank you. I don't want to leave you. I don't think I could exist without you."

She hugged him back, barely able to get her arms between him and the wall. "Yes, you could. Besides, it's not like I'm going to be around forever. I think after this I'll become a pirate or something. Xander's been telling me all about what life on the Continent is like. It might be fun to run amok."

Paulo choked out a laugh and let her go. "You can't be serious."

She shrugged. "I think neither of us should shut ourselves off to opportunities for happiness. I just hope you'll cheer for me when I become a pirate queen, and you're still stuck here playing the peacock marquess."

"Actually, I've been thinking about turning my feathers in."

"Really?" She plopped down beside him. "I was wondering why so many of the villagers' wardrobes had somehow gotten a bit brighter."

"Noticed that, did you? Jenkins did a marvelous job purging

my wardrobe. I think even you'd approve." The weight of Paulo's eyelids was starting to become too much. He closed his eyes but kept the back of his head resting on the wall behind him.

"Paulo? Are you all right?"

He squeezed his eyelids together, trying to ease even a sliver of the pain before he opened them. He met Diana's concerned gaze. "Yes, I'm just trying to make amends too."

A frown brought her eyebrows together and she grabbed Paulo's arm. "Come on. Let's get you to bed. We've got a battle to prepare for and it wouldn't do for you to look anything less than ferocious."

Paulo let her pull him to his feet, grateful for her steady hold. He nearly toppled back to the floor when he got to his feet.

"Sweet Gaia, you're as wobbly as a lamb."

Paulo would have ripped his arm from her grasp if he thought he wouldn't fall over. "Brat."

"Maggot."

31
THE TOWER

Lake Luna will surge forward, the water collecting into the shape of a hand. It will race across the torn-up ground around Iatrus Castle and punch into the northwest tower. Laurel will fall, the surge of water smashing her into the ground.

"Master, they're coming for the western wall."

Laurel sprang from her chair in the sitting room. "How many?"

"Five hundred strong," Conley answered. "And there's another mangonel being hauled around the lake."

She strode through the door. "Your couillards are going to come in handy then."

"If we hurry, we might be able to shoot down the blasted machine before they can even load it."

They raced out of the castle. Laurel felt the weight of exhaustion wash away as adrenaline rushed through her veins. She would have to make sure to rest that afternoon if she was going to be of any help to anyone by the end of the day. Sleep had completely eluded her that night. The air buzzed with the coming fight. Even if Paulo hadn't been an oracle, Laurel would have known it was on the horizon.

The sky was red with the sunrise, as if it too was portending the blood this battle would spill. *Fitting.*

Laurel sent Conley off to the southwestern tower as she headed for the northwestern. She approached the damaged portion of the wall. The stone mage had been able to build a walkway in the gap, once again connecting the wall and making it easier for all of them at the top to get from tower to tower. He'd been hard at work getting the wall back to its former state. The magic made that section of the wall weaker, but it would at least keep the rebels from scrambling through. Laurel passed by the one weather mage in the castle, who was in the process of gathering clouds right above them. Laurel really ought to learn the man's name. He'd been one of their most helpful fighters. She'd ask Paulo about him later.

Declan had been put at the mangonel in the upper bailey, his silver hair a beacon in the crowd below. He almost singlehandedly loaded the large boulder that had been sitting next to the machine into the sling.

A throng of men met Laurel at the northwest tower. She nearly had to shove people aside to get to the couillard at the top. When she finally got through, she found Paulo leaning against the deadly war machine. She paused long enough to witness him patting it like his prized mare in the stables. She'd already seen Conley's schematics and he'd told her exactly how it worked. Like the mangonel, it used a long arm with heavy weighted baskets on one end and a sling on the other to launch projectiles. In this case, old pieces of castle wall. She and Conley would work the couillards on the west wall. Xander was in charge of the springald on the center tower and Captain Isaac had a team on their own mangonel in the southern section of the outer bailey. They'd had to haul the blasted thing from the eastern side the day before, but they would hopefully be able to use it to attack the encampments in the forest.

"What are you doing here?" she asked him, approaching the machine and checking the lever.

"Trying to help," he said. He set his hands to his hips. "Figured you could use a squire. I know Mare is staying with Mater in the sitting room so she can send out messages as information comes in, and Serene is scribbling fire charms into the bolts Xander is shooting out of the springald. Even Diana is helping with the archers. I wanted to be here to help."

Laurel narrowed her eyes at him. The dark circles under his eyes had grown more pronounced and his red hair, while usually a bit mussed by his fidgeting, stood on end. "Have you seen something?"

"Maybe," he replied, exasperated. "There were so many little pieces last night—"

A splash rippled out in the middle of the lake, cutting off his words. Laurel turned to see Xander standing at the springald, his hands flailing as he began shouting.

"Stay here," Laurel ordered and headed off in Xander's direction.

Paulo didn't listen, of course, and followed after her.

When she reached Xander, his face was twisted in a scowl.

"What's going on?" she asked.

He gestured at the springald, but Serene was the one who answered. "One of the skeins just popped."

Laurel went to the side of the machine, finding the skein that would pull back the bow arm on the left had indeed broken apart. She ran her fingers over the fibers, finding a few had broken, but it looked like some had been cut. Someone had sliced through most of the skein, just enough that when it was loaded for the first time, it would snap.

"We'll have to go without it for now," she said, coming back around the machine and looking for Paulo. Where she expected to find him waiting for her to give a report, he instead was looking at the mangonel down in the bailey below them. His narrowed eyes danced with magic.

Xander blew out a breath. "Conley's going to be livid. I'll probably have to sell off one of my finest jackets to pay for whatever new weapon will appease him."

"I'll speak with him," Laurel said, turning back to the tower. "Serene, you go help Conley. We still might be able to use the fire charms. Xander, you go down and help Declan with the mangonel."

"And here I was hoping you'd send me to the command center

so I could kick up these feet." He gave her a playful grin and a dramatic bow. "As you command."

Laurel watched Xander trot away, Serene already halfway to the other tower, nearly tripping on the untied laces of her boots. Honestly, her loose laces would get her killed one day. Laurel turned to the men gathered around the springald. "Get this machine out of the way. Don't break it further or you'll be facing more than just the wrath of your captain."

The men scrambled to get the springald away from the crenelled edge of the wall, and Laurel turned to make her way back to her post.

Paulo followed right behind her, a silent shield at her back.

"It was cut," she said when they were out of earshot of anyone else.

"I was hoping it wouldn't be."

Her shoulders sagged. "Who did it?"

"Declan."

Her head whipped back to look at him. "Do you know when?"

"It had to be last night. The skeins weren't put on until after supper."

"Curses."

Declan had just become their most potential traitor.

"Get that blasted rock loaded!" Laurel hollered, the sound of clashing blades and dying screams ringing in her ears. The men around her, soaked to the bone from the rain lashing at them, grabbed the largest boulder from the pile. The stone mage— according to Paulo, his name was Eric— had pulled more than three dozen large boulders from the ground in the large outer bailey on the other side of the castle. Both him and the weather mage, Eden, were probably the two single most effective fighters on the wall.

The rock was loaded onto the sling, the entire machine rocking with the weight.

"Clear!" she hollered above the rain.

The men around her dove for the edges of the tower.

Gritting her teeth, Laurel yanked down on the lever.

The arm of the couillard snapped up, hurtling the large stone across the field.

The arc of the stone would land it right in front of the rebel's trebuchet.

"We'll need another!" Paulo barked over the cacophony.

As soon as he said the words, light erupted on the field ahead of them, a beam of pure heat shooting up into the sky. It hit the flying boulder, not breaking it, but bumping it just enough to take it off course. It smashed into the ground a hundred paces in front of the trebuchet.

Blast.

Laurel spun to help load the couillard but had to practically leap out of the way when Diana jumped up in front of her to stand on the crenel, bow in hand and white fletched arrow nocked. The iron tipped arrow flew from her fingers. Laurel could barely follow the streak of white in the deluge as it hit the bedraggled fae woman in the chest.

"How many cursed fae do they have?" Laurel asked no one in particular.

"There's only half a dozen more," Paulo answered, coming up behind her.

"We need to take them out," Laurel bit out, wiping tendrils of wet hair from her face. While killing the fae made her gut twist into knots, there was little they could do to protect the castle from their magic besides taking them out of the fight.

Paulo looked past her to where Diana remained on the edge of the wall. "I don't think we'll need to worry about them for too much longer."

"*Come on!*" Diana screamed. "*Is that the best you can do?*"

Paulo stiffened next to Laurel, his eyes turning pearlescent. He blinked and it was gone.

"Blast it, Diana!" He hauled Diana off the wall. "Get off the tower!" he roared over the rest of the crowd.

Laurel followed his lead, not doubting for one second that he knew what he was about. "Let's go!"

The men all rushed for the stairs. There were two flights

between the top of the tower and the wall level. Only two men could walk through the opening at a time and there were at least thirty men on top of the tower.

Laurel grabbed the crossbow she'd taken from the armory and slung it over her shoulder.

"Diana!" Paulo snapped from behind her.

Diana had run to the side again and shot down at a few rebels who were in the process of raising a ladder up by the wall below them. Laurel jumped to join her, quickly loading her crossbow. Two well-placed shots and the help of the men on the wall brought the ladder down before the first man had stepped up the rungs.

Laurel left the rebels to their fate and found the rest of the men had made it through the door.

"Come on!" she shouted, jumping down.

Paulo pulled Diana from the wall once again, her shouts at the rebels disappearing as Laurel stepped down the stairs. She tried to take the steps down two at a time but had to slow to let the men ahead of her work their way down. She shoved her way past a few of them, trying to clear a path for Paulo.

"Move!" Paulo's command rumbled through the stone around them and the men increased their speed.

The steps under their feet shook.

Laurel braced herself against the edge of one of the arrow slits along the wall and watched several of the guards lose their footing. She spun around, looking for Paulo.

Her eyes snagged on the blurry sky outside the arrow slit.

A giant wave of water hit the tower.

The stones broke apart.

Laurel braced herself, but it was the wrong move. The water hit her, sweeping her off her feet. The stairs beneath her boots fell away. There was no up or down, right or left. Only water.

But something grabbed her arm.

The water disappeared and she found herself dangling over the edge of the hole. She looked up and found Paulo half hanging outside of the tower, eyes bright with magic and teeth gritted. With a roar, he pulled her up. Diana appeared next to him and Laurel reached with her free hand for Diana's proffered one. They lifted her together, and when she was in reach, Paulo grabbed her belt and pulled her over the edge. She fell into him, and he fell back onto the stairs, cradling her to his chest.

"Sweet Gaia, Laurel," he gasped, "you've got to quit trying to die."

She allowed herself thirty seconds to catch her breath before she pulled away from him. At least a third of the top of the tower had been ripped away by the water. A gaping hole had been left by the attack, taking a good chunk of the stairs with it. Pieces of limp lake grass and algae hung from the jagged edges like broccoli stuck in teeth. She carefully looked down at the ground below the tower as clumps of stone tumbled over the few foolish rebels still scuttling around the base. The rest of the rebels had vacated the area but were quickly regrouping.

The remains of the couillard littered the ground.

She sighed. "Seems Xander won't be the only one buying Conley a new sword."

32
AN UNEXPECTED CHARM

Paulo leaned against the table, his hands gripping the edges as he studied the maps in front of him. He wasn't lounging on one of the couches or staring out the window. He was at the table. Xander stood on one side of him and Laurel on the other while Captain Isaac and Mater stood across from him.

"I've got a dozen men patching the hole," the captain said, pointing at the northwest tower, "but it's going to be a weak point for us if we can't truly repair it."

They'd lost their stone mage. Paulo ran a hand through his hair. The rebels had swarmed the tower. The water had punched a hole large enough to throw a trebuchet through, and the staircase made defending the hole difficult. The mage had been shot trying to repair it. Two arrows had been all it took.

It seemed the rebels were done waiting. Their numbers, while mighty, had dwindled far more than the castle's. With Captain Isaac's help, Paulo had estimated a total of nearly two thousand that had come to take the castle. With the high ground, the castle had been able to take out a good third of the rebel forces, not to mention the Aigeans. Which meant the rebels were getting desperate. They were ready to take the castle.

And they would, if Paulo didn't come up with a solution.

"How many men do we have on the west wall?" he asked.

The captain pulled a black notebook from his jacket pocket and flipped through it. "I've got a hundred."

"The rest of them?" Laurel asked.

Captain Isaac didn't even blink at her question which would have made Paulo smile if the situation wasn't so dire. "I've got another seventy on the north. The south wall has fifty, thirty on the front gate, and two dozen on the bastion. The east wall is being held with fifty men."

Less than four hundred men to fight against the rebels. To save the castle.

Paulo pointed at the eastern wall. "Get all but a dozen of those men on the west wall. Have the men on the bastion help keep that side defended and relocate men back to that side if the fighting moves."

"Yes, my lord."

Xander leaned forward. "How long are you going to leave Conley on the tower?"

Paulo opened his mouth to answer when his magic slammed into him.

Serene, sitting on one of the crenels of the wall, tossing pages of sketches off the side.

He'd seen similar versions of the vision, her location changing, but the motion was always the same. Serene, pen in hand, ripping out pages.

But the visions after had changed.

A collection of knots. A pile of silver coin. A silent lake behind the rebels' backs.

The magic disappeared as quickly as it came and he stepped away from the table, striding for the door. He could hear Mater take control of the room as he left, asking about getting the men food.

Laurel appeared next to him, her silent steps keeping pace with his. "Where are we off to in such a hurry?"

"I need Serene."

Laurel took the lead. "I just got word from her on the east wall."

"I know."

"Of course you did." Paulo could hear the eyeroll in her voice. "What did you see to make it so we need Serene so badly?"

"I saw us get the upper hand."

Laurel went ahead and jogged backward, eyes wide. "Are you going to keep being cryptic or are you going to share?"

He pulled forward, grabbing her hand. "Better to get it all out in one go, don't you think?"

They raced through the castle. It was easier to get to the north wall by taking the upper bailey wall to where it met the outer wall on the south side. How many more times would he have to walk these stones? Would it ever stop?

Paulo pulled Laurel behind him, the feel of her hand grounding him as his magic tried to push itself forward. He needed to see Serene first, then he could figure out what they needed to do next.

They found Serene near the bastion, her untied boots tucked up under her to hold her sketchbook in place and a magelight strapped to her head by a few pieces of leather. She looked up when they got close, shining the light straight into Paulo's face.

He put up a hand. "Curses, Serene."

"Sorry!" she dimmed the light and stood up. "What are you two doing out here?"

"We came looking for you," Laurel answered. "Paulo saw something."

Paulo knelt down next to the short wall where Serene sat. It had to be there somewhere. He grabbed the satchel laying there and opened the flap.

Serene ripped it from his grasp. "What on Gaia's green earth are you doing?"

"I need your charm book. You were on to something, and we need to finish it. *Now.*"

Her dark eyes narrowed, but Laurel set a hand on her shoulder. "If he steals any of your charms, I'll gut him for you."

Serene slowly reached into the bag. "If he steals any of my charms, he'll beg for us to gut him." She drew out the book and passed it over.

"Yes, yes, I get it." A pox on him and all that. They acted like they didn't trust him or something. He untied the leather strap wrapped around the entire thing and flipped to the last few pages where a good chunk of them had been ripped out. When he saw the faint knot at the top of the last page, he stopped. "This! We need this."

Laurel leaned forward to look at the page. "What is it?"

Serene took the book back from him. "It was just a knot I was working on right before I finally gave up for the night. I've been thinking about that cursed water attack on the tower for hours and I was wondering if it would be possible to charm the water."

"Charm it for what?" Laurel asked.

Paulo looked out at the lake over their heads. "Charm it to be impossible to manipulate. And you can."

Serene shook her head. "No, I can't. I can't cover the entire lake with the charm and if I draw it around the banks, it will simply get ruined in the battle."

Paulo ripped the page out of the notebook. "I know how to do it."

"Hey!" Serene snapped. "You can't just rip things out!"

But Paulo was already at the stairs, Laurel and Serene on his heels.

"What did you see?" she asked.

Paulo hit the bottom of the stairs. "We'll need Mater and the servants to raid the castle for every spare coin we can find. We have five blacksmiths in the larger bailey with cooling forges. We'll need them back to work. If we can get whatever coins we have stamped with the charm—"

"We can get them into the water and make the lake unusable," Serene finished. "Oh, it's brilliant. While the tiny charms may only influence a small section of the water, enough of them will slow if not completely cut off the Aigeans' power over the lake."

"But we won't be able to get the coins scattered through the water from the banks and we can't send anyone out on boats so close to the fighting."

"We have two water mages," Paulo said. "They can at least get the water moving enough before the charms touch it that we can get the coins in."

"Besides," Serene added, "anything the Aigeans do with the

lake will only mix the coins up more. While they won't be able to control the water, it will move it until the entire lake is useless."

Laurel gave Paulo a serious expression. "How long do we have until the next attack?"

He didn't need his magic to tell him again. "They attack an hour before dawn."

She pulled the sleeves of her tunic up her arms. "Then I suggest we get moving."

It took three hours before the first batch of charmed coins made it to Paulo's hands.

He'd been standing at the blasted table in the command center, preparing the men for the last stand and witnessing the hands of his pocket watch slowly count away their chances of success. They would either thrash the rebels and send them packing, or they would fall.

"How?" He picked one out of the bag in shock. The silver coin that had once depicted the profile of King Dion was crudely stamped with the intricate knots he'd seen in Serene's sketchbook.

Laurel folded her arms, a streak of ash smeared on her nose. "The mage girl you had working as a scullery maid because she could keep the tarnish off the silver? She can also manipulate the metal to soften it and make it malleable. She crafted two dozen metal stamps within half an hour. She got offered jobs from every blacksmith in the outer bailey. I don't think you'll get to keep her on here at the castle."

"That's unfortunate." He stood, tying off the bag and tossing it back to her. Mater would be disappointed. She loved Grandmother's silver candlesticks. "How many more do we have?"

The coins jingled as she tossed the bag up in the air and caught it. "There's four more bags of this size, and I'm praying we can triple that amount within the next two hours."

"Then what are we waiting for?"

She tossed the bag back at him. "Just your most honor-ableness."

He caught the bag. Who was the cheeky one now? He chased her out of the command room. They passed by servants shuffling around the castle, carrying bed linens to be torn into bandages, broken furniture to be thrown into furnaces, and water through the various hallways. The blacksmiths had put up their shops on the other side of the upper bailey wall, right next to the front of the castle.

Donnie strode across the great hall, an armful of cloth strips in his arms, when Paulo made it to the top of the stairs.

"Have you seen Mater?" Paulo asked.

"She's been in the infirmary with the healers. I'm headed to her now."

Paulo grabbed his arm. "I don't know if I'll be back in the castle before dawn. Will you make sure she stays inside the castle tonight?"

"Of course," Donnie replied. "Did you see..."

Paulo shook his head. "Not anything worse than usual, but it would make me feel a lot better if I knew someone was watching out for her and she was out of harm's way." Especially if this idea went off the rails. There were too many fates twisted into this mission.

"I think she'd say the same for you," Donnie replied. But he straightened his shoulders. "I swear to you, as my friend, I won't let any harm befall Mater. The rebels will have to tear me to pieces if they want to get to her."

Paulo released his arm and nodded. "Thank you." By the Goddess, he was glad Donnie was here. While he could be ridicu-lous, he was just the right kind for Paulo.

"Just—" Donnie hesitated, eyes flicking to Laurel who waited by the door before meeting Paulo's. "Just don't do anything I wouldn't do."

Paulo barked a laugh. "That doesn't limit my options very much."

Donnie shrugged. "Then make sure that if you do something stupid, you do it with enough flare that even the Goddess claps you on the back when you get up there."

33
THE LAKE

There were three things about the coins that would cause problems.

The jingle they made in the bags, the cursed weight, and the way they glittered with the moonlight.

Two of these problems could be easily solved.

Laurel watched the clouds drift toward the bright moon ahead. If they timed it perfectly, Eden the weather mage would have the clouds in place right as they reached the edge of the lake.

The fabric padding in the sacks helped reduce the noise by half, but the charms Serene had quickly sewn into the linings of each of the eight bags had muted the jingle entirely.

Which left the weight.

From climbing down the wall to crossing over the debris at the base of the walls to getting to the abatis pit, she could already feel the fatigue begin to nip at her calves. She used the collar of her shirt to wipe the sweat from her face as she across the thin plank of wood held down on one end by Mare and the other end by Conley. Mare had been the first across, not fearing the plank sliding into the ditch under the abatis and getting stuck underneath. Quite a few of the sharp stakes had fallen into the pit below, creating a maw of jagged teeth.

Fully across, Laurel continued toward the lake. She didn't

need to help hide the plank. Conley and Mare would remain behind and wait for their return.

Too bad Conley wasn't one of the ones carrying the bags.

Behind her, she prayed the others got across. There were eight of them. Xander, Laurel, Paulo, Diana, Declan, Serene, and the mages all carried the sacks of coin. Serene accompanied the two water mages, acting as guard but also would hopefully be able to help them if something went wrong.

The length from the castle wall to the lake was approximately a quarter of a mile, but it felt like a whole one. Mater said that each pack contained about thirty pounds worth of coin, all collected from Iatrus Castle's vault and other safes around the castle. Collecting the coins had been the easiest part of the endeavor. Once those in the castle and upper bailey heard they were collecting the coins, they arrived at the blacksmiths' anvils in waves— many donated from the villagers themselves. The pack wasn't so heavy she was in danger of not being able to move quickly, but it would be cursed difficult to fight with if it came to that.

The ground under her feet grew viscous as she crept closer to the lake. With the way the Aigeans had been pushing the water around, the soft ground had been turned up and the sludge from the bottom of the lake brought to the banks.

Paulo pulled ahead and turned slightly, making his way a little to the right of her. The rest of their group spread out much the same way, stretching across the east side of the lake. The sound of the quiet lapping of the water met Laurel's ear before she found the edge. The water line rippled at the bank from two feet below. The Aigeans' use of the water had drained quite a bit from the lake. The drop from the top to the water wasn't straight down, but it was steep.

When everyone made it to their positions, Laurel slid down the embankment and pulled the pack off her shoulders. Praise the Goddess for Serene's charms because the blasted thing fell with a thump on the muddy ground, and it would have definitely made a ruckus if it hadn't been charmed. She crouched beside the pack, doing her best to be as quiet as possible while she pulled the drawstrings apart to open it. The coins jingled slightly, the charm unable to hide the sound now that the bag was open. Slowly, she stepped into the lake.

The clouds fully covered the moon, blocking out most of the light.

The coins trickled into the water.

She took slow steps farther into the lake, the black water sliding around her. It wasn't until she reached a dozen paces that she felt the water move under the surface.

At the center of the lake, the two water mages were creating a whirlpool.

Laurel dipped the mouth of her bag under the surface. She couldn't see anything due to the lack of light, but she could feel the weight of the bag grow lighter as the coins fell into the water. It was difficult to gage how many were falling, but she did her best to make it slow so the current would have the chance to spread them out instead of clumping them all together. They needed to cover as much area of the lake as they could.

The water began to slow against her legs, the coins distributed far enough by everyone else now that they were affecting the mages' own magic. Laurel stuck her arm into the bag, picking out the last handful of coins caught in the bottom of the pack.

A scream ripped through the air.

She straightened, dropping the pack into the water and backing up toward the bank.

The scream had sounded like it had come from their side of the lake, but the water and the trees distorted sound. She couldn't completely trust her own hearing, but she wouldn't stand out in the open if someone was screaming.

A ripple played in the water a dozen or so feet away from her.

She bolted.

The water behind her crashed as something shot out from the surface.

As she lunged for the final stretch to the bank, she spun, getting a good look at the sharp-toothed seal making a lunge for her.

She punched the beast square in the face.

The hit caught the seal by surprise. He fell to the side of Laurel, both of them hitting the bank at the same moment. In the time it took for Laurel to draw her dagger from her thigh, the seal had transformed into a man, the dark pelt whipping around his waist.

It really wasn't fair the blasted creatures were able to transform the clothing and weapons they wore with the pelt.

The selkie grabbed the bone handle of his blade, but Laurel was on him before he could draw it. He wasn't Caspian by any means, but he was still a brute of a male. He tried to spin out of her reach, but she stretched her arm, slicing her blade across his back. He yelped, the sound a bit seal like, and finally got his knife out of his belt.

Laurel drew the other blade she had. She didn't have time for a fair fight.

The selkie growled and charged her.

She spun the blades in her hand and took two long steps toward him before she slid onto her knees.

On instinct, the selkie leapt into the air, like he had known the exact moves to this dance they were performing.

With the blades in her hands, she raised them above her head and sliced at the tendons on the backs of his ankles.

The selkie's feet hit the ground, but his legs couldn't properly hold him up and he staggered.

Laurel leapt to her feet when he fell to his knees, pulling at the knot on his selkie pelt. She placed both daggers against the sides of his neck.

He stilled, his face turned to the lake.

She sliced his throat and kicked him into the water.

Most Aigeans could recover from a stab wound or a deep slice, but even this selkie wouldn't heal before he bled out in the lake.

Leaving the beastly creature to his fate, she jumped and pulled herself up the bank, mud coating her arms and torso. She rolled onto her back once she got to the top. Her legs were exhausted from running and fighting. She did a quick once over, making sure her adrenaline wasn't masking any injuries. The front of her left pant leg had ripped open and exposed her torn up shin, but it wouldn't impede her. *Good.* Hauling herself to her feet, she tried to find the others along the banks of the lake.

Shouts rang all around, but she headed in the direction she'd seen Paulo go. Her soggy clothes weighed her down, but she sheathed her long daggers and pulled a pair of throwing knives from the bandolier strapped to her chest.

She found Paulo knee deep in the water, going toe to toe with a merman.

Cocking her arm back, she threw her throwing knife.

It sank into the merman's shoulder, eliciting a bellow of pain from him.

Paulo took advantage of the distraction and used the sword in his hand to knock the wicked-looking harpoon from the merman's grip.

The merman roared and dove back into the water right as Laurel reached them.

Laurel would have thought the mermen all to have scaly tails like the one she'd seen in Iatrus Castle's courtyard, but this merman's tale flashed completely smooth and gray as it sank into the water.

Laurel grabbed Paulo's sleeve, yanking him backward. "We need to get out of here."

He allowed her to drag him back toward the bank and helped pull him to the top.

She looked him over as he got to his feet. His right bicep had been slashed, but it looked shallow. There was a rather nasty slice on his outer right thigh as well. The merman must have been lefthanded.

Another scream, one of fury rather than fear, had both of them whirling toward the noise.

"Diana," Paulo murmured. He took off at a run, not even looking back to see if Laurel would follow.

But she did.

They found Diana on the bank closest to the trees. A black shadow leaped out of the water toward her, and she shot an arrow, sticking it in the torso. The yowl of pain the seal gave off sounded as biting as a curse.

"I'm going to kill you!" Diana screamed as the water stilled around her ankles. She drew another arrow, her sharp eyes on the surface.

Not even Laurel could see the black shape of Caspian's seal form in the dark water.

But Diana must have seen something, because she fired off two shots, and Caspian's seal form soared up from the water with a roar, two white arrows sticking out of his back.

Paulo ran past Diana, sword in hand. He slashed at the selkie, but Caspian dove backward, avoiding the blade and slipping back into the inky lake.

Laurel stopped next to Diana. "Let's go."

"No, I'm done playing games. I'm going to kill him right now!"

Her tirade was ended as Paulo raced back toward them and scooped her up, throwing her over his shoulder.

"Put me down, you idiot! I had him!"

Laurel followed behind, clambering up the bank as Paulo carefully stepped so his jogging pace stayed even. *Curse mages and their magic that only make their lives a hundred times easier.*

Diana gave him a rather hard hit to his kidney that made him stagger.

Laurel winced. Perhaps she'd spoken too soon.

"Put me—" Diana's words cut off as she glanced behind Laurel.

Laurel had her two long daggers out as she spun.

A wall of water rose over the top of the lake.

"Go!" Laurel barked.

Diana finally got her freedom and stumbled when Paulo dumped her onto her feet. The three of them sprinted forward, dodging large stones and broken wagons. Laurel checked over her shoulder again, seeing the wave hop onto the shore. While it might have been smaller than any of the other waves the Aigeans had used in their attacks, it would still crush them if they didn't get to cover.

Pushing every bit of energy she had into her legs, she raced forward, looking for anything they could use.

Ahead of them, she spotted four bobbing shadows scrambling around a turned over wagon.

"Hurry up!" Declan bellowed.

The twins turned in his direction and Laurel pushed past them. The wave was decreasing, likely picking up coins as it tried to build up across the lake, but it still towered over the trees.

She slid to a stop where Declan stood, smearing thick mud onto the face of the wagon. Serene stood on the other side, connecting lines of mud with others.

"Get under the wagon," she snapped. "This beauty has one shot and you better be out of the way if you don't want that giant wave to crush you against the castle wall."

Laurel gave a sharp nod and followed orders, the twins trailing quickly behind.

"How much longer is this going to take?" Declan asked.

"Shut your trap and get under the cursed wagon!"

Declan dove beneath the wagon, the ground underneath them shaking with the wave.

"Serene!" Laurel called out. "What's taking so long?"

"Almost there!" Serene said in a way too cheery voice. As if there wasn't a giant wall of water eating up the ground between them.

Paulo grabbed Laurel's arm. She turned, biting words on her tongue dying when she saw the whirl of his magic. He blinked, the magic still swirling, but his attention back in this time as well. He yanked Laurel behind him, and she fell backward as he lunged for the side of the cart.

The water crashed into them.

"*Serene!*" Laurel screamed.

The wagon above them shuddered for a split second but held. The wave rushed past them, crashing over the ground until it hit the castle wall ahead of them. It rose up a few feet over the wall before falling back, whatever magic it had held to propel it forward running out.

Laurel scrambled for the side of the wagon where Paulo was pulling himself to his knees.

In his hands, he held one of Serene's untied boots.

Laurel burst out from under the wagon, slipping on the slick mud under her boots. She whipped her head left then right.

No, no, no. Not Serene. Not Serene.

It wasn't until she saw Mare, practically throwing herself

down the wall and sprinting toward the ditch separating them that Laurel found her.

Laurel fell to her knees.

Serene hung limply from the abatis, one of the spikes of bright wood sticking out of her chest.

34
AN UNEXPECTED VICTORY

THE REBEL TREBUCHET BOUNCED AS THE ROCK IN ITS SLING HIT OPEN AIR and soared toward the west wall.

"*Get down!*" Paulo bellowed.

The men around him dove below the crenels as the boulder struck the west wall. Screams rent the air as bodies went flying.

Paulo was up before the stones under his feet quit shaking. He ran to the edge of the southwest guard tower. The boulder had crashed into the section of wall right next to where Eric, the stone mage, had put a patch of stone and magic together to repair. Half of the patch crumbled, not meant to outlast another hit without the old stone bricks to support it on either side.

Curse whoever killed my stone mage.

The blasted trebuchet had already made two solid hits on the castle, one taking out the top of the ballroom and the other the northwest tower near the guard barracks. If this lasted much longer, they were going to take out the entire castle, and they wouldn't have anything left to pillage.

"Fill the hole!" he bellowed, pointing the bow in his hand at the wall.

The rebels cheered in victory as the dust cleared enough for them to see the hole. They swarmed like ants, skuttling over debris toward the opening.

But the castle guard was ready.

They'd been ready since Paulo rallied them the moment he returned from charming the lake.

From failing to save Serene.

The guards poured out of the gap, a hundred strong, with shields shining and swords poised. Captain Isaac stood on the front line, his voice booming over the guard as he held his shield up next to his comrades'.

Paulo bolted for the stairs and the archers followed. He took them three or sometimes four at time, his magic keeping him from slipping or missing a step. He outpaced his men and made it out the door leading out onto the west wall. He nocked one of the arrows in his quiver, pulling it back and shooting a rebel that had made it to the top of one of the ladders. The man fell, screaming. Paulo wrapped both hands around the end of his bow, and when the next head popped up, he whacked the man square in the face. The man's head whipped to the side, and he fell next. Leaving the ladder to the men behind him, Paulo didn't stop as he pulled another arrow from the quiver and jumped to the very top of the wall. The crenelation was spaced three feet for every crenel and five for the top. He sprinted across the wall, nocking arrows and shooting any rebels he spotted until his quiver emptied. He leaped back down onto the walkway, grabbing an abandoned half quiver of arrows from the ground without stopping.

At the edge of the gap, a ladder had been pushed against the wall and several rebels had made it to the top. A few of the guards were pushing them back toward the broken section.

Paulo's magic flared in his head, and he followed it as he leaped forward, grabbing the very top of the ladder. A rebel climbed up two rungs from the top, but Paulo's weight pulled the ladder to the side and with most of the rebels abandoning the bottom of the ladder to attack the captain, the thing was top heavy.

It slid down the wall.

As the ladder fell, Paulo swung out to the open side and slid down. He jumped the last few feet and rolled to a stop as the ladder crashed onto the rebels pouring into the opening.

A few of the rebels turned in his direction, but he nocked

another arrow before they could point their blades at him, and he shot down the tallest one.

Then, he was on the move again.

And not once did the water of the lake move.

Captain Isaac saw him, and a small gap appeared in the line of shields, right at the guards' feet.

Paulo ducked a slice from one of the rebels and dove through the small gap. He rammed into a few of the soldiers in the middle of the group, but they only staggered for a second before pulling him to his feet.

"Out, your lordship!" was all the acknowledgement he got before he was shoved to the back of the horde of fighters and spit out into the outer bailey.

He staggered, but a strong arm kept him from faceplanting.

"Back on the wall with you!" Conley snapped. "Laurel needs you at the gate!"

Paulo ran, his legs still feeling like jelly from the ladder trick and raced for the front gate. He passed into the upper bailey and through the bustling tent sea. Men, women, and children raced about, hauling supplies into med tents or weapons to blacksmiths for repairs.

Peter stood in in the center of it all under a large post with the MacGregor standard fluttering from its top. Paulo's pace slowed as he made eye contact.

"Report," he said, not slowing, but instead jogging past.

Peter stayed at his post. "Fifty in the tents. Thirty in the graveyard."

"The wall went down," Paulo said turning to jog backward and cupping a hand around his mouth. "Those numbers are about to go up."

Peter's face paled, but he nodded and called for the injured to be moved if possible and more tents prepared for more injured.

The last of his orders faded into distant hollers as Paulo cut through the tents and back out into the outer bailey on the north side of the castle. He raced to the left tower that held the gate, rushing up the stairs and allowing his magic to guide him to Laurel.

Diana stood at the top of the tower, her bowstring pulled back with a white-fletched arrow that went flying a moment later.

"What are we at, Xander?" she called.

Xander stood at the other end of the tower closest to the gate. "Seventy-three."

Another arrow materialized in Diana's hand. "That gives us another quiver each."

"So glad you can do basic math," Xander quipped, sending three arrows into the horde below them in quick succession.

Paulo swept past Xander and onto the walkway over the gate. He found Laurel at the top of the wall, a crossbow at her shoulder. She shot down at the men holding up a large battering ram. The one at the front fell.

"We've lost the west wall," he reported, not waiting for her to address him.

"Then what on Gaia's green earth are you doing over here?" She cranked the bowstring back on the crossbow.

"I'm here to take out the battering ram."

She loaded a bolt into place. "Oh yes, because it's going to be so simple to just take out the blasted battering ram."

How dare she doubt him! He huffed, looking about for what he really could do.

The rebels below them were slowly being fed by the men and women crossing the dirt with the enchanted plates, the paths having been easily drawn now that so many of them had crossed that way to get to the castle. One at a time, the rebels made their way across the field.

Paulo grinned.

He pulled one of his six arrows left in his quiver and backed up slightly, letting his magic flood him. He played through a hundred different scenarios, pushing his magic and letting it coat his consciousness until he found the only lines where he made direct hits.

The arrow flew from his hand.

It arced over the wall, lifting higher and higher until it reached its peak and made its descent.

Paulo didn't even see it land, but the earth exploding in light told him he'd hit exactly where he'd needed to.

"Xander!" Laurel snapped. "Keep Paulo supplied with arrows!"

Xander gave a sharp nod, collecting his quiver and tossing it at Paulo's feet before running off.

The schola followed Laurel's command to the letter and Paulo never ran out of arrows.

The rebels quit crossing their border after Paulo had blown up fifteen of their men with their own weapons. Seeing there wouldn't be any reinforcements, the rebels abandoned the battering ram, running for the west side of the castle where their comrades had gathered to push for the break in the wall.

Paulo and Diana shot down a third of them before they made it around the northwest tower.

Laurel directed men to the wall, the tower still in a state of disrepair. Half a dozen men had been put on patrol of the only hole in the temporary wall. While they appeared haggard and bloodstained, there was a fire in their eyes as they continued to push the rebels back.

They were holding. Praise the Goddess, they were holding.

Someone smacked him upside the head.

He spun and found Diana, eyes wide with admonishment.

"There's no time for lollygagging!" she said and sprinted out onto the west wall.

Paulo growled but followed behind. He'd show her lolly-gagging.

Laurel stood right outside the door, cranking back the crossbow string again.

"Where is the best place for me to go?" Paulo asked.

"Like I'm blasted supposed to know." She gritted her teeth and set the last bolt in her quiver on her crossbow. "Aren't you the cursed fortune teller?"

"Just wanted you in on the conversation." Paulo raced past her, letting his magic free again. His head ached something fierce, but the blood pumping through his veins kept him moving forward. He flew past Diana, then Xander, and stopped at the edge of the wall, this side still holding onto some of the magical stones Eric left behind.

Captain Isaac had fallen back, the rebels pushing the guard

back through the hole until they were barely keeping the rebels from breaking into the outer bailey.

It was going to break.

Paulo raced back the way he'd come, snatching up a fallen sword.

"Follow me!" he bellowed.

The men on the wall answered.

Several stayed behind, fighting off the slowly decreasing number of ladders hitting the top of the wall. Most, however, followed Paulo down the stairs of the tower and into the bailey.

The rebels broke through the moment before Paulo reached the line.

He dodged a blade, sliding his own into a set of ribs and moving on.

It was a blur of fate and blood and steel in front of him.

One man's line turned white with death. Then another. And another.

Paulo could feel the cuts and bruises against his skin, but he was so swept up in the magic he couldn't think of anything else except his next step. The sun fell below the horizon, but the sky was bright with fire and the knowledge that there would be no other fight after this. That they would make a stand here or they would die protecting what they loved.

He heard Captain Isaac call for an advance and felt the surge of Iatrus Castle's guard at his back. The rebels began falling back through the wall. Paulo didn't allow a single one within his reach to get past him. His sword flew through the air, no longer the silver of steel but the red of blood.

He pushed forward with a shout, startling the rebels around him, who took one look at him and scrambled away.

The men of Iatrus Castle were right there with him.

"For Olympia!" someone called.

"For Delphine!" said another.

"For Iatrus Castle!"

With a ferocious cry that rattled the very walls around them, they pushed forward, shoving the last of the rebels through the wall.

A horn blew out across the water, the sound barely breaking through the pounding in Paulo's ears.

He knew that sound.

"*Retreat!*" someone screamed.

Paulo gritted his teeth, looking past the rebels to see what new curse the rebels would bring.

But it was they who ran. They who retreated.

The call was not for Iatrus Castle.

It was for The Cartographer's men.

By the Goddess, it was over. They'd won.

Paulo lifted his sword over his head and roared.

Iatrus Castle roared with him.

35
AN UNEXPECTED PROPHECY

Donnie will skip down the halls of Iatrus Castle,
grabbing two petite chairs from one of the guest rooms as
the servants pass by him with six-foot armoires and
entire bedframes. A wicked gleam will spark in his eye as
he marches down the stairs behind them.

"What do you think Laurel wants?" Diana kept stride with Paulo through the halls. The quickness of her steps matched the pulse of Paulo's heart. "We've beat the blasted rebels. Can't we have a day off from training?"

While she complained about training, there was a certain energy to her limbs. A darkness that made her practically vibrate next to him. Hopefully, Laurel's idea would expel some of it. Would bring a little light back to Diana's eyes.

Paulo followed Conley down the stairs, doing his best not to grin and give anything away. He'd seen what Laurel had been planning for that morning, but he wouldn't be the one to ruin it. Not even for himself. He'd done his best to squash down his magic as much as he could over the course of the morning. To allow himself to relish in this moment of peace.

There was certainly still an ache in all their chests. Losing Cal had been a blow, but Serene's death had taken a piece of all of them with it. He still couldn't believe he hadn't been able to catch her. They'd had to wait to bury her until after the siege had ended. They laid her next to Cal, her coffin a simple oak box, since this was one death Paulo hadn't foreseen in the weeks before the siege started. Even he'd been caught by surprise.

But death came for everyone, and he knew that better than most.

They finally reached the hallway leading to the ballroom, finding the rest of the scholae gathered in front of Laurel and Donnie.

"Welcome to our team building exercise." Donnie's grin stretched as he met Paulo's eye. "We'll be playing capture the flag, except this particular version will be played a bit differently than some of you may be accustomed to." He held up a golden neck-cloth, the cloth trimmed with laced beyond comprehension.

He went through the rules, but Paulo only listened with half an ear. The defensive team would hide the flag. The team on offense would have fifteen minutes to get the flag and hand it to Donnie at the back of the ballroom, or they lost. The teams would play to best three out of five. Paulo grinned. He wouldn't need that long for his team to beat the other.

"Now, no game is worth playing if there aren't stakes." Donnie grinned mischievously.

Paulo watched Diana out of the corner of his eye. While her countenance was still dark, she seemed curious enough to at least listen.

"All right, old boy," Paulo drawled. "Don't leave us all in suspense."

Donnie slipped his hand into his jacket pocket and withdrew a handful of folded papers. "For the player with the most flag recoveries, I have here a receipt for a new hunting knife from one of the blacksmiths in the upper bailey. He offered to craft one while he waited for Paulo to release the villagers."

Both Diana and Conley visibly perked.

"For the quickest team to get their hands on the flag, I have a note from the kitchens with promise of a fresh slice of *portokalo-*

pita after supper since we got the first wagon of fresh groceries yesterday."

Paulo's mouth watered. He wanted that cake. His magic stirred in his head, but he pushed it down. He would need it for the game.

"And the grand prize for the overall winners will be that each member of the team can ask a boon of Master Schola here."

All eyes turned to Laurel. A boon from an assassin was no small thing. It was a contract without a payment. It was a promise to do whatever the other party wanted. Was she mad? They were still trying to figure out if the scholae wouldn't stab her in the back. Yes, they'd narrowed down the possible traitors, but still. She wanted to give them something over her?

"Are you not playing?" Diana asked.

Laurel gestured to the group. "It would be uneven."

"What are the teams?" Xander asked.

Donnie unfolded his last slip of paper, brandishing it theatrically before unfolding it. "The first team to attack will be Diana, Mare, and Declan."

The six of them split into their teams.

Diana gave Paulo a cocky grin. "Good luck."

"I certainly won't need it." Paulo rolled up his sleeves, heading toward the door.

Xander chuckled. "Those are some famous last words."

The ballroom door creaked open, and Donnie led Xander into the room, followed closely by Conley.

Paulo stopped next to Laurel and gave her a half smile. "I'm sorry you don't get to play."

"Why are you sorry?"

He'd watched Laurel's life for years. Watched her play this game with Aspen in Stellatus Hall over the years, both of them falling into fits of giggles as they tried to outsmart the other. Listened to them talk about her father being the best player out of any of them. Heard the joy as they swapped memories about their best games when he'd still been alive.

"I know how much you love this game." He slipped into the ballroom before she could respond.

They'd made it to the fifth round.

How on Gaia's green earth did Diana's team get this far?

It really was obvious how, but Paulo still couldn't find it in himself to accept it. Laurel had known what she was doing when she'd put Mare on Diana's team. He'd known but seeing it and living it were two very different things.

The woman could move almost as quickly as Paulo could while his magic was taking the wheel. Honestly, he wouldn't be at all surprised to find out that somewhere in her ancestry she had some fae blood. Likely the Night Court with how the shadows seemed to bend to her whims. Women with shining white hair shouldn't be able to hide in shadows half as well as she did.

But maybe she just really wanted the hunting knife Laurel promised to the person with the most recoveries on the defensive side.

Paulo would have to settle for the cake they'd won the first round on offense. He'd gotten to the flag within thirty seconds, and no one had beat him yet.

Not that anyone had been surprised. Xander had whooped and hollered on about the mighty marquess that could jump off castle walls and fought with the ferocity of a lion. He wasn't the only one to say such things either. Paulo had caught the ends of whispers all around the castle, about how no one in Delphine could believe the marquess had been down in the main battle. About how he'd practically flown as he'd ran along the walls, his arrows never missing their mark.

The attention made Paulo's neck prickle with heat far more than any of his other antics had over the years. He hadn't fought to garner more attention. He'd done it to save what he loved.

His carefully curated mask was being disassembled quickly. It wasn't surprising. He knew it would happen, but he hadn't expected it to happen this fast. He'd had plans to carefully expose what he could do to the rest of the kingdom. To protect what little bit of privacy he had.

But it was inevitable. People would believe him to be some kind of hero, and he'd get asked to do all sorts of things that he didn't want to do.

Donnie leaned back in his chair at the back of the ballroom, his lips curled up in a wicked smirk. That goading twist had grown as each round had progressed. His blue eyes practically sparkled with amusement.

"Stop that," Paulo said, folding his arms over his chest.

"Stop what?" Donnie asked, a bit too innocently.

Conley sighed, but Xander was practically vibrating next to Paulo.

"We just have to win. We have to. If we can keep tabs on Mare when she comes into the room and not let Declan get his hands on any of us, we can do it."

The rather large goose egg on his forehead stood as a testament to why no one should let Declan get their hands on them.

Paulo allowed his magic to continue to guide him as he moved about the room, looking for the best place to hide the flag. Donnie must have collected every piece of furniture from the entire castle and put it in the ballroom. It wouldn't have been too hard considering a lot of it had been left in the halls to dry out after the flooding. But still. There were *beds*. Chairs had been piled up into teetering towers and armoires laid on their sides. How Mater had been convinced, the Goddess only knew, but she'd come in during the previous round and clapped with glee when Mare had been found curled up with the flag in a chest only as big as Paulo's torso. When Diana broke one of grandfather's old side tables, Mater's brow had quirked, but that was all.

"Could we hang it from the ceiling do you think?" Conley asked.

The first round, they'd tucked it into a secret compartment Paulo had known about in one of the chests littered around the room. Diana had known about the hiding spot as well and got it within the first five minutes. The third round, after they'd found where Declan had hidden the flag under Donnie's chair, they'd tied the neckcloth around Xander's neck, which had resulted in the head injury.

Paulo looked up at the broken ceiling above them. While most of the ballroom had been repaired, the glass roof was still caved in and left open to the elements. It would be cause for concern in the winter months, but they were still a ways off from that. He'd have time to get some repairmen in here before then.

He shook his head. "It'll take us ten minutes to climb up there."

"Three minutes left," Donnie happily chirped.

Paulo echoed Xander and Conley's curses.

The clip of their boots grew more frantic. At least, Paulo's and Xander's did. Conley's steps were still silent.

"On the balcony?" Conley asked.

Xander ran to the edge of the room. "Behind the painting?"

"I could stuff it in my shoe." Conley obviously hadn't learned from Xander's experience wearing the flag.

They called out idea after idea and each one had to be shot down because Paulo watched them lose.

Blasted Mare.

Donnie laughed. "One minute."

"Here!" Xander called. Conley raced past Paulo, and they followed Xander's voice.

He laid halfway under a bed, a small knife in his hand. "Let me see it. I can stuff it in this mattress."

Conley passed him the fabric and Xander stuffed it into the slit he'd made into the bottom. A vision of Mare snatching it crossed Paulo's vision.

"Thirty seconds!"

"Curses," Paulo hissed, "this will have to do."

The three of them raced away from the bed, getting as far as they could before the double doors cracked open on the other side. Xander skidded out of view behind a wide leather chair. Conley tucked his feet and closed the door of a thick wardrobe—likely the only one the man had ever been able to squeeze into.

Diana led the charge, taking in the room and beginning to search for the flag. Declan came in behind her, gray eyes promising violence for anyone that got in his way.

But Mare wasn't with them. She hadn't been with them any time they'd come into the ballroom.

Paulo pulled on his magic. The ache behind his eyes turned to a drumbeat. Hopefully, he could convince Mater to have tea made up in the sitting room.

He ducked down behind an overturned table, dodging a pillow thrown by Diana.

"Why do you always throw pillows at me?" he whined.

"Because I want to hit you with something harder, but Mater told me not to do that anymore after I knocked your tooth out when we were nine. Said I would have to go to a ball in a dress if I ever did it again."

Paulo snickered at the horror in her voice.

He moved on from the table, taking cover behind a chaise that had come from the library.

A cheer went up above him.

He glanced over the back of the chaise toward the balcony. The servants had started trickling into the ballroom during the second round, likely wondering what all the furniture they'd had to drag through the castle was for.

The game had become quite the spectacle and most if not all the servants now crowded the edges of the balcony. Even Jenkins stood at Laurel's elbow, cheering.

Perhaps Paulo would get the valet a little flag to wave about next time.

Mare ghosted past him, a staff in her hand, and Paulo pounced.

She stepped out of his reach with the frilly neckcloth tied around her neck.

They'd blasted found the flag.

Mare raised her staff and smacked him on the shoulder when he lunged for her again. He rolled to the side, avoiding a hit to his head. She followed him step for step, doing her best to fend him off.

Diana skidded into view. She pointed a stern finger at him. "No. Don't even think about it."

A grin stretched over his lips, and he lunged for Mare.

She took off.

Paulo chased after her as she bounded through the furniture, throwing chairs and coatracks in his trail as she zipped through the maze. His magic blazed around him, though she bounded through the furniture quicker than a blasted rabbit. Paulo reached out his hand, his fingers brushing against the back of her black jacket.

Declan came out from around an armoire and plowed straight into him.

By the Goddess, it was like getting hit by a boulder. They tumbled to the ground, rolling over the floor until Declan smacked into the legs of a sofa. Paulo grabbed one of the cushions and smashed it into Declan's face.

Unable to breathe, Declan grabbed for the cushion, releasing his grip on the back of Paulo's shirt.

Paulo leapt to his feet, scrambling to gain distance between him and Declan, who had freed himself from the cushion and was grasping for Paulo's boots.

So, Paulo stepped on his fingers.

Declan hissed, wrenching his fingers out from under Paulo's boot and curling them against his chest with a curse.

Another cheer went up.

Mare was almost to Donnie. Conley was on her heels, but she outpaced him by two strides.

Paulo grabbed another cushion, pulling his arm back to throw it. If he could just hit her, she would stagger just enough for Conley to get the flag and keep Diana's team from winning.

The cushion fell from his hand as Declan took him out at the waist.

They toppled into a leather chair, the entire thing flipping and sending them to the ground.

Paulo's head smacked the ballroom floor.

Magic flooded him, blocking out everything.

Declan disappeared.

The game.

The castle.

Everything around him was gone.

Penny hugs a girl with blond hair tinged green, a scraggly blue ribbon in hand. The girl seems familiar.

The High King of Faerie stands with others Paulo has seen in snip-

pets of futures. The Lòchran, with his pale eyes and humongous arms that make even Paulo feel a bit small, stands next to the other Winter prince, with his bright purple hair pulled behind his tapered ears.

Queen Carnation pleads with Penny. They stand in a sitting room, the windows outside filled with snowy peaks and glittery stars.

Penny crosses over a patch of gray gravel, a sea of sand behind her where the High King stands and toward the grassy ground where a few other fae await her.

Appears through a portal inside what looks like the Hermen's front sitting room, a scream rending the air that has her running up a set of stairs.

Steps onto the very bottom stair leading up to Iatrus Castle, her green eyes wide.

Stands on the docks of Eleusia as dawn brightened the darkened town, a stern expression on her face as she glares at Lady Barclay. Bedraggled fae surround them, their faces drawn in exhaustion, but their eyes bright with hope.

On the beach below the royal palace, huddling against the wind next to Queen Carnation in the sand as Lady Barclay and King Dion argue back and forth.

In the grand hall of the palace, holding Lady Barclay's hand as the duchess sits in a chair and scowls at everyone that passes by them.

At the border of Faerie, her arms shining with magic as trees shoot out of the ground around her. Huge oaks grow for miles with her magic.

In the snow, her sword locked with Adira Durant's before the High King grabs her by the throat.

But Penny wasn't the only thing Paulo saw.

Mare pulls a pack onto her shoulder, silently gliding through the front door of Iatrus Castle and disappearing into the night.

Declan nose to nose with Laurel, a dagger in his hand.

Xander lying in a pool of blood.

Teagan standing in the middle of a frozen lake, watching from the sidelines as the fae press the rebels back. The man leaves Adira Durant to her fate and make his way back through Faerie. He collects what men he had and takes a ship down the coast. A ship filled with fae.

Then Laurel, on the ship, her long daggers in each hand. She charges Teagan, a dance of silver and black.

Paulo watched all of it over and over again.

Every moment.

Every possibility.

Every unchangeable fate.

He watched until his brain was too full of magic that it shoved him into darkness.

36
THE HEART

The moment she heard Paulo's head crack against the ground, Laurel saw red. Her feet moved of their own volition, and she shoved her way through the crowd on the balcony. The carpeted steps flew beneath her feet as she took three stairs down at a time. Her dagger was in her hand when she hit the bottom step. She hurtled over an overturned desk and dove through the posts of a bed before she reached them.

Paulo lay still on the ground.

She slid onto her knees beside him. His breathing was quick, his face pale as she placed her fingers at the pulse under his neck. His heart beat at an accelerated rate. She slid her fingers over his temple, finding the quickly swelling bump on his head.

"Cursed marquess," Declan muttered. He shook out his arm, walking toward the door.

Laurel sprang to her feet. She slammed into Declan, her knee digging into his spine as he fell forward.

He grabbed her arm and threw her over his head.

The air went out of her lungs, but she rolled to the side and shot to her feet.

He mirrored her, his lip split from hitting the ground.

She didn't give him a moment to recover.

The dagger in her hand flashed as it came up to his neck and she shoved him up against one of the wardrobes. Her nose was nearly pressed against his as she gritted her teeth. "Give me one good reason that I shouldn't gut you right this second."

His arm swung up, a dagger in his fist.

Laurel jumped back to avoid the swing, but recovered quickly enough that she could slice her own blade toward him. It made contact, leaving a line of blood along his arm.

Declan roared and lunged forward.

She quickly drew her other dagger.

The collar of her tunic jerked, choking her as she was dragged backward.

She flipped the dagger in her hand and stabbed behind her.

The grip on her tunic disappeared.

She spun, fire burning in her chest as she spotted Conley. "Stay out of this," she growled.

Declan chuckled, a dark, ugly thing. "Is that all you've got, Master?" He was obviously goading her. He'd been looking for a fight since he'd arrived at Iatrus Castle.

But Laurel couldn't get the crack of Paulo's head on the ballroom floor to stop echoing in her skull. She pulled a throwing dagger from her wrist.

Before she could even pull her arm back, Mare was between them, her face stern as she raised her hands between them. While she said nothing, the message was clear. This fight wasn't going to get them anywhere.

"Why isn't he waking up?" Xander said from where he and Diana were crouched next to Paulo.

Laurel sheathed her blade and stalked over to Xander. "Move."

He scrambled to his feet and Laurel took his place.

Diana leaned down, carefully prying Paulo's eyelids open. "Curses." She sat up.

"What? Is it a concussion? Is he completely unresponsive?" Laurel glared up at Declan. "If you gave him a brain injury, you're going to wish it was you lying on this floor."

"Sweet Gaia, Laurel, calm down!" Diana said. "It's his gift. He's gone into a magic coma again."

Laurel stiffened. She'd seen Paulo in a similar state at the palace, when he and Donnie had drunk themselves into a stupor and Paulo's magic had completely taken over his mind.

She stood, whirling toward Donnie. "You were involved the last time as well."

He tsked. "Correlation does not imply causation. I certainly couldn't have gotten him that drunk in the five minutes since the last time you saw. Besides, the man can hold his drink far better than I can."

Diana set a hand on Laurel's arm. "We just need to get him somewhere comfortable."

Still standing near the wardrobe, Declan asked, "Does this mean we won?"

Laurel shot to her feet, but Conley grabbed her arm and dragged her toward the door.

"What the curses are you doing?" she asked, her voice still carrying a bite with it.

Conley's hold on her tightened. "Diffusing the situation. Look around."

Laurel looked up and saw the servants still standing on the balcony, their eyes wide as they watched her get dragged out the door. Mater clutched the black collar of her dress, her own eyes still on her son as she quickly raced down the stairs, Jenkins on her heels.

The fight drained out of Laurel as Conley yanked her into the hallway.

"You can let go now."

Conley chuffed. "I'll let you go when we get far enough from the ballroom that you can't hear Declan say anything else that will get him killed."

Laurel grimaced, allowing Conley to drag her farther into the palace.

He finally stopped at the door to her rooms and let go of her arm so she could get her key out.

"None of us got our own rooms," Conley said.

"I'm not Master Schola just for the fancy title. The job comes with perks." She opened the door and gestured for him to proceed her inside.

He gave her a flat look but did as she asked. It was a show of trust on his part, putting his back to her and stepping into a room without drawing his weapon. She followed, closing the door behind her.

Conley strode toward the modest sitting area next to the fireplace, taking a seat in the plush blue chair across from the white fainting couch. He pointed at the couch.

Laurel rolled her eyes. "Great Goddess, you're bossy."

"I only have to be bossy when you're acting like a maniac. Now sit."

She did and in a very unmaniac-like manner. "You're right. My instant reaction to Paulo's injury was uncalled for."

Conley leaned forward to set his arms on his knees in that very serious way of his. "I don't think uncalled for is the right word. If circumstances were different perhaps, but my main concern is it seems like this might create a problem that needs to be addressed now."

Laurel leaned back, laying an arm over the back of the white couch and setting a booted foot across her other knee. "You think Declan is going to retaliate?"

"No. I think if you don't get a hold on your emotions, there's going to be blood."

She frowned. "I don't understand."

"Great Goddess, help me." Conley wiped a hand down his face. "Have you ever been in love, Laurel?"

Laurel's frown deepened. "Why are you asking me that? What does this have to do with anything?"

"It has to do with everything. Just humor me and answer the question."

"If you're talking about romantic love, no." There had been boys in the past that had caught her eye. Even Xander had interested her until he'd opened that big mouth of his and never shut it again. But nothing had ever come from any of it. Kissing had been a part of training as much as swordplay had been, so there'd never been a dreamy first kiss with a boy she'd been dreaming about. She'd had no time for it. Not while she was fighting off threats from Teagan and keeping Aspen from getting herself killed.

Conley scratched at his goatee. "I didn't think so, but I wanted to be sure. What do you believe romantic love looks like?"

She tapped her fingers on the back of the couch. "From what I hear, it's all butterflies and moony eyes. Aspen talked about how Luc would bring her gifts, or they'd sneak out to Vale every so often. Sounded like a lot of trouble."

Conley chuckled. "Aye, that's usually how it goes. But every love is different. I told you about my wife."

"Gaylynn. I remember."

He smiled softly. "It took me six years to convince her that she loved me."

"That's a long time to pine after someone."

"I met her when we were practically children. Both of us had a lot of growing up to do, me in height and her in wisdom. She had her eyes on another lad when I came around, but eventually I wore her down."

"What convinced her?"

That soft smile turned wistful, and he looked toward the window. "When I asked her what it was— stature, age, position— she said it was that she couldn't imagine not having me in her life. We'd become good friends, and when she thought about what our lives would be like when I finally gave up on chasing her and found someone else, she realized we wouldn't be able to be the kind of friends we were. That someone else would naturally come between us, and Gaylynn wasn't going to cause someone else to ever worry about my loyalty to them because she had held it first. But she also couldn't imagine doing the same and inviting someone else into the bond we shared. When I was out on a scouting assignment one winter, she sent me a letter, telling me she realized that she was in love with me. I returned three weeks later to propose, and we were married late that spring."

"That's quite the story," Laurel said, her throat a little tight.

"I didn't tell you that to garner your sympathies, Master. I told you because not everyone experiences love the same way. While Aspen and Luc experienced the exciting kind of love that made them feel alive and adventurous, there is a love that can feel like it just makes sense. It doesn't have to be a bright flash of fireworks. It can be a slow thaw, or you just wake one morning with a simple understanding that it's the only conclusion. It can creep on you until you realize that it had been there for far longer than you even realized."

"What does all this have to do with me attacking Declan?" she asked.

"Because of *why* you attacked him."

She crossed her arms over her chest. "He hurt Paulo. It was out of line."

Conley straightened in his chair. "He hurts everybody. That's what makes him such a brute in real combat."

"We were in a mock battle."

"You saw him ram Xander's head into a table. You didn't have any complaints then."

Laurel clenched her jaw. There wasn't a logical reason for her reaction to Paulo's injury. Yes, Declan was brutal. Far more than he probably needed to be, but it kind of came with the territory. Provocationists were some of the most violent fighters in Stellatus Hall because of the way their minds could detach from emotional decisions to find the most effective options. Declan had been one of the most intense provocationists because he really had no regard for anything except his job. He might have had a few friends, and he did his best to protect those under his charge, but he could make the tough decisions when it came down to it.

"Master. *Laurel.*"

Her eyes snapped up at the use of her name. Conley wasn't one to break protocol.

He tilted his head. "What made you so upset about Paulo getting injured?"

The tightening in her chest when she saw Paulo hit the ground returned. She hadn't even been able to think. Hadn't had a single other thought than that she was going to kill Declan for hurting him. That he was too still on the ground.

Conley held up a handkerchief.

She blinked and only then felt the tear roll down her cheek.

Ignoring the offering, she wiped away the offending drop with the back of her hand. "What are you trying to get at, Conley?"

He sighed, tucking the cloth back into a small pocket against his abdomen. "You're in love with him, Laurel. You're in love with Paulo."

Like an idiot, she choked on her own spit. As if her very body rejected the idea, and she couldn't even swallow it. She coughed until her face burned.

"What?" she finally got out. "What would make you think that's even a possibility? He's a moron!"

"We both know that isn't true. He's one of the only men you've ever met that can surprise you. That can keep up with that miraculous brain in your head."

She scoffed. "He dresses in the most ridiculous clothing."

"To get a rise out of you."

"And he says the most atrocious things."

"My last answer stands."

"He lies until he's blue in the face."

Conley gave her a flat look. "You're literally an assassin. Lying is the least of your sins."

"He's ridiculous!"

"Every single man you will ever meet is ridiculous. What else?"

"What else?"

"Aye. What else is there? Do you have things you admire about him?"

She sank farther into the couch. "No."

Conley raised one dark eyebrow.

"Maybe." But she wasn't going to tell Conley about her obsession with Paulo's freckles. "He's a good marquess."

Conley stretched his feet out in front of him. "I agree. He's a fantastic marquess. I've never seen such loyalty from a nobleman's people."

She bit her lip trying to look past all the pomp and remember who Paulo actually was. "He's also a good brother. A good son."

"His family loves him very much."

"Yes." The thoughts started to snowball. "He's also very skilled. I saw him catch one of Aspen's throwing knives without even a scratch. Even I can't do that. He showed his ferocity on the battlefield. He's strong and takes care to keep his body strong."

Conley hummed. "What about him as a man? A person?"

"He's respectful, even when he's being a dolt. Somehow, every child he comes across loves him and he treats each of them with high regard. He cares about doing right by people, even if he has his more selfish moments." Her words slowed, but her mind didn't. He was a selfish man, a vain man, but he did good. The consequences of his gift made him have to keep people at arm's length and forced him to make decisions that no man should ever have to make. It would make anyone selfish. The power to manipulate fate would drive most men to destruction, and while Paulo had caused destruction, he'd done it with the intent to do good. Which was more than she could say for anyone in Stellatus Hall. For herself.

A puff of breath blew out across from her and she refocused on Conley.

"Are you attracted to him at all? Have you felt any kind of draw to him?"

Laurel snorted. "Have you seen him? He's like a walking statue of perfect masculinity and he can kiss like a starving man."

Conley's brows rose. "While I can't say I noticed his *perfect masculinity*, I didn't realize the two of you had kissed."

Laurel drew up short. "It wasn't a real kiss." She hadn't even really known who he was when she'd accosted him in the palace's darkened hallway. She'd done it to keep her identity concealed. Not that telling herself that had helped her forget how his lips felt against hers. How he'd held her, gentle yet demanding at the same time. The way his red hair felt like silk under her fingers.

"Do you want to do it again?"

She mashed her lips together as her cheeks burned.

A deep laugh burst out of Conley's chest. "Honestly, Master, I can't believe you're this far in and haven't realized you're absolutely smitten."

She hid her blazing cheeks behind her hands. "I can't believe you're making me talk about this. I should make you do laps around the outside the walls. Or pick up every single piece of glass littering the gardens in front of the castle."

Conley's laugh died off, but he wiped his eyes. "I'm not trying to embarrass you. My intent is to show you that your feelings for Paulo are deep, and they need to be addressed. You need to figure out how to handle them so the next time someone bashes his head into the ground, you won't pounce on them like an angry lioness."

Were her feelings for Paulo that deep? She'd been angry, so angry with him. Had it hidden what she actually felt. Did her anger only prove how much she actually cared about him? Yes, she was attracted to him. She couldn't deny that. But was what she felt something other than attraction? And what did that mean for them? For the battles they still had ahead of them?

Laurel laid her head against the back of the couch. "What am I supposed to do? If I actually do have feelings, do I tell him?"

"That's entirely up to you, but whatever you need to do, do it soon." He stood. "And you probably will want to go check on him. And apologize to Declan."

She blew out a breath and closed her eyes. "You're probably right." She got to her feet, making her way to the door. "I'll go talk with Declan. Will you help make sure the ballroom gets put back together for training in the morning?"

Conley gave a sharp nod, opening the door for her. "Of course, Master."

Laurel stepped through first this time. She turned to head in the direction of Declan's room but paused.

"Conley?"

"Yes?"

"Thank you."

She walked off, not waiting for a reply, though she swore she could feel him grinning at the back of her head as she strode out of view.

Declan and Xander's room wasn't far from her own. The windows along one of the hallways had almost all been destroyed and wooden boards had gone up to keep the worst of the summer heat from pouring in, but the hallway was still sweltering as Laurel passed through. She found the hallway leading to the scholaes' rooms and paused outside of Declan and Xander's. The door had been left slightly ajar. She looked up and didn't see the string of their trap in place.

Her blade was in her hand, and she shoved the door open.

Declan knelt on the ground, tucking something into his pocket.

"Master?" he asked, pushing himself to his feet. He looked to the blade in her hand. "Come to finish what you started before Conley dragged you off?"

She twirled the blade in her fingers before sliding it back into the sheath at her thigh. "No. I came to apologize. I shouldn't have attacked you. I'm sorry. I overreacted and I'm going to do my best to avoid doing it in the future."

If her conversation with Conley was anything to go by, there might be a few more overreactions before she could figure herself out, but she would try better not to lash out at her team.

Declan's brows lowered and his shoulders eased a fraction. "You're actually sorry? Why?"

She shook her head. "It wasn't fair of me to attack you when you didn't do anything wrong. We are all part of the same team. I care about each one of you. As a show of goodwill, I'm keeping my end of the deal for the game and allowing your team to claim their boons. I hope you'll use it wisely."

He stood there as if she'd just presented a complicated puzzle to him. As if he didn't know what to do with her apology.

A hand slipped into his pocket almost self-consciously. "All right. Is there anything else?"

"No. I've sent Conley to make sure the ballroom is set back to rights. I won't force you to go, but he might appreciate the help."

Declan nodded and followed her out the door. He reset the string this time and didn't speak as he followed her back down the hall. They had to pass by Paulo's room together before he would continue on to the ballroom. Hopefully, Paulo would wake soon and the tightness around her chest would loosen.

A loud crash sounded down the hall, coming from the direction of Paulo's room.

Laurel had her dagger out and Declan had unsheathed his own blade. They were halfway down the hallway when a door burst open and Paulo staggered out, the front of his white shirt stained with what looked like ink.

He turned, meeting Laurel's gaze with clear blue eyes.

"She's coming."

37
AN UNEXPECTED REUNION

Paulo stood at the door of his closet, frowning. This wouldn't do at all. He had royalty set to arrive. He wouldn't settle for such paltry offerings.

"We don't have anything else? I know I said to throw it all out, but I still have to look like a marquess."

Jenkins sighed and walked past him. He pulled a key from his pocket and popped open one of the trunks at the very back of the small room. A rainbow of colors that made Paulo feel like he needed to shade his eyes burst out of the top.

"By the Goddess, did I really wear all those colors?" It had been nearly two months since he'd let Jenkins purge the peacock marquess wardrobe. Paulo hadn't worn more than a thin trim of lace or more than one fob hanging from his waistcoat. It was jarring to look in the face of the mask he'd worn for so long.

In regular Jenkins fashion, he muttered as he pulled a few pieces out. Since their conversation all those weeks ago, the suspicion that the valet was actually cursing Paulo with those mutters only heightened.

Paulo waved him back. "I don't want to wear them, but we might have need of them. Just get my best blue jacket and a nice waistcoat. Our visitors will be here today, and I don't want them thinking anything is any more amiss than they have to."

The lid snapped shut on the trunk, but Jenkins didn't lock it.

He sorted through the half dozen jackets and waistcoats Paulo had hanging up and picked out a bright blue jacket and brown waistcoat.

"Thank you, Jenkins."

"Of course, my lord."

A knock sounded on the door and Mater stuck her head in.

"Aren't you dressed yet?"

Paulo spread his arms out wide. "Perfection takes patience, Mater. You of all people should know that."

She stepped fully into the room. "Because I'm perfect or because I'm patient enough to be considered a saint?"

"Yes." Paulo grinned as Jenkins hung his clothing up on the peg next to the mirror. The valet pulled the waistcoat from the hanger and held it out for Paulo to put his arms through.

Mater chuckled. "Save that flattery for Laurel. I have a feeling you're going to need it today."

Paulo paused buttoning the front of the brown waistcoat. "You think there's going to be problems?"

Mater's lips formed a thin line in the mirror. "Call it intuition, but I think today is going to be a long one."

He frowned, pulling his magic to the front of his mind. Penny would arrive that afternoon, her band of companions clothed in peasant garb. The male fae she had with her would complain. He'd seen most of this already.

What he hadn't looked for was Laurel in the equation.

He'd asked her to have the scholae conveniently absent during Penny's visit. While Paulo trusted Penny, he didn't need her asking questions and getting involved in things that would distract her from her mission. She needed to find Lady Barclay and get back to the border. He didn't get that blasted goose egg on his head two weeks ago for nothing. If Penny got it in her mind that he needed help, she would stay here. She was good like that, putting others before herself.

Magic pulsed behind his eyes.

Penny, bringing up Queen Carnation's loss.

Laurel, running through the woods.

He blinked the magic away, gut twisting. Laurel knew most of it, of course, having been there, but she didn't know about the babe. There hadn't been time to talk about it. Honestly, Paulo hadn't *wanted* to talk about it. He knew if he'd told her in the beginning, she would have run back to Aspen and gotten herself killed. By the time Laurel had been willing to talk to him, they'd been in the middle of a siege. There hadn't been a good moment. Not one that would come with consequences he would be happy with.

Blast it all. Laurel would blame herself for everything Aspen did. The girl was a cursed nuisance.

He should tell Laurel.

But when?

Paulo turned from the mirror to face Mater. "Well, then, we need to make sure everything goes as smoothly as possible. I have a rather risky idea I may need your help executing."

"Oh?" Her brows rose on her forehead, accentuating the few wrinkles she had there. "What were you thinking?"

"How much do you think Laurel will be opposed to wearing a dress?" He took the jacket from Jenkins and folded it over his arm. If Mater could distract her for long enough, Paulo could speak with Penny for a minute or two, then sequester her somewhere in the castle and speak to Laurel afterward. He would reveal his hand in keeping the information from her. He'd promised her that he wouldn't keep lying to her. He would tell her. Tonight. After he spoke with Penny.

Mater's surprise turned contemplative. "She's worn dresses before."

"But I mean a *real* dress. I don't think it's wise for Penny to know Laurel's true occupation. At least, not right now."

Mater's face smoothed into understanding. "I can certainly talk to her."

Paulo gave her a peck on the cheek. "Thank you, Mater."

If the sitting room didn't have carpet, Paulo's boots likely would have driven the entire castle absolutely mad with his pacing. His magic whirled around him, flashes of Penny's arrival blinking in and out of his consciousness.

"You'll ruin Mater's favorite rug if you keep this up," Diana drawled from where she had draped an arm over her eyes and stretched out along a chaise. That particular piece of furniture had a large crack in the backrest, having been the victim of one of Conley's blows.

Paulo didn't stop his pacing. "What's taking Laurel so long?" It shouldn't take so long to put on a blasted dress.

"You've been in here for five minutes. Besides, Mater's probably doing a little jig over the fact that she gets to dress up another girl. There's no reason to go ruining it for her."

"Fine," Paulo grumbled.

Diana lifted her arm. "Are you going to need to go down to the front gate to let Penny in?"

Paulo shook his head. He'd spoken with Captain Isaac about their visitors. Lord Stone Hermen would be accompanying the group, and the castle was already well acquainted with him, so there likely wouldn't be any issues with the guards recognizing them. The last of the villagers had returned to their homes yesterday, clearing out the inner bailey which would allow Stone to drive straight up to the front door. The villagers' departure wasn't a consequence of Penny's arrival, but Paulo couldn't say he wasn't glad to have them gone. Penny, saintly lady that she was, would have wished to help, but Paulo needed her to come in, have some tea, and head out before something bad happened.

Like her telling Laurel about the loss of the queen's babe.

That would be a disaster.

He needed to tell her.

He should tell her.

His pacing halted and he looked out the window one more time. His magic still had Penny arriving within half an hour. Laurel was still sequestered in Mater's rooms. There was time.

Diana shot up from her seat as he strode from the room. "Where are you going?"

"I have to speak with Laurel."

She sighed. "Good luck trying to steal her away from Mater."

It shouldn't be too difficult to take a minute with Laurel. She'd probably punch him right in the eye, but it would be done. He pulled on his magic again. Saw him get to Mater's room. Saw him sent away multiple times.

Every time.

His hands grew a bit clammy as he stopped outside Mater's door and knocked.

A maid quickly answered. "Yes, my lord?"

"I need to speak to—"

Mater appeared at the maid's side. "Paulo?" She stepped out into the hall and shut the door behind her. "What's the matter? You look rather peaked."

"Can I have a moment with Laurel?"

Mater quirked a brow at him. "My dear, she's not in a position to take company at present."

"I just need to speak with her for a moment." He grabbed the door handle.

"Paulo!"

Mater tried to pull him back, but it was too late. He stepped fully into the room and froze.

Laurel stood in the center of the room, a maid at her back yanking on laces.

To a corset.

Which she wore over only a thin chemise that tucked into her leather breeches.

His mouth went completely dry.

The maid gave a little squeak, making Laurel look over her shoulder. Her brown eyes went wide at first, then narrowed to dangerous slits.

"What the curses are you doing in here?" she hissed. "Get out!"

Mater was finally able to pull him from the room.

He couldn't even speak, no coherent thought making it past the vision of Laurel's bare shoulders and the way the corset had accentuated her figure. And the breeches. Those cursed breeches. She wore them with regularity, but always with a long tunic or a jacket.

A pair of hands pushed at his mid back, and he had to practically shake himself from the thought of Laurel for him to realize it was Mater.

"How about you head down to the entry hall, hm?" Mater said, her cheeks a flaming red color.

Paulo's chest tightened and all thoughts of Laurel fled. "I'm sorry. I didn't mean to embarrass you or Laurel."

Mater stopped shoving him down the hall. "I thought I taught you better than to barge into a woman's room." Her tone was as reproachful as he'd ever heard it.

"You did. I wasn't thinking." No, all he'd been thinking about was getting to Laurel before Penny could expose him for the liar he'd been for the last five months. For hiding things from her.

He could see it. Laurel would learn the truth and it would break what tender trust had been sprouting between them.

The tiles below his boots told him he was at the entry hall before he realized he'd walked across the entire castle. Diana stood next to Hiatt, both of them looking at him as if he were wearing a lady's turban.

He reached up on top of his head to make sure he wasn't. His fingers only met hair. "What?" he asked.

"You didn't hear Hiatt?" Diana asked. "Penny's here. The cart just pulled up to the front step."

Blast. He was out of time.

"I think we've got it, Hiatt." Paulo slapped his most charming smile on his face, though it felt a little stiff, and marched past the butler.

Hiatt gave a slight bow of his head, though his lips were turned down in quiet disapproval as he stepped away from the door.

Paulo reached for the handle and swung the door open.

At the top of the stairs, Lord Stone Hermen stood, his white teeth blinding as he smiled at Paulo with mischief in his eyes. Oh, Paulo was certainly going to have to be on his guard with the Minister of Trade in his house. Especially with Peter still residing at the castle. There was sure to be a great recounting of their exploits at dinner tonight.

Behind him stood two fae, though both were glamoured. One was blonde, with dark brown eyes. He recognized Farrah, the fae that could make portals and had helped Penny on a few parts of her journey. Beside her stood Prince Dair, though his long purple hair was glamoured brown and his tapered ears rounded.

Then, there was Penny.

He couldn't help himself.

"Penny!" he hollered, hearing his own voice echo with Diana's beside him, the two of them completely in sync again.

Penny's foot rested on the bottom step as she looked up at them. Her green eyes practically glowed, her queenliness shining through. Paulo met Diana step for step as they barreled toward her and those green eyes widened. Diana grabbed her first, scooping her up into an embrace. Paulo wrapped his arms around them both, feeling something in his chest click back into place. He hadn't realized how worried he'd been about her until he saw her, *really* saw her.

"We've been so worried about you," Diana said, echoing Paulo's own feelings.

Penny laughed. "About me? I've been going mad not knowing what's been going on with you. When Angelica sent word that you'd been under siege, I was heartbroken."

Paulo's chest tightened just a fraction. This whole time, as she'd been tormented by the rebels, attacked by fae assassins, and facing an all-out war, she'd been concerned about them.

He tried to look casual as he tucked his hands into the pockets of his trousers. "It was nothing we couldn't handle."

"Obviously," Diana helpfully tacked on.

Paulo didn't look up at the still broken windows of the castle or the ruined gardens. They were alive. They'd made it through. Besides, Penny had been through so much worse than they had. Had faced some terrible things since they'd seen her last. He wouldn't give her even an inkling of what had happened. She didn't need that.

But her eyes glanced between them, taking on a glistening quality.

"I'm so sorry," she said.

Paulo reared back as if he'd been slapped. It certainly felt like it. "What on Gaia's green earth do you have to apologize for?" It had been his fault she'd made it to Faerie, that this war had even started, that they were all in this position. If anyone should be apologizing, it should be him.

The corner of her lips twisted down. "I should have stayed. I should have been here to help you, to help everyone. Perhaps none of this would have happened if I'd stayed in Olympia."

By the Goddess, she blamed herself? She couldn't blame herself. A lump settled in the back of his throat as he placed his hands on her shoulders. "Listen to me very carefully, Penelope Barclay. I saw that future. I saw where you stayed behind and tried to help from this side of the Mist. Let me just say that I had that pack ready for you after the wedding and would have told whatever lies I needed to get you to go. That should give you answer enough, *Your Majesty*."

"Don't you think it ought to be 'Your *Mage*-esty?'" Diana snickered, her freckled nose bunching up with mirth.

Penny rolled her eyes, and Paulo could do nothing but grin. He'd missed this a lot more than he thought he would and having the three of them together like old times felt so right he couldn't imagine what he would do when Penny had to leave again.

"I think 'Your *Mage*-esty suits much better. Glad we got that sorted, as there are introductions to be made"— he glanced up at the others, taking in their roughshod clothing, especially the prince who looked so ready to peel his skin off it made Paulo grimace—"and obviously some clothing to be burned."

The prince nearly sagged to the floor. "Stars, yes."

Paulo gestured for them to proceed into the castle.

Now, he just had to figure out how to keep Laurel from slitting his throat.

38
THE LIE

Laurel will sit beside Penny, her interest piqued in the slant of her eyes and the set of her shoulders. But Penny will reveal what she knows about the queen. Laurel will run from the room, leaving Penny behind.

LAUREL'S JAW WAS PRACTICALLY ACHING FROM ALL THE GRINDING HER teeth had been doing. She'd really believed Paulo to be the great manipulator of MacGregor House.

He had nothing on Mater.

Absolutely *nothing*.

Mater stood behind her at the vanity, rubbing oils into Laurel's hair. The smell of the stuff was lovely, a mix of lily and coconut— neither of which Laurel could use to poison the cursed woman. However, it did make her dull brown hair shine like silk. It really wasn't fair when she wanted to strangle someone.

Even after more than half an hour since Paulo had barged into the room, her skin still prickled.

It was completely unfair. He shouldn't be able to look at her like a starving man and leave her heart racing and palms sweaty. Not after the conversation she'd had with Conley. Not when she couldn't decide what to think. She didn't know if she was in love with Paulo. She didn't really know if she even *liked* Paulo. He was annoying. Selfish. Maniacal. Sarcastic. All of it.

But the way he'd looked at her...

"Stop it," she muttered to herself.

"Stop what?" Mater said, a little too cheerily.

Laurel narrowed her eyes. Oh, the woman was a pest. She'd practically let Paulo into the room. Her look of unfettered delight at Paulo's complete stupor was nothing short of diabolical. Her cheeks had pink slightly when Laurel had glared at her as she dragged her son out of the room, but the unrepentant smile she gave Laurel when she shut the door told her the blush was more from holding back laughter than any real embarrassment. By the Goddess, Laurel would be cursing every member of this household before her stay at Iatrus Castle was through.

"Why are we wasting time in here?" she asked. "I have the blasted dress on already. Shouldn't you be down in the sitting room receiving your guests?"

"Penny is far more Paulo and Diana's guest than she is mine." Mater put the oils aside and began picking through a selection of perfumes she had laid out.

Laurel groaned.

"Are you in such a hurry to get down there?" Mater grabbed a skinny, cream bottle. "I figured you'd rather be hiding with your scholae rather than meeting Penny."

It wasn't just Lady Barclay's daughter Laurel was eager to meet. While she couldn't quite picture the sweet girl the twins had spoken about the few times they'd mentioned her, Paulo said there would be fae in attendance. There was the smallest inkling of hope in Laurel's chest that she could speak to them about Teagan and see what she could do to help the fae he was attempting to smuggle back to the Continent. If she was going to put a stop to Teagan's reign of terror, she needed to figure out how to help the fae.

"If you're really in such a hurry," Mater said, "I suppose we can get going."

Laurel jumped to her feet. As she passed Mater's freestanding mirror, she allowed herself a once over. The cobalt-blue dress was a thing of beauty. While the style looked a bit outdated, it was still a lovely day dress made of fine sturdy linen. The square neck-line flashed just enough of her collarbones to be alluring while keeping the rest of it modest. Her hair was completely smooth down her back and her brown eyes didn't look boring. She looked rather put together. The leather string was wrapped around her wrist, the lead weight heavy for a moment as she glanced at it in the mirror. The brown boots peeking out of the bottom were a little off point, but no matter what Mater said, she wore boots and trousers underneath. By the Goddess, they'd just ended a siege. She would be wearing proper fighting clothing for a while yet.

Mater swept past, lips curling up in the mirror at Laurel.

Blast it. Now Mater was going to think Laurel appreciated the pampering. Which she had. Not that she'd admit it. Not when Mater looked so cursed smug.

Laurel whirled away from the mirror, the skirts flaring. "Don't think this gets you off the hook for the stunt you pulled with Paulo earlier."

Mater grinned innocently as she opened the door. "I have no idea what you're talking about."

Sweet Gaia, Laurel should have just hidden herself in the billiards room with Declan and Xander. Or taken guard duty with Mare. Something.

Mater shut the door behind them but turned in the opposite direction as Laurel. "This way. We have one more person to grab."

Rolling her eyes, Laurel followed. It didn't surprise her one whit when they stopped in front of Donnie's door and Mater knocked gently.

The door practically flew open before Mater finished the knock, revealing the catastrophe that was Donnie's room. By the Goddess, he was worse than Serene. There were clothes strewn about the entire place. Was that a pair of breeches hanging from the ceiling. How was that even possible? Laurel glanced at Donnie. The knot on his cravat was slightly askew, but the rest of him looked as put together as he always did, from his perfectly pomaded hair down to the polished shine of his boots.

"Ah, good afternoon, ladies." He shut his door behind him. "I assume the guests have arrived?"

Mater reached up and fixed the set of his necktie. "I believe they've all collected in the sitting room." She gestured for them to follow her as she walked back down the hall.

Donnie shuffled next to Laurel. "My fair lady assassin, you do clean up rather nicely."

"Pretty words mean little to those who put no stock in them," she said.

"You value my compliments so little?" Donnie set a hand to his chest, as if wounded. "I'm hurt, Laurel."

"Save it." Laurel glared. He'd find no sympathy from her today. Not when her ribs kept compressing around her lungs and the back of her neck prickled. By the Goddess, it felt like bees had taken up residence in her body and their buzzing kept getting louder and louder the closer she got to the sitting room.

Mater glanced over her shoulder at them but said nothing.

"She bites today," Donnie said. "This doesn't have anything to do with Paulo, does it? I thought the two of you had been doing so well."

"Of course not." The words hastily flew from her mouth. She didn't need Donnie guessing at what happened between them. Sucking in a deep breath, she tried to recenter herself. "Sorry."

Donnie hummed, unconvinced. "If it did have something to do with Paulo, I was just going to tell you that the second you show up in that dress, you're going to win."

"What is that supposed to mean?"

A smirk spread over his lips. "It means Paulo's going to be groveling at your feet for one scrap of your attention looking like that. Not that you weren't a radiant woman before, but whatever Mater did has you looking like a goddess."

A blush stole up Laurel's cheeks. "Stop being ridiculous."

"I'm not being ridiculous."

Mater grabbed both of their arms. "Honestly, the two of you are both being ridiculous. Laurel, you do look stunning, and Paulo is going to notice, so stop worrying. Donnie, stop trying to get a rise out of her."

"I'm not worrying."

"I was definitely trying to get a rise out of her. Look how lovely she looks with that scowl."

Laurel felt the scowl deepen as they arrived at the door, Mater hauling them behind her.

"You're an absolute nuisance," she hissed.

"And you're lying to yourself if you think whatever this thing is between you and Paulo is going to keep being ignored. Stop playing around and trying to break my best friend's heart."

Donnie broke off from her inside the room, calling, "Penny! I'm so relieved to see you in good health."

Laurel watched him saunter in the direction of one of the chairs.

A woman stood, barely making it to her feet before Donnie practically bowled her over. When he finally pulled away, Laurel got her first real look at the woman.

Penny Barclay was... petite. Laurel had seen glimpses of her at the palace for the few weeks they were both there, but only from afar. She stood no taller than Donnie's shoulders. Her mother hadn't been a tall woman either, but she'd filled a room with her presence. Penny used her height to come across as unassuming, but when Laurel met her eye, there was a deep, old power there. Like Penny had been through and understood more than Laurel ever would. She wore one of Mater's old gowns that Laurel had seen hanging in the wardrobe previously, a pink thing with ruffles at the bottom, but while ill-fitting, Penny stood as if she wore a ball gown.

Penny's attention turned to the divan next to her, and Laurel found Paulo getting to his feet, his blue eyes bright with that hunger she'd seen in him earlier. It made every inch of her skin prickle.

"Laurel, you look lovely." He practically purred the words. They rumbled through her and made her hackles only rise further.

He wasn't going to undo her with a sultry glance and that deep timbre of his voice.

She jutted out her chin, meeting his eyes and not daring to show even an ounce of the effect he had on her. "Take your compliments and stuff them with the rest of your unmentionables, Paulo."

Diana laughed from her seat. "You tell him, Laurel."

Paulo's eyes widened the smallest bit, but his smile only grew slightly. Like he knew exactly how much she'd been thinking about him today. As if her snapping words only proved how he'd affected her.

Blast it all.

Paulo grabbed her hand.

By the Goddess, the awareness of him was going to undo her. Even after their kiss in the palace, she hadn't been this affected. But with Conley's words running through her head and the image of Paulo standing dumbstruck in Mater's room flashing with every beat of her heart, she felt her head going a bit light.

Paulo led her to the divan he'd been sitting on, pulling her down beside him as he turned to Penny and introduced her. He didn't say anything about Laurel being an assassin, as she knew he wouldn't. She was supposed to be a completely normal person for this interaction. She would really have to figure out how to approach the fae with her questions without tipping them off to what she was. That wouldn't be too difficult, considering how she could use the siege as motivation for her inquiries.

The clearing of Paulo's throat next to her brought her back to the conversation. There was the faint glimmer of magic leaving his eyes as he turned to her.

But the blue held panic.

Sweet Gaia, had she missed something?

"Laurel, this is High Queen Penelope of Faerie."

All thoughts of Paulo fled as her attention snapped to Penny. There was no point to her ears, no litheness to her limbs. In fact, she was almost stocky in comparison with her toned arms and curved hips. Not that she'd really expected to find any. Penny was a Barclay. Lady Barclay was human, a mage even. Penny was her exact copy, excepting the faint difference of eye color and general demeanor. She couldn't have been adopted or something. There was no way a fae would mingle with a mage knowingly. That, Laurel knew, was taboo. But perhaps she'd tricked the fae into thinking she was bronty?

"But you're not fae," Laurel said.

The purple-haired fae across the room laughed. "No, she certainly is not."

Laurel worded her question carefully. "How did a human become High Queen?"

Paulo leaned back in his chair. "That's a little anticlimactic. Penny, do tell her what's absolutely worse than being a human queen."

Penny's green eyes rolled back, making Laurel like her all the more if she thought Paulo was just as ridiculous as Laurel did. She raised a hand, and a green and black glow sprang up over her fingers and stretched up to her elbow.

By the Goddess. She definitely hadn't tried to trick the fae then.

"You're a *mage*. How are you not dead in a Faerie ditch somewhere?"

Mater tsked at the brash words, but Laurel couldn't find it in herself to care. The fae's distaste for mages was somewhat known, though Laurel hadn't ever learned why exactly. The access Stellatus Hall had to fae knowledge was quite limited, considering there usually weren't jobs taken in Faerie due to the Mist having been a barrier. But what little resources they did have told of the fae's abhorrence of the human magic users.

Penny chuckled. "Luckily, I have some very good friends... and extremely sharp knives."

Oh, this woman was going to be Laurel's favorite of Paulo's friends. No wonder the twins adored her so much. Laurel stood, yanking on Paulo's arm. The look he gave her was a mixture of annoyance and frustration.

Laurel yanked again. "If you insist that I sit by you, then you'll let me sit by her so I can at least pretend you aren't in the room, *my lord*."

She saw the reprimand hit him. His cheeks flushed the slightest bit. He was definitely thinking about his un-lord-like conduct earlier.

But he set a hand to his heart, his expression morphing into another mask. "You wound me!"

She shoved him one more time, getting him to finally scoot enough for her to sit closest to Penny.

Mater cleared her throat and asked for Penny to give an account of what had happened since they'd seen her in Olympia.

Penny gave Mater a bright smile. "Of course. I suppose I'll start with the day I left. You all probably know about Diana getting me to the portal. After that, I went into the Mist..."

Laurel did her best to keep her questions to herself. She felt like she knew next to nothing about the magical kingdom as Penny spoke about shapeshifters, flying carpets, and cities built on the tops of mountains. There were little men who dipped their red hats in the blood of their enemies and old women that had walked the earth giving guidance to the fae since the Goddess had still appeared to Her creations. She spoke about the war with the rebels, how they'd torn apart their cities and burned down their sacred trees. There was a fire in her green eyes as she spoke about her plans to help Olympia and find Lady Barclay.

Every bit of it sounded like a fairytale. Like something Father would have told Laurel and Aspen he heard whispered across the ship that came from faraway lands.

Penny asked about her mother, the rest of the room filling in when they'd seen the duchess last. Laurel looked to Paulo, waiting for him to mention the bit about Declan helping Lady Barclay lay plans to take Eleusia back from the rebels. He blandly talked about how angry Lady Barclay had been about his involvement in Penny's adventure— conveniently leaving out the part where Laurel had threatened to slit the woman's throat if she attacked Paulo— but he didn't mention what Lady Barclay's plans were. Just talked about how the duchess had tried to get to Penny.

Penny sagged back into her chair. She nodded when Paulo finished speaking. "King Dion mentioned he hasn't seen her either."

Laurel's full attention returned to the conversation. "You've spoke with the king? Is he planning on taking back his palace?" Her throat tightened the smallest bit. "Did you see the queen?"

"Oh absolutely." Penny's brows puckered together. "I don't know what their plans are for taking back the palace right now. I've come to find my mother and then see about how we can get the king and queen back on their thrones. It was Shaunie who actually asked me to come, and I couldn't say no. Not after what she lost."

Her tone was heartbroken as she finished, her bright-green eyes downcast as she spoke about Shaunie. The queen had been through so much, but she'd pulled through. The palace had fallen to the rebels, but King Dion likely cared more about that than Shaunie did. But Penny spoke more like Shaunie was mourning a death rather than an inconvenience.

Paulo shifted beside Laurel, sitting up and nearly pressing his chest against her back. "Yes, it's all very—"

Laurel's hand shot up, silencing him as her thoughts were trying to catch up with the turn in the conversation. "It doesn't seem like you're only talking about a palace. Who did she lose?"

It felt as if everyone took in a collective breath.

Paulo seemed to become a statue behind her.

By the Goddess, this was an absolute scheme.

She kept her focus on Penny, not even daring to glance at anyone else in the room. A cold calm came over her, her heart building up defenses against a blow she could feel coming.

Penny glanced past her for a split second, her eyes trained on Paulo, before meeting Laurel's gaze again.

"She lost a babe."

The words didn't fit correctly in Laurel's head. A babe? Shaunie didn't have children. She'd only been married a few short months.

But that was long enough to be with child.

Long enough to be poisoned while with that child.

To lose that child.

Great Goddess, that explained all the blood that had stained Shaunie's dress that night. Why the poison had acted so quickly when Aspen had only been in the palace a few weeks. The reason for King Dion's devastation.

She'd lost a baby.

Aspen had killed a baby.

She was on her feet within a second, the dagger she'd had tucked into the back of her dress under her hair in her hand. Her fingers curled into Paulo's neckcloth, and she hauled him up.

The room burst into an uproar, but Laurel couldn't even bring herself to care.

All she saw was the resignation in Paulo's blue eyes.

"Did you know?" Her chest nearly creaked with how tight her ribs banded around her lungs. How had she not realized? How had no one told her?

But of course, this had Paulo's puppeteering fingerprints all over it.

He didn't look away from her. Didn't try to hide behind his mask or bring his magic to light. He met her head on.

"Yes," he said, "I knew."

Something broke inside of Laurel. "She promised. She swore to me no innocents would get hurt." Laurel had even pointedly asked. Had made sure Aspen hadn't fallen so low, hadn't been influenced so much by Teagan's darkness, that she would stoop to kill those who didn't deserve it. That she didn't become the very monster Laurel had been striving for years to not let her become.

Laurel shoved Paulo back. She couldn't even look at him. Couldn't see the pity or the regret in his eyes. She should punch him in the face. Should kill him.

"Laurel—"

"Don't!" she snapped. She spun, finally remembering they had an audience. That everyone could see her fall apart.

She should run.

"I need to go." Gathering her skirts at her knees, she took off, not caring who got a view of her trousers underneath or the weapons she had strapped to her. Not caring at all what these people thought.

"Laurel, wait!" Paulo called behind her.

But Mare— good, wise, insightful Mare— passed by Laurel and swept into the sitting room.

Laurel ran down the hall, cursing Paulo's name as she bolted for the front door.

39
THE TRUTH

LAUREL RAN FOR THE FRONT GATE, HER BREATHING RAGGED.

Control. She needed control.

But there was no control inside the castle.

All that waited for her back there was lies.

Why on Gaia's green earth hadn't Paulo told her? What made him think keeping that information from her would have ever been an option?

She ordered the gates opened. When one of the guards got a good look at her, they didn't even hesitate. The gates swung outward, letting her slip through.

She ran straight for the forest.

How had she not blasted realized the queen had been with child?

The signs had all been there. King Dion had told the city Shaunie had gone to stay with her family in Speculo. But the palace had known. She'd been sick for weeks. Hadn't left her bed. When Laurel had seen her, the signs of Stellataen Arrow poisoning had all been there. Had completely implicated Aspen's involvement in her condition. If Ashton, the mage that could heal any ill, hadn't been there, Shaunie would have been dead alongside her babe.

Assassin work had consequences. People died. There had been more than one person who Laurel had been contracted to kill that she didn't believe truly deserved it. But no one was perfect. Everyone made mistakes and hurt people. Everyone could be a villain. Even her.

Until she'd seen what this rebellion was doing, she'd thought it didn't much matter what lives she took. All that mattered was that she got the money to buy her and Aspen's contracts and get out of the hall. She thought if she could get Aspen away from Teagan, they would have the freedom to do what they wanted. That Aspen could finally be free from his forked tongue and poisonous ideas. But it had been too late.

There was no way Aspen hadn't known Shaunie carried a babe. Not with how the poison reacted to pregnancy. There had been plenty of studies done on the poison in the years since its discovery. While most times the poison was slow acting, slowly killing the organs from the inside out until it was too late by the time the victim noticed, pregnancy expedited the process. It made the symptoms a thousand times faster. The signs would have been there from the very beginning and Shaunie had obviously been given more than one dose of the poison.

Aspen had known.

And she'd lied straight to Laurel's face.

Had brushed it off as if Laurel's worries were completely unfounded. As if Laurel had been ridiculous to even think it.

King Dion would kill Aspen if he ever got his hands on her.

By the Goddess, Laurel might do the deed herself.

While she might have killed, she'd never made the mistake of killing anyone outside of her contract or self-defense. It was the one guideline most of Stellatus Hall trained into their assassins early on. The one rule that saved her. Killing innocents was messy and often came with repercussions no one wanted. There were several assassins in Stellatus Hall that had no qualms about getting their hands messy, but the majority of the hall did their best not to bring revenge seekers knocking on Stellatus Hall's door.

Killing a babe would bring an entire kingdom down on Aspen's head if the king decided to seek vengeance for his family.

Laurel shivered, realizing she'd already made it to the trees. Her lungs were near to bursting, and the blood rushing in her ears was going to make her heart explode. Her knees hit the ground. She couldn't push herself up as she fell to her hands. There wasn't enough air. There wasn't enough anything. Not enough time. Not enough space. Not enough of her.

A branch broke behind her and she was on her feet in an instant, dagger up. She hadn't dropped it in her run from the sitting room apparently.

Paulo stood a few feet away, his red hair a mess of waves atop of his head.

By the Goddess, all of this was his fault.

If he hadn't let Adira Durant go, this war would have never started. Laurel would have never had the geas with Adira and Teagan. She wouldn't be trapped on this cursed isle. Aspen would have never come here. Would have never had to poison Shaunie. Would have never killed a babe still in its mother's womb.

He raised his hands slowly. "Laurel."

As if the sound of her name on his lips was some kind of spell, she snapped.

Her blade came up and she slashed at his throat.

He was gone.

She twirled, her boots skidding in the dirt. The dagger in her hand flashed as she spun it and stabbed at his midsection.

His hand came around her wrist and he pushed the blade past him, wrapping an arm around her waist in the process and tucking her against his chest.

"I wanted to tell you."

She screamed, a ragged, horrible sound that ripped from her throat. Her knee came up to kick him in the groin.

He released her, stepping back to avoid the blow.

"I swear, Laurel, I was going to tell you."

"When?" she demanded. "When were you going to tell me? After I saw Aspen again? After I figured out how to get rid of this cursed geas keeping me trapped here? After I had to look the queen in the eye and tell her I didn't know my sister literally killed her child? After I was blasted to bits by King Dion because I didn't know, and he sought out revenge against Aspen through me? *When were you going to tell me?*"

"Today!" He threw up his hands. "This morning. I came into Mater's cursed room to tell you."

"*Today?* Paulo, you've had months, *months,* to tell me. Was it because Penny arrived, and you saw her telling me? That you decided you were going to get caught so you had to circumvent it. Was that why Mater practically kidnapped me into her room? Because you didn't want to tell me?"

Paulo's tight expression fell, and he closed his eyes. The Paulo sign for "you caught me in my lie."

Her hand flew up and she slapped him across the face.

Paulo staggered back. "Curses, Laurel."

The words kept pouring out of Laurel's mouth. "You could have told me when we got out of the palace. You could have told me when we were traveling through Olympia to get here. You could have told me any cursed time since we ran, *and you didn't.*"

"You're right." He rubbed at the side of his face, the skin of his cheek already turning a bright red. "You're absolutely right. I should have told you. I know I should have told you. I'm so sorry you didn't hear it from me."

"I should have heard it from you! How dare you keep that from me! I had every right to know."

"You did. You absolutely did."

The words didn't fix anything, but they did unknot some of the twisting in her stomach.

Laurel slumped onto the forest floor. Standing took too much effort. Her head fell into her hands as she tried to hide the tears she could feel building. Now was not the appropriate time to cry. Not when she felt like she would either explode or simply fall to pieces.

"I thought we were done with the lies," she whispered. "With all the masks and deceit."

She heard Paulo fall to the ground in front of her. "I can't promise there won't be moments I lie to you, Laurel. I simply can't. I know I can't."

"Then what are we going to do?" she asked. "You say you want me to trust you, but every time I feel even an inkling of trust or allow a moment of vulnerability, you practically throw it back in my face. I already told you, I'm done playing games. I refuse to be your puppet."

"Oh, Laurel. You've never been nor ever will be my puppet. If anything, you're my puppet master. Anything I can give you within my own powers, it's yours." He let out a long sigh. "I'm trying to do better, to *be* better about telling you things. Today, I was an idiot. I know that. I knew better and I should have acted better. I'm sure there will be other times when I'm an idiot, but I hope by then, you'll know that I really do trust you. That I want you to be my partner in all this."

Laurel looked up. Did he actually mean that? Was this another moment he was simply saying the things she wanted to hear? She needed something else. She needed assurances.

"Then I propose a pact," she said. "A geas if you will."

He met her gaze, his eyes that forget-me-not blue. "All right. What do you propose?"

"I want you to tell me everything. If you see something to do with me, I want to know about it."

"Laurel—"

She cut him off. "I'm not finished. I don't need the little things like what I'm going to choose for breakfast or when someone is going to come around a corner. I just want the big things. Either the moment the vision comes or at least see them in that sketchbook of yours the next time I see you."

Paulo kept his mouth shut, but she could see the objections trapped on his tongue.

"If you promise to do this, I'll promise to take your direction on what to do. If someone's going to die, I'll trust you to make the call. If I have to sacrifice something I love, I'll trust you to know best how. I'm going to put my faith in your choices."

His brows shot up. "You're not going to fight me on them?"

"Oh, I never said that. I'll fight you tooth and nail for something if I think I need to, but I'm going to hear you out first. I'll listen to your reasoning. I won't put myself in danger unless I think it's completely necessary."

He gave her a flat look. "You always think putting yourself in danger is necessary."

"I'll try not to. I'll try to be better about listening to you. But you have to tell me when things are happening and trust me to also make the best decisions. I want to work together on bringing the rebellion down."

"What about Aspen? Or Teagan?"

Laurel's throat grew tight, but she shoved the tightness back down. "When it's time to face Aspen, I will. I know Teagan isn't done with this place yet, but I hope if we can work together, we can take him out."

"And if you never get the chance?"

He asked the question, but it felt like he was asking something that would never happen. Teagan wasn't one to leave loose strings. Based on the somber draw of Paulo's face, he knew it too.

"Is there a chance I don't ever see Teagan again?"

Paulo's magic flooded his irises, but his eyes retained their clarity. "No."

"Then we don't have to worry about that right now." She pushed herself to her feet, the fire in her gut still roiling around, but manageable. Now, she would move forward. Now, she would figure out how to fix all of this.

She offered her hand to Paulo. "What we need to do is figure out how we're going to learn to trust one another."

Paulo's palm slipped into hers. His strong fingers encircled her hand, and he used his grip to pull them together slightly. "I do trust you, Laurel, and I'll spend the rest of my life proving it to you."

40
AN UNEXPECTED FRIEND

PAULO FOUND PENNY IN THE LIBRARY. SHE STOOD RIGHT BENEATH THE gargantuan boar head Mater had removed from the front entry hall nearly a year ago. Her hair glowed red with the soft light of the magelights above her head. Mater had told Paulo to bring Penny down for supper in half an hour, but he didn't know if he'd be able to. There were so many questions he wished to ask her. So many things he should apologize for. Her eyes trailed over a map laid out on a table.

"It's not polite to linger in doorways," she said, not taking her gaze from the map.

Paulo leaned into the doorframe. "Whoever told you I'm polite is either a diabolical liar intent on your demise or trying to sell you something."

She looked up then, her green eyes full of mirth. "You can't fool me, Paulo. I've seen what impolite looks like. If I didn't have the talents of a fae healer, I'd have the scars to prove it too."

Right. The fae didn't particularly like that Penny had come into Faerie and shaken things up. He had to swallow back a lump. "How are things? Are you truly all right?"

Penny straightened, abandoning the map to come around the table. She leaned back against the edge of it, watching him.

"If you want the truth, it isn't as pretty of a picture as I told in the sitting room."

"I know." He looked down at the hardwood floor of the library. "I likely know most of the things you omitted. How Adira Durant starved you in her camp. About how your magic had basically been torn to shreds. How the fae really tried to kill you."

"I wondered when you'd finally admit to knowing more than you let on. Ever since our dance at the solstice ball all those months ago, I've remembered you saying you've seen things. That there are things that need to happen."

"There were. There still are."

She walked back around the table, the dress she borrowed from Mater skimming the floor.

Paulo finally left his place in the doorway, stepping into the full light of the library. When was the last time he'd walked into this room? Diana was a more avid reader than he was, but he still read. But he certainly hadn't been in here since the siege started. It was on the south side of the castle, farthest from the study. Paulo probably passed by it a hundred times in a day going from place to place, but the doors were almost always closed. It wasn't like the palace library in the capital with people bustling about at all hours. Iatrus Castle didn't have anyone running the library besides a couple of the maids who came to dust every few days. The books sat quietly in their shelves around the perimeter of the room, content to be left to roost on their own. A bit of their calm settled on Paulo's shoulders. He needed to come in here more.

"So," Penny said, "what's been happening here since I left? I mean besides the siege and all that."

Paulo approached the table. "You want more than a siege? My, you're difficult to please."

A smile stretched across her cheeks. "Well, I am a queen now you know. I'm bound to be a bit of a snob."

"What do you want to know?"

Her green eyes grew sharp. "Tell me about Laurel."

He couldn't stop the corners of his lips from turning up. "You want to know about Laurel? Out of all the other things you could ask me about, she's the topic you want to bring up?"

She shrugged. "I've got enough of a grasp on the rest of the kingdom, and Mater spoke to me and Lord Hermen earlier about what possible route my mother might have taken from here. I want to talk about something that doesn't have to do with war or death or destruction for longer than five seconds. So, humor me. How did the two of you meet?"

A chuckle burst from Paulo's chest. "Do you want the easy answer or the complicated one?"

"You choose."

Which should he tell her? The long of it and how he'd been having visions of this woman since he was a lad? How she'd plagued him for years and tortured his every waking moment? How he dreamed about her?

He fiddled with the sleeve of his jacket. "We met at the palace. She worked in the kitchens."

Penny settled her hip against the table. "What did she think about a marquess taking an interest in her?"

He grinned. "She hated it."

"I can imagine." Penny laughed. "She came with you from the capital though. She must trust you a great deal."

"Oh, I wouldn't be so sure." He blew out a breath. "She's trapped here. She can't return to her old life."

"Does she want to?"

Paulo opened his mouth, but no words came out. Did Laurel want to return to her life? He knew her goal had been to leave Stellatus Hall, but did she actually wish to return to the Continent? With the scholae here, did things change for her? The realization that he didn't actually know what her plans were made his gut twist. She talked about getting back to Aspen, but what about after? Did she even know herself?

"Might be a good thing to talk about," Penny said. "I've recently learned communication can be very important between two people in love."

Paulo laughed. "I can't say Laurel's in love with me."

"You didn't come back to the castle in pieces," Penny said. "I saw that wicked dagger she had. I would've stabbed you if I'd been as upset as she was."

Perhaps introducing the two of them hadn't been such a great idea. Was this what Laurel felt like when he and Xander were together? "She definitely tried."

One of her auburn brows quirked. "Laurel gets more interesting by the second. I can obviously tell you're in love with her. She definitely feels *something* in regard to you or she wouldn't have reacted so violently to you keeping the truth from her."

"She does get rather violent when I keep things from her."

The other auburn eyebrow lifted to meet its twin. "I thought she was a cook. I didn't realize they could be so violent."

"She is. By the goddess, I've never had better *loukoumades* than when she makes them. I swear, hiring her was the best thing the palace ever did for their kitchen."

"Has she been working in the kitchens here then? Paulo, you better not have hired her if you're going to be trying to court her."

He scoffed. "What do you take me for? I might be a cad, but I'm not despicable."

"Good." Penny's shoulders eased a bit. "I can't imagine how she's feeling, being taken out of her life and placed in the middle of all of this."

"What? You probably know better than anyone. You are literally queen of a kingdom that hates you."

Penny shook her head. "But I chose that. I chose to go after Aiden, and I chose to say yes to becoming queen. I could have said no at any time. Could have simply walked away and gone back to my mother and waited everything out. I would have hated myself for it, but I had the choice. It doesn't seem like Laurel has had many choices given to her."

Laurel hadn't, had she? She'd gone from one mission to the next, taking orders from one master or another. The one thing she had chosen was that she wanted to free Aspen from Stellatus Hall and the two of them would create a new life together. But that choice had been taken from her too. Paulo had stolen it from her when he'd kept her from killing King Dion.

"How do I give her a choice, Penny? How do I help her while also keeping her safe?"

Her mouth twisted in thought. "Sometimes, you have to trust them not only with your heart, but with your peace of mind. You have to become partners. Have to make decisions together."

"And what if you know bringing them into a decision will hurt them?"

"I can't guess what it would be like to know the future, but I do know what it's like to be left behind on something that I know I could help with. Honestly, there will be more hurt done if you don't give her that trust and instead make the decisions for her. Neither of you will ever move from this place unless you both give in a little and stop trying to do things on your own. You have to rely on each other. You'll find that when you do that, the future is brighter and those dreams you thought you could make reality are much more attainable."

"By the Goddess, I thought the romance books made you mushy. That king of yours has made you even worse than you were before."

She didn't blush and roll her eyes as he expected her to. She looked down at her hand, her finger twisting around the amber ring circling her finger. "When you find that one person you would do anything for, you'll do whatever it takes to be with them. You'll overcome any obstacle and make any bargain because you know they're worth it— even if it's you that needs to get out of your own way."

Penny left the next morning.

It hurt more than Paulo thought it would. It had been inevitable. She didn't belong in this place anymore. She was destined for magic and wonder not found in the mortal cities of Olympia. Her fate was meant for greater things than him.

But it still made his chest ache.

The two fae trotted next to her on some of Paulo's mounts, Lord Hermen riding his cart in the opposite direction.

"May the Goddess be with you," Paulo muttered, watching the horses until they finally disappeared into the trees.

Mater appeared at his elbow. "I do hope she finds Dominique."

"She will." Paulo had seen it happen within the next couple of days. He'd tried to give her just enough information to lead her in the right direction. Penny would do better finding her mother on her own rather than having Paulo give her all the answers. "I just hope we can be ready for when she finally does."

"What do you mean?"

Paulo turned to her. "Once Penny finds Lady Barclay, there's only one more promise she has left to help fulfill. She's going to help take back the palace."

"They're going to have to fight Aspen." Mater's lips thinned. "If they take Aspen captive, they'll kill her."

"Yes." If the king even got close to Aspen, there would be less left of her than there had been of Luc. She would find no mercy from the royal couple.

Mater smacked him on the arm. "Well? What are you going to do to stop them?"

He turned back to the window, watching as Lord Hermen tilted his hat at the cart that passed him.

"I already sent a letter."

41

AN UNEXPECTED SELKIE

of thatch for the roof he was standing on only lifted an inch at a time, but eventually it made it to the top far enough for Miles to grab onto it and lay it on the edge of the roof. Paulo released the rope and rubbed his gloved hands against his trousers, the skin smarting.

"Should be the last of the thatch, my lord," Miles said, using a ratty handkerchief to wipe his balding head.

Paulo leaned down and grabbed the hammer at his feet. "Good. Your family deserves to sleep in your house tonight."

Only a few of the houses in the village had been damaged during the siege. Miles's had been the worst; the entire roof having caved in from the heavy rains. His family of six had been all sharing a single tent for the last three weeks as they worked to fix the roof. It had taken almost an entire week to collect the thatch, as most of it had had to be purchased from outside of Iatrus Castle. Luckily, there were quite a few farmers between Delphine and Tauros that hadn't yet been affected by the rebellion, though Paulo had to pay a pretty penny for the straw. He should have done a better job fortifying the village before the siege and making sure the villagers had something to return to after, but he'd pay his penance in expensive straw, blisters, and an awful sunburn if he had to. By the Goddess, his skin was going to be peeling off his neck in sheets by tomorrow.

Paulo grabbed his bucket of spars that he'd been using and carefully maneuvered himself up to the top of the roof.

He kept his magic at the front, making sure he didn't fall and meet his untimely death.

He was an idiot for deciding to help the villagers work on repairs.

But it was better than being in the castle.

For two weeks, he'd watched Laurel pace the halls, her anger still palpable. They barely spoke. Barely looked at each other.

The chasm between them was killing him. While they had come to an agreement, she had asked him to give her some time. But time was something neither of them had. Would she simply abandon him and go off on her own? Would she go find Penny and help her take back the palace without telling him? Paulo had finally been able to reestablish communications with the Hermens since Lord Hermen's visit, but he'd found out the king was no longer with them, though the queen was. She stayed to take care of Angelica Eile after she had her babes.

There was another family who had paid the price of Paulo's decisions.

"My lord!" Paulo looked down the side of the house and found one of the village lads standing below. "My lord, the dowager asked me to fetch you. Says she'll meet you at the village well."

Mater hated it when people called her "the dowager."

Paulo straightened from his position. "Well, Miles, it looks like I've been summoned. I'll send someone to come finish helping. We should have it all done by sundown."

"Aye, my lord."

Paulo climbed down the rickety ladder leaning against the almost finished house. He allowed his magic to fade, though it still pushed against his mind as if vying for his attention. With a sigh, he allowed it free reign once he reached the bottom. He'd been ignoring it too much of late and to his detriment. The vision swirled in front of him.

Diana, running through the forest, the bracken a whir of green under her feet.

An orb of water around her head.

Paulo nearly knocked the ladder from the side of the house as he staggered back. He steadied it before taking off toward the center of town where he found Mater at the city well. She flipped through a short stack of papers as one of the village women looked over her shoulder, pointing at something on the pages in Mater's hand.

Mater must have felt Paulo approach because she looked up, her brown eyes meeting his.

"Oh, perfect. I just wanted to ask you..." She frowned. "What's happened?"

"Have you seen Diana?"

Mater passed the pages to the woman next to her. "I just sent her back to the castle. We need some candles for the chapel, and I know I saw some in our stores. She also went to check in with Laurel and the scholae to see if they were coming down to the village today."

They weren't. Paulo had already checked. Not that he was watching Laurel's lines or anything.

He took off toward the castle. Praise the Goddess he was wearing some of his worn boots. They ate up the ground as he sprinted through the rest of the village and into the trees. The village itself was on the other side of a section of the forest south-west of the castle. The main road wound around the trees to get to the castle, so it was easier to go through the forest.

Which Diana would have done.

The trees were full of leaves, the oaks and plane trees heavy with foliage from all the water over the summer. The ground even was thick with ivy and ferns. Paulo's boots nearly caught on multiple occasions, but his magic flared around him, searching for Diana.

He turned when he saw himself colliding with her. His heart thumped against his ribs as if it would explode.

He had to get there.

His magic told him he'd be tackled two seconds before he was.

He only had enough time to turn so he didn't land face down in the mud. He rolled with his attacker and when he came to a stop, he was underneath Laurel.

Her brown eyes were intent on his and she brought a hand up to his mouth to keep him quiet.

The snap of breaking foliage sounded to their right and Laurel quickly shot to her feet, steps silent. She grabbed his arm and hauled him up. It took all his focus to keep his steps quiet as she dragged him behind a thick pine tree. His bare forearms scraped against the rough bark as she pressed into him, carefully peering around the tree. The steps got closer, and Laurel carefully pulled Paulo along the side of the trunk as the tread of boots stomped behind them. He made sure to keep his focus on his magic to guide his steps. His heart may have jumped when she set a hand on his chest, but he did his best to ignore the sensation while they waited for the passing footsteps. Praise the Goddess for ignorant idiots who didn't know how to walk in a forest.

Laurel went to remove her hand from his chest, but he grabbed onto her.

"We need to find Diana."

She nodded and he finally released her. A dagger appeared in one hand as she took off in the direction Paulo had guessed Diana to be. He trailed behind her. She moved through the forest like she was one of the trees. As if she could not only see the world around her but feel it under her feet. Likely, all that time out here with Diana had made her comfortable in the forest. She probably knew it well now, having seen most of it. The way her mind could capture things still amazed him.

She slowed at a small copse of trees, her head tilted as she listened. Her head whipped to the west, and she pulled Paulo back behind another tree trunk. This time, her hand rested at the small of his back and she stood a bit behind him, allowing him to look around the trunk if he wished. Well, at least he assumed that was why she positioned them that way.

This time, he did feel her. His skin prickled with awareness at where her fingers were carefully settled along his spine. She didn't move a hair, but every inch of his body reacted to her.

It had been days since they'd spoken, but it felt like years.

Her nearness was intoxicating.

Did she feel the same? Likely not. She was so focused on everything else, she probably didn't even realize she was touching him. He looked over his shoulder at her. As he suspected, those dark-brown eyes were scanning the forest in front of them. As the sound of whispers started to reach his ears, she looked up at him. There was still distrust in her eyes, but he also saw something else spark there as well. Did she lean a bit closer to him? It felt like her fingers pressed a little harder into his back, but he truly could have been imagining it.

When the whispers grew loud enough to understand, she dropped her hand and crouched, sliding past Paulo's legs to peer around the trunk.

Paulo stiffened when he heard Caspian's familiar voice.

"My informant within the castle hasn't spoken to me in some time, though I do not know if he's still alive or if he's just gone dark."

There was an informant inside his blasted castle? Paulo's teeth ground against each other. How the curses hadn't he caught them?

"While today may not have been successful, I am sure we will find another way in," a watery voice replied.

What had happened today?

He looked to Laurel, and she shook her head. She didn't know either.

But now they knew the rebels were definitely still trying to get into the castle. It was a good thing Captain Isaac hadn't let up on the patrol rotations even after the militia had returned home.

Caspian sighed. "We may need to make a move on the village and draw them out."

Paulo would have jumped out from behind the tree if Laurel hadn't grabbed onto the back of his pant leg.

A roar sounded.

Paulo's head whipped around the tree just in time to see Diana land on top of both Caspian and the merrow he was with.

They all fell, a tumble of limbs and curses. Caspian was the first to his feet, grabbing the spear he had strapped to his back.

Diana knocked against it with her bow and rolled away from the merrow's needlelike teeth.

Water began pooling around Caspian's hand.

Paulo charged out from behind the tree. He tackled Caspian to the ground, distracting him from Diana. They hit the dirt hard enough for it to knock a bit of the air from Paulo's limbs. He shot to his feet before Caspian did and made a grab for the spear. He really needed to start running about with more weapons if he was going to have to continue to fight all the time.

Caspian rolled away, taking the spear with him.

Paulo looked back just in time to see Laurel plunge a dagger into the throat of the merrow before he whipped back around, hands up ready to fight.

Caspian was gone.

Diana nearly ran into him in her haste to get to his side. She crouched next to the ground where Caspian had rolled and moved the largest of the bracken leaves.

Paulo pulled on his magic.

The selkie had gone west, charging for the creek that fed into Lake Luna.

She shot to her feet, but Paulo grabbed her arm. "He's headed to the creek. He'll beat us there and either kill us where he stands or use the water to escape."

Diana yanked her arm away from Paulo with a growl. "I'm starting to get the feeling that you don't want to kill Caspian."

"I don't. Not yet at least."

"Why on Gaia's green earth not?"

Laurel stepped up beside him, wiping her blade on a cleaning cloth now red with blood. "Because he just let us know he's trying to get in touch with a contact of his in the castle."

"And," Paulo finished, "without him, we'll never figure out who it is unless he can reach them again."

Diana blinked. "There's a traitor in the castle? Who is it? I'll kill them where they stand."

But Laurel laid a hand on Paulo's arm. "It's one of the scholae, isn't it?"

Paulo brought his magic back up and plucked at the strings of the last three scholae he was truly worried about.

He sighed. "Both Declan and Xander could meet with him."

Laurel sheathed her blade. "Then we have our work cut out for us."

42

THE SIREN

> *Declan and Conley will walk down the stairs of the guard tower. At the bottom, they will see the guards on patrol walk past the gate. As they do, a shadow will slip past them. Conley will yell and Declan will tackle the intruder to the ground.*

Laurel wasn't avoiding Paulo. She wasn't.

There was little she could do about the fact that he wasn't around for her to speak to since Penny had left nearly a month ago. She wouldn't seek him out. He hadn't really sought her out. In fact, all of them had been working tirelessly in the village for the last several weeks trying to get everyone from the castle back to normal life. There obviously wasn't much for them to speak about since neither of them spoke much.

Except that he'd lied to her.

And she'd tried to kill him.

Then one of his best friends had left.

Not to mention that Diana had caught half a dozen rebels trying to break into the castle a week ago. She'd followed them into the forest and discovered Caspian there. Laurel had watched her disappear when she'd come back from a practice session with Xander in the trees before she'd given chase. It hadn't been until after they returned to the castle that she'd noticed Paulo had disappeared.

By the Goddess, maybe he was avoiding her.

Mare sat next to Laurel on the bench in the training room, her arms crossed over her chest as she watched Xander. He had a target set up on the other end of the ballroom, a crossbow in his hands. They had yet to move the training room back outside. It wouldn't be too hard to do, it just seemed like such a waste and the builders hadn't been called in to fix the ceiling yet, though it had been boarded up. Paulo had ordered it done the week before and it had finished right before a storm had swept through. It had been raining for two days straight.

The weather had been acting a bit off since the siege. From the records Laurel had perused when she'd researched the castle's history, it was a little late in the year for such storms this far south. The clouds had been tinged green, and hail had pounded the roof of the palace, nearly as large as the kumquats she used to make spoon sweets.

The doors to the ballroom burst open. Laurel shot to her feet as Declan and Conley, fully masked in their silver, dragged someone in between them.

"Caught this one trying to sneak in through the back gate," Declan said, finally dumping the person on the ground in front of them.

A head of wine-red hair whipped up to meet Laurel's gaze. The sea green eyes snagged her thoughts for a moment before a burn started up between her shoulder blades.

Laurel sauntered closer. "Lady Delmar. A pleasant surprise."

Lady Delmar pushed herself to her feet, though her hands were tied behind her back. "Laurel, please tell your goons to untie me before I do something particularly nasty to one of them."

Conley took a step forward, but Laurel raised a hand. "What are you doing here?" She wasn't totally sure where Lady Delmar's allegiances lay. She'd been the next spymaster after the youngest prince had disappeared to Faerie, but Laurel couldn't be sure she wasn't in Adira Durant's pocket.

Lady Delmar gritted her teeth. "I was invited. Now, untie me before—"

The boarded-up doors along the back wall burst open, a giant of a man barreling through them. Conley was the first to engage the intruder. The man unsheathed a sword from behind his shoulder with a roar.

Four blurs of color burst through the open door. Xander screamed like a child and dove to the ground as one flew right over his head.

It took a second to recognize Sir Heff, his wild hair pulled back from his face and the thick armor plate strapped to his chest completely altering his appearance. This wasn't a blacksmith. This was a knight.

Conley didn't last long under the man's onslaught and Sir Heff gave him a brutal kick to the sternum that sent him staggering back into a pile of weapons.

Declan and Mare engaged the man as one unit.

Laurel drew her daggers, only to have to dive out of the way of a jet of flame coming right at her face.

Four dog-sized dragonets circled the room.

Xander remained quivering to the side, his arms tucked over his head as he curled up under one of the tables. Declan still engaged Sir Heff, but even he couldn't match the brute force of the blacksmith's bastard sword. Conley had recovered and joined him. Mare was in the process of weaving through the pillars of the room, leading the dragonets on a merry chase through the ballroom.

When Lady Delmar attempted to get to her feet, Laurel knocked her legs out from under her and the siren fell to her rear. She glared up at Laurel.

"Wait!"

Laurel turned to see Paulo skid past the ballroom door, his wet boots making him shoot across the hardwood floor. Not even a moment later, he raced back into view, his red hair dark and dripping. Something in her stomach did a flip.

"Wait!" he shouted. "I asked them to come!"

The scholae paused in their advance, none of them taking their eyes off Sir Heff, who shoved past them to get to Lady Delmar. He crouched down next to her, pulling a knife from his boot to slice the ropes tying her arms behind her back. He looked up to Paulo and muttered, "Your charm, Rissa."

Laurel followed his gaze and found Paulo standing in the doorway, his jaw a bit slack and eyes glassy. The charmed tattoo against Laurel's spine burned something fierce. The lady siren's magic was tenfold what Caspian's friend had flaunted.

Lady Delmar quickly drew out the string of leather with the tiny shell and clasped it around her neck. When it finally lay against her chest, Paulo blinked himself back to life, his blue eyes clearing until they met Laurel's, and he gave her a nod of greeting.

That was it. A nod.

"Apologies for the unorthodox welcome," Paulo said.

Sir Heff glanced about the room and gave a short grunt, sheathing his blade over his shoulder.

Lady Delmar looked him over as well, her sharp eyes flicking over every inch of him before turning to back to Paulo. "It's good to see you actually take your castle's security seriously, darling. I never seem to know with you."

Paulo's lips curled into a smirk. "What fun is it if I can't keep everyone on their toes?"

Lady Delmar hummed, though if it was in agreement or not was difficult to decipher. She turned and met Laurel's gaze. The woman's full lips stretched into a sparkling smile. "It's good to see you, lady assassin. Are these all friends of yours?"

The scholae strode through the room, coming to stand beside her in a show of solidarity. Laurel continued to meet the siren's gaze, keeping her face blank. She didn't answer, knowing better than to give Olympia's new spymaster any more information than she needed. Lady Delmar was wily enough as it was.

The lady's grin deepened. "Lord MacGregor, thank you for inviting us into your home. When I received your letter, I didn't know what to believe. It was quite... informative. I had to come see everything for myself."

Laurel glanced over at Paulo for a second before looking back to the two newcomers.

He blew out a breath. "I told them about your relationship with Aspen."

She tried not to react, but Paulo read her too well. He took a step toward her. "I didn't give any condemning information. Simply that if she wanted help getting to Aspen, talking to you would be the best option."

"Yes, King Dion has certainly expressed a desire to get Aspen out of his palace. He's wished rather vehemently for it to be on an undertaker's cart, but Lord MacGregor expressed a particular interest in not letting that happen."

Laurel didn't look to Paulo again, keeping a blank mask in place even as a scream built up in her chest. While he might be on her side— praise the Goddess— Paulo was likely the only one in this blasted kingdom that didn't want to see Aspen dead, the king more than any other. Of course he wanted to kill her. She'd seduced him, took his castle, poisoned his queen, and killed his child. Vengeance would be the only thing on his mind. He'd been absolutely humiliated. His life completely ruined. Laurel could understand the logic behind it, but it still made everything inside of her boil.

"Is the king still with the queen?" Paulo asked.

"Not at present," Lady Delmar answered. "When they returned from Faerie, the king took his leave of their safe house and has relocated to allow the queen some space."

Laurel read what she didn't say in the small frown between her brow and the thin bare of her teeth. The king had left his queen behind. He really was a blackguard when he wanted to be.

"If the king and queen aren't in any serious danger, what brings the new Lord of the Underworld here?" Laurel asked.

There was the slightest shift behind her. The scholae hadn't known this was Olympia's new spymaster. She could practically feel them coil up like snakes.

"Lady Penny Barclay has returned from Faerie and come to help take Olympia back from The Cartographer." Lady Delmar set her hands behind her back. "Her and Lady Barclay have taken back the city of Eleusia and have rallied their people to help push the rebels out of the rest of the duchy. They have gone to meet with the queen and rally forces to take back the palace."

Declan and Conley shared a smirk, them having been the most present during the planning with Lady Barclay, but Laurel's ribs tightened around her lungs. The Barclays were going to speak with the queen? After what she'd been through?

"I've come to ask for your help," Lady Delmar said. "Your sister has made getting into Olympia's palace difficult. Paulo mentioned you may have a way into the palace."

He'd told the siren about the caves? Laurel did look to Paulo then, but he gave a small shake of his head. He hadn't revealed the tunnels then, just mentioned a possibility. He was giving her the option to share what she knew. Allowing her to choose whether or not she wanted to betray Aspen and let these people into the palace.

But what was the best option?

If she did tell the spymaster about the tunnels, they would storm the castle. There would be a massacre, and Aspen would likely find herself on the sharp end of a sword. She would at the least be shoved into a dungeon to await a public execution or become a smear on the floor like Luc. Laurel wouldn't put it past the king to simply rid himself of Aspen the moment he saw her. If she gave the locations of the caves, Laurel would completely betray Aspen and it would be by choice, not like when she'd left because she hadn't had a choice.

But if Laurel didn't tell the spymaster, there would be no way for them to get into the palace. Adira Durant would have something to fall back on if Queen Penny and her husband were able to reclaim Faerie and drive the rebels out. Teagan would have easy access to Aspen and might even take her back to the Continent without Laurel ever seeing her again.

As if sent by the Goddess Herself, Mater appeared in the doorway.

"Ah, Lady Delmar, Sir Heff. What a pleasure to see you. Would all of you like to join us for luncheon? I've just had the kitchens bring it up in the dining hall."

No one moved.

The scholae stayed at Laurel's back, their eyes likely trained on the dragonets now perched on the balcony above them or on the couple standing in the middle of the room. She could still feel Xander shaking beside her. None of the scholae, including her, had ever trained to take out a dragon. They weren't a problem anywhere on the Continent. At least, not that Laurel had ever heard. The siren and the blacksmith stood in the middle, their hands loose at their sides.

Paulo was the first to move. "Thank you, Mater. Yes, let's continue this conversation in the dining room." He gestured for Lady Delmar and Sir Heff to follow Mater.

They did, though Sir Heff kept his attention trained on Laurel.

Once they were at the door, Laurel gave a nod. The scholae swept past her, following the couple with silent steps. While Lady Delmar might not have been a true threat, Laurel wanted her to know that the scholae certainly were one.

She followed behind, gliding past Paulo.

He snagged the back of her tunic. "This is your decision, Laurel."

She looked up at him. "Why?"

A soft, sad thing curled his lips in what was supposed to be a smile but only made him look more miserable. "Because I want you to have choices, and I'm sorry I haven't been better about giving them to you. I trust you to do what you think is best here."

"And what consequences will my choices have?"

He shrugged. "There are always consequences. We just have to choose the ones we can live with."

She rolled her eyes. "I'm not trying to be cryptic, you oaf. If I give them information to get into the palace, what happens to Aspen?"

The colors of his magic swirled in his eyes. "It's very possible she dies. There are some futures in which she's subdued and put in the dungeons, but those options aren't good either."

Was he actually giving her a straight answer? Laurel licked her dry lips. "What if I don't tell them what I know?"

"They don't gain access to the palace. Adira Durant may return to the palace and the war will continue on, though the end of that is a bit murky. Aspen will remain in the palace until either Adira kills her or Teagan takes her back to the Continent."

"Why would he take her back? There's nothing left there."

"Again, it's a bit muddled, but from what I can gather, he plans to make her the new Master Schola and reform the group with the fae acting as their own personal weapons arsenal. Any of the other scholae that may return are slaughtered. Aspen becomes his personal puppet and may accomplish atrocities in his name or die trying."

Laurel ground the heels of her hands into her eyes. "I have to stop him."

There was no way she was going to allow any of those things to happen without her at least trying to fix them. If she didn't want the king to kill Aspen, she needed to get her out of the palace. If she didn't want Adira and Teagan to achieve their aims, she needed to get the Olympians in the palace.

Paulo snatched her hand, his fingers a vice around hers. "If you go, there are multiple times where your own life will be in danger, and I won't be there to help you."

Her fingers tightened around his. "What do you mean you won't be there?" He hadn't let her out of his sight in months. Hadn't left her side through everything they'd faced.

"If I go, you'll have no chance of beating Aspen." He swallowed, a slight tremor in his hand. "The Goddess has made that very clear and no matter how I look, if I go with you, you die. Every time."

A small piece of Laurel eased a fraction. If he didn't go with her, she wouldn't have to worry about him. Wouldn't have to worry about how Aspen would react to seeing him. Could focus on Aspen and getting her out of the palace. He would keep everyone else safe.

"But," he continued, "if you go with Lady Delmar, once you get to Aspen, there's a hundred different ways it could go. Incapacitating her is going to be difficult. Half the time you get her down to the palace grand hall, half the time you don't. She will kill you. You will kill her. The king will kill you both. You won't get her out and the rebels will collapse the tunnels on your heads."

"What about successes?"

"You knock her unconscious and drag her to the entry hall. The king doesn't kill her, but when she wakes, she escapes. From there, there's another slew of possibilities."

"I just need to get her out of the palace, and I'm going to need to do it quickly."

He blinked away the magic, his brows furrowing. "I don't

know how you're going to bring her all the way back here without losing her either. Any poisons you use to keep her unconscious for such an extended period of time will have ill effects. Without seriously maiming her, it will be difficult to even keep her in a wagon."

She set her hands to her hips. "There's something we can do, we just have to figure it out."

Paulo shuffled in front of her, his mouth twisted in thought as he stared with blue eyes down at his boots. "Whatever you decide, Laurel, I'll support you."

"Are you sure this is wise?" Conley asked, leaning against the doorframe of her rooms.

Laurel threw her jacket into the rucksack on her bed along with one of her spare daggers. "If I don't go, there will be consequences."

"If I was you, I'd leave the little chit to her own devices," Declan said from his seat near the window.

Mare passed Laurel the slim box of poisons she'd retrieved from Cal's trunk. She'd finally been able to go through it after the siege. He'd had so many devices and mixtures it had taken her several days to get rid of the truly dangerous stuff not even she would mess with and divvy out the stuff that the rest of the team could use as well. The one thing she hadn't been able to decide what to do with was his research journal. The contents of that journal weren't just the formulas for the simple poisons Laurel used, but some of the most dangerous things Laurel had seen. They were notes from his previous mentor on all the different ways chemicals reacted to different parts of the body. How different chemical compounds could do certain things when mixed with other chemicals or even exposed to the very air itself. Cal's work with bat guano was especially ingenious and had the potential to change how warfare was fought for the rest of time. Laurel could see where he'd left off, trying to find the right ratio of saltpeter to sulfur to get the powder to blow at certain rates. He had a drawing that looked like it had been done by Conley of a barrel that a large ball of lead could be fired out of. If someone were to get their hands on the notes, they would have the power to destroy armies with little effort. It was a terrifying thought. Her first gut reaction was to throw the cursed notebook in the fire and never think on it again, but she felt it a complete offense to Cal's memory if she just threw all his life's work away.

So, the journal remained at the bottom of her trunk. She would have to decide what to do with it soon.

She tied off the top of the rucksack and threw it over her shoulder. "None of you will convince me to stay."

The tips of Xander's boots tapped on the ground. "At least let one of us come with you. While I'd like to follow your wishes and remain behind to guard the castle, wouldn't it be wise for one of us to have your back? Declan especially might be helpful, as sieges are certainly under a provocationist's purview."

Declan glared at Xander, his gray eyes easily communicating the threat of bodily harm, but it was Conley who answered him.

"If our master believes us staying to guard the castle is the best use of our talents, we'll heed her orders." He folded his arms over his chest. "We may not particularly wish to follow those orders, but we will regardless."

"I appreciate your understanding." She looked to Mare. "I'd especially appreciate someone watching out for Diana."

Diana had taken to watching the castle walls like a phantom since the rebels' latest attack. She didn't come inside the castle for meals or training. She paced the outer wall for most of the day and far into the night. Her anger and emotional turbulence had simmered down to a brooding focus. She was no longer prone to emotional outbursts but had become a single thought, and it was Caspian's end that kept her at the castle walls. She'd reached the end of her leniency with him and was fully ready to take him out the next time their paths crossed.

And Laurel would help in whatever way she could.

Mare gave Laurel a single nod of acceptance, and Laurel believed she would remain at the castle even with her tendency to go places that she believed she would be wanted. But perhaps she saw how much Diana needed her here.

Laurel walked past Conley out the door.

The scholae didn't follow but interpreted her orders as the goodbye they were and went their separate ways— except Conley who trailed behind her. He had already expressed his desire to speak with Sir Heff about his sword before they left.

She was nearly to the entry hall when Paulo came around the corner. Laurel slowed, but Conley kept on his way, his steps quickening as he disappeared out of sight. He absolutely abandoned her to Paulo.

Coward.

Paulo turned back to her with a smirk. "Is he so enchanted by Heff's talents?"

"Something like that." She readjusted the sack on her shoulder. "Was there something you needed?"

He studied her, his blue eyes flicking about as he stared down at her face. He held his expression in place, but she could see words he wished to say.

Her voice came out quieter than before. "What is it?"

"I don't want you to go." He swallowed. "I don't like the idea of you being there without anyone to watch your back."

She reached forward and gave his arm a squeeze. "I'm a tough girl. I can handle myself."

He chuckled. "Of that, I have no doubt, but it still makes me want to throw fate to the wind and pack a bag right now."

A piece of her chest warmed. While his words felt contradictory, she understood them. There was something about leaving him behind that sat wrong in her chest. They'd been in the same space for months. It didn't feel right to leave him here with the threat of the rebels trying to come back for the castle. With Caspian still running around the march. But the confidence he had in her abilities was another kind of care. She knew he didn't need her to help him guard the castle, but she wanted to be here. They were slowly becoming two halves of a whole.

She quickly dropped her hand from Paulo's arm. By the Goddess, she needed to stop that line of thinking. Conley's conversation with her had put all sorts of ridiculous thoughts in her head.

She cleared her throat. "Is there anything else I need to worry about in the capital? I'll do my best to help Penny."

Paulo stared down at her, all the emotions that had been swirling there only heightening. Slowly, as if making sure not to spook her, he carefully trailed a finger over her cheek.

"Don't worry about anyone else if you can help it. Just make it back here with Aspen."

Gently, he moved toward her, brushing his lips over her forehead.

Before Laurel could even take a breath, he walked away.

She watched him go, the warmth of his small kiss reaching all the way to her toes.

Conley's voice echoed in her head.

Have you ever been in love, Laurel?

Yes, it was a very good idea that she go to Olympia.

43

AN UNEXPECTED GAME

Paulo sat in the library, his head leaning against the back of a sofa with his newest sketchbook lying across his lap. He stared up at the screaming boar's head. Mater really had been right about putting it there instead of the entry hall. It wasn't just the placement of it on the wall that made it fit, but the irony of a screaming beast in a library.

There were so many things he needed to do, but he couldn't get up from the chair.

The scholae still posed a problem. Conley was fully on board to follow Laurel. He'd been convinced. Mare's future continued to elude Paulo, her string of fate so like Donnie's in that there were so many possibilities, so many ways she could react to a situation based solely on a whim. Her loyalties were only to herself, but she could be convinced to see staying was in her best interest.

That left Declan and Xander.

Paulo's magic fluttered over his mind, sifting randomly through pieces of their futures.

Declan, stabbing a knife into Laurel's neck.

Xander, kneeling at the feet of Teagan Obscuritas with Laurel's mask in his hands.

Death, betrayal, destruction.

Trust, victory, life.

Declan was unpredictable in all the worst ways. Unlike Mare, all Paulo saw was him sneaking about, looking through Laurel's things, killing Xander, attacking Conley, standing in the dungeon, speaking with Caspian and holding a shell in his hand. There were so many things. So many possibilities and all of them condemning.

Xander was much the same. He met with Caspian in the forest. He walked away from a burning Iatrus Castle. He stood on a boat with Teagan, fae slaves surrounding him. He lay in a pool of his own blood in the middle of the woods.

The magic buzzed about, not settling on any one future, all of them as possible as the next. They still hadn't decided where their loyalties lay. Their wills torn in two. The visions circled over and over again as Paulo tried to put the pieces together. Would one of them eventually betray everyone? Should Paulo stick both of them in the dungeon and be done with it? He didn't have any solid proof— at least, nothing condemning. He had his visions, but these were only possibilities. He couldn't read their hearts, only their choices and none of them were looking good.

Paulo didn't even realize he wasn't alone until Donnie sat on the sofa next to him.

"If I didn't know any better, I'd think you were a man too far in his cups."

Paulo tilted his head to their left. "See that desk? If you twist the knob on the lamp clockwise until it clicks, it'll reveal an entire bottle of brandy in the wall."

Donnie burst out laughing. "Your grandfather's doing?"

"Absolutely."

Donnie popped out of his seat and sauntered to the hidden cubby. He popped it open and grabbed the two glasses along with the crystal bottle of brandy. He poured two fingers worth of brandy in each before closing the cubby and handing one to Paulo.

The cool crystal felt good against Paulo's fingers, but he didn't bring the glass to his lips.

Donnie drained the brandy in one go. "Och, that's awful. I miss wine." He set the glass down on the short table in front of the sofa. "So, are we going to be moping around the castle the entire time Laurel is gone, or are we going to do something fun?"

"Do you have any suggestions?"

"Dozens, but when we consider which ones Mater would certainly not approve of, I've narrowed it down to two. Either we can challenge the scholae to cards and take their silver masks off them or we can drink ourselves into a stupor for old time's sake."

What Donnie thought Mater would approve of and what Mater would actually approve of were two very different things. Paulo pushed himself up, so he was sitting straighter in the sofa. "How about you help me solve a mystery?"

"What kind of mystery are we talking about here? The last time we played detective, it was to see if Lord Discordia actually did wear—"

"Not that kind of mystery," Paulo cut him off. He had been pushing that particular evening at Lord Discordia's house party far from his mind for years. "I'm thinking of something a little more dangerous."

Donnie set his glass on the table. "You know me, I'm always game for a good game. What are we looking for?"

Paulo set his untouched brandy next to Donnie's empty glass. "We're looking for a mole."

The door to Declan and Xander's room was locked.

Paulo knocked on the door.

"If you're really wanting to give them the element of surprise," Donnie whispered, "you have to—"

"Wait! Don't—"

Donnie lifted his booted foot and smashed it into the doorhandle. The door popped open, snapping the string at the top corner.

Paulo tackled Donnie, sending both of them sprawling as the sack of ink fell from above the door and exploded on the ground. A few droplets sprayed onto Paulo's boots and the backs of his trousers.

"Blast it, Donnie." Paulo shoved himself to his feet, smacking Donnie on the side of the head in the process.

"Ow!" Donnie rubbed at his head and sat up. His eyes went wide as he took in the ink staining his own boots. "Curses, that would have been the devil to get out of my jacket."

Paulo shook his head, summoning his magic to check the repercussions. Declan would be livid, telling off Paulo for allowing someone to break into their rooms. Xander would be anxiously looking for something, but neither of their futures changed besides that.

"How are we supposed to get in there now?" Donnie asked. "We'll leave boot prints all over Mater's floor if we step in that."

Paulo looked about the hall. There was a single table with an empty vase, a picture of a weeping woman at a stream that had always made Paulo's skin prickle but Mater loved, and a tapestry of the MacGregor family seal.

Paulo went to the tapestry. "Quick, help me get this down."

Donnie abandoned the doorway and joined him in pulling down the tapestry. The thing fell from the wall like a ton of bricks, landing right on top of Donnie and knocking him to the ground.

At that moment, none other than Hiatt walked around the corner, his polished buttons gleaming when the magelights above their heads hit them.

Paulo froze, hovering over a sprawled Donnie, lying still under the heavy tapestry.

Hiatt blinked languidly when he noticed them at the other end of the hallway. His brows pulled together in a slight frown when he saw the puddle of ink now staining the hallway, but he didn't hurry his steps to reach them. Instead, he passed by at a sedate pace.

Paulo was about to reach for Donnie again when Hiatt said, "The dowager will not be pleased that you stained the carpet."

Then, he disappeared.

"I told you Mater would be mad about the floor," Donnie hissed, pulling his legs out from under the tapestry.

"She'll understand." *Hopefully.* When he and Diana had been eleven, they'd accidentally torn a hole through the billiards room wall and into the hallway. They'd been fighting over something ridiculous that Paulo couldn't even remember. Mater had discovered them, covered in the rubble, and ordered them to fix the wall in complete silence. They weren't allowed to speak until the wall had been fixed or Father would put them in the dungeon. They believed her, knowing Father would do whatever Mater said he would. It had taken them three days of silence to fix the wall, but they'd done it. It had been an absolutely terrible job that Father had to have a real builder redo the entire thing, but the lesson had been learned.

Iatrus Castle was to be treated with care, or the wrath of Mater would be unleashed.

Paulo dragged the heavy tapestry across the hall. He tried to toss it through the doorway of Xander and Declan's room, but it only half covered the ink.

Donnie set his hands on his hips. "Well, we can probably jump it."

Paulo nodded, stepping onto the thick tapestry. There was about three or four feet of ink between him and the other side of the puddle. He jumped, clearing the black liquid. Donnie followed suit, but the brandy must have hit a little harder than Paulo would have guessed, because he nearly stumbled into one of the beds.

Grabbing the back of Donnie's waistcoat, Paulo kept him from faceplanting. "You should really lay off the drink."

"You wouldn't like me half so well without it," Donnie quipped. He straightened his clothing and glanced about. "What are we looking for?"

Paulo did the same, taking in the room. The left side was messy, clothes and fletcher's instruments strewn about. The right was a tidy contradiction, the bed made and nothing personal left out. Paulo crouched down next to Declan's bed, reaching underneath it and finding the slit Laurel had.

There was nothing there.

"Did your grandfather happen to make any secret little compartments in here?" Donnie asked.

Paulo knelt all the way to the ground, looking under the bed to see if anything had fallen. "I couldn't tell you. Not even Father had found most of them before he died. Diana and I took a whole summer once to see if we could discover all of them, but we still find them from time to time."

"Well, this writing desk has a lamp similar to the one in the library."

Paulo stood, turning to look at the lamp. The indigo glass of the lampshade was an exact replica of the one in the library. When Donnie tried to lift it from the top of the desk, it didn't move. He twisted the knob clockwise until it clicked. The bottom section of the windowsill above the desk popped out. Donnie pulled on it, revealing a hidden compartment.

One that wasn't filled with crystal decanters, but pages of notes.

Paulo pulled one out, finding Captain Isaac's handwriting laying out a guard rotation schedule. There were schematics on weapons that Conley had drawn, ironed pages of Serene's scratched out sketches, and even strips of paper with Mare's straight script sharing communications she'd had to write out.

"By the Goddess," Donnie said quietly, "you do have a mole."

"Yes, but which schola is it?"

Donnie looked up at him. "What do you mean which one? Don't you already know?"

"Both Xander or Declan may betray Laurel. I can't see the past to see what decisions they've already made. All I can see is the fate the Goddess has decided, and the choices offered to Her children. I can't see what either of them has decided to do. I'm not like the Sireadh that can read a person's heart."

"Then stick both of them in the dungeon."

Paulo tucked the pages back into the hidden compartment and slid it shut. "If we lock them in the dungeon, we lose the element of surprise."

"Aren't we past that point now?" Donnie gestured to the hidden compartment. "Do you want to give either of them the chance to get this information into rebel hands? We don't want Caspian hanging around anymore."

Paulo stayed silent.

Donnie's jaw dropped. "You *do* want Caspian hanging around. Why on Gaia's green earth would you want to subject Diana to that again?"

"Because the only way we really stop the Aigeans is by taking out Caspian. If we get rid of our mole, Caspian disappears. If we get rid of Caspian too soon, whichever schola it was will wait out the storm until he can betray Laurel in a worse way. If we can catch the either one in the act of betraying us, we can trap him and take out Caspian at the same time."

"And you're willing to risk Laurel to wait? Honestly, it makes more sense to get rid of both suspects and let Caspian go back to the Isles."

"But if Caspian returns to the Isles, he'll come back and use Prince Evan as his bargaining chip." And the prince needed to stay on the Isles. The Goddess had deemed that necessary. "We have to kill Caspian here. He's known as one of the Aigeans' best warriors. It wouldn't just be a matter of taking out good fighters but would be a blow to their morale as well."

Donnie blinked at him. "You've thought about this a lot."

Paulo nearly laughed aloud. "This is all I've been thinking about as of late."

"So, what are we going to do?"

Paulo set his hands to his hips and stared at the drawer.

"We're going to set a trap."

44
THE CAVES

Laurel will walk through the caves under the palace, the late night howling as the wind turns in their direction. She will march at the front of the group until they reach the entrance but pauses at the end of the passage, her eyes drawn to a shallow alcove.

Laurel rode in front of Lady Delmar and Sir Heff. Apparently, the knight turned blacksmith didn't trust Laurel to ride behind them.

That suited her just fine.

It gave her time to think without having to watch her back. They needed her far too much to do anything untoward and the dragonets swooping from tree to tree would likely keep an eye out for any attackers on the road.

She had no idea what to do about Paulo.

How he could adapt so quickly to things almost made her head spin. It hadn't been so long ago that she had expressed her wish for him to trust her. She hadn't expected him to take to it so quickly. Their conversation in the hallway, the fact that he shared the visions he had with her had been... nice. She hadn't really had to drag them out of him or try to decipher his intentions. He gave her the facts. But then he'd also allowed her to choose. He hadn't told her which one he wanted but allowed her to make a decision and respected it.

To say it had been easy to get him to understand what she wanted from him would be a lie, but the fact that he was actually trying now did strange things to her head. People couldn't just change like that could they?

But this wasn't the first change he'd implemented since she'd been around him. He'd been more somber since the siege, not wearing ridiculous clothing and attempting to be part of serious discussions instead of a bystander who would yell out quips as the rest of them scrambled to keep everything from falling apart. She'd seen him walk to the village every day for an entire week to fix roofs and replace windows. He'd never been an absentee marquess, but it was different now. Like he was actually part of it all.

"Laurel, how long have you been an assassin?"

The question jarred her, and she looked back over her shoulder at Lady Delmar, who was pushing her horse forward to ride beside Laurel's bay mare.

"Why do you care to know?"

"Because we have one more day of travel and I'm bored to tears. When did you join the Order of Stellatus?"

There had to be more of a reason for the spymaster to be asking, but besides collecting profile information on her, Laurel couldn't really see a way for Lady Delmar to use her history against her. "I was seven when my mother left me and my sister at the doors of Stellatus Hall."

Lady Delmar tilted her head. "I heard it was mostly orphans that made their way to the assassins' hall."

"Orphans make up a great number of the hall's occupants, but there are plenty of parents with debt collectors at their doors."

"They sell their children," Sir Heff said, his tone dark.

"Yes."

"And you were one of them?" Lady Delmar asked.

The question didn't warrant a response, so Laurel remained silent.

Lady Delmar hummed knowingly. "What would drive a mother to sell her own children?"

Laurel had seen plenty of desperate souls leave their children at the door to the halls, knowing they would at least get some coin out of it where they wouldn't if they left them at an orphanage. Most of the children left by their parents didn't make it far into training, the abandonment breaking them. Laurel and Aspen had been one of few who didn't break, but it had likely been because they'd already been broken. They never suspected to ever find Mother at their house next to the coast. Mother had taken the money at the door of Stellatus Hall with a smile on her thin red lips as if she had gotten the better end of the deal. The cursed woman would never return. No one would be waiting for them if Laurel or Aspen ever tried to leave the hall.

"So, you've been an assassin for what? Ten years now?" Lady Delmar asked. "Your mother left you, and Stellatus Hall has been your home. What made you decide to switch sides and take on The Cartographer?"

The question made Laurel's stomach twist. Her automatic reaction would be to say that she had no choice, but that was a paltry reason in comparison to the reality. Aspen was one motivation. The fact that Adira Durant was tearing good lives to shreds was another. But the one that kept her silent came with forget-me-not blue eyes and enough freckles to dot the skies. Instead, she turned the question on the siren. "What made you abandon your people?"

Lady Delmar's eyes grew dark. "That's easy. I murdered my stepfather and faced an execution if I ever returned."

"I think you and I are probably more alike than either of us would care to admit."

"You're probably right, darling," she agreed.

Laurel readjusted her position atop her mount. It had been too long since she'd ridden a horse, and four days in a saddle was killing her legs. She'd have to make sure she added horse riding to the training regimen when she returned to Iatrus Castle.

"How much longer until we reach the palace?" she asked.

Rissa pulled out a plain silver pocket watch from the pocket of her dress. "Should be there before midnight tomorrow."

Laurel looked up at the glaring sun still high above the trees.

"So, your sister is a real piece of work, huh?"

By the Goddess...

The crash of the water on the beach brought back so many memories to Laurel's mind that she felt her hackles rising. She could have sworn she'd seen red sails off the horizon, but when she'd looked again the color had disappeared. The wind pulled at the bottom of Laurel's knee-length jacket, but she kept her hands empty, ready to grab her daggers at a moment's notice.

The palace above the cliffs had been encapsulated by a dome of magic. Lady Delmar had told her as they traveled that the royal palace had magical defenses that were built in. This shield was the largest, but there were others. Few lights glimmered in the palace windows, relegating the beautiful building from a shining pinnacle of royalty to a greasy beggar with missing teeth.

Laurel trailed behind Lady Delmar and Sir Heff. Apparently, opening up about her past had convinced the knight she wasn't going to stab him in the neck.

Hopefully, she wouldn't have to.

Voices caught the wind and sailed to Laurel's ears. She heard the sound of Lady Barclay's sharp tone and the deep rumble of the king's timbre.

Perhaps the beach would swallow her whole right then and there. Or maybe the king would take one look at her and zap her into oblivion, not even giving her a chance to have to face him or the queen.

Two fae, Penny, Lady Barclay, King Dion, Queen Carnation, and a handful of humans she'd never seen before all sat in the sand. Laurel ducked behind Sir Heff as her hands started sweating in her gloves. She could run. She could dart past them and make it to the tunnels. If she did it before any of them realized she was there, she could make it through and to the top. She could climb into the palace herself and get to Aspen. The entire palace would be distracted by the attack at the front gate. It would give Laurel plenty of time to get to Aspen and figure out how to get her to Iatrus Castle alone.

"Laurel?"

Curses. Laurel found Lady Penny walking toward them. The need to fall back on old habits she'd developed in Olympia took over and she gave a small curtsy. "Hello, Your Majesty."

Lady Delmar looked between them. "You've met?"

"High Queen Penelope came to Paulo's estate at the beginning of her endeavors in Olympia." Laurel refrained from meeting Penny's eye. There had been little time for them to get to know one another before Penny had left. Not that Laurel had really wanted to get any closer. The news of Queen Carnation's loss had plagued her for days even after the high queen's departure.

But Penny obviously felt no such ill feelings.

"What are you doing here?" she asked. She stood on her tiptoes, though with her petite frame she likely couldn't see over Laurel's head, let alone past Sir Heff who had taken position behind her again. "Did Paulo come as well?"

Laurel shook her head, trying to keep her expression neutral at the sound of Paulo's name. Something in her chest twisted a bit at his absence. "This isn't his battle."

Movement from behind Penny had Laurel's entire body stiffening.

Queen Carnation stepped carefully toward them, her blue eyes sharp on Laurel.

Sweet Gaia, the woman looked like an avenging goddess herself.

Laurel swept past Penny and when she was two steps away from the queen, she fell to her knees in the sand. If the queen wanted to take a crack at her, she would let her. Laurel would take the punishment for Aspen's sins if it would appease Queen Carnation enough to let Laurel take her. She would bargain whatever freedoms she had. She would grovel. She would beg.

"Your Majesty," she said, her words like tar in the back of her throat, "I can't begin to say how sorry I am. If I'd known—"

"Enough."

The queen's voice had Laurel's jaw clicking shut. The back of her eyes prickled as Queen Carnation's chest deflated the smallest bit with a sigh.

"I know it wasn't you. Dion told me everything that happened that night. You're the reason we all made it out alive, and you being here now only proves you're on our side."

The backs of Laurel's eyes prickled and she bowed her head. How could the queen say that? How could she not take one look at Laurel and see what Aspen had done? Laurel may have helped them, but it was only after she'd tried for months to kill the king. It was only because of Paulo that they were here. He was the one who had saved her. He was the one who had saved all of them. Laurel had almost made her decision too late. If he hadn't taken her away from Aspen and the rebels, she would still be helping them. The Goddess only knew how many more innocents would have fallen if she'd stayed. If she hadn't had Paulo to show her what Aspen had become.

But because of Paulo, she hadn't stayed. He'd shown her there was more. He'd given her a choice. If she hadn't been so mule-headed about it, she would have seen it for what it was. Instead, she'd acted as if she'd known what was best. That she'd believed she knew what she needed.

Curse you, Paulo MacGregor.

Laurel looked up and met the queen's eyes, trying to blink away the moisture gathered at her own lashes. "If I'd known what she was going to do, I could have stopped it. I could have convinced her to leave. It's because of my own selfish blindness that this happened, but I swear I'm here to fix it."

"What?" Penny asked, completely confused.

Lady Delmar met Laurel's eye and Laurel shook her head. The knowledge of who she was hadn't been shared with the new Faerie Queen.

Rissa stepped in with her sparkling smile. "Penny, may I formally introduce Laurel Flumen, a Daughter of Stellatus Hall and one of the Continent's most skilled assassins."

Laurel blinked. Well, Lady Delmar had certainly been doing her research.

Penny's nose scrunched up. "You're an assassin?"

Was she an assassin? She'd broken the codes of her order. She'd failed to fulfill her geas. She'd betrayed everything she'd ever stood for and would continue to do so because now she had the choice to.

She bowed her head, the tears that had been gathering finally falling.

"Not anymore."

Laurel led the group through the tunnels, as Adele, one of the Underworld's spies, unraveled the spool of thread behind them so if they got separated, everyone could find their way back through.

It was like Laurel had never left.

The tunnels were completely unchanged, the shallow nooks still dusty and the silent howl of the wind still whistling through the caverns. Some of the tunnels opened up into rooms empty of anything except for the tree branches and Faerie creatures carved into the walls. Some led off into other tunnels that would take them to the side of the cliff. Some were collapsed.

But Laurel remembered the path back up.

When they reached the last tunnel, Laurel stopped, her eyes drawn to the alcove just off to the side.

"Almost to the exit," she said. "Keep heading that way."

The others passed by her, but she crouched down next to the dust covered bag and ripped it open.

There, sitting right where she'd left it, was her mask.

She drew it out, wiping the little bits of dust from opening the bag off it. The filigree carved into the silver shimmered in the glow of the magelight in her hand. She pulled the hood of her jacket up, having taken the clips from one of Cal's jackets and sewing them into this one. Her poison jacket lay at the bottom of the bag, but she didn't want it. Didn't need it.

The mask settled on her face like a second skin. It felt like she could breathe. Like she'd been wearing someone else's face for so long and this was her true one.

She would have to come back for the bag before they left. The rest of the company had passed by her, and she rejoined them at the back.

Lady Penny looked at her over her shoulder. "What does the mask mean?"

The question rang a bit in Laurel's head. What did it mean? She could no longer claim a place in Stellatus Hall. She didn't want to. But her sect meant everything to her. Conley, Mare, Declan, and Xander— even Paulo and Diana— had become something else to her. This silver mask had brought them all together. Had given her a chance at a life she had always dreamed of.

"It means," she finally said, "I'm taking my fate into my own hands."

The rest of the group turned off their magelights at the bottom of the dirt ramp leading up to the palace wall.

Lady Delmar turned to them, her eyes flicking over every face. "The opening here is just inside the shield. Once we climb over the palace wall, we'll be splitting up into three teams."

Laurel's gut sank. They weren't all going as a group? Even if most of them had some weapon training, there were still a few untrained.

After giving a small kiss to Sir Heff's fingers, Lady Delmar met Laurel's eyes. "Dion, Shaunie, Laurel, and Heff will be going off to take care of the shield. Since Dion is the only one here who knows how to deactivate it, the rest of you have to do whatever you can to get him there."

Laurel's attention flicked over to the royal couple who were both staring at her. King Dion's expression was especially thunderous as he watched her, but he didn't outright reject Lady Delmar's direction. Queen Carnation's face held a hint of worry, but her blue eyes glittered with determination.

Lady Delmar continued, "The next group consists of the Barclay women, Dair, Farrah, and Jolly. Somewhere in the palace, the rebels are holding fae prisoners. If we can get them released, the rebels won't be able to use them in the coming skirmish."

At least they were thinking of the slaves. Lady Penny and her fae companions practically bristled at the mention of them. Was the young fae boy still here in the palace? Laurel hadn't seen him since she'd met Aspen and Luc in the great hall before they'd gone to the royal sitting room. Was he even still alive?

Lady Delmar continued with the last group, pointing to Harper. "You, me, and Adele will go into the Underworld headquarters beneath the palace. I know Durant would have had the place ransacked, but Hart—" she cleared some emotion from her voice— "he had caches of supplies— maps, palace schematics, and even some defense charms— hidden in there just in case Durant ever came back." She turned to meet Penny's gaze. "I know Aiden prayed she'd never return, but Hart feared that more than anything else and always made sure we wouldn't be defenseless against her."

Whoever Hart was, it sounded like he knew Adira Durant well. Laurel would have put together an entire stockpile of weapons to use if she ever thought Adira would be coming to attack her. Hopefully, the cursed woman wouldn't see it through the end of this war, or Laurel would have to talk to Paulo about stockpiling.

If she returned to Paulo. If she made it out of this palace alive.

Lady Delmar tied off the golden string at the mouth of the tunnel and tucked the glittering spool in her pocket. As the rest of the group climbed up onto the surface, Lady Delmar stayed behind, grabbing Laurel's arm as she went to pass.

"Once we're finished, my team will join you. Heff will guard Shaunie with his life, so it will be up to you to make sure the king doesn't get himself killed."

Laurel pulled her arm from Lady Delmar's grip. "The king's death is not the one I worry about."

45
THE PALACE

Sir Heff took point this time. While the man was as big as a bear, he stepped as silently as Laurel did through the palace gardens. The clamor of battle rang in the air around them, the attack on the gate in full swing.

They needed to hurry.

Laurel trailed behind the king and queen, keeping pace with them while also checking over her shoulder in case anyone came upon them. King Dion seemed like he was keeping himself calm, but the ends of his hair continued to rise, and he had to discharge his electricity into the cane slung over his shoulder more than once. The queen followed behind him, not touching him, but staying close.

Sir Heff stopped at one of the doors leading into the servants' quarters. Likely the main hallways were being patrolled by a scant few while most of the rebels had gone to defend the gate. With his sword in his only hand, Sir Heff used his chin to direct everyone to stay put while he slipped through the door.

"So, Laurel— if that's even your real name— how much trouble are you going to be when I kill your sister?"

Laurel looked up and met the king's gaze, which practically glowed with his magic. Little bolts of electricity danced over the amethyst shade of his irises. She didn't look away at the flash of power. Didn't move to take one of her daggers. This was a test. He wanted to push her to betray herself to him, to see if she was actually on their side.

He didn't trust her.

She didn't blame him.

"How much trouble are you going to be when I save her?" she asked.

A slight breeze tugged at the end of Laurel's jacket. The clouds above them were forming, drawn to the king and his power. If he didn't quit showing off, he was going to get them caught.

"Dion, stop being an idiot." Queen Carnation's voice cut between them. "You of all people should know better than to threaten someone's sibling. You know exactly how Laurel feels. If Denny or Evan were in the same situation, you would tear this palace apart to get to them no matter what they'd done."

The king whirled on his wife. "You would defend *her*? Even after what she's done?"

Queen Carnation's face was set in a stubborn tilt. "I'm not defending *her*. I'm defending Laurel, the one who saved your life and helped us get back here. I want justice as much as you do, but we can't let our feelings overrule our heads. We can't blame Laurel for her sister's mistakes, nor can we expect her not to wish to save her."

The king's face fell, his magic dissipating as he took a few long breaths.

"She isn't going to get out of this without consequences," Laurel said. "She broke laws where I come from. There will be retribution for her actions."

The king gave her a disbelieving look. "I hope that's true, assassin."

Sir Heff returned, practically appearing out of nowhere. "Let's go."

The queen followed after him first, switching places with her husband in the lineup. She trailed behind the knight closer than she had even her husband.

King Dion shadowed his wife, continually checking over his shoulder at Laurel.

The servants' quarters looked much the same as they had when Laurel lived there. They passed Esther's office, where she and Cook would meet with Queen Carnation to discuss castle matters. The magelights in the sconce on the wall slept in their perch as Laurel glided by.

As they walked farther in, the air around them grew warmer. Soon, the hiss of voices broke the silence. Laurel slowly wrapped her fingers around one of her long daggers.

Sir Heff stopped at the door leading to the kitchens, carefully sliding it open to peer through it. He tapped his foot and Queen Carnation turned back to Laurel, six fingers raised.

Six people on the other side.

Laurel slipped past the king and stopped next to the queen. She pulled one of the small daggers from the bandolier on her chest and handed it to her.

The queen took it with wide eyes.

Without a word, Laurel unclipped her mask, tucking it into her jacket and pushed through the door.

The clamor of a kitchen sang in her ears. Steam hissed, pots clanged, and knives clipped a beat on cutting boards.

Next to the door hung several aprons. Laurel grabbed one and threw it over her head, tucking stray hairs behind her ears.

Next to the archway, she found a sack of potatoes.

Cook would have slaughtered someone if she saw dirty potatoes next to the washbasin.

"Dan! Hurry up and get those pitas out of the oven. The captain said the men would want a victory feast when they ran the royalists away from the gate."

Laurel had to duck her head to hide her grimace at the grating voice.

Delilah.

The wretched girl had taken over the kitchens. Laurel grabbed the sack of potatoes and walked into the kitchen.

The room had much been changed.

A little girl stood next to the washbasin, her hands raw from scrubbing at the piles of dishes towering around her. Grime covered every square inch of the floor, an abandoned mop leaning against the table.

The table where Galen sat.

Laurel nearly dropped the potatoes.

The mage was completely gray, his cheeks sunken and garnet eyes dull. He looked as if someone had brought him back from the dead and all he was now was a husk. He didn't even look at her as she passed by him.

Laurel quickly shuffled through, taking the potatoes to the single stool sitting at the other end of the table.

"We need more flour!" Delilah screeched.

Laurel finally found her. She was sitting in a chair by the ovens, her cheeks ruddy and her blond hair piled on her head. She wore a dress Laurel suspected had come from the queen's closet, though it had become stained from working in a kitchen. Dan stood at the oven beside her, his solemn face the same as when Laurel had last seen him. When he'd stabbed Galen in the back.

There were two others, a man and a woman, in the room. The man stood over a stove, stirring a large pot that was black around the edges while the woman skittered in the direction of the pantry.

"Hey, we don't need potatoes, you stupid girl," Delilah said.

Laurel turned back to her and met her eyes.

Delilah's face went completely white. "Sweet Gaia."

Dan turned toward Delilah.

Laurel dropped the potatoes and was on him within a heartbeat.

One dagger slid into his ribs, while the other came around and went straight through his spine.

He gasped and was dead before he hit the floor.

Delilah screamed.

The man at the stove sprang at Laurel, a large butcher knife in his hand.

Laurel let him get within her guard but used his momentum to pull him past her and sank her dagger into his stomach.

He dropped the blade and fell to the floor.

Laurel barely had time to crouch before a bucket flew past her head.

The other woman had returned and grabbed the boiling liquid from the stove. She threw the contents right at Laurel's face.

Laurel dodged the scalding liquid, but the man with the new

stomach wound screamed when the boiling slop hit him in the back.

The woman staggered as she tried to right herself.

Laurel used the momentary opening and stabbed her in the throat.

Delilah's screams had gone from shocked to hysterical. The undercook was crawling on the floor, blubbering as she made it to Galen who still sat in his chair at the table.

It was then that Laurel noticed the manacles around his ankles.

Ice crept through her midsection as she stalked toward Delilah. The woman was shaking Galen, screaming in his face.

"For once in your life, do something useful and *save me!*"

Galen just looked up at her with empty eyes.

Laurel twirled the daggers in her hand.

"Sorry, Delilah. You exposed me and I told you what would happen if you tried. Do you remember?"

Delilah started shaking, her face completely white.

"I told you I would tear that sad, weak lump of flesh you call a heart out of your chest and make you gag on it."

Delilah's eyes rolled into the back of her head, and she fell to the ground in a heap, her head smacking against the wall behind Galen.

Oh, by the Goddess. The girl was a lightweight. She couldn't even stay conscious long enough for Laurel to actually draw blood. Laurel watched her until she could count three solid breaths and turned to the wash basin.

The little dishwasher was trembling on the floor in front of the sink, curled up in a ball with her face smashed into her knees. It was only then that Laurel noticed the tips of her ears peeking out between the riot of brown curls.

A fae child.

Laurel sheathed her daggers and knelt by the little girl's side. "Hi, sweeting."

The girl's trembling turned to all out shaking. A little sob hiccupped from her.

"I don't think you want to be here." Laurel didn't touch the child, but she pushed a few of the dishes away from her. "I've brought some friends with me to help you. Is it all right if I let them in?"

The girl's shaking didn't stop, but she gave a subtle nod.

Well, Laurel thought it was a nod. She stood, but before she could take a step away, the door to the servants' quarters opened and Sir Heff stepped through, going straight to Galen's table and looking over the manacles.

Queen Carnation knelt by the little girl, touching her shoulder. "We're here to help you. Can I find you a better place to hide?"

The little girl looked up at Queen Carnation, her sapphire eyes wide with fear. She didn't say anything, but she allowed the queen to help her to her feet.

"We'll need to be quick," Laurel said. She met the girl's wide gaze. "You look like a smart girl. Do you know any good hiding spots in the kitchens?"

The girl tucked herself closer to the queen but gave a short nod.

Laurel crouched down to her level. "I need you to listen carefully. Your High Queen is here. Her name is Penny. She's freeing the other fae trapped here in the palace with one of the Winter princes and another one of your kind. We need you to find your hiding spot and not come out until Queen Carnation here or her husband, King Dion over there, comes to find you. Can you do that?"

The little girl's eyes were still wide, but they sparked with hope, and she nodded emphatically.

"Go," Laurel commanded.

The girl disappeared into the pantry, moving faster than any human child could.

Queen Carnation turned back to Laurel. "Why me or Dion? Why not come back for her yourself?"

Laurel pulled her silver mask out from inside her jacket. "Because I don't suspect you'll want me around for longer than absolutely necessary once all of this is over."

How had it come to this?

Laurel peeked around the corner once more.

Six guards stood at the other end of the hall, each of them holding a crossbow. Their faces were covered in black masks not unlike the one she'd put back on her face. Was Aspen trying to replicate the sect? To create her own twisted version of it?

Cursing, Laurel pulled back and crept down the hallway to the slightly open door halfway down. She slid into the room, keeping the door open just enough not to let the locking mechanism click.

"Well?" King Dion whispered.

"They've got a half dozen crossbows in front of the door. We walk out and we're pincushions."

He scoffed. "I can take out that many with a snap of my fingers." He snapped to emphasize his point, lightning crackling with the sound.

"We need a distraction," Queen Carnation said. She looked to Sir Heff, who was standing sentinel near the door. "What do you think?"

Sir Heff's rough voice carried across the room even as he spoke in low tones. "You and I are the best options."

The king straightened with indignation, but the knight was right. Laurel would be best served as double to the king as she was the best fighter out of the four of them. King Dion was needed to take out the shield. The queen and her knight would just need to outrun them until Lady Delmar and the others could meet up with them. Sir Heff likely knew where his wife would be and could take the queen to safety while Laurel and the king took out the shield or at least didn't die before Lady Delmar joined them. If she'd completed her mission and hadn't gotten herself killed.

But all Laurel had to do was get to Aspen. She just needed to talk to her. Just convince her to come back to Iatrus Castle. Somehow.

The queen stood, the king following right after.

"You can't be the distraction," King Dion argued. "It's too risky."

The queen set a hand on his cheek. "We're going to be fine Dee. Heff has seen me through worse scrapes than this. Trust me. Trust *in* me. I'm just as responsible for this kingdom as you are. Let me do my part so we can take back our home."

The king crushed her to him. The queen's eyes were wide as she was practically smashed against his chest, but her arms came around him and she squeezed back just as fiercely.

When they finally parted, Queen Carnation followed behind Sir Heff, her hand still wrapped around her dagger. They disappeared through the doorway.

Laurel and the king took up a post next to the door, Laurel peering through the opening to view Sir Heff and Queen Carnation glide down the hallway.

The king stood across from her, his hands sparking with magic.

"If she dies, I'll kill you."

Laurel didn't look up at him. "Your Majesty, if it was my fate to die at your hands, Lord MacGregor would have never let me leave his castle. Take whatever scrap of comfort you can from that and shut that big mouth of yours before I knock you over the head and leave you here for the rebels to find."

The king's teeth clicked as he shut his mouth, but he remained quiet as Laurel watched out the door.

The staccato of half a dozen crossbow bolts against a wall rattled down the hall.

A shout sounded, but it was a shout of surprise rather than pain. Laurel opened the door a little more and watched as four of the six rebels ran down the hall in pursuit of Sir Heff and the queen.

Laurel pulled the door all the way open. "Let's see you show off that flashy magic, Your Majesty."

King Dion gave her a feral grin and strode past her.

She hadn't forgotten what his magic felt like.

It crackled against her skin, making the air feel heavier. The king's hair rose until it was a halo around his head.

Before the rebels at the other end of the hall could even blink, the king's magic shot forward out of his hands. Laurel had to shield her eyes as that white-hot magic vaporized the two guards. When Laurel finally blinked the stars out of her vision, not even their masks remained on the ground where they'd stood. Laurel took lead as the king touched the rod at his back, dispelling his magic. He had to have an entire storm's worth of energy in that thing by now.

The door to the royal sitting room had been replaced. Instead of the enchanted door that only opened for royal blood, the new door had been constructed of iron and had a slot for a window a third of the way down.

"How many do you think are on the other side?" the king asked.

Laurel shrugged, crouching down to look at the doorknob. No charms were carved into the handle, but that didn't discount the hundreds of them carved into the door. Any of them had the potential to blast her fingers from her hand. Carefully, she wrapped her hand around the round knob.

None of the charms immediately tried to kill her.

"You know how to pick a lock, right?"

Laurel stood from her crouch, her hand still on the knob, and twisted it.

"Never mind then."

She pushed the door open, not moving into the room. Instead, she stood on the threshold, her eyes following the beam of light that trailed across the floor until it landed on the legs of a table in the middle of the room. A faerie glass orb sat on the table, a careful pulse of magic beating out of it.

The king attempted to take a step forward, but Laurel's arm shot out across his chest.

A shadow stirred behind the orb. It stepped into the light the door let in.

A mask of silver and black hovered over the orb.

"Hello, Laurel."

Laurel dropped her arm.

"Hello, Aspen."

46

THE SHIELD

Laurel will lie at Aspen's feet, a dagger in her throat.

THE SHADOWS IN THE ROOM TOOK FORM AND SHOT TOWARD LAUREL.

She would have thought it was fae shadow magic except she could hear the squeak of their boots on the polished floor and saw the flash of their eyes behind their masks.

Laurel stabbed the first one right through the eye hole in their mask.

The king's magic flared, lighting up the room as he zapped one of the assailants and left them twitching on the ground.

But in the flash of light, Laurel counted their numbers.

There were seventeen masked fighters between her and Aspen.

The next one launched himself at the king, a wicked hunting knife in his grip.

Laurel intercepted him, kicking his knee hard enough to disconnect the ligaments. The man fell with a roar, slashing his blade at her. She spun, her feet carrying her around so she ended up behind him. Her blade slid easily across the skin of his throat, and he fell.

The king roared and blasted his magic forward. The two

attackers coming toward them dropped and Laurel finally stepped into the room.

She needed to get the king to the orb.

Another attacker charged her with a sword. Laurel slid to the side, locking her daggers into the hilt of his sword, and popped the pommel from his grip. She cut both of his arms, making him unable to fight, before moving onto the next attacker.

Two came at her and she had to dip backward to avoid losing her head. Two swords crossed right in front of her nose. She allowed herself to fall backward and kicked her feet out, catching both of them in the shins. The two fighters staggered forward, and Laurel sent her feet over her head and landed in a crouch. She sprang forward before the first man could get his feet under him. Her dagger sank into his chest, and she let go of that blade long enough to draw a throwing knife from her vest and flick it toward the other sword wielder's neck. She retrieved her dagger from the first but had to abandon her throwing knife to the second as she saw a flash of silver out of the corner of her eye. She ducked and another throwing knife sank into the wall behind her.

Aspen had joined the fight.

Gritting her teeth, Laurel looked up and found the king only a few steps into the room, his magic crackling around him. Clouds had gathered on the ceiling over his head as he struck down two more opponents.

Eight left.

King Dion ripped the cane from where it hung over his shoulder and slammed the handle into the face of another attacker.

Seven more.

Aspen stood next to another woman behind the orb, her hand swinging back.

Laurel ripped another blade from her chest and threw it before Aspen could throw hers.

It sank into the neck of the masked woman beside Aspen, making her topple and knocking into Aspen as she threw the dagger.

The blade sank into the wall just next to the king's head.

He dove behind a sofa.

Aspen screeched, grabbing three more daggers and throwing them in quick succession at the couch where the king had hidden himself.

One of the fighters attempted to sneak from the room, likely going for whatever backup they could find. Laurel threw another throwing knife, hitting him in the spine. He went down.

Five.

Aspen launched herself at the couch, a thin dagger in her grip. She jumped over the back, her dagger poised to strike.

Laurel's heart seized as she shoved past another attacker. The king wouldn't hesitate to fry Aspen if she got close enough.

But there was no lightning.

Aspen shot to her feet, her eyes darting around.

The king wasn't there.

He burst out from behind one of the chairs closest to the orb, taking out the two masked fighters standing guard with the handle of his cane.

The other three leapt to take their place.

"*Sit*," a cold but soothing voice commanded from the doorway.

Laurel's knees buckled slightly before the skin between her shoulder blades burned like it was on fire. She gasped, shaking her head to clear the muddled magic from her brain.

Aspen screamed and grabbed her leg, likely feeling the same fiery brand in her skin.

The rest of her fighters sat like obedient dogs and the other members of the Underworld quickly set to incapacitating them. The spies' ears were stuffed with what looked like wax and they did their best to keep their eyes ahead of them.

Lady Delmar strode the rest of the way into the room, her sea-green eyes flashing. She opened her mouth but looked to see the king also sitting on the ground.

Sir Heff strode in behind his wife, his bastard sword red with blood. He positioned himself between Lady Delmar and Aspen.

"Your Majesty," Lady Delmar cooed, "please turn off the shield."

The king nearly leapt to his feet. He grabbed the orb and turned it around. There, on the bottom of the orb, was a gap.

Aspen laughed, a broken, raspy sound. "You thought I wouldn't take precautions? I destroyed the mechanism. The shield will not fall."

Lady Delmar's face turned thunderous. "You really should stop talking."

A hiss cut through Aspen's laugh as Lady Delmar's magic hit her again, but she was getting to her feet. Her movements seemed slow but were calculated. Patient. Waiting.

Laurel took a step toward her, the burning in her back a dull ache now. How was she going to get Aspen out of here?

"You've lost, Aspen," Laurel said, coming to stand next to Lady Delmar. "Your little game is over."

Aspen's body was as taut as a bowstring. "You think this is over? I haven't even gotten started."

Laurel saw her shift.

They'd fought enough times Laurel had learned how Aspen moved.

Knew when she was preparing for a strike.

Laurel had her dagger in her hand.

She jumped forward.

But Aspen knew her too.

Aspen spun out of reach, snatching her throwing knife from the sheath against her forearm.

The knife would hit the king. He couldn't move without Lady Delmar's direction.

The siren.

Laurel flipped her dagger in her hand, letting herself push past Aspen and opening up her left side.

Aspen saw the opening and brought the knife toward Laurel's stomach.

Laurel sliced her dagger across Aspen's thigh, severing the charm she knew was tattooed in her skin.

The knife in Aspen's hand faltered, leaving a shallow cut in Laurel's side.

Laurel smacked into the floor. "She's uncharmed!"

Lady Delmar struck. She moved with a grace that could have outdone Mare. With one hand, she gripped Aspen's jaw and brought her face close to her own.

"*Sleep.*"

Aspen's eyes rolled back into her head, and she slumped to the ground. Laurel leapt forward and caught her before her had hit the floor. She carefully laid her down, staying at her side.

Lady Delmar stepped over her legs and turned to the king. "Is the orb made of faerie glass?"

The king nodded emphatically, his amethyst eyes glazed over.

She cursed and pulled her charm from her pocket and clasped it around her neck.

The king's legs buckled slightly as the magic in the room evaporated. "By the Goddess, Rissa. *Never* do that again."

"Apologies, Your Majesty." She looked down at Laurel. "We have two minutes before your sister wakes."

"The shield?" Sir Heff asked.

Laurel looked to the king, who was holding his cane in front of him. There was a latch at the bottom of the staff which he carefully pulled open. A metal rod shot out of the bottom. He pressed the button at the top of the cane and exposed the piece of metal he'd been tapping anytime his magic had gotten out of hand.

His hair stood on end as he brought the end of the cane over the orb. The air in the room grew so heavy it pressed down on Laurel. Clouds gathered above the king, green and roiling.

"Close your eyes," his voice boomed, punctuated by white lightning in the clouds above his head. The entire room rattled.

Sir Heff grabbed his wife and threw himself over her.

With a roar, the king brought the cane down on the orb.

Laurel ducked over Aspen as the entire room exploded.

White light burned even through Laurel's closed eyes. The room around her groaned as thunder shook the walls. Laurel clamped her hands over Aspen's ears to protect her however she could as the sound reverberated through every bone in Laurel's body.

Magic shot out from the center of the room, shoving her back. She couldn't hear anything. Couldn't see anything.

Was this what death felt like?

Because if it was, it blasted hurt.

She felt hands prod at her side where she'd been cut. She grabbed the arm that touched her, and the person stilled, but didn't attack her further. Laurel tried to blink the spots of white away from her eyes until eventually Queen Carnation's face came into view. Laurel quickly unclipped her mask, wanting to make sure the queen knew it was her. She pulled her hood from her head and slipped the mask into her jacket.

"Where's Aspen?" she asked, though she couldn't really hear herself speak.

The queen's lips moved, but only a muffled sound broke through the ringing in Laurel's ears. Laurel shook her head and asked again. Queen Carnation shifted and pointed behind her.

Both Sir Heff and the Underworld spy, Harper, stood sentinel over Aspen. She still lay on the ground unconscious. The black part of her mask had broken off, exposing half of her face. There were shadows under her exposed eye and her skin looked pale.

The queen came between them again and gently tilted Laurel's head back and forth. She pulled and handkerchief from her pocket and pressed the silky cloth to the back of Laurel's jaw. The queen drew the cloth away and turned it to show the smear of rusty blood staining the white fabric.

Sweet Gaia, the king had wrecked her ears.

The queen gestured for someone and one of the Underworld spies, Adele, stepped forward. She looked over Laurel's injuries before saying something to the queen. The queen got up and hurried away and the spy met Laurel's gaze again. She pointed to her own ears and then her side, mirroring Laurel's injuries. She then gave a questioning look.

"I don't think there are any other injuries."

Adele nodded and settled in to sit with her.

Laurel watched the rest of the room whirl around her.

The king sat on one of the chairs, wiping his face of the tiny smears of blood from the broken orb. Someone had wrapped his hands already. The cane that had held his magic was a twisted hunk of metal on the ground next to the table where the orb had sat.

Only the glitter of miniscule shards of glass around the room was left of the orb.

Laurel's attention strayed to Aspen as movement started up

around her. Aspen's brown eyes were open, and she was trying to push herself to her feet.

Lady Delmar descended on her, taking off her charm.

Aspen slumped to the ground once again.

Adele bumped Laurel's shoulder and pulled her attention to a scrap of paper in her hand. Curling script had been scratched over what looked like meeting notes.

The shield has been down for fifteen minutes. The Hermen's were able to get over the wall ten minutes ago and Queen Penny released the fae just before. We're still rounding up rebels, but it won't be too much longer. The palace is ours.

Laurel let her head fall back against the wall. They'd done it. By the Goddess, they'd actually done it.

Lady Delmar clasped her charm back around her neck and came to where Laurel was still slumped against the ground. The siren had a small gash on her cheek that healed quicker by the second. What Laurel wouldn't give to have some of that fae healing.

The siren crouched down next to Adele, though she focused on Laurel as she spoke.

Adele scribbled a few more words onto the page.

Aspen needs to be taken care of.

Laurel nodded. "I need to get her out of here before the king decides he's ready to seek justice."

Lady Delmar spoke, and Adele dictated again.

I'll have Heff get a cart.

Laurel pushed herself to her feet and out into the hall. She needed to get out of that room. Needed to breathe fresh air.

She held onto her side as she stumbled out into the hallway. The drain of adrenaline left her weak as she trailed through the hall. She stopped at one of the windows, pushing it open and letting the humid air wrap around her. There were still clouds above the palace from the king's magic, and the wind stirred up the ocean. Red compass flags had been stuck on the poles at the tops of the towers. She looked at each one, searching out the color and counting the flags. It would be miserable for the palace staff to replace all those.

Another streak of red caught her eye, but it was far from the castle.

A ship with red sails was turning back out to sea.

Laurel smacked her hand against the windowsill. The ship on the horizon hadn't been a mirage.

The Shining River had come to Olympia.

But it had come too late. If they'd been maybe an hour later, she would have seen it. She could have sneaked on board.

But she couldn't. She couldn't leave the boundaries of this cursed kingdom.

She'd never wished to stab Teagan with his blasted geas blade more.

47
AN UNEXPECTED RETURN

PAULO PACED ON THE WALL ABOVE IATRUS CASTLE'S FRONT GATE, HIS eyes never leaving the road leading up to the castle. Never once glancing away from the curve that would lead to the village. With the sun behind him, he watched the shadows of Iatrus Castle grow longer with every second.

If he hadn't seen his horse throw a shoe, he would have ridden out of the castle gates and met the cart. If Peter hadn't come that morning to discuss the flocks, he would have left at sunrise. If his absence wouldn't have given Declan or Xander enough room to make a move, he would have left all of them behind and gone after Laurel the day she'd left.

The Goddess certainly had her way of forcing patience on him.

The chair Donnie sat in creaked. "Seriously, you ought to sit down. No woman wants a man who pines after her."

Mater tsked from her own chair. "Don't listen to him. Being honest about your feelings is the best way to a woman's heart."

"If that were true," Donnie said, "you would have married me ages ago, Mater. I've told you a hundred times how much I adore you."

The smack of a hand on an arm cracked behind him.

Diana jumped up onto the wall in front of Paulo, strands of red hair plastered to the sides of her face. Paulo hadn't even heard her coming, her practice with the scholae vastly improving her abilities. She'd just come from practice, her eyes still bright with whatever fight she'd taken part in.

"Conley's ready," she said.

Paulo gave a sharp nod. Both Conley and Mare would be needed for Aspen's arrival. With Lady Delmar's gifts used to keep Aspen subdued, no one but the scholae would be helpful. Xander and Declan had been assigned to guard Aspen during the evening and were getting some shut eye before their shift.

Paulo thought about it all week. How he would set a trap for both of them.

When he saw Laurel traveling with Aspen, it came to him.

Aspen was the perfect bait.

If one of the scholae was working with the rebels, that meant they were likely still in Teagan's pocket. And Teagan wanted Aspen. He wouldn't leave the isle without at least trying to get her.

Whoever decided to actually betray Laurel would do their best to let the rebels know she was here.

And they would likely do it that very night.

Paulo allowed his magic free reign.

Declan, his face twisted with ferocity as he yelled down at Laurel. As he brought a knife to her throat. "You let him die!" he roared in her face.

Later, him storming into the pitch-black forest and coming upon Caspian.

"You're late," Caspian snaps.

Then, Xander climbing down the wall of the castle in complete dark. walking through the woods and finding Caspian near a stream.

"I didn't think you'd make it out here," Caspian says.

Were both of them the mole? Were they working together? Caspian only mentioned one contact, but did he have more? Paulo searched through the fate lines, but without being able to see what choices they'd already made or what they were thinking, he couldn't know. Perhaps it was time to put both of them in the dungeon and simply be done with it. But Laurel wouldn't approve. She wanted to give them both the chance to change. To become more than they could on their own, and imprisoning them would tear that chance to shreds, especially as they were both on the cusp of their loyalty.

Movement in the present snapped him away from the magic of the future.

A cart trundled around the corner, pulled by a horse that had to stand nearly twenty hands high. Flashes of color flitted about the cart, zipping from the trees to the cart and back again.

Paulo's tightened chest loosened with the first real breath he'd taken in days.

"Open the gates!" Donnie called, his voice carrying a humorous note with the command. Mater chuckled in her chair beside him.

Diana hopped down from the wall. "Do you think Sir Heff will let me buy that horse?"

Paulo ignored her, turning toward the stairs. He took the steps two at a time, feeling Diana match his pace at his heels. They burst out of the gatehouse just as the front gates widened enough for Paulo to slip through.

The cart was still a ways off, but he could make out the riders. Sir Heff sat at the front, his hand holding the reins to his tall horse. Beside him sat his wife, her head of wine-red hair leaning against her husband's side. Paulo could feel the barest traces of her magic touch him from that distance and he had to tear his eyes away from her. The blacksmith's dragonets swirled around their heads, the gold and blue beasts chirping excitedly as they got closer.

In the back of the cart, Laurel sat straight, her silver mask gleaming. Praise the Goddess, she'd made it. He'd seen her as she traveled, but he hadn't let himself relax until he saw her with his own eyes. Next to her sat Aspen, her body hardly moving as the cart swept up the hill toward the castle.

"Time to go," Paulo said, grabbing Diana's arm. He needed to get out of there before he could allow the siren's magic to sweep him toward them. No matter how much his heart tugged at him to just look at Laurel and make sure she was all right.

Her body shuddered. "Sweet Gaia, Lady Delmar's magic is potent."

Paulo nodded and walked back to the gatehouse. Mater and

Donnie met them at the door to the gatehouse and walked with them back to the castle. He took Mater's chair, hoping having something to do would help distract him. He wanted nothing more than to run back out the gate, siren magic be hanged.

Paulo stopped at the front step, handing the chair he carried to Hiatt.

"You're not coming inside?" Mater asked.

"I'm going to meet them at the dungeons."

He left the front door, walking around the side of the castle. The dungeons had been built under the northwest tower, right next to the guard barracks. While the top of the tower had been destroyed in the siege, the dungeons beneath were perfectly sound. The only access, however, was on the outside of the castle. It was wise, since it would place any escapees outside the castle proper rather than inside and would trap them within the upper bailey next to where most of the guards were.

Paulo strode toward the doors to the dungeon and found Conley and Mare just ahead of him.

"Diana said you have the cell ready," Paulo called to them.

Conley glanced over his shoulder. "The little chit won't be able to pick her way out of it. The only one who could probably escape it would be Mare, but only because she could wriggle through the bars.

Mare bared her teeth.

The dungeon door stood wide open when they arrived, and Captain Isaac hovered at the threshold, his hazel eyes narrowed.

"Are you sure you don't want me around for the prisoner transfer?"

By the Goddess, the captain was uptight.

Paulo quirked a brow. "You're more than welcome to stay and get in the way."

Captain Isaac huffed but turned away and walked to the barracks. The other guards milling about followed after their captain, filing into the barracks behind him.

"I'll come once Lady Delmar is able to release her magic," Paulo said.

But Mare shook her head.

"You think I ought to stay and get in the way?"

Conley chuckled. "You've had no problems doing so in the past, but that's not what she's saying."

Mare reached into her pocket and pulled out a string of twine. On the end hung a twisted knot of silver. It was an exact replica of the tattoo stamped into the side of Mare's neck. She held it out to Paulo.

"Place it under your shirt," Conley said. "It needs to be touching your skin for it to work."

Paulo took it, slipping his head through the loop of twine. He pulled off his cravat and slid the silver under his shirt. He folded up the neckcloth and stuffed it into his pocket.

"We really ought to find you someone who can tattoo it on somewhere," Conley said. He looked past Paulo. "Laurel could probably do it if we asked her."

Paulo turned as the cart came fully into view. His heart skipped at the sight of Laurel before magic washed over him, brightening the colors around him and drawing his attention to the siren at the front of the cart.

The silver began burning against his chest.

"Curses," he hissed, his consciousness snapping back into reality. The colors around him faded back to their normal hue, and Lady Delmar no longer held the strong allure she had only seconds before.

"Bites, doesn't it?" Conley said, slapping Paulo on the shoulder. He sauntered toward the cart.

Paulo followed, the silver still burning against his skin. Was this how the tattoo felt? It would be miserable to have that kind of sensation under your skin. Maybe Conley's idea of Paulo getting the tattoo could remain an idea.

Mare ghosted past him as the cart came to a stop. She held out a hand to the giant horse, who studied her for a second before lipping at her palm. A smile bloomed on her face, a real smile, and she grabbed hold of the horse's bridle.

Sir Heff stepped down from the cart, making the entire thing tilt back and forth under his weight. He took his wife's hand and pulled her from the bench.

Lady Delmar looked minutes away from a dead faint.

Laurel jumped out of the back, silver mask glinting in the

fading sunlight. The urge to rush to her and wrap his arms around her was staggering. He'd watched her die a thousand different deaths after she left over a week ago. Seeing her completely fine in front of him loosened the bands that had slowly been closing around his chest.

She stopped at the back of the cart, her face turned to the last occupant.

Aspen still sat, her brown eyes completely glazed over. Her face was almost gaunt, and the blankness of her expression made her seem almost unreal. As if she were a wax statue rather than a living human.

Lady Delmar turned to her. "Get out of the cart." Her voice was scratchy, barely more than a whisper, but it held enough magic for the silver against Paulo's chest to flare with heat.

Aspen snapped into motion, launching herself out of the cart and onto the ground next to Lady Delmar.

The siren leaned against her husband. "Walk behind Laurel and do whatever your sister says."

Aspen trailed behind Laurel, her eyes darting back to look at Lady Delmar as they all followed them into the dungeon.

Conley pushed to the front beside Laurel, directing her to the cell they'd prepared for Aspen. Mare stayed with the horse, though her blue eyes followed Aspen with a sharpness Paulo had only seen on the battlefield.

"Any rebel trouble recently?" Sir Heff asked. He pulled his wife close, holding her against him with his single arm.

"Not too recently. They're still haunting the woods, but they haven't made another major effort since the siege ended."

Sir Heff grunted his pleasure at the news but didn't ask anything further.

Paulo leaned forward to glance at Lady Delmar. "Is there anything you need, my lady?"

She swallowed but kept her words to herself.

"A bath," Sir Heff answered, "with all the salt you can spare."

Lady Delmar looked up to him with gratitude.

"I'll have it done as soon as we finish here."

Aspen disappeared down the stairs behind Conley and Laurel.

Paulo sucked in a breath as he took his first steps down into the dungeon. It wasn't as scary a place as he'd heard some dungeons could be. It wasn't used very often, so there was no reek of despicable humans or musty mold. There were three cells, each separated by stone walls and pure iron bars with a barred window the size of Paulo's shoe that let in a few inches of light. The two cells closest to the stairs were empty of everything but what was kept for prisoners: a small pallet that could be softened with straw, a wooden pail used as a chamber pot, and a stool.

The one against the far wall had been completely transformed.

The stone was completely bare of any straw. A metal pail sat in one corner, the handle removed from the rings on either side. There was no bedding, nowhere for Aspen to sleep. The window of the cell had been blocked with a sheet of metal that looked like it had been melted to the bars. The wooden door matching the other cells had been replaced. Instead, a metal plated door now took up the wall. There were no exposed bolts, the metal completely smooth. There was a single slit in the door, just big enough to pass a bowl through. Unlike other cell doors he'd seen, there was no small door to cover it.

Laurel took Aspen's arm and guided her into the cell.

Aspen looked back to Lady Delmar who nodded at her. The grin on Aspen's face turned almost manic at the siren's tiny smile.

Conley shut the cell door and slid the lock into place.

Aspen's brown eyes appeared in the small window, finding Lady Delmar.

The siren let out a long breath and pulled her charm out of her pocket. She placed it around her throat.

The magic in the room evaporated.

Lady Delmar sagged into Sir Heff's side, and he hoisted her up.

A scream shattered the space around them.

Paulo jumped and looked toward the cell.

Aspen's brown eyes had disappeared from the window, but he saw her hand reach out and grasp at the door. She pushed and pulled at the edges of the metal, her knuckles white with strain as she tried to find a way out. The release of magic had turned her completely feral inside her cage. The cage Paulo had put her in.

Another rage filled scream ripped through the dungeon.

"*I'll kill you! I'll kill every single one of you!*"

Conley stepped farther away from the cell, his hand on the sword at his waist.

The iron door thumped as Aspen rammed into it.

"*Laurel! LAUREL!*"

Laurel turned away from the cell. Her fingers hooked Paulo's sleeve and pulled him after Sir Heff. She said nothing as she walked away. Didn't look back as Aspen's screams echoed through the dungeon and followed them up the stairs.

"When I get out of here, I'll kill *all of them*! I'll paint my blades with their blood! Do you hear me? *All of them!*"

48

THE PROVOCATIONIST

LAUREL'S HANDS SHOOK AS SHE POURED ANOTHER BUCKET OF SALT INTO the tub in Mater's washroom. Mater had her own bathtub in her room, set up with its own water pump and everything, so it was easier to get Lady Delmar into a bath there rather than waiting for the servants to haul the copper tub to one of the spare bedrooms.

Bubbles floated up from Lady Delmar's nose as she met Laurel's eyes. It was slightly eerie watching the siren breathe under the water, the gills at her throat expanding with every breath.

Sir Heff had shortly explained that the siren needed the salt water after using her gifts so much. That was the only explanation he gave before leaving Lady Delmar in Mater's care and disappearing.

"Do you need any more salt?" Mater asked, setting the last bucket next to the tub. "We have more in storage, but this is the last of it from the pantry, and it will take a minute for the servants to gather more."

Lady Delmar shook her head, her red hair swirling around her face as she mouthed "No more." Her gills, three on each side, flared as she breathed, but there was a pair at the bottom that didn't open. In fact, they were nothing more than scars. It wouldn't have even crossed Laurel's mind that they were gills if she wasn't looking at the others.

The entire thing was odd, from watching a siren breathe underwater dressed in only a chemise to the fact that Aspen was locked in a dungeon across the castle from them.

How had the world come to this?

"Laurel, I can take care of Lady Delmar if you'd like to wash up as well. I have supper set to serve at eight."

The light out the window in Mater's room showed a full night sky.

Laurel nodded, taking a step away from the tub. She should probably check in with Conley and Mare before their shift changed at the dungeon in a few hours. It might be good to talk to Aspen. The sheer insanity that had been in her voice had hopefully calmed. Hopefully.

The water moved and Lady Delmar sat up. "Laurel," she said, her voice still rough, "I wouldn't recommend seeing Aspen tonight."

"Why not?" Laurel asked.

Lady Delmar's sea-green eyes flicked over her, searching. "We all had a long journey, her included. Being under the influence of my magic will have numbed her of all her own emotions for days. Those emotions will be a raging inferno in her now. It will be like feeling them all over again."

"Then I should be down there." Laurel's fingers clenched. "No one should have to feel all of that at once."

"That may be true but send someone else. Let your men take the brunt of it. If she channels all of it toward you, I fear it will only tear you apart further. She'll need you in the coming days to help her put it all back together. To figure out how she actually feels now that she's gotten to the base of them."

Laurel bit the inside of her cheek. "How do I fix this?"

Lady Delmar dipped back down into the water until her neck was below the surface. "I don't think this is something you can fix. Only the Goddess can change hearts. We just have to pray She changes Aspen's sooner rather than later."

Laurel stared at the ceiling of her room for hours.

Unfortunately, her mind wasn't like others' were. She felt every second that passed, could count back the seconds with a precision that rivaled a clock. But it made it difficult to let her mind filter out time, so she was only left with the mess she was dealing with.

She couldn't sit there.

She needed to do something.

Throwing her blankets off her legs, she got out of bed. Her toes curled into the fur rug under her feet as she stood and grabbed the long jacket laying across her trunk. She buttoned it over her chemise, feeling slightly better as she padded out of her room.

Her bare feet led her down into the kitchens, as they always seemed to when her mind was too full. She stopped at the door of the cold room. a towel-covered bowl sat on one of the many shelves. When she peeked under it, she found leftover *kataifi* dough from the wraps they'd had at dinner. The kitchen had put out quite the feast for Lady Delmar and Sir Heff. The kitchen was likely thinking of using the scraps for breakfast the next morning. Recipes flipped through Laurel's head until she landed on one in particular.

Ekmek kataifi.

With a sigh, she left the cold room. *Ekmek kataifi* was probably her least favorite dessert, but Aspen loved it. In the pantry, Laurel gathered a lemon, the jar of cinnamon sticks, and a pot of honey. She set the ingredients next to the stove and grabbed a saucepan. It took several minutes, but soon enough, the cinnamon and lemon peels were boiling in water over the fire she'd gotten stoked. She removed them from the heat and poured a good glob of honey into the mix and stirred it in until it no longer stuck to her spoon.

She left the syrup to cool and went back to the cold room to grab the *kataifi* along with some butter. A metal cake pan hung on one wall next to the pantry door and she grabbed it from the hook. She slathered the pan in butter and set some in a bowl on the hot stove to melt, then pulled the shredded dough in the bowl apart until it untangled. Half went into the pan before she drizzled the melted butter on top and added the rest. She set the pan in the oven and started counting down the half hour until she would need to flip the dough. The syrup had darkened, and she stuck her finger in it to taste. The tart lemon mixed perfectly with the sweetness of the honey. It wasn't as cool as she would like it to be, but she would just throw it into the cold room for a bit if it didn't cool by the time the dough had baked.

The custard would have to wait until the dough was done so it had time to cool. Laurel took the empty bowl from the dough to the sink. She could chop the pistachios for the top though. Her fingers wrapped around the pump above the sink.

"Can I help?"

Laurel spun around.

Paulo leaned against the doorframe to the kitchen. He'd abandoned his waistcoat somewhere and stood only in his shirt-sleeves. He still wore his boots, which meant he hadn't gone to his rooms, or he likely would be wearing slippers or something. Laurel curled her own bare feet.

"There's not much to help with," Laurel said, turning back to the sink as warmth spread up her neck.

She felt more than heard him move toward her. He sidled up next to her by the sink, reaching out to grab the handle of the pump.

The dirty bowl. *Right.* She grabbed one of the rags next to the sink and held it under the water as it came out of the spout.

"What are we cooking up tonight?"

"*Ekmek kataifi,*" Laurel responded, wiping the bits of dough that had stuck to the sides of the bowl.

"You hate *ekmek kataifi.*"

She looked up at him. "How do you know I hate it?"

He took the bowl from her and grabbed a drying towel. "That's actually a really funny story. I was watching along your fate line a few years ago when I saw you and Aspen having an argument about it. You had one lemon left in the cupboard that you'd been hoarding and Aspen found it. She begged you to make it for her and you said you'd been saving it for *lemonopita.*"

Laurel remembered that day vividly. It had been right after she'd gotten her own rooms in Stellatus Hall when Laurel had been fourteen. She'd broken into her savings to buy the rooms to share with Aspen after Teagan had said something about Aspen taking missions to get her own room away from the other girls in the hall. Laurel had seen the gleam in her eye and decided it would be better for both of them if she simply got them one to share. The kitchen had been installed only a week later.

"I lied to her," Laurel said, walking over to the oven.

"What?" Paulo asked.

"I was saving the lemon for *ekmek kataifi*, but she wasn't supposed to know. It was her birthday two days after that, and I had planned on making it a surprise. So, I told her I was using it for something else." Aspen had been spitting mad for the rest of that night, but Laurel had never seen her smile so big as she did when she saw that cake the morning of her birthday. It had been the first celebration they'd had in their new room. For just a moment, it had felt like old times. Like it was just the two of them and the rest of the world didn't exist.

Paulo barked out a laugh. "When I saw the vision, it was on my birthday. Well, mine and Diana's. It was finishing my last year of school and wishing I could be with her. When I saw that vision, I remembered all the fighting we'd done as children about the day and realized I didn't miss her *that* much."

Laurel took the bowl from his hands and walked to where the others were stacked. The smell of the dough in the oven told Laurel it was probably ready to flip. She turned toward the table to find a spatula, only to find Paulo standing there, one already in hand. He offered it to her.

"Thanks." She slipped it from his hand and turned back to the oven.

"I really hope the two of you are able to get past this."

The pan was hot as Laurel grabbed it with a towel. "Me too." She used the spatula to flip the dough and set it back in the oven.

"It's going to burn."

"Oh? What makes you say—"

The door to the kitchen burst open and Declan stormed in.

Paulo was in front of Laurel before she could even speak. "Not another step," he warned.

Laurel grabbed his arm, ready to shove past him when she met Declan's eye.

His face was twisted into a sneer, his gray eyes dark and angry. "Is it true?"

"Is what true?" Laurel asked, pulling away from Paulo.

Declan pointed a dagger at her accusingly, jaw ticking as he ground his teeth. "Were you the reason Luc died?"

"I didn't kill him, Declan." Laurel held out her hands but felt the blade tucked against her chest weighing down the front of her jacket. The explosion of emotion from him was more than she thought he would give. While Declan and Luc knew each other, came from the same town and had grown up together, she didn't think Declan would have cared this much.

"That's not what Aspen just told me." He took a step forward, but Paulo made a low rumble in the back of his throat. Declan glared but didn't take another step. "She said you stabbed him. That because of you he faltered, and the king took him out."

Her arms fell back to her sides, her heart sinking. "That did happen, yes." The memory of the Luc's scream and the smoldering floor flashed through her mind again.

His eyes widened slightly, as if surprised by her confession. "So, you turned against one of your own to protect a man you'd sworn to kill. To help a kingdom you don't even have allegiances to. Were you so ready to abandon your life that you had to throw it all away? Who are you going to throw at the king's feet next? Conley? Me? Do you actually want us to believe all that fluff about you wanting us to be a family when you literally betrayed one of the only people that truly cared about your family? You killed the last person I had, all because a pretty boy flashed his magic smile at you. You killed Luc to get into a mage's bed."

Something in her snapped and she shoved past Paulo to stand right in front of Declan. "If you think that's why I did what I did, you're more of an idiot than Luc was. Do you know what would have happened if the king had died? What destruction would have been wrought? You weren't there. You didn't see what they were doing to the fae. What they were doing to *children*. I couldn't let it continue, and I knew if the king died, there would be no stopping the rebels from taking the palace for good. Not stopping Teagan from taking innocent fae from their homeland."

"This is *war*."

"Yes, one we should have never been a part of." Her chest heaved. "This was never our fight, but we were forced into it, just like everyone else. The least we can do is figure out which side is the right one."

Declan laughed, the sound lacking all humor. "There's no 'right side' in a cursed war. There's only one and the other. You chose the one that betrayed everything the scholae have built. You betrayed the people who trusted you most."

Laurel straightened her shoulders. "You're wrong. I betrayed those who would rather see the world burn than fight for what's honorable. I refuse to fight for someone who wants to destroy people simply because the Goddess made them different. Look at those fae, Declan! I won't fight for someone who believes one life is less than another and so they should be treated as animals rather than people. I refuse to fight for someone who does that. That thinks everyone is simply a rung in their ladder to step on so they can rise to the top.

"Isn't that what your little lordling has been doing all this time? He hasn't cared one whit who got hurt as long as he got what he wanted."

"I thought that once," Laurel admitted. She didn't look back at Paulo as she said it, not wishing to see the hurt she was sure would be in his eyes. "But since returning from the palace, I realize there's a stark difference. Paulo, while misguided at times, does it to save, while Teagan and Adira Durant only do it to harm. Do I think any of it is right? Maybe not, but Paulo is incomparable to them because he doesn't want to watch the world burn."

Declan's eyes narrowed into dangerous slits. "Well, maybe I do."

He brought up the dagger in his hand.

Paulo tackled him to the floor.

The two of them grappled on the ground, Declan spewing every nasty curse he likely knew in Paulo's face.

Laurel snapped out of whatever spell had shocked her into place and grabbed one of the butcher knives from the block on the counter. She couldn't let Declan hurt Paulo. Couldn't let him hurt anyone. She watched the two men, waiting for an opening.

Paulo only showed grim determination as he got the upper hand. He ripped the dagger from Declan's hand, flipped it around, and knocked him in the temple.

Declan went silent.

Paulo stayed where he was, straddled on Declan's chest. His shoulders rose and fell with heavy breaths as he stared down at the schola. His knuckles went white around the dagger before he tossed it away from him and stood.

"What are we going to do with him?" Laurel asked.

He wiped a hand down his face, still staring down at Declan as his eyes shifted color. "We'll have to put him in the dungeon. I won't have him threatening you like that again. If we just let him go, he'll go right to Caspian."

"Are you sure?"

"I saw it. I found things in the room he shares with Xander a few days ago. In the vision I saw after, Caspian had been waiting for him in the woods. I knew tonight would be the night either he or Xander would make their move. He has to be the one who's been passing information on to the rebels."

She looked down at the schola. "He's been the mole this entire time." In her head, it made sense he was the one who betrayed them. He'd been the most vocal about them fighting in this war. He'd disagreed with it from the start. But something in her chest didn't sit right.

Paulo turned to her, the lines of his face stark in the light of the oven behind her. His attention strayed over her shoulder.

She spun around, finding the *kataifi* dough had burned to a crisp.

49

AN UNEXPECTED PAST

Paulo stood at the door to the dungeon and let out a long breath. His blood still boiled at the sight of Declan holding that dagger. At the memory of Aspen threatening Laurel through the door of her cell.

They'd both been in the cells for two days. Captain Isaac had put a guard rotation on the outside of the dungeon while Xander, Mare, and Conley all rotated shifts on the inside.

Paulo had offered to take Conley's shift at breakfast to give the man a break. The schola had taken one look at him and clapped him on the shoulder before striding away and disappearing. He probably thought Paulo would take back his offer and made himself scarce.

But there was enough at stake that Paulo would take the shift.

He nodded to the guards at the door. One of them pulled a key from the ring at his belt and unlocked the thick wooden door.

Silence, hungry and waiting, greeted him on the other side.

"Here," one of the guards said, passing him a magelight. "It gets a bit dark down there in the evenings."

Paulo nodded his thanks and took the magelight. He slipped it into his pocket and descended the stairs.

The door closed behind him like the top of a coffin.

Slowly, he stepped down the stairs until the cells came into view.

A pair of brown eyes peered through the door at the far end.

"Well," Aspen drawled, "it seems the lord of the castle isn't so proud to avoid mingling with the likes of us little people."

The creak of metal sounded from Declan's cell, but he didn't come to the barred window in the wooden door. Conley hadn't remodeled the cell as he had Aspen's, though there was a shiny new padlock in the door that hadn't been there before. At least, not that Paulo remembered.

Paulo found a small stool settled near the wall opposite Declan's cell. He sat, crossing his feet in front of him. There was nothing quite like pretending ease while two predators paced in cages only a few feet away.

"Did Laurel send you down here because she finally grew tired of looking at you?" Aspen drawled. "I know I already have."

Paulo pulled a smirk onto his face. "I'm flattered. I imagine taking in all this gloriousness would be like staring at the sun. Even my eyes grow weary with my own magnificence."

"Are you always such a preening idiot?"

"Not at all. I just have to reserve all piety for worship days. I can't walk into the Goddess's own temple and outshine Her. It wouldn't be in good taste."

Aspen scoffed. "Surprising to hear you would worship anything besides yourself."

"I can't disregard the artist for the art. I at least know how to give credit where credit is due."

"You say that as if I don't."

Paulo shrugged as he tried to slow his pulse. "You can make whatever inferences your guilt directs you to. It's certainly not my prerogative to tell you what an ungrateful hag you are."

Movement stirred behind Declan's door. "Ignore him, Aspen. He's just trying to get under your skin. He does it to everyone."

"Admit it, *Dec*," Paulo said with a grin, "you like it when I get under your skin. It makes you feel all warm and fuzzy inside."

Declan grumbled curses from behind the door but said nothing else. They'd been around each other long enough for him to know better.

"Is that how you got my sister to betray all of us?" Aspen said. "I figured you'd have to get more than under her skin to persuade her. I certainly know how a good roll in the sheets will tempt even the most stalwart of hearts to betray their loved ones. You can ask your king about that if you doubt it."

Paulo set a hand on his chest in feigned exasperation even as his blood boiled at her implication. Laurel would rather die than allow someone to use her like that. "If only your sister were so easy to persuade. Her heart is a steel trap that has ensnared me wholly. She's like the stars in the sky, gracing me with her loveliness, yet always so far out of reach. She is the moon, brightening my darkness with her light. I would likely perish at just the taste of her lips on mine." His heart had certainly stopped the first time she'd kissed him.

Declan's cell had grown very quiet at Paulo's words. Had he swooned? Paulo smirked at the idea of the brute fainting at the thought of such a declaration, as exaggerated as it was.

"Honestly, I'm surprised she hasn't just poisoned you at this point and taken your castle for herself. You're more of an idiot than I thought."

"I am a fool for love."

"We can agree on that. Laurel is unlovable. She's a snake that makes you feel like you mean something to her then strikes when you get too close."

Paulo pursed his lips in feigned consideration. "My sister had a snake once. A little whip snake. The creature had been injured and was hanging limply from a tree when she found it. She brought it home half dead and nursed it back to health. When she tried to release it, it kept slithering back into her rooms and she would find it curled up with her in bed in the morning. After a few days of it happening, my sister had a little terrarium made for it so it could be comfortable in her rooms, though the top always stayed open so it could slither back into her bed. Unfortunately, one day she woke up to find it lying on the ground near her bed, dead. Twisted in its grasp was a viper. When we finally figured out how the viper had gotten in, we realized the whip snake had been protecting her all those weeks by sleeping in her bed with her."

The two snakes had very obviously been fighting over a giant mouse that had gotten into Diana's room, but that was beside the point.

"Touching," Aspen spat. "And I imagine you'll tell me all about how Laurel is so great and has saved your castle and all that. Listen, I appreciate the effort— bravo for having the guts to come down here— but you don't truly know her. You don't know what she's really done. You don't know her like I do."

Paulo leaned forward on the stool, resting his elbows on his knees and setting his chin atop his hands. "I saw your sister for the first time when I was eight years old."

Brown eyes, narrowed in confusion, looked through the slot in the door. "What?"

He nodded. "I saw her make her first kill. Watched her as she had to stab a man in the chest. When the vision passed, I threw up all over my father's favorite coach. I saw the vision three more times after that, watched her as she killed this man over and over again. It wasn't until the third time that I realized why she killed him."

"She was an assassin. She killed people for a living."

Paulo shook his head. "This wasn't her first kill after training. This was in the girl's dormitory. She killed one of the other assassins."

Aspen's eyes lost their narrowness, widening with understanding. "I remember seeing a dead assassin in our dormitory. We all woke up and he was lying there with a dagger sticking out of his back. No one confessed to it and the whole dormitory got reprimanded for it. We had double the amount of training as the boys that day and all of us went to bed that night with lashes on our legs from the master's cane. I was so angry I told whoever it was to fess up."

"I remember," Paulo said. "Do you recall her coming to training the next morning with a bloody nose? She'd gone to do what you told her, but it turned into her reprimanding the master in charge over the children. She gave him a concussion."

Aspen's brows furrowed. "What? That didn't happen. She couldn't have taken out a master. She was the same level as me. I surpassed her in training when I was ten and she had to stay back with me."

"Didn't you ever wonder about that?" he asked, leaning back and folding his arms over his chest. "Somehow, she always stayed right next to you in training. Always got the same score as you in bouts. Always seemed to copy everything you did."

"She didn't have the talent I did. Ask any of the other assassins here. They'll tell you that Teagan always got on her about letting me surpass her. She had to practice outside of regular training hours just to keep up. She couldn't even graduate when she turned twelve like the rest of her class. It was only because of me that she was able to stay. I was the one who went to Teagan and asked for him to give her a chance."

A laugh rumbled from Declan's cell, the first sound he'd made since Paulo's flowery declarations. The laugh built until it echoed.

"By the Goddess, you're more delusional than Teagan." Declan's face filled the window, and he leaned an arm against the top of the bars. "With that ridiculous memory of hers, she didn't need extra training sessions. She could memorize strikes after one bout in the sparring ring. When she trained with us, she could watch us and perfectly replicate every spar and show us where we missed the mark. Could recall the name of every poison when she heard it for the first time even when Cal couldn't, and he'd created the cursed things. She wasn't practicing outside of training because she was behind, it was because the other masters saw her potential and wanted to give her more specialized training. They only pretended it was because she was behind in her studies to keep Teagan off their backs. She probably would have qualified to graduate at ten rather than having to wait for you to turn twelve and graduate with you. I was there when Master Schola approached her when she was fourteen, but she said she wouldn't join until you were further along in your own career. He pestered her for two years before she finally joined because of you."

"That's a lie!" Aspen shoved away from the window in her door.

Declan rolled his eyes. "Believe whatever you want, but I was there too. I saw the things she could do. I might not agree with what she's done, but there's a reason she became Master Schola."

"She tricked all of you, just like she tricked me! She's a liar and she doesn't care about anybody. Do you know she wasn't even going to stay at Stellatus Hall? Teagan told me she was one contract away from leaving it all behind. That killing the king would free her. That she would be able to pay off her contract leave all of us in her dust."

"Is that what he told you?" Paulo said. "Aspen, she could have paid off her own contract two years ago."

"No, she couldn't. She had to take this job. Teagan showed me the accounts. The payout from killing the king would pay hers off and she would leave."

"He didn't tell you what he'd promised her in the geas?" Paulo asked. "Laurel bargained for your contract. If she killed the king, Teagan would give her your contract and she could pay off the rest of hers. She was freeing you both."

Aspen's door rattled. "No, Luc was going to free us. It's the entire reason I came to Olympia with him. The reason I've stayed to complete his mission. He's the one who bargained for my contract. He told me he was going to kill the king to free us from Teagan and Laurel. She killed him for it. She killed him for trying to take her own victory from her. For trying to save me."

"By the Goddess, you really are a brat," Declan grumbled.

"And you're a gullible idiot who's following blindly behind a lying witch!" A rather hard thump shook the iron door. "She's faking it. She's trying to convince all of you she's better than she actually is."

"And what about you?" Declan bit back. "You're the one who was wearing a cursed scholae mask without taking the oaths. At least the rest of us can say we actually earned our silver."

"Teagan gave me that mask!"

"Teagan Obscuritas is a bigger liar than the rest of us. The only way he made it to the top of the food chain was by making promises he has no intention of keeping and killing children. He goes to bed at night with a guard at his door because he knows one day those sins are going to catch up with him, and when they do, he'll wish he'd jumped from the top of the hall and saved us all the trouble of having to kill him ourselves."

Paulo pretended to pick lint from his trousers. "All this talk about Teagan is making me nauseas. Let's get back to talking about Laurel."

"I think I'm done talking to both of you." Aspen's shadow disappeared from the little window.

"Good riddance," Declan muttered. He walked away from the door, going back to his silent corner.

Paulo let out a sigh. "I really wish Laurel hadn't burned the *ekmek kataifi* last night. It would have been nice to share a bowl with her before I had to come be around you lot."

"Laurel hates *ekmek kataifi*," Aspen said, her voice a bit muffled.

Paulo pulled what he hoped looked like a confused frown onto his face. "Oh? Why would she have been up in the middle of the night making it then?"

Aspen remained silent for the rest of Paulo's shift.

50
THE SHED

Xander will rise from where he lays in the bracken of the forest, his brown eyes darkening. He will pull a blow dart from the pocket of his trousers. As a shadow walks toward the water, he'll load the dart into a tube and raise it to his lips.

THE WHIP OF LAUREL'S FISTS HIT XANDER IN THE STOMACH WITH QUICK succession.

He let out an audible wheeze as the air left his lungs. He was able to get one of his arms wrapped around her neck though and brought her to the ground.

She slammed her head into his face then reached up to jab her thumb into the pressure point of his elbow. When his arms loosened, she elbowed him in the gut and rolled to her feet.

"Great Goddess, Laurel." He coughed, trying to get some air into his frozen lungs.

She straightened, dusting off the dirt and bits of straw from the sparring ring. They'd finally been able to move the training grounds back outside to give the builders space to fix the ballroom. With the capital back in King Dion's hands, the kingdom was beginning to turn a corner. She watched as Xander struggled to get air. "You need to work on guarding your front. I shouldn't have been able to get that many hits in."

He pushed himself up to sit. "Good thing I don't plan on getting in too many hand-to-hand fights then."

"Don't get cocky." She turned to where the servants usually left water.

She jumped back as Paulo nearly barreled into her.

He skidded to a stop at the edge of the ring and spun around. "Hello, Laurel. I saw you were out here instead of at lunch where I had originally intended to see you. Did you miss me? Xander, do you have any blow darts on you?"

Laurel wiped a hand down her face. "What?"

Xander got to his feet, patting down his jacket. He reached into the pocket he usually carried them in but came up empty handed. "I actually left them in my room this morning."

Paulo blew out a breath. "Shame."

"Is something the matter?" Laurel asked, watching Paulo study Xander.

"Not anymore," Paulo said, turning back to her. "Are you done for the day? I was hoping to talk to you about what our plan is for the prisoners."

Laurel turned to Xander. "Looks like you're good to head to lunch. I would talk to Mare about setting up a time to work on your guard."

"I'll ask her about it." He gave the both of them a little salute and marched away.

"I really would like him more if I didn't keep seeing visions of him doing assassin things."

Laurel shrugged. "Maybe he's more like Mare than we thought."

Paulo came up beside her. "Maybe."

"Did you actually come out here to speak with me about Aspen and Declan?"

"Partly. I saw Xander with a blow dart yesterday. Lucky for him, he left them behind. I can't wait for this blasted war to be over so I can quit worrying about everyone trying to kill us all the time."

It really must have been weighing on him because his eyes

were a bit darker than they usually were and his voice carried a serious note she still wasn't accustomed to hearing from him often.

She stepped away from him and grabbed the ladle next to the water bucket. "If you want to work off all that anger, I'm still feeling like a fight." She took a large gulp of the tepid water. The summer heat was trying to linger even though autumn had technically come the week before.

"You want to get thrashed so badly?" he asked.

"Oh, is that how you think it's going to go?" she chuckled, setting the ladle down and turning back to him. "I've been out here practicing while you've been lounging around your fancy castle all day."

He quirked a brow, pulling his arms out from his dark-green jacket. While he didn't reply to Laurel's taunt, his broad shoulders defied her quip about him lounging. He was wider now than he'd been before the siege. The extra training he'd been doing had only honed him into a perfect specimen.

Sweet Gaia, she was ogling again.

She cleared her throat. "Swords? Or would you rather spar with staffs?" What other long reach weapons were there? The idea of getting too close to him sounded dangerous right now. Her stomach had been doing strange things in his presence for weeks, and it was starting to turn into a problem. She didn't need this right now. Not while her sister was trapped in a dungeon.

His deft fingers quickly untied the simple knot at his throat. "I think staffs might be the best option. You seemed a little intense when you fought with Xander, and I'd rather not get stuck on the end of the sword." He folded the cravat and set it on top of his jacket.

Laurel ripped two of the staffs from the rack. "Are you done undressing or do you want me to go get Jenkins to help?"

A wicked smile stretched across his lips. "Why get Jenkins when you'd probably be so much better at it?"

She scoffed and threw the staff at his face.

He caught it, his eyes a miasma of color. The staff spun in a lazy loop as he circled the ring.

Laurel matched his movement, mirroring his every step as he made a full lap around the ring.

The side of his jaw twitched. "I spoke with Aspen."

The flutter in her abdomen fell. "I figured you would when you took Conley's shift. I hope she wasn't too bad."

Paulo chuckled. "The conversation was certainly enlightening. It's always a novelty to speak face to face with the people I have visions about."

Laurel knocked her staff into his, halting its spin. "What are we going to do with her?"

His staff twisted in his hands, pinning hers under it. "I don't know yet. Her future isn't set. She still has quite a few decisions to make."

Laurel's staff slipped from its pin, and she took a step back. "What do we do next?"

"We wait. I'm not sure for what yet, but I think the Goddess is waiting for something. I haven't had many new visions lately. It's happened a few times, when there's a precipice that needs to be faced. There have been many world-altering decisions made of late. The lines of fate have never been so intertwined."

"There you go again, getting all mystic on me." Laurel sent a jab at him.

He dodged it and swung at her legs. She jumped over the staff and struck at his shoulder.

Words were replaced with the whir of the staffs. The slow cadence of their steps grew frenzied. The crack of the staffs against one another bounced off the castle walls. Paulo met her strikes hit for hit and she did her best to keep him on his toes as she seamlessly moved from defense to offense. Her heart was a steady beat against her chest, counting out the steps only she and Paulo knew. Neither one touched the other, but they drew closer, their breaths in sync as they whirled around one another.

The dance was intoxicating.

Laurel felt everything around her fade away, all except Paulo. He was bright in her view. His eyes danced with magic, and she felt herself pulled toward them.

He had to have felt it to, as he seemed to be drawn in by the same pull she was.

They got so close that when Laurel swung at his shoulder, he was able to step right up to her, locking their staffs between them. She could feel the flutter of his heart under her fingers now trapped against his chest. The magic that had danced in his eyes fled, leaving only that bright blue she could drown in.

"Paulo—"

His lips crashed into hers.

That flutter in her stomach erupted.

She grabbed the front of his shirt, dropping the staff between them.

His staff fell on top of hers and he wrapped both arms around her, sinking his fingers into her hair and pulling her toward him until they were flush against each other.

The kiss grew into two, three, four, each one more urgent than the last. She wrapped her arms around his neck, and he leaned down to sweep her up into his arms, only taking his mouth from hers to move it to her neck as he walked them across the sparring ring.

She couldn't breathe as he pressed his mouth to her throat, her jaw, her ear. This kiss was nothing like what they'd shared in that dark hallway in the palace. That had been a moment of whim. That had been two bodies struck by want.

This, this was *need*.

He kicked open the door to the old weapon's shed and set her back on her feet only long enough to press her into the wall at the back. The door behind them creaked closed, but she lost herself back into Paulo when he returned his lips to hers. Lost herself to the feel of his fingers in her hair and the press of his body against her. He shielded her completely from everything around them, filling her mind with nothing but him. Nothing but his lips against hers.

By the Goddess, she would never kiss another man. There was no one else for her but him.

She loved him.

She loved him *deeply*.

She had for a long time, and she just hadn't wanted to accept it. Told herself that it wasn't possible. That it was a trap.

But if it was, Paulo was just as trapped as she was.

She felt the thrum of his quickly beating heart under her palm. Felt the untamed desire in his palms as he cradled her jaw in his hands and tilted her chin up to deepen the kiss.

Something pushed against her mind.

At first, she thought it was just the fierceness of Paulo's kiss muddling her thoughts. His teeth dragged against her bottom lip and the feeling dissipated. Her fingers dug into his silky curls, and he moaned, making her stomach flip. His hands slid down from her face and to her hips, his fingers curling around her belt and pulling her closer to him even as his broad frame crushed her into the wall behind them. He demanded every inch of her, every bit of her attention, every beat of her heart. She could do nothing but comply, her own need demanding the same of him with every press of her lips to his. With every beat of her heart against his chest.

Her knees buckled and he wrapped his arms around her, his mouth moving from her lips back to her neck. Every inch of her came alive.

But the push in her mind came again, and she turned to it.

Her mind exploded with magic.

Colors, smells, sounds, all one after another. Lines of color woven into a tapestry of time. Of fate.

She heard Paulo gasp the same time she did.

The magic settled on a green line, ripping her from the present and into the future.

Penny will storm through blood-spattered snow, her arms glowing green as she wields a sword. A scream will rip through the air, and she'll spin, following the sound.

The youngest prince, the new High King, will watch as a fae with pale eyes will fall to the ground, a sword of shadow dissipating from his chest.

Another scream will rip through the air and Prince Dair will charge against the king. Penny will use her magic to pull him away from the fight.

Adira Durant will turn to Penny, manic glee in her eyes as Penny summons a ring of trees to surround her, The Cartographer, and the High King. A man will step through the trees, as if a ghost. The High King will engage him as Adira will attack Penny.

The magic evaporated and Laurel fell to the ground, Paulo falling with her. They landed in a heap, sending several jars on the shelf next to them crashing to the ground. Paulo's forehead rested on her shoulder. Their breaths were labored between them, and Paulo's arms tightened around her.

"You saw."

All she could do was nod.

"By the Goddess, you can see my visions. You..." His lips pressed against her neck, gentle and light.

Her heart skipped at the touch.

"Do you realize what that means?" he asked. "Do you know what you seeing my magic actually means?"

It took her several seconds for her mind to settle enough for words to form.

"What?"

He pulled back, just enough to meet her eye.

"It means, you Laurel Flumen, are in love with me."

She blinked at him. "What? No, it doesn't."

"It absolutely does. The magic wouldn't work otherwise. I can only share my magic with those I have a deep connection with. Someone who has made a mark on my soul. I've only ever been able to share it with my family— much to King Dion's frustration. Most mages only can share it with their close family members and their life partners."

Heat flared in her cheeks, and she tried cover it up with a glare. "By the goddess, Paulo. This is not the time to make another one of your fake proposals."

He laughed then cradled her face in his hands again. "If you let me, I would marry you right this second because now I know what we have is real. Even if you don't see it yet, the magic recognizes it in you. I can wait as long as it takes for you to recognize it, but it's true. We have something beautiful between us, and I'm not going to let you try to lie your way out of it. Not now. Not after that."

Something lodged in the back of her throat, and she had to swallow it back down. He couldn't know, not when she'd just realized it for herself. Not when she hadn't come to terms with it yet. Loving Paulo came with things she didn't know if she could handle. Love wasn't going to win them this war. Love wasn't going to save Aspen or defeat Teagan. They didn't know how all of this would end, and she couldn't tell Paulo she felt something for him only to have them ripped apart. She couldn't make him promises she didn't know if she could keep. She needed to figure out if love between them was even possible.

"I love you, Laurel, and I'll wait an eternity for you to figure it out," he said, as if reading her thoughts. "I'll follow you to the very ends of the earth if that's what it takes but know I'm never going to give up. I'm never going to let you go."

"Paulo—"

His lips captured hers once more and the protests burned away.

51
AN UNEXPECTED SISTER

IF PAULO'S HEAD WASN'T POUNDING SO HARD, HE WOULD HAVE BEEN dancing. Or singing. Or some other loud boisterous exclamation of everything he was feeling.

Laurel felt something for him. Something deep. That was the only explanation for why his magic would have connected with her. Mage gifts could only be shared with those the mage shared a connection with. A two-way connection. Like the bond between a parent and child. Or siblings. Or lovers.

The fact that she saw his magic should have him shouting from the rooftops.

Gaia just had to put a dampener on this as well.

He looked up from the sketchbook in his hand and grabbed the cup of ginger tea he'd poured himself before he'd started the sketch. The cup was cool to the touch. *Blast it.* He drank the lukewarm contents in one big gulp, nearly gagging when it slid down his throat. It hit his stomach like a rock, but hopefully the ginger would help ease the pain behind his eyes.

The sketch in his lap wasn't his best work, but it would do. The High King knelt in the mud, Penny in his arms and the resurrected Hart next to him, as the sky fell from above them. He jotted down today's date and stuck the pencil between the pages. If he had to guess, he'd estimate this battle would happen within the week. It was too large a fate to happen in the distant future, when a thousand different decisions could throw it off track. He'd combed through it, looking for each thread of fate tied with this battle. Each string turned white. Each life hanging in the balance. There would be consequences of this battle that would ripple through generations.

With the drawing done, he closed his eyes. He'd have to check Laurel's fate tomorrow.

Just thinking of her brought a string to the forefront of his thoughts.

A string of steel turned white.

He shot up from his chair, the magic falling away instantly.

"No," he whispered.

He reached for the string again, shoving his hands into his hair.

There, on Laurel's fate, shone the color of death.

He plunged himself into the magic, pulling the string right before it turned white.

Paulo will hold Laurel's limp form in his arms, the sky red above them as he screams.

And no matter how many ways he looked at the line of fate, it never changed. Every path they took, every choice they made all led here. All led to him losing her.

Paulo ripped his consciousness from the vision.

How was he going to change this? He'd done it for Queen Carnation, her fate changed by the decisions Laurel made before the palace was taken. But who could save Laurel? What would it take to ensure this future never came?

"My lord?"

He looked up and found Jenkins standing in the doorway, the pitcher from Paulo's washstand and a towel in his hands.

Jenkins's head tilted to the side. "Is everything all right? You look as if you've seen a ghost."

Paulo scrubbed at his face. "I don't know. I don't know what I saw. It was the fate of a ghost. The ruination of everything I've worked for. The death of life and love and a future worth having."

"That sounds rather awful." The valet's eyebrows shot up. "Is there anything I can do?"

Paulo plopped back down into his chair. "I don't know. I don't even know what to do."

Jenkins walked through the small sitting room and into the bedroom where the washstand was. He returned empty handed and hesitantly sat in the chair across from Paulo's.

"How dire is it?" he asked carefully.

Paulo swallowed. "Very."

"Then there must be a way to change it." Jenkins steepled his fingers against his chin. "I don't think the Goddess would give you such a vision if there wasn't something you could do to alter it. Or at least understand how She wanted you to turn it around. You've had dire visions before and there's generally a reason for them. I'm sure there's something—"

"Jenkins."

"Yes, my lord?"

"Shut up."

"Yes, my lord."

Paulo blew out a breath. If there was a way to stop Laurel from meeting that fate, he would find it. If he could convince her not to get on that boat or maybe they could get to the ship before Teagan could. There were so many pieces. He would have to comb through every one. Fiddle with every possibility. He'd seen Queen Carnation's fate change from white back to blue. He could figure out how to change Laurel's. He would.

"Sorry, Jenkins. I shouldn't have told you to shut up."

Jenkins shrugged. "I understand. I was letting my thoughts get away from me." He stood, giving Paulo a smile, though worry still pulled at the corners of his eyes. "I think perhaps some rest will do you good, my lord. There will be more answers when the sun is there to shine on them."

Paulo rubbed at his temples. "I hope you're right."

Paulo's eyes opened.

His bedroom greeted him. There was soft light coming

through the window behind him, the moon shining through which meant it wasn't close to daybreak.

He blinked. Why was he awake?

The scratch of paper being flipped sounded behind him.

He sat up, pulling his magic to the front of his mind.

Aspen sat on the floor under the open window. Her golden hair glowed silver with the moonlight. He only saw the side of her face, the light coming from the window highlighting just enough for him to see her eyes trained on the book in her hands.

A sketchbook.

"You're rather good," she said, flipping the next page.

He rolled out of bed, coming to stand on the side opposite to her. "What are you doing in here, Aspen?"

She flipped another page. "I came to kill you. I figured if Laurel was so willing to throw away her life for you, your death would be the heaviest blow, and I didn't know how many I could take with me before she finally killed me."

Paulo's fingers curled into fists. "Then why am I not dead?" How had she even gotten into his room? How had she escaped the dungeon?

"Because I saw the book next to you on the bed. It was open to a page with Laurel's face on it. You said you'd seen her for years, so I got curious." She turned the book so he could get a glimpse of the pages. On the left page was the vision of Laurel getting her silver mask. On the right was one of her and Aspen sitting next to each other on a bench, both of them laughing.

"I don't remember what we were laughing about in this one."

Paulo swallowed. "I think it was when Luc accidentally dyed his hair orange."

A smile touched her lips. "I'd forgotten about that. He'd used the shower in our rooms and had used one of Laurel's cleaning bottles, thinking it was some kind of hair soap. She always used whatever bottles we had on hand. He had to shave his entire head. He wouldn't talk to me the entire day because he was so embarrassed. That was the same week I told him I loved him."

Paulo kept his mouth shut. He wouldn't lie and say he was sorry for her loss. He wasn't. Luc had been a blackguard who tried to hurt Laurel. Anything Paulo said would come out bitter, so it was better to stay silent.

Aspen quietly flipped through a few more pages. "Ah, this one I remember."

It was a drawing of Laurel crawling through a window, a long box in her hand.

"It was a dress, wasn't it?" Paulo asked.

Aspen shook her head. "A coat. It was this beautiful red coat I saw in a shop in Vale after returning from a mission when I was fifteen. I'd taken Laurel to see it after, but it had been gone when I went to look. She sneaked out the next day and asked the clothier about it and ordered a special one made for me. I wore it until the seams were practically bursting. I'd grown six inches from the time she'd bought it, but I wore it until I couldn't even move in the thing."

Paulo leaned against the post of his bed. "She does care about you, you know."

"I don't know what to believe anymore." She pulled another sketchbook into her lap. "Like this. You marked it as happening four years ago, but it could have only happened last year." She raised the book up and showed him the picture of Laurel slicing her hand with the geas blade, Adira Durant and Teagan sitting around the desk with her.

"I saw her coming to Olympia then. I saw what path Teagan would go down with Adira."

She flipped through a few pages, landing on another. "And this one?"

The image of Laurel lying in a pool of her own blood screamed at him from the page.

"I saw a few days after."

"But it didn't happen."

"Not all of my visions come to pass. Sometimes, the present can be changed to influence the future. Some things are inevitable, but some aren't."

She shut the journal with a snap. "I've been through most of these now and almost all of them have images of Laurel's death."

The bands around Paulo's chest squeezed his ribs. "Yes."

"Why does she keep dying?"

"Because she can't help it."

She looked up at him. "Can't help what?"

"Dying for what she believes in."

Aspen grabbed another notebook and opened it to another image of Laurel's death, this time with a sword in her stomach. "What happened in this one?"

"She was discovered snooping around the palace looking for you after she hadn't heard from you for a few days. Six guards were returning from an early patrol, and she didn't know about the change. They caught her by surprise."

"Why didn't it happen?"

"Your taking over of the palace didn't take as long. The timeline never reached that point."

"What about this one?" She flipped to a page with Laurel lying on the ground surrounded by pieces of pottery.

"An accident. The flowerpot dropped from two stories up and smashed into her skull. She died from a head injury on her first day in Olympia."

"And?"

"I distracted her long enough that she wasn't right under the pot when it fell."

"And this one?" She held up a picture.

Paulo had to bow his head. "That was what happened if she stayed in the palace after the king escaped. She would try to free some of the fae slaves."

She tapped where a long dagger stuck from her neck. "This is Luc's blade."

"He was the one who caught her. He was able to call for enough men and they overwhelmed her."

"Luc would have never killed her."

Paulo quirked a brow. "He looked pretty serious about killing her when they fought in the palace."

Aspen's lips thinned but she didn't deny it. "Why does she keep dying?"

"I don't know."

She looked up at him. Tears hung at the corners of her lashes. "I know I said I wanted to kill her, but I don't want her to die. I don't actually want this."

Paulo slowly walked around the bed so he was on the same side she was. "What do you want, Aspen?"

A sob cracked from her chest. "I just want things to go back to the way they were. I want to wake up in Stellatus Hall to the smell of Laurel's cooking and the sound of Luc's laugh. I want to look at the hideous flowers decorating the kitchen cupboards and the chipped cups set next to the sink. I want my family back. I want Laurel to stay with me instead of disappearing all the time. I want to bicker about stupid things like how almond biscuits are better than butter biscuits. I don't want to hate her anymore. I want her to stay with me."

He crouched down. "Laurel's still here, Aspen."

Aspen wiped her face with her sleeve. "She left me behind. She ran from me during one of the worst moments of my life. Didn't try to fight for me or stay for me."

"Would you have actually let her? You're the one who told her to leave."

"But I didn't expect her not to come back! She completely abandoned me and has been frolicking around this castle like it's her own personal fairytale. She was supposed to come back for me, to say she's sorry and fix it like she always does."

Paulo gritted his teeth. "Would her return have actually fixed it? Because from where I've been sitting, it never did."

"What is that supposed to mean?" she bit back.

He grabbed one of the sketchbooks and flipped open to the page in the back. "See this? This is what happened if she tried to come back to the palace on her own."

Aspen covered her mouth with her hand.

The two sisters took up both pages. Aspen had her hands around Laurel's neck, her face twisted in unadulterated hate as she screamed down at Laurel, who looked up at the ceiling with empty eyes.

"This would have happened three months ago, if Laurel had decided to go to you. The siege stopped it from happening. There's more if you'd like to see them. I can show you what happened if the king had fallen in the takeback of the palace. Or when Caspian Delrio dragged her back to the palace in chains when our defense of the castle fell to the rebels."

She dropped the book as if it burned her. "I don't want to see."

"I may not be able to read people's thoughts, but I can see their hearts based on the decisions they make. If Laurel had come back to you at all, she would have died by your hand."

She covered her face, her whole body sagging against the wall as a muffled sob shook her.

"And that's not even the worst of it. Tonight, I saw fate pull taut."

The door behind him burst open and Conley stormed in with five guards.

Aspen leaped forward, grabbing Paulo's shoulders. "What did you see?"

He met her tear-filled eyes. "I saw her die to save you."

The guards ripped her away from him, but she didn't fight.

No, the fight had left her completely as they dragged her limp form over the dozens of sketchbooks.

All with Laurel's death tattooed on their pages.

5²
THE ESCAPE

Declan's cloak will conceal him as a squad of guards runs past the tree he's hidden behind. He'll tuck his hood lower and head deeper into the woods. He'll count under his breath, his silver mask trained down at the ground until he arrives at his destination. Caspian will be waiting for him.

"He's disappeared."

Laurel slammed her fist into the door of Declan's cell. "How on Gaia's green earth did he get out of his blasted cell?"

Xander shifted, gently prodding his broken nose. "I don't know. One second, he was behind the door and the next he wasn't."

With a growl, she stomped toward Aspen's empty cell. "How could you let them both escape? Neither of them should have made it out of here, let alone both of them. You were supposed to alert the guards if anything happened."

"I—"

The dungeon door burst open, and an entire squad of guards hustled down the stairs. Aspen's gold hair, greasy from lack of a proper bath, hung limp in the middle of the group.

Conley trailed behind the guards, his dark eyes never leaving the back of Aspen's head.

"How did you find her?"

"It wasn't hard. She was sitting on the floor of Paulo's room."

She stiffened. "What happened? Is he all right? Did she hurt him?"

"He's fine. It looked like all they'd been doing was talking."

Well, that was completely unbelievable. Laurel spun on her heel, marching toward Aspen's cell. The lock slid into place right as she banged her fist on the door.

"If you hurt him, Aspen, I swear on every cursed star in the blasted sky—"

"I didn't hurt him," Aspen said, her voice quiet. "I barely touched him."

"Don't lie to me."

"I'm not!" Aspen's eyes filled the window. "If you're so worried about it, you can go check on him yourself. I didn't hurt him."

"Why should I believe you?" Laurel's voice lowered. "Why should I trust anything you say when you'll lie straight to my face?"

Aspen's eyes clenched shut. Two silver tears slipped from the corners of her eyes. "I deserve that, but I promise I truly didn't hurt him. I couldn't hurt him. Not after what I saw."

Laurel's chest tightened. "What? What did you see?"

She opened her eyes and more tears fell. Her lip trembled with so much emotion Laurel nearly stepped back.

"Laurel!"

She whirled at the sound of Paulo's voice.

He pushed through the crowd in the dungeon, and she met him there. There was no blood anywhere. No discoloration around his nose or mouth. She ran her fingers around his neck, but there were no needle marks. She grabbed the front of his shirt.

"Love, I don't think you want to undress me in front of everyone. We wouldn't want to give them the wrong idea."

She froze, meeting his eye. His face was a bit drawn and his hair a complete mess, but he

looked completely fine.

"You don't feel dizzy or like you're going to throw up? What about feverish?" She reached up to check his forehead.

He wrapped his fingers around hers. "Laurel, I'm completely fine."

Air finally seemed to be able to enter her lungs and she sagged. Her arms wrapped around his waist of their own accord, and she pressed her face into his chest. "Praise the Goddess."

"I told you," Aspen said.

Laurel dropped her arms and turned back around. She set her hands on the pommels of her daggers and stepped toward the iron door. "How did you get out?"

Aspen leaned her face against the door, her eyes red-rimmed. "Your little schola let me out once he busted from his own cage."

Conley stepped up beside Laurel. "Did you see how?"

"He had a key to open my door, so I imagine he had the same for his."

Laurel looked to Conley. "Was his door tampered with?"

He shook his head. "It looks like he actually did get his hands on a key."

Which meant someone had either been lax in their duties or he had gotten help.

"Was there anyone else in the dungeon when he escaped?" Laurel asked.

Aspen shook her head.

Laurel turned around and found Paulo studying the door. "How did we not see it coming?"

He glanced back at her then crouched down next to the door. "I was occupied with larger fates this evening. He must not have been plotting it for long since I didn't see it over the last few days."

"Do you know where he's going next?"

Paulo stood, his magic whirling.

"Yes. He's going to meet with Caspian."

Rain poured down the glass of the sitting room window. The storm had appeared seemingly out of nowhere. Iatrus Castle's resident weather mage, Eden, had said it was likely the consequence of so many magically induced storms, the atmosphere around Olympia had to reset itself. There would likely be more freak storms, and the winter months would either be too dry or too wet.

Magic always came with a cost.

Laurel cradled a cup of tea in her hands. The fine porcelain of the cup was painted indigo, with swirling suns of gold leaf glimmering around the top edge. She hadn't brought the cup to her lips. Her stomach was in too many knots.

"You can't go off in this storm, Diana," Mater said, pouring herself another cup of tea. "Not even Caspian will be running about in this. We'll wait it out and send the guard to search the forest. There's no sense in you going out there right this second."

Diana paced in front of the crackling fireplace. "I know he's still out there. Paulo saw them in the forest. They could be right outside the castle. There are plenty of spots to tuck away to keep from the rain. I could go look through each of them."

"Then what? Are you going to fight them on your own?" Mater picked up an almond biscuit. "At least for the guard, don't go out in this. Wait until the storm passes."

"I'm tired of waiting," Diana growled. "It's been three days since Declan escaped and I'm tired of sitting around while Caspian's scheming plans to attack us again. I'm tired of this cursed war."

"Here, here," Laurel said, raising her cup.

Mater turned to her. "Laurel, what news from your sister? Have you spoken to her yet?"

"We had a brief conversation." Three days ago. Where Laurel accused Aspen of hurting Paulo. Which she hadn't. Why hadn't she? There was no way that hadn't been her intention, but what had actually stopped her?

"I'm glad she had a chance to speak with Paulo," Mater said. "Oracles always know the right things to say."

How true those words were. Every argument she'd had with Paulo always dissolved rather quickly. He always knew how to diffuse a situation as efficiently as possible. If Laurel wasn't so cursed logical, she might have been angry. But she wasn't. It was likely what had kept Aspen from slitting his throat.

Diana grumbled by the fireplace.

"Why don't you go see what Oliver is up to?" Mater suggested. "I know he and Ariana were going to take a walk this afternoon, but it looks like the storm will be around for a while longer. They might be up for something more to your liking."

Diana's steps slowed and she let out a sigh. Her mouth opened with a retort, but she glanced at Mater and whatever she was going to say died.

"Fine." She stormed from the room, her steps more of a stomp than her usual stalk.

Laurel carefully set her cup down. That had been much too easy.

Mater stood and went to the open door, shutting it behind Diana. She turned around and set her hands on her hips, a wicked grin on her face.

"So, are you going to tell me what has been going on between you and Paulo? Or am I going to have to guess?"

Oh, sweet Gaia.

Laurel kept her gaze. "What are you talking about?"

Mater returned to her seat. "I'm talking about the fact that my son has been vacillating between grinning like a lovesick puppy and staring out of windows like he's died and haunts the halls of this castle."

"I've barely seen him since they caught Aspen in his rooms." Between trying to track Declan down in the woods and whatever fate searching Paulo had been doing down in his cave, they'd barely spoken. Laurel hadn't really had time to even think about the kiss they'd shared. The touch of his lips on hers. The feel of his magic. The vision he'd seen. The way he'd looked at her after. When he'd told her he loved her.

All right, so maybe that was all she'd been thinking about.

"Oh my," Mater said. "He's gotten to you, hasn't he?"

Laurel straightened. "What?"

Mater's lips curled up in a knowing smile. "He's finally broken you down. You've realized you're in love with him."

"I don't know what you mean." She snatched her cup off the table to give her hands something to do.

"I think you know exactly what I mean. You two have been dancing around each other since the moment you arrived at the castle. The two of you have changed so much in the past few months it seemed it was only a matter of time."

Laurel sighed and slouched back in her chair. "I don't know what to do."

She hadn't said the words out loud until now. She really felt as if she were being pulled in a hundred different directions. There was this war to think about. And Aspen. Declan. Teagan. There was her geas and the fact that Stellatus Hall had been taken. There was the other scholae to worry over. The war in Faerie. It seemed like there were a million other things that should be taking up her attention, yet her heart pounded at the very thought of Paulo's smile and the deep desire she had to count every single one of his freckles. Of feeling the press of his lips against her skin again. Of telling him how she felt.

"Love isn't often convenient," Mater said. "Especially love with an oracle. Take me and Phineas for example. I was nearly an old maid by the time we found one another. Not for lack of trying on his part. It is rather difficult to meet when you live on different continents."

Laurel sat back up. "What do you mean 'different continents?'"

"My dear, Paulo takes after his father in more than his looks and magic. It seems his romantic tastes are much the same. I came to Olympia from the Continent when I was twenty-eight and married Phineas a year later."

The teacup in Laurel's hand nearly splashed all over her in her haste to set it on the table. "How did I not know you were from the Continent? Where are you from?"

"Manifesta, on the southern end of the coast. My father was a tradesman. When Olympia had really started opening up to trade under the Tyrant King's father's reign, my father was one of the first to travel here. I remember him coming home after his first trip with stars in his eyes. He told my mother that very day that when they were ready to sell the business, they would pack up and move to the magical isle. I'd been fourteen and he kept his word. Fifteen years later, my parents packed our things. I was the youngest in my family, all three of my older sisters having already married and left the house, so it was just my parents and I that made the trip."

"That must have been quite a journey." Manifesta was hundreds, maybe even thousands, of miles down the coast from Vale. Laurel had never even gone that far south, and she'd been all over the Continent, even going to the far north where the mountains were too tall to climb. Where the people told tales of frozen wastelands on the other side of the mountains, home to giants and women with the power to control the elements.

"It took us nearly three months on a boat," Mater continued. "An experience I never wish to relive. I was seasick the entire journey and have sworn off ever setting foot on a boat again. I still have nightmares about it."

Laurel chuckled. "You've been trapped on this isle as much as I am."

"In a sense. I will say, stubbornness is not the same as forced imprisonment."

"That's true." Laurel stared at Mater, seeing her in a completely new light. While the woman's hair had grayed, it had been dark once. The deep brown of her eyes and more olive tone of her skin certainly spoke to her heritage. Even the shape of her nose wasn't the straight pert things Laurel saw throughout Olympia. It was a strong, Continental nose. It had all been easy to overlook in Olympia, as the people on the isle were all so colorful due to the proximity to Faerie, but now that Laurel knew, she could see it.

"But I remember vividly that first day we got off the boat in Eleusia. While it wasn't as bustling a town as it is now, it was still like walking into an entirely new world. I remember seeing my first mage. It was a mage filling and selling magelights on a street corner. I bought one right there and carried it with me for years after that. It still sits atop my vanity, though the magic ran out ages ago. But I can't get rid of that first taste of magic."

Laurel could easily imagine the feeling. While she'd had a little more exposure to magic before she'd arrived on these shores, she was still awed by the enchantment of it all. The wonder.

Mater chuckled. "That was nothing in comparison to meeting Phineas."

"I'm not going to rise to the bait and ask how that came about."

"Well, I'm going to tell you anyway."

What felt like magic unfolded from Mater's story.

Mater had been invited to her first real society event within her first three months of living in Olympia. Her parents had bought a house just north of Eleusion and had become next door neighbors to Patricia Byrne, who married Lord Hermen. The two had become friends and Patricia's father was the third son to a baron who had served as one of the king's knights, so they were involved in just enough society to make connections. Patricia had invited Mater to a picnic, where Lord Phineas MacGregor had also been invited.

"I remember him walking into the room for the first time. Every eye followed him. 'The marquess,' they all said. I could barely keep my eyes off him. He had very obviously been looking for someone when he entered and when he met my eyes, that search ended. He smiled so widely my heart had nearly handed itself to him right there and then. He almost plowed through the crowd around him before he made it to me. With no introduction he said, 'Hello, Ms. Absconditus, I would like to dance with you.'"

Laurel snorted. "So, the ego comes with the magic then."

"It would seem that way, but I've never met a humbler man than Phineas. I'm pretty sure Paulo got his self-confident streak from me. After all, I told Phineas that he would be sorely disappointed to find I would not like to dance with him."

"Good for you, Mater."

She grinned. "I wasn't going to be one of those pattering flirts that seemed to follow after him just to get a whiff of his title. I was a woman who knew what she wanted and had spurned many a man before him, much to my mother's dismay. Patricia nearly fainted at the slight, but Phineas's smile only grew and I knew this man was it for me. That I had found someone worthy of my regard. Little did I know what an adventure it would be."

"Did you know he was an oracle right from the beginning?"

She shook her head. "He told me three weeks into our courtship. We were walking in a park, and he saw a child fall from a tree and break his leg. Phineas left me standing in the middle of a path to run through the bushes like a madman. He barely caught the child as he fell, but the only casualty had been Phineas's coat. He'd torn it running through a bush. It was when I asked him how he'd known that he told me about how his magic worked. Then, as cocky as I was, I asked him what he'd seen about me. Sweet Gaia, the look on his face had me blushing like a debutante during her first dance."

Laurel shook her head. "The MacGregor men seem to know how to really get under the skin."

"We courted for six months before he finally asked me to marry him. When I asked him later why he waited for so long, he said he didn't want to ask until there was absolutely no way I would have said no. He didn't want there to be any other possibility but my absolute agreement to the match. He wanted it to be fate. We had a lengthy engagement due to my family having to travel to get to us, but we made it to the temple and said our vows."

Laurel bit the inside of her cheek. "And everything was happily ever after, right?"

Mater met her eyes, the wistfulness falling to contemplation. "Certainly not. I had no idea what I'd gotten myself into. That first year of our marriage was fraught with disagreements. Neither Phineas nor I were much for yelling, but we certainly cried at each other plenty. Sometimes, it felt like he was manipulating every situation and doing everything he could to keep me happy with no regard for himself. It took us quite a few years to figure out how to work together, to find happiness together instead of trying to make happiness for the other. It also didn't help that it was a struggle for us to have children. I felt guilt every time my body wouldn't allow a babe to grow, but Phineas was always so optimistic. He of course knew Paulo and Diana would come, but it was still difficult. It takes a strong will and a patient heart to know the future and yet wait for it. But we learned how to find joy together, and in that joy came so much love that I would have never imagined for myself standing across from him and denying him that first dance. If I had known then, I would have demanded he marry me right then and there."

Laurel watched as Mater smoothed out the dark gray skirt of her dress. The color of mourning. "Was it worth it? Even though you lost him?"

Mater's eyes limned with tears. "Absolutely. I would never trade the time I had with him even if it was to erase the heartache of his passing. Nothing could have prepared me for his death, even if we had known it was coming for years beforehand."

"How did he die?" Paulo had never told her, only that it was a tragedy.

"The doctor that did the autopsy said it was a complete fluke. His heart just stopped working. One moment he was walking back to the castle from his early morning ride, the next he was gone. Paulo was the one who found him. He was thirteen."

And he blames himself for it. Laurel had seen it in his eyes whenever he spoke about his father. About how he would never live up to his greatness. She could see the guilt over not being able to save him, even though there was nothing he could have done even if his magic had seen it. Perhaps it had been a mercy for the Goddess to keep it from him. Knowing when someone would die and knowing no one could stop it would be torture of the worst kind.

"All this to say," Mater continued, "loving someone who can see the future is no easy thing, but it can be the best decision you ever make. There will be no greater adventure than the life you can build together. It was never easy with Phineas, but it was always worth it."

Laurel dug the heels of her hands into her eyes to get rid of the prickle that was starting up. "I don't know if I can give him what he wants. I don't know if I'll ever be able to give him the kind of life he deserves. I'm not one of your court ladies with their fancy dresses and good pedigrees. I come with baggage. I don't know if we'll go to bed one night and wake up with blades to our throats. I don't know if I'll be able to stay with him if we don't win this war. I don't know how I'm going to be able to be what he needs me to be."

Mater set a hand on Laurel's knee and gave it a squeeze. "I can't tell you what to do. I can't say that there won't be times that you wish you'd chosen something easier, but if you feel for him as deeply as he feels for you, I think you should at least give it a chance."

"How do I do that?"

"You let yourself fall."

53
AN UNEXPECTED TWIST

Paulo stared down at the swirling letters in front of his eyes. His pounding headache made reading nearly impossible. The last several days had been filled with trying to find Declan while also trying to get rid of the white on Laurel's fate line.

Neither of which had been successful.

"You look like you need a stiff drink."

Paulo folded the paper down far enough to see Donnie lounging in the chair on the other side of his desk.

"Drinking doesn't solve everything."

"Then maybe you need something else. I saw Laurel wandering about the castle a little while ago. Perhaps she could use some company."

Paulo straightened the paper back up, concealing Donnie's smug grin once again. He was doing his best to give her time. Forcing his feelings on her wouldn't get him anywhere. He'd seen her speaking with Mater a few days before and realized she needed time to straighten herself out without his interference. Without her feeling like he was manipulating her. Not that it was easy. Every few seconds, he had to talk himself out of marching out of here to find her and kiss her senseless. Which was why he'd had Donnie come sit in the study with him while he waited for Captain Isaac to bring the latest report.

Today was the day they would find Declan.

But how they would find him was still up in the air.

A knock reverberated through the room and Hiatt opened the door.

"My lord—"

Captain Isaac burst into the room, not waiting for the butler to finish. "He's in the castle."

Paulo shot to his feet. "How did he get in?"

"He slipped through the west wall. Sent us on a merry little chase through the forest opposite the lake, but it was all a misdirect. He sneaked into the castle while we were distracted."

"Curses. Where is Laurel?"

"I don't know. Mare was sent to track her down, but we don't know where she is."

Paulo's magic flooded him.

Laurel sits on a stool next to an empty cage, piles of cloth-covered furniture surrounding her.

Paulo grabbed the sword leaning against the wall next to the desk and raced out the door, leaving both Donnie and Captain Isaac behind. He passed by guards combing the halls, and Mater called after him, but he ignored them all as he strapped his sword to his hip. The front door burst open as he shouldered his way through it. The rain from the previous few days had left the grounds a muddy mess, but he ran toward the northernmost tower on the outer wall even as the mud tried to pull his boots from his feet. The door to the base of the tower was open and he threw himself down the stairs.

At the bottom, he found Laurel standing in the middle of the room, daggers in her hands.

"Oh, great Goddess." She sheathed the daggers at her thighs. "I come down here to try to mull over what to do about you alone in the dark where I don't think anyone will find me and here you are, just bursting in. How am I supposed to figure all this out when you insist on intruding on every moment of self-reflection I try to take?"

His brain wasn't quite able to wrap around her words, his pulse still spiking. "What?"

She rolled her eyes. "Don't act like you didn't know exactly what I was doing."

"I don't know what you've been doing." He looked around the room. "It doesn't matter right now anyway."

"So now you aren't going to stick your nose into my business?"

He gave her a flat look. "Your business is my business. Like how Captain Isaac just came to tell me Declan is in the castle."

Laurel's brows rose on her forehead. "Oh. That's way more important."

She tried to walk past him, but he snagged her sleeve.

"What were you doing down here?" All of Cal's experiments had been removed from the space, Laurel having deemed them too dangerous to have lying around. All that was left from his time down here was a few empty vials and the empty cage where Cal had kept a few bats.

"I thought it would be quiet enough for me to think. Cal had the right of it. There's little to distract you from your own mind down here."

"You say that as if it's a bad thing."

She huffed, but it was more amused than frustrating. "My mind is much louder than it needs to be right now."

Without meaning to, he found himself reaching up to rub his thumb over her cheek. "You can always come to me, you know. I'm always happy to help quiet your mind."

She glared up at him, but there was something in her eyes that made the expression feel false.

It made his stomach swoop the tiniest bit.

The scuff of a boot sounded behind Paulo.

"As touching as this is, the two of you really need to quit trying to undress each other with your eyes and focus."

Paulo spun around, pulling Laurel behind him and drawing the sword at his hip.

Declan stood on the bottom step, his gray eyes narrowed at them.

Laurel stepped up beside Paulo, though she kept her daggers sheathed at her sides. "Have you come to turn yourself in?"

He met her gaze. "No, I've come to cash in my boon and help you find a traitor."

She frowned at him. "What do you mean?"

He leaned against the opening, pulling a broken arrow from the pocket of his jacket, the black fletching catching the light as he twirled it with his fingers.

"Have any of you seen Xander recently?"

Conley pushed the top of Declan's head down until he plopped into the chair in the middle of the sitting room. "Don't think because you used your boon to plead for clemency that I won't hesitate to stab you if you so much as twitch in a way I don't like."

Declan glared up at him, straightening his jacket.

Paulo stood opposite them. It wasn't the most intimidating interrogation room, but it was the only place all of them could fit in.

Laurel stood next to him on one side and Captain Isaac stood on the other. Mare had placed herself at the window beside Diana. Six guards took up a post on either side of the room and two more stood outside the door. Mater sat in a settee close to the fire, a cup of tea in her hand. Paulo knew better than to ask her to leave.

"Talk," Conley demanded.

It had been two hours since Declan had revealed himself at the bottom of the tower. He had willingly returned to his cell once Captain Isaac had finally caught up to Paulo. The hunt for Xander had begun right after. Paulo had searched the man's fate line, but all he saw was forest and him finding Caspian near a stream. He couldn't tell exactly when it would happen, but it was all he could see. As if Xander's fate hung in the balance of what Declan would say.

Declan straightened his jacket, giving Conley a slight glare, before turning to Laurel. "Xander has been betraying us from the beginning, and I was two days away from proving it when you all got it in your heads that it was me."

"Explain quicker," Conley demanded.

Declan rolled his eyes. "I caught him sneaking back into the castle one night, weeks before the siege. He said he'd gone to take a walk, but he'd been acting weird since we arrived in Olympia, disappearing at odd times and always knowing the strangest things. He was the one who figured out you were here in Delphine when none of us could figure out where you'd disappeared to after the capital. He said he learned it from one of the rebels that had come out of the palace, but it didn't sit right with me. I kept my eye on him after that. When he sneaked back into our rooms that night, I knew something was going on."

"You're wasting time," Conley drawled.

"I'm getting there!" Declan snapped. "After that, he started talking to himself, going over things like guard numbers and patrol rotations. It was odd for him since he didn't usually care about anything outside his own responsibilities, but I chalked it up to us being in a new place. It wasn't until stuff started going missing during the siege that I began to suspect him."

"You mean the things we found in your room," Laurel said.

Declan nodded. "That's when I knew he was a mole."

"Why not bring it to one of us?" Conley asked.

"Because I wasn't sure none of you were helping him. Mare only has allegiance to herself now that Serene's gone, and you couldn't decide whether to stick around to help Master Schola or pull all of us from this cursed place. Cal was the only one I might have told because it seemed he had enough sense in his head, but he died before I was sure."

"Why not tell me or Paulo?" Laurel asked.

"And put the rest of the scholae on their guard? No. If I went to you two, it would have marked you as untrustworthy and I knew if we left, you lost the siege. We were too far into it to risk the upheaval, and I didn't have enough proof to make it a sure thing."

"So, you didn't trust us and instead allowed a traitor to run around for months," Conley said accusingly.

"I couldn't figure out how he was getting the information to the rebels. It wasn't until I got a hold on the blasted shell that I realized how."

Paulo looked to Laurel, whose eyes had gone wide. The white shell. The one Laurel had found under Declan's bed.

"It wasn't just a normal shell, was it?" Paulo asked.

"It was a communication device. Xander kept it tucked in the breast pocket of his jacket. When I was trying to look for where he was hiding the reports he'd stolen, I found it. It was lying on the floor by his bed, and I knew it would get stepped on. I stuck it in my pocket to give him later but forgot. I didn't know what I had until he went on a rampage looking for it. Said it was his lucky shell, but he was frantic looking for it. It sounded off to me, so I hid it inside my mattress. You know how assassins are. We don't keep sentimentals. So, I looked at it again. Turns out, if you pressed it to your ear, it wasn't the sound of the ocean you heard, but the person on the other side listening in."

"By the Goddess," Laurel said.

Paulo ran a hand through his hair. *By the Goddess is blasted right.*

"That was enough to implicate him," Paulo said. "Why didn't you use it?"

"Because whoever was on the other side heard me too. They figured out I wasn't Xander and killed the enchantment."

"You lost your proof," Paulo said. And so had Laurel. They must have found the shell after Declan scared the Aigeans off. If they'd been quicker, if Paulo had worked harder... He shook his head. "But you still could have brought it to us."

"Except I thought Xander would stop. He seemed to like you, Lord MacGregor, and I thought with the loss of the shell, it would give him an excuse to let it go. But he didn't. More things kept happening that shouldn't have, so I started sabotaging everything he was doing. I tried to make him look the fool so you would all look in his direction."

Laurel took a step forward. "You cut the springald's skein."

He nodded and looked over her shoulder at Conley. "They shouldn't have known about the catapults you built. The strike on the tower where Laurel fought was completely intentional. It was the least threatening, considering it was the farthest away from any of the enemy encampments. No, the rebels knew what they were doing when they took out the tower. I just couldn't figure out how they knew until I got my hands on one of his arrows."

Captain Isaac pulled the broken arrow from where he'd stowed it when they'd taken Declan into custody. "It's hollow."

Declan nodded. "He'd been sending things through the arrows. I can't be sure, but I suspect the rebels knew about Laurel's whereabouts because of the springald bolt that went into the lake. It wasn't a misfire, but an intentional one. While it sank into the water, the Aigeans must have been watching for it and pulled it from the lake during the fight. That's why they were the ones that targeted the tower."

Laurel rubbed at her forehead. "You could have brought any one of these things to us, Declan."

He scoffed. "None of you would have believed me. This kind of evidence would have never held up in Stellatus Hall. You would have taken his word over mine since I had disagreed with staying the most. You would have never suspected him of it, so I needed to have solid proof."

"Except we already suspected he would betray us," Paulo said.

Declan's attention snapped to him. "What do you mean you already suspected him?"

Paulo set his jaw and met each of the scholaes' gazes. "I suspected each one of you of betraying us."

All three sets of eyes went wide.

"How?" Declan asked.

Paulo looked to Laurel. He hadn't fully confessed all of this to her.

But she gave him a nod to proceed.

With a sigh, he explained how the first day they arrived at Iatrus Castle he started to have visions of each of them betraying them. Of Mare's disappearance. Of Conley's coup. Of Declan's assassination attempts. He explained about the others' too, how Cal would have poisoned Laurel, and Serene would have gone to the rebels along with Xander. Their faces grew more and more pale as he explained each time he'd stopped them from making that choice, even if they didn't realize it.

"The reason Xander was able to make it this far was because his treachery was the least cause for concern. Most of what I saw was him meeting with Caspian once then keep talking to himself. It wasn't until just before your capture, Declan, that I saw him meet with Caspian again."

"That's because I finally figured out they were meeting. I

found that broken shaft floating in the lake. I'd gotten out on patrol ahead of Xander and was waiting at the shore when I saw it. I snatched it out and read the note inside before whatever enchantment it had on it made it evaporate. It gave some coordinates and told Xander to meet there in two weeks, saying they'd received word from Teagan."

"Curse that man," Laurel said under her breath.

"I was going to tell you, Laurel, and have us catch them in the act. Then you returned with Aspen, and I didn't have the chance to say anything before I was put on babysitting duty and your sister got into my head. When she told me you killed Luc, I lost it. He was the only link I had to my past. My own family. When Aspen told me you killed him, it felt like the betrayal I'd been thinking you would make. Been *wanting* you to make. I knew how Luc felt about you and Aspen. You three were as close to family as anyone could get in that cursed hall. At first, I didn't understand why you didn't tell us when you had Diana lay it all out when we first got here, but I get it now. You knew we weren't trustworthy, and you were right. If I'm being honest, I'd been looking for a reason to take you out since I arrived, and when she said that, all those thoughts came roaring back. I should have listened to you. You've proven to be the master we needed, and I let rage blind me to that."

He looked to Paulo. "I shouldn't have said those things about you that night. I can see now that you're the reason all of us have made it this far. That this side is the right side."

"If you knew all that, where have you been?" Conley asked.

"I went to the meeting with Caspian. I waited at the spot, watching for Xander to show up, but he never did. They must have thought he got the first note and never sent another. When Caspian was about to leave, I showed myself. He thought I was Xander at first, then realized I wasn't him. He ran."

Paulo nodded his thanks but turned to Captain Isaac. "So now we need to figure out where Xander is going to meet Caspian. All I have is a vague location near a creek. It could be anywhere in the blasted forest."

Diana stepped forward.

"I can help with that."

54
THE REVENGE

Diana will fly through a star-studded sky, an angel of death and revenge as she releases the arrow between her fingers.

IT WAS LIKE THE FOREST WAS HOLDING ITS BREATH.

No birds chirped their indignation at Laurel and Diana's invasion of their territory. No trees bristled in the cool autumn wind. Even the sky above them was still, as if the very stars stared down at them with unblinking eyes.

Diana was a wolf next to Laurel, completely silent as she stalked her prey. Laurel was more than attuned to Diana's movements, having shared far too many hours in this forest with her. She was able to match her stride as they raced through the trees.

Xander and Caspian wouldn't last the night.

Laurel's blood was cool in her veins, an iciness taking over every bit of her body. Her silver mask likely reflected the blank slate of her face under it.

She was no longer a creature enraged by the betrayal of one of her own.

No, she was the monster fate had molded her into.

The sound of babbling water brought their quick pace to a

slow jog. Diana turned south, not going straight to the water, but keeping them close enough to still hear the creek.

Laurel shadowed her.

Their pace slowed as they approached a bend in the shallow river. The water funneled together to fall a few feet. Not a far fall, but the crashing water was enough to mask the hum of voices.

Diana darted from tree to tree until they could see the creek.

And next to it stood two cloaked shadows.

The figure closest to them shifted, the hood of his cloak unable to conceal the curling grin of his silver mask.

Declan had been right.

Diana ducked down, staying as low to the ground as she could while also keeping her feet. Being so close to the water gave them thicker vegetation to blend into, and Diana used it to her advantage.

But Laurel didn't.

She glided through the shadows, dancing through them as if she were trading one partner for the next. She flicked back the tails of her long jacket and pulled two throwing knives from their sheaths at her waist.

Xander was the first to realize she was there.

He tried to run.

With a flick of Laurel's wrist, she sent a throwing knife into the back of his leg.

He tumbled to the ground.

Caspian drew a spear from his back and threw it. Laurel dodged it, though just barely. It caught the very edge of her sleeve against her bicep. The selkie was wicked fast, but his aim still wasn't good enough. When Caspian attempted to get to the water, Laurel threw her other throwing knife. In order for him to avoid it, Caspian had to leap back toward the trees.

Laurel got between him and the river.

He brushed the sandy dirt from his shirt. "Laurel is that you? I didn't recognize you without Paulo panting after you. Is he on his way then?"

The attempt to get a rise out of her only made the ice in her gut thicker.

"We don't need him for this."

"We?"

Diana struck.

She leaped from the trees, her bow drawn with an iron arrow.

Caspian turned right as she let go of the string.

The arrow lodged itself in Caspian's shoulder.

He didn't even have time to scream before Diana was on top of him. They hit the ground, but Diana didn't fall. She rolled off him, coming to her feet a few steps away.

Xander tried to crawl away while he thought Laurel was distracted. She slammed one of her long daggers into his cloak, the edge of the blade glancing off his leg. He yelped.

"Shhh." Laurel stepped forward, running the tips of her fingers over his hood until she could grab his mask and gently turn him to face Diana. "I want you to watch. I want you to see what happens to those who betray a hunter's trust."

Diana switched her bow to her nondominant hand and drew a buck knife from her waist. The bone handle gleamed in the starlight as she charged Caspian.

The selkie bared his teeth, pulling a long, needle like blade from his waist. He dodged Diana's jab, parrying with one of his own.

She ducked low, using the tip of her bow to smack Caspian's ankle.

He yelped, jumping back.

But it opened him up.

Diana slashed her blade across his selkie skin.

The sealskin fell to the ground.

Caspian yowled, a keening, desperate sound, as he reached for it.

Diana slammed her knife into his hand, stabbing through both his palm and the pelt under it, pinning him to the ground.

He screamed.

Diana pulled one of the arrows from her quiver and used it to saw through the sealskin.

Caspian screamed as if she were skinning him alive. He writhed until he finally pulled the buck knife from his hand. He slashed at her with the blade and Diana jumped back. With bloodied hands, he reached forward and grabbed the pelt. He made a mad dash for the water, but when he tried to use the pelt the magic took far longer than it should have to help him transform.

Diana stepped up to the bank and nocked an arrow. She shot him in the shoulder halfway through his shift.

He reverted back to a man.

"*Diana!*" he screamed. "*Please, Diana!*"

She shot him again.

He dodged the arrow, diving below the water and swimming a few feet up stream. The magic finally took, and with a roar, his seal form barreled forward through the water.

Diana watched, the white fletching of her arrow against her cheek.

A single tear fell.

Then another.

Yet, she didn't shoot. Something in her eyes, that darkness that hadn't let up since the moment Cal had died, disappeared.

Caspian swam, the splash of his panicked swim fading as he disappeared.

Diana didn't lower the bow until he was completely gone. Her eyes found Laurel's and she gave a small nod. While Caspian still lived, she'd gotten what she wanted. She'd found her justice.

And now it was Laurel's turn.

Laurel grabbed the top of Xander's hood and drew it back.

Xander yelped as she ripped the hooks from the mask and tore the silver from his face.

His brown eyes were wide as they met Laurel's. "I'm sorry, Laurel."

Laurel tossed the mask toward Diana, who had grabbed another arrow from her quiver and trained it on Xander.

"I don't want apologies, Xander." Slowly, Laurel circled him. "I want answers. How long have you been spying on me for Teagan?"

Xander swallowed. "From the moment you joined the scholae."

She absorbed the answer, letting it settle next to the ice in her gut but not break through it. This treachery wasn't new for Xander.

"How did he get you involved?"

"It shouldn't be hard to guess. I have another twenty years on my contract. He said he would cut them down to ten if I reported to him about you when you made schola. I didn't have much of a choice, so I said yes."

Teagan would do something like that. Laurel's grip tightened on the blade in her hand. It wasn't enough that he had her contract. That wasn't enough control for him. He had to pull on Xander's leash too. He'd been angry when Laurel had taken her oaths as a schola. He'd berated Master Schola right in front of her for even suggesting such a thing. But Teagan had no say over the scholae. He couldn't decide who would be invited in and who wouldn't. He hadn't been asked to join and that had certainly left a mark on him. Master Schola had told him to "stop throwing a tantrum" and hadn't even blinked when Teagan threw a slew of curses at his back.

"What kind of things did you report to Teagan?"

Xander's face had lost most of its fear as the confession continued. "Everything. He asked about training regimens you took part in. Asked about what Master Schola had you doing. Asked about your relationship to Aspen. Asked if you ever had any relationships with any of the other assassins. It was all asinine up until you became master. After that, he started having me look through your files, compiling information on the other scholae and what missions we were given. He became obsessed with trying to get rid of you before you could pay off your contract. He knew if you left, there would be a shift. That if you went to start your own guild, he'd lose half the hall."

"Then, the Olympia job showed up," Laurel concluded.

"Then the Olympia job showed up," he parroted. "I wasn't part of that conversation, but he approached me after you left and said once he had confirmation of your death, he would call my end of the bargain fulfilled and would knock my contract down to those ten years."

Laurel stood from her crouch. "Unfortunately, I didn't die."

"No, you didn't. You were in that palace for months without even being caught, and it was driving him mad. When he realized he couldn't go with Aspen to the palace and had to go with Adira to Faerie, he brought Luc in. Made a deal with him for his and Aspen's contract if he killed you and the king when they took the palace."

"But I escaped."

"I didn't even know you escaped until I received word from him. The Mist had finally fallen, and I got a missive from Teagan, saying you were still alive and running about Olympia. That he wanted me to come and help him find you. I got that letter two days before the hall was taken. I'd already bought passage to Olympia, but Conley insisted we stay together. So, I convinced them to come to Olympia to look for you. I figured it would be far easier for six of us to track you down rather than just me. I bought the rest of the scholae passage, them never knowing that I had already paid my way."

"How did Teagan get in contact with you once you were on the isle?"

"He'd told me to go to the capital and wait for *The Shining River* to come to harbor. The ship was going back and forth from Faerie, transporting fae slaves to the palace from the Summer Court. Teagan told me to speak with the captain. When I finally met with the captain, he told me one Caspian Delrio had spotted you at Iatrus Castle and was preparing to lay siege. He told me to get into the castle and make contact with Caspian."

By the Goddess, it was all so much worse than she'd thought. Teagan's disdain of her had been growing for a long time, but she hadn't realized how deep it had run. She knew he didn't like her, knew he wanted her dead, but this? This was far more than distaste. This was hatred. This was envy. This was a man who would see the world burn just to make sure Laurel didn't get what she wanted.

And all she'd wanted was to leave him to his little paradise and never look back. If he'd just let her leave, he probably would have gotten everything he wished for.

"I was just the mole," Xander said. "It was just a job. You of all people should be able to recognize that, Laurel."

She nodded. "You're right. I do understand. Thank you for telling me, Xander."

He visibly sagged. "I'm so glad you see reason. I really do like you, and I'm glad you've stuck it to Teagan all these years. I'm eager to see you knock him from his throne."

"But you won't see it, Xander."

He frowned. "Well, maybe not from a dungeon, but still."

"You aren't going to see the inside of a dungeon either."

He blinked. "What?"

Laurel's arm whipped out and her blade slid across the flesh of his throat.

He gagged, his hands coming up to wrap around the wound.

She stood over him as he bled out.

"You won't see any of it because you'll be dead. You're the reason Cal is dead. The reason Serene died. You're going to bleed out in this forest alone and even the scavengers that feast on your body will celebrate your death. You are stripped of all the honors of a schola and cursed to face the consequences of an oath-breaker in this life and in the life to come. May the Goddess have mercy on your soul, though I doubt She will."

He fell to the ground, his life bleeding out onto the forest floor.

But Laurel wouldn't even give him the honor of being there when his heart finally gave out. Without another word, she walked away, Diana following right behind her.

55
AN UNEXPECTED PANIC

Paulo couldn't even see the ceiling of the cave as the magic whirled around him.

Laurel. Dead.

Dead.

Dead.

Dead.

Her line of fate stayed that bright glaring white no matter how many possibilities he ran through. No matter what he tried to change. It was like the Goddess was laughing at him. Like She'd been toying with him all this time, making him believe he could save Laurel when he could do nothing but watch her die over and over again.

He slammed his hands against the stone underneath him and roared at the ceiling.

The magic exploded around him.

Penny, opening a package with the MacGregor seal.

Paulo, cradling a limp Laurel in his arms as red lightning flashes above them.

Penny's maid, Sissy, holding a glowing spear.

A shadowy figure running from something through an oak forest when hands reach out and pull them into a tree.

Paulo, laying a headstone on top of a grave in the castle graveyard.

Prince Evan, dragging himself onto a sandy shore.

Aspen, crying at the foot of a newly filled grave.

"No!"

The magic fled from him, leaving only black spots at the edges of his vision.

His lungs couldn't get air into them. He couldn't breathe. His breaths were shallow and fast. He couldn't get enough. Couldn't make his lungs expand.

"Paulo!" Mater called from somewhere behind him. Her face appeared before him, her brown eyes wide. "Darling, breathe!"

As if his body recognized the command of its creator, his lungs finally drew in air.

Laurel appeared next to her. "What's happened? What's wrong?"

Mater went to her knees and set her hand on his chest. "He's panicking. Keep your hand on his chest. Encourage him to breathe. Help him recenter himself in this time. I'm going to run for Jenkins." She hurried to her feet and disappeared.

Laurel quickly took her place, setting one hand on his chest and wrapping her other around his fingers.

"Breathe, Paulo. Look, like this." She took a deep breath in and let it out slowly, then repeated.

Paulo tried to copy her. Tried to meet her slower pace. His chest shuddered with every breath.

"Do you feel my hand on your chest? Try to focus on making that go up and down slower."

The weight of her hand suddenly seemed like all he could feel. It was heavy and it trembled slightly. Was Laurel frightened? He took another deep breath, this one easier than the last.

"Do you hear the spring? Seems like your flood door is open. I can hear the water going out."

He could just hear it over the blood rushing in his ears. The soft gurgle of the water escaping out into the tunnels.

Laurel lifted his hand that she'd been holding and brought it to her chest. "It smells like damp earth down here. You smell like it too. Under your fancy cologne, I get a whiff of this room whenever you brush by me. I didn't know what it was until I came down here for the first time."

He couldn't smell it, but he could smell her. She smelled like fresh forest. She must have gotten back from tracking down Xander and Caspian. It was the reason he'd come down here in the first place. He'd wanted to send men if they needed them. But his magic had pulled him in. Had brought him back to Laurel's death over and over again.

"Hey, hey, don't go back. Stay with me." She reached up from where she'd had her hand on his chest and brushed a hand through his hair. "I'm right here. It's going to be all right. You're going to be all right."

He watched her, studying her face as his breathing slowed again.

"Diana?" he asked, unable to get any other words out.

"She's fine. She just went up to her rooms to change. I came to find you and found Mater instead. We both heard you yell and came rushing down here. She's going to get Jenkins."

Paulo nodded. Mater had said that.

"Do you want to sit up?" she asked, setting her hand on his shoulder.

He nodded again, and she helped him up to sitting. He still shook, his body completely spent. He felt the pulsing of his head, but it was still dull in comparison to the squeeze around his chest.

Laurel rubbed a hand down his back. "Do you want to talk about it?"

He shuddered.

"All right, bad question. That was a bad question. Um, did you know that pistachios aren't actually a nut?"

He blinked. Had she really said pistachios? "What?"

"Pistachios aren't nuts. They're actually a drupe. It's a type of fleshy tree fruit. Almonds aren't nuts either. Their technically seeds."

"How do you know?"

"I read it in a cooking book when I was younger. There was a bookstore in Vale I liked to peruse. I would quickly skim every new travel and resource books they had and buy the ones I knew Aspen could use later. Every once in a while, they got in a recipe book, and I would read those too."

He shook his head. "You were stealing knowledge from the bookstore."

"Hey now, I bought some of them. Stellatus Hall didn't have a very good selection, as books were regularly pilfered for coin and the valuable ones were hoarded. I had to get my hands on my own knowledge somewhere."

She laid her head on his shoulder but kept rubbing his back. With every stroke, the bands around his chest loosened a fraction and his breaths came easier.

"Thank you," he said.

"For what?"

"For helping me. For not being frightened by all this."

She rubbed the side of her nose against his shoulder, likely getting rid of an itch. "Please. This is the least scary thing I've gone up against. Besides, I just watched your sister nearly tear Caspian to shreds. Now, *that* was scary."

He blew out a breath. "He's not dead."

"No," she said with finality, "but he left, and I took care of Xander. We don't need to worry about them anymore."

A breath stuck in his lungs, but he pushed it out. "That couldn't be further from the truth."

Mater and Jenkins arrived, Mater's face creased with worry and Jenkins muttering up a storm. Maybe Laurel could recommend a few recipe books for him, and he could take up cooking as a hobby.

"I knew you'd help him, Laurel. Here, dear, give Jenkins your other arm and we'll help you up."

Paulo allowed Laurel and Jenkins to pull him to his feet. His legs had gone completely numb and he hadn't even noticed. He teetered as he walked, but Jenkins kept him upright.

"I've got him from here, Miss Laurel, if you would like me to take him."

Laurel wrapped an arm snuggly around Paulo's back. "I'd like to see him to the top of the stairs if that's all right with you."

They got Paulo up the narrow steps and out into the office. They sat him on the sofa and Jenkins set to getting a fire going in the fireplace.

Laurel grabbed Paulo's hand in hers once again. "Is there anything else I can do?"

He pulled her closer, settling their clasped hands over his still rapidly beating heart.

"Just stay here. Don't leave me."

She looked past him at where Mater stood, but he was too tired to turn his head to see what had captured Laurel's gaze.

"I'm not going anywhere."

Paulo slept through all of breakfast and barely touched his lunch the next day. Donnie offered on multiple occasions to track down more of Grandfather's secret stashes to share, but Paulo declined the offer. He couldn't allow himself to get lost in his magic again. It would only drive him mad.

Laurel hadn't been at either meal, so he went looking for her. He didn't use his magic, instead allowing whim to pull him one direction or another. The rain had returned, so he guessed she wouldn't be outside in the training yard. She wasn't in her rooms or the sitting room with the other three scholae. She wasn't with Diana either. He swept past the open library door to ask Mater when a shadow in the library window caught his eye. He back tracked and there she was.

Her head lay against the window, her eyes closed. A large tome sat in her lap atop a thick blanket she must have found in the trunk next to the fireplace. She was sound asleep.

He carefully crept across the room. He couldn't ever remember seeing her sleep, not in visions or in present time. It was like she was always moving. Always making decisions that would change fate over and over again.

There wasn't much light filtering through the rain clouds, but he could make out the softness of her lips and the scar near her ear. She'd gained another handful of scars over the last few months. He prayed there wouldn't be more.

When he went to sit in the window seat, her eyes opened.

"Paulo?" She sat up.

He set a hand on her knee and pulled some of the blanket onto his lap. "Sorry I woke you."

She closed the book she'd been holding. "What is it?"

He swallowed. "There's something I need to tell you. Something I need to ask you."

She shifted, closing the book in her lap and setting it on the floor. "That doesn't look very promising. What's going to happen?"

Paulo felt the lump in his throat growing. "Teagan is coming to Iatrus Castle."

Laurel took in a deep breath. "We knew that was going to happen, especially after we found out about Xander."

"It's more than that. Xander was able to get information to Caspian before he escaped. The blasted selkie is going to tell Teagan everything before running for the Isles of Aigean like the coward he is. Teagan's going to come to the castle. He's going to take Aspen."

"How?"

"He'll walk into the dungeon and say he's freeing her. Drag her out kicking and screaming. She'll be happy to see him. Angry. Sad. I don't know. There's too many things."

"All right. We can try to figure something out."

He shook his head. "That's not it. If he takes her, we go after her. He gets her on a ship. A ship with red sails. They try to leave. You make it onto the ship. You give yourself to Teagan to try to free Aspen. He kills her. He lets her go. He shackles her to the ship. There's a hundred different things he does, but it ends the same way. You fight him. He kills you. You kill him, but the ship gets out to sea, and you die because of the geas. No matter what, you die. Over and over again, you die. I don't know what to do. I don't know how to stop it from happening."

Laurel touched his shoulder. "We'll figure this out, Paulo. There's always something we can change."

He ran his fingers down his face. "I can't see it. By the Goddess, Laurel, I'm so blasted scared."

Laurel gave a shaky laugh. "I don't see what's so scary. I die all the time, right?"

"This is *not* the time for sarcasm."

"Sorry." She chewed on the inside of her cheek. He could see her mind going through things, shrugging off the fear of her death to focus on solving the problem. "What if Aspen isn't in the dungeon when Teagan comes? What if she's somewhere else?"

"We can't put her anywhere else where she won't escape."

Laurel picked at the threads of the blanket. "What if we convince her not to escape?"

Paulo let his magic through the walls he'd built up. A new fate opened up, one where Aspen didn't want to go with Teagan.

Aspen will leave the confines of Laurel's room and attack Teagan outside the castle.

Aspen will stay in the room and Teagan will find her.

Aspen will remain hidden in the room and Teagan will run for the ship.

Paulo's eyes flew open. He looked to her. "There's one where Aspen's not taken."

Laurel grabbed his arm. "That's a start."

"We just need to convince her to not go with him. That it's better if she stays." He stood. But how? Even after he'd spoken with her, there had been no change. That future hadn't even come up until he'd told Laurel—

"It changed."

"What changed?"

He whirled, grabbing Laurel's face in his hands and pressing his mouth firmly to hers.

"You're brilliant. By the Goddess, you're brilliant."

She pulled away from him. "Yes, but why?"

"It's you. You're the one who's going to change Aspen's mind. Now that you know, you have the power to change it."

56
THE DUNGEON

If Paulo really believed Laurel had the power to change Aspen's mind, he really might be mad. Never once in their childhood had she ever changed Aspen's mind about anything. Aspen would argue a point until she was blue in the face, certain she had the right of it the entire time. At least, until further down the road when it became more convenient to change that opinion.

Laurel pinched the bridge of her nose as she walked out the front door of the castle. How was she going to reach her?

The small lead ball hanging from her wrist bounced against her nose and she sighed.

The walk to the dungeon was far shorter than she would have liked, but she didn't stop at the door or let herself think. If she thought too long about it, she'd just walk away, and the future Paulo had seen wouldn't happen.

She stomped down the stairs, not even caring if the noise was ridiculous. Master Schola was probably twitching wherever in the world he was.

Conley sat at the bottom of the stairs and stood. "Master."

"I'd like a word with my sister. Go ahead and let the guards at the door know you'll be back in a half hour and to not come down here until then."

He gave a sharp nod and swept up the stairs, much quieter than Laurel had descended them.

Aspen peeked out of her cell, her brown eyes guarded. *She should be wary.* Laurel curled her fingers and felt the lead weight rest against the heel of her hand.

Father would want them to mend this rift between them. He would tell Laurel she was the oldest and it was her responsibility to be a good example— even when the example was one of mercy. Even when she wanted to be the one to show what justice looked like.

She let go of the bead and reached into her pocket. Aspen watched her carefully but said nothing. Her footsteps were quiet as she approached the cell and grabbed the key in her pocket. It slid into the lock and the iron lock clicked. She pulled the door open. Aspen stood quietly on the other side, the only sign of her fear the flutter of her racing pulse at her neck. Paulo must have ordered a few things brought in for her because there was a wash-basin in the corner of her cell as well as a pallet. Her hair looked much cleaner than it had before, and she was even wearing a new dress.

"Hello, Aspen."

"Hey."

Laurel stepped to the side and gestured to the outside of the cell. "Care to join me outside?"

There was a slight narrowing of Aspen's eyes, as if she couldn't quite believe Laurel would let her out. As if it was some twisted game. She took a step, testing the waters. Laurel pulled the door open wider and Aspen jumped through like a fox sprung from a trap.

Laurel gestured to the stool. "You can sit there if you'd like."

Aspen plopped down onto it. "What did you come down here for?"

"Like I told Conley, I want a minute to speak with you. We're due for a good long conversation."

Aspen's back retained its stiff posture. "I agree."

Laurel blew out a breath. "I'm so furious with you."

Aspen twisted her fingers in her lap. "I know."

The shadow of boots passing by the other cell window flashed over Aspen's face. There was a yelp and the sound of rain hitting stone blocked every other sound.

"It rains here a lot," Aspen said.

"They say it's because of all the magic. The weather mages in the kingdom have been using their gifts too much and it's taken a toll on the atmosphere around the isle. The weather is trying to right itself, but it's causing some unusual storms."

Aspen nodded, staring down at her hands. "That makes sense."

Laurel watched her. What should she say? Was it wise to just lay the blame at Aspen's feet? To call her out? To wait for her to speak?

Laurel blew out a breath. "What happened to us, Aspen?"

Aspen met her gaze. "What happened is you decided to be a hero and made me a villain." She said it lightly, as if trying to make a joke, but it was much more accusatory than funny. The bitterness made it sharp enough to bring Laurel's guard up.

"You were never a villain to me."

"Oh really? Is that why you yelled at me and called me a liar and a thief in the palace all those months ago? Is that why you nearly tore my head off when you found out I was in your precious marquess's room? Why you've kept me locked in a cell for *weeks* without even talking to me?"

Laurel rubbed a hand over her face. "I didn't know how to talk to you. I knew if I tried, we would just end up screaming at each other and nothing would get fixed."

"Is that how you think this conversation is going to go? Well, you should just leave me in here for a few more weeks and come back when it's more convenient for you."

Laurel's jaw clenched and she had to take a breath. "It's never going to be convenient to talk to you about how you lied to me and killed a babe."

Whatever protest Aspen was about to spew died on her lips. "It was part of the job," she said quietly. "I had to poison the queen."

"You know, I've been hearing that a lot lately— that it was 'just a job'— and I can't tell you how cursed tired I am of that excuse. I took more jobs than anyone in Stellatus Hall and I never once killed a baby or betrayed those I had sworn to protect and treat as family."

"Teagan—"

Laurel growled. "And he seems to be the root of it all. But guess what? I was in the same position as all of you. By the Goddess, I had it even worse because he hated me and sent me off to do things no person should ever have to do. But did I kill anyone outside the bounds of my mission? No. Did I kill people who didn't deserve it? Probably, but I didn't kill any innocents."

"We can't all be as perfect as you, Laurel," she spat.

Laurel barked a laugh. "You think I'm perfect? All I've been doing for the last ten years is failing to keep Teagan from sinking his claws into you and get us out of Stellatus Hall so we can have a real life."

"We had a real life! One you were just too proud to notice. You were too caught up in the past to let us have a future we both wanted. Too busy trying to be smarter than everyone else."

"What on Gaia's green earth is that supposed to mean?"

Aspen clenched her fists in her skirts. "It means you were running around trying to make everyone else look like a fool instead of actually caring about our family. You couldn't just do what needed to be done to get us out of there. You had to be better than everyone else at everything, including your cursed honor. You couldn't just let Teagan win so we could get out."

"Do you think that's what would have happened? If I'd just let Teagan ground his heel in my face that we would have gotten out of there? He was worse than Mother. At least with her, we knew what to expect when she got home. That she would rage at us and tell us how useless we were. With Teagan, it was a game. He would draw you along until you weren't of use to him anymore and that's when he would strike."

"But he wasn't like that with everyone."

"Oh, you mean like with you? Do you know how many times I had to stop him from hurting you? How many times I threw myself in front of him because I knew he was frustrated with you about something? Remember when you were fourteen and you and Luc decided to sneak out of the hall for the first time? Did you know that Teagan knew you'd left?"

Aspen's face grew pale. "He did?"

"Yes. He was on his way to drag you back from the city by your hair and planned on killing Luc for going with you. I had to practically throw myself on his sword to stop him." In fact, she'd told him she would go to Master Schola and accept his invitation to join the scholae. Teagan's anger had completely shifted from Aspen to her in a heartbeat. It was one of the reasons she'd actually joined the scholae soon after. She'd known she could protect both Aspen and herself if she took the position.

"You didn't have to protect me. I knew exactly what I was doing. I knew the risks."

"Except no fourteen-year-old should feel like a prisoner. I wanted you to feel like you had a real life. One like we had when Father was still alive."

Aspen rolled her eyes. "Again, you with Father. He died, Laurel. He died and left us with Mother. He wasn't this great man you always say he was. You don't have to keep living your life trying to make him proud. He's gone."

Laurel's jaw tightened. "Yes, he was a great man. I live my life the way he taught me to because I want to be the person he knew I could be. He was the only person in our lives that ever cared about us."

"No, he's the only person *you* ever cared about. You put him on this grand pedestal and idolize him even now. No one else will ever be good enough because you've painted him as this perfect man that no one can ever get close to touching. He was just a man. He made mistakes. He had to if he thought marrying Mother was a good idea."

"Of course he made mistakes! He snapped at us when he was tired. Fought with Mother when she poked at him. He lost his temper and broke down when we needed him to be strong. Burned food and spent money he didn't have. He wasn't perfect, but he cared. He cared about the kind of people we would become. About our dreams. He pushed himself past the limits of any man so he could provide a life for us that he knew we needed."

"But he didn't give us that life. Instead, he left us to this. He left us behind to fend for ourselves."

"You can't blame someone for dying!" Laurel yelled.

"You can't blame me for surviving either!"

"I certainly can when that survival looks like becoming a madman's puppet. When I nearly killed myself to give you choices and you still chose wrong. You chose to be Teagan's golden girl and do whatever he told you so you could have whatever you wanted instead of fighting for it yourself."

Aspen clawed at her cheeks and screeched. "You can't even take one second to get off your high horse. I get it, you're smarter than everyone and better than everyone, and you didn't have to dirty your hands to get where you are. You're some great big hero, and you can't concern yourself with the woes of us little people."

"You think I haven't gotten my hands dirty? Aspen, I'm not like you. I have a broken brain that makes it so I remember every detail of what I've done. I don't have the luxury of making a mistake and allowing time to help me forget about it. I relive the sins I've made over and over again. I can look down at my hands and see every spot of blood they've taken. I can recount every life I took. I can tell you how long it took them to die and what their final words were verbatim. You think my hands are clean? I'm pretty sure their far bloodier than even Teagan's. At least he has the excuse of being human enough to forget the wrongs he's committed. Death doesn't dog his every step as it does mine."

The last words struck Aspen somehow. She sagged in the stool, her head in her hands. She shuddered. Was she crying?

"I'm sorry," she finally said. "I didn't want to fight with you. I've been telling myself if you came down here that I wouldn't let my anger get the best of me. That I would ignore this burning in my gut I've felt for so long. That I would do whatever you said. I know I've made mistakes, and I'm sorry. I'm sorry I've done what I've done. You say your plagued by the memories of those you've killed? I can't close my eyes without seeing Queen Carnation. Without hearing her sobs as the poison wracked her body. When I realized she was with child, I didn't know what to do. I gave her more Stellataen Arrow to try to speed the process along. It just made everything so much worse. I'd never seen what that poison does to a person. Never realized what we did to people when we gave it to them. Something broke inside me when she lost her babe. I know I'm irredeemable. I know the Goddess won't have any mercy for me. I know She's cursed me because of what I did. She's going to leave me completely alone."

Laurel crouched down in front of her. "I'm right here, Aspen. I've always been here."

Aspen's sobs grew louder. "But She's going to take you from me too! I saw it in Lord MacGregor's sketchbooks. You die. You keep dying and it's all my fault. All of this is my fault."

Had Paulo told her about his vision? About what Teagan was planning? He must have. That must have been how he kept Aspen from killing him when she'd escaped. He'd opened up about what was happening.

"You can't take all the credit for this," Laurel said, laying her hand on Aspen's knee. "This is on Teagan."

Aspen shook her head, but Laurel tightened her hold on her knee.

"Listen to me. He's the one who started all of this. He's the one who tried to come between us. He's the one who's been whispering poison in your ear. And we have a chance to stop him. We have a chance to make things right."

Aspen looked up at her, tears falling from the end of her nose. "What are you talking about?"

The door to the top of the dungeon burst open.

Laurel shot to her feet, pulling her hidden dagger from under her jacket.

Paulo raced down the stairs; his eyes frantic as they met hers under his dripping hair.

"He's here. Teagan's at the front gate and he's demanding we release Aspen."

57
AN UNEXPECTED THIEF

Teagan will come to take Aspen.

ASPEN SHOT TO HER FEET. "I'LL TALK TO HIM. I'LL TELL HIM TO LEAVE and never come back. I'll tell him what a lying, horrible black-guard he is and send him packing."

Paulo met Laurel's gaze and shook his head. Letting Aspen anywhere near Teagan was a bad idea. He knew that much at least.

She turned back to Aspen. "We have a plan, but that means I need you to trust me."

Aspen glanced at Paulo out of the corner of her eye. "What do you need me to do?"

"We need you to stay in the castle." Laurel grabbed her arm, leading her to the stairs. "I'll take you to my rooms. If you can stay there while we take care of Teagan, it might give us a chance to stop him from hurting anyone else."

At least, it would give them more time to come up with how to stop him. Paulo wiped his sopping-wet hair from his forehead and stepped ahead of Laurel. If Teagan left, they'd be able to regroup. Hopefully, the king and queen would be in a better posi-tion to send aid. There would be more stability in Eleusia. Paulo would have time to gather allies that he knew he could rely on.

They could take Teagan out. The snake had nowhere else to go. No hole to slither back to. He would get desperate. He'd make mistakes.

Paulo took the stairs back up two at a time. He stopped at the top, ordering the two guards stationed there to follow Captain Isaac to the main gate.

"Go with them, Paulo," Laurel said from behind him. "I'll get Aspen into the castle. You go to the gate and stall them."

Paulo nodded and headed toward the gate. When he came around the corner, he found Captain Isaac at the gate, directing men to different positions. The castle guard had become a well-oiled machine over the past several months. They followed their captain's command with silence and precision.

"Where's our unwelcome guest?" Paulo asked.

"Still at the bottom of the gate, my lord."

"*Laurel!*" a raspy voice shouted over the gate. "Come out and play you little witch!"

Fire spread through Paulo's chest at the insult. He nodded to the captain and marched up the stairs to the top of the gatehouse. Declan stood just out of sight of the door, his silver mask dark in the shadows. He flicked his fingers at his side. He counted two and pointed to the other side of the gate.

Conley and Mare were on the other side then.

Paulo swept through the door and finally got his first glimpse at Teagan.

The man was a spindly creature, shorter than Paulo thought he would be. He likely only stood a couple inches taller than Aspen. His hair stringy from the rain soaking all of them. Fifty men stood in a semi-circle around him, a dozen made up of iron-chained fae.

"Ah, Lord MacGregor," Teagan said, his eyes taking in Paulo's figure as he made it to the middle of the walkway. "My name is Teagan Obscuritas. I've come to take back the treasure that's been stolen from me."

Paulo leaned his forearm against the wall. "The only thief I see here is you." He made sure to look directly at each of the fae he had shackled.

Teagan's mouth stretched into a sharp smile. "I can assure

you; I paid every piece of gold due for these lovely trinkets. You'll find no theft on that score."

"Slavery is thievery of free will, Mr. Obscuritas, and you will find no tolerance for it here. If you don't wish for trouble, you'll unchain those you've stolen from their homes and leave."

Teagan shook his head, spraying water onto the men and women around him. By the looks of them, they were all assassins except for the fae. "Sorry. I didn't come to negotiate with a half-beat lordling. You'll either allow me to speak with Aspen or I'm going to slaughter every one of you that gets in my way."

Paulo's fingers clenched into fists. "We've withstood one attack from your ilk already. I don't think you'll find it so easy."

Teagan's gaze shifted down the wall. "Laurel! I've been calling for you."

Laurel ghosted up beside Paulo, her silver mask in place under her hood. Her finger hooked around his pinky and gave it a slight squeeze. He felt the slight tremor in her hand as she did, and he hooked his finger tighter around hers.

"I've come to retrieve Aspen from you," Teagan said. "As you were unable to uphold your part of our geas, her contract remained unfulfilled, and she must continue her service with me."

The rain fell in thick sheets around them, soaking the assassins as she stared down at him. Thunder sounded a way off, but it did nothing to deter any of them.

Teagan's face darkened. "Don't be obstinate, Laurel. You've always tried to act like you know what's best, but you don't. You've never been able to take care of her and you certainly can't do anything for her now, trapped on this cursed isle as you are. Why, I imagine she'll be more than happy to return with me and leave you to this sorry little castle. After all, you've been holding her back for so long. Coming between us and keeping her from becoming the glorious creature she's destined to be with me. Don't be selfish. Stop trying to hide her from me. She's going to come with me and take back what is rightfully mine."

Silver glimmered out of the corners of Paulo's eye. The other scholae glided over the walkway and took up positions on either side of them. Teagan's eyes narrowed at their arrival.

Paulo pulled a smirk onto his face, allowing his magic to flood him.

"I think that's as solid a 'no' as I've ever seen. Come back when you learn how to say 'please.'"

Teagan's face twisted into an ugly mask of fury. "Aspen is mine! She's mine and I will take her!" He turned to his men. "Get rid of the gate!"

The assassins moved forward, the sound of iron chains ringing out over the falling rain. Three fae were shoved to the front, two adults and a child.

Laurel grabbed Paulo's hand in a steely grip, her brown eyes wide as she stared down at them. "I've seen that child before."

Paulo's magic flashed across his vision.

Light and fire blasting through the front gate.

He jumped for the other side of the wall. *"Abandon the gate!"* he roared.

The guards standing below him looked up at the command, but their weeks together had taught them to listen when Paulo spoke. They scattered, diving to the sides of the gate. Captain Isaac barked orders, hollering for the men to get out of the way. He ran down the middle of the host, shoving men into a retreat.

Light shot through the entrance, blowing the doors from their hinges.

Four guards didn't get away quick enough. They didn't even have time to scream before they were burned to nothing but ash.

Captain Isaac hadn't made it out of the magic's path, his blackened sword all that was left of him.

Bile crawled up Paulo's throat. *By the Goddess.* Jenkins would be devastated.

The assassins surged forward.

Paulo raced for the gatehouse.

Diana appeared in the doorway, her bow already drawn as she leapt on top of the wall. She shot down at the fae, taking out the two adults that had blasted the gate.

Like a whip, Laurel snapped forward, pulling Diana from the wall.

"Don't kill the little fae boy that did this! Try not to kill any of the fae if you can help it. This isn't their fault."

Diana gave her a sharp nod and spun back toward the fight, an arrow flying and sinking into an assassin's chest.

Paulo stormed down the stairs of the gatehouse, grabbing a sword from a rack by the door. He burst out into the bailey.

"Defend the hole!" he hollered, rallying the guards around the gate. The guards readjusted, responding to the call of Paulo's command as easily as they had their captain's.

The assassins poured through, their blades clashing against the guards'.

"Conley! Secure the upper bailey."

Conley raced for the gate to the upper bailey.

Declan skidded to a stop next to Paulo. "If we keep them at the front gate, they'll be able to escape. We need to push them to the side so they can't get out if we want to make sure we trap Teagan here."

Paulo's magic flicked through possibilities. "Push them east. We don't want the fight getting close to the inner bailey if we can help it."

Declan drew two short swords and ran into the fray.

A hand tightened around his arm, and he turned to Laurel.

"I'm going for Aspen," Laurel said. "I need to make sure someone is there in case Teagan gets through."

His magic shifted to Aspen's line.

She will barrel through the assassins, cutting her way to get to Teagan, the promise of death on her face.

He whirled toward the upper bailey. A shadow hung from the stone wall.

"*Stop!*" he roared.

Aspen slipped the last few feet from the upper bailey wall, wearing one of Laurel's jackets and streaking toward the assassins.

Blasted girl! Paulo raced to intercept her, casting his magic out further to see how to best reach her. His magic flared. *A rock smashes into his skull.* He had to slow to avoid the fist-sized rock. The cursed thing nearly brushed his nose as it flew past. Too close. The assassin that had thrown it charged out of the fray toward him, a long ax over his head.

Paulo saw the sharp tip of the ax come for his neck and he

dodged it. The assassin's side opened up and Paulo came up on the inside of the assassin's guard. His sword slid easily between the man's ribs, and the assassin dropped before he likely even realized what had happened.

Aspen nearly reached the assassins when Laurel tackled her to the side. The two of them rolled off the road. Laurel pulled Aspen up, shaking her and yelling. Paulo couldn't hear the words over the sound of the rain, but he saw the fear in her face.

Aspen's eyes were wide as she glanced back toward the fight.

Teagan had spotted her. He grabbed hold of one of the fae, directing her gaze toward Aspen.

The fae's magic shot forward.

The rebels had used Day Court fae for much of their fighting. With their attack on the Summer Court first, they had been able to enslave many of those with light magic.

But this fae was from the Night Court.

"Run!" Paulo roared.

Laurel yanked Aspen into a run, but they didn't make it more than a few feet before the Night fae stuck. Shadow slammed into both of them, sending them sprawling into the grass. Aspen screamed as the shadow wrapped around her and pulled her back toward the assassins.

"Aspen!" Laurel chased after her.

Paulo wove through the fight, dodging blades and magic as he ran to where the fae stood next to Teagan.

When Aspen was nearly to the circle of assassins, Paulo lifted his arms over his head and threw his sword. The blade spun tip over hilt, and it was only because he saw how to throw it that it hit its mark.

The fae went down and the magic cut off.

Aspen fell, landing on her side.

Shoving through the crowd, Paulo kept his eyes on her as she pushed herself to her feet. His magic flicked through possibilities as quickly as Diana's bow could shoot off an arrow. His heart beating like a raging drum in his chest. Almost there. He was almost there.

Teagan appeared at Aspen's side, his cold eyes gleaming.

She screamed, angry and frightened.

The assassins closed in around the pair, blocking Paulo's view of them.

"Aspen!" he hollered.

As if from every assassins' nightmares, Laurel flew into their midst. She slid through their ranks like oil, her daggers dancing in front of her as she pushed through them. The moment an assassin realized she was there, they were already bleeding out.

Paulo jumped to join her, pushing through the assassins to get to her. He could carve a path for her. Could get her to Aspen before Teagan escaped with her. He shoved the remaining assassin between them.

Fire burst out across the sky.

Paulo dove, grabbing Laurel and getting her to the ground before the flames could touch her.

Men screamed, guard and assassin alike.

The fire stopped, and Paulo dragged Laurel to her feet.

Teagan stood on the other side of the gate, Aspen nowhere to be seen.

He grinned, his blue eyes shining in the light of the roaring flames between them.

Then, he reached up, sliding a ring onto his finger.

And he vanished.

58
THE FATE

LAUREL SHOVED THE PAPERS OFF THE TABLE IN FRONT OF HER. GLASS, paper, ink, books, all of it went crashing to the ground.

He'd taken her.

After everything they'd done to keep Aspen from Teagan, he'd taken her.

Laurel's stomach still twisted at the memory of Aspen running across the outer bailey. Laurel had nearly torn her head off when she'd caught her. When she'd said she wouldn't sit in a castle like some damsel when she could take care of Teagan herself. When she could fight too.

By the Goddess, how wrong she'd been.

Laurel sank to the ground next to the table. She slammed her fist into the floor, one punch after another until her knuckles split. Her heart crashed against her ribcage, trying to find release from the vice that had wrapped all the way around her chest.

She brought her arm back for another swing, but someone grabbed her.

"That's *enough*, Master," Declan snapped.

That hadn't nearly been enough. She yanked her arm from his grasp. "I'll be blasted done when Teagan is black and blue and choking on his own blood!"

"And we'll help him get there." Declan took a step toward her. "*After* we hear back from Mare and Diana about which way he took Aspen. We need to make sure no other assassins decided to circle back for another shot at taking the castle after all the others took off after Teagan disappeared."

Laurel ground her teeth. "None of those cowards would dare take another shot at the castle."

"I know quite a few of them stupid enough to try, especially with fae at their disposal. Don't let your own hunger for vengeance make you stupid, Master. Teagan couldn't have gotten Aspen far, but trying to chase them down without knowing where they're headed won't get you any closer to him. We need to come up with a plan. We need Paulo to tell us what to do next."

"So now you've decided to trust him?"

"Yes, and you should too. He told you to wait here for news, and that's exactly what we're going to do."

The fight in her fizzled out and she buried her face in her hands.

"Sweet Gaia, he's going to kill her. The moment he decides she's not worth the hassle, he's going to slit her throat. If she gets it into her head to try to take him on, he won't even bat an eye."

"You're right. He won't. But if we're going to give her the best chance of making it out of there, we have to play it smart. Teagan will be expecting you to charge after her because you've always sacrificed yourself for her. You can't play into his expectations, or you'll lose."

She looked up at him, taking in the severe set of his shoulders. and stony expression. "If you were him, what would you do?"

He ran a hand through his damp hair and blew out a breath. "Teagan likes to be in the best position he can be. He'll run back to whatever fortifications he's made for himself. Go back to the rest of his men. There were at least three dozen assassins unaccounted for last night. They're probably watching over whatever other fae he's taken. He'll want to get behind those lines. He's a strategist, but he's also a coward. He'll go on defense rather than attempt another offense, especially since he got what he wanted."

Laurel nodded. "You're right. We just need to figure out where he's going."

Declan walked around the mess she made and plopped

himself into one of the chairs. "I'm sure Mare or Paulo will be up here any second with news and we can make a decision then."

Laurel pushed herself to her feet. "I don't know how you can remain calm right now."

He shrugged. "I can't let myself get caught up in the things I can't control. If I'm always reacting to things, I'll never get anything done. Sometimes, the hardest part is in the waiting, but it's always worth it in the end."

"Until you wait for too long and wind up in a dungeon," she muttered.

The corners of his lips tipped up. "But even that worked in my favor. I was able to prove my innocence, and you took care of the problem."

"Right, because me killing him was all part of your master plan."

"It's important to know when and how to delegate things."

She shook her head. He was mad. He was right, but he was still mad. She really should have trusted him more. Listened to him more. That was one thing she'd realized when she'd spoken to Aspen earlier. She'd never been very good at listening to those around her. She'd relied on herself for so much and figured she'd known best. But she didn't. She needed these people to help her.

"Thank you, Declan."

"For what?"

"For being here. I don't think any of us would have made it this far without you."

He snorted. "I know you wouldn't have."

The sitting room door swung open, and Mare strode in, her cloak and hair splattered with mud.

"Did you find them?" Laurel asked.

Mare plucked the map of Olympia from the pile Laurel had tossed. She shook it out, sprinkling shards of glass onto the floor before setting it on the table.

"Where?" Declan asked.

Mare's finger trailed a line through the forest, cutting around the lake and turning south. She ran her finger all the way to the river.

"Boats?" he asked.

Mare counted six on her fingers.

"Which way are they going?"

Her pale fingers trailed south down the river.

Laurel settled her hands on the pommels of her daggers. "They're going to Eleusia."

A crash sounded in the hallway. Laurel drew her blades as Paulo staggered into the room. His eyes were wide with magic, the colors whirling.

"The ship with red sails. Red lightning. Red blood. All red. Everywhere is red."

Laurel raced over to grab him before he fell over. How much had he seen? "Paulo, let it go. Let the magic go."

The colors disappeared from his eyes, and he blinked until nothing was left but the blue. His face creased in pain as the magic dissipated, and he slammed his eyes shut.

"His ship will be in the docks at Eleusia," Paulo hissed. "He's got a hundred fae on the ship with the rest of the assassins. He's planning to take Aspen and the others back to Stellatus Hall."

A stone sank in Laurel's stomach. This was about more than Aspen. Teagan couldn't take those fae back with him. She'd seen what a few of them could do to a castle guarded by an oracle and hundreds of guards. The Continent wouldn't stand a chance. Teagan would take out every warlord that came for him and make the others pledge allegiance to him. And that wouldn't even be enough. He'd never be able to leave these isles alone. Not when he knew how to keep the fae under his control. Not when they were what kept him in power. He'd return, but he'd bring an army with him.

Paulo grabbed Laurel's shoulders. "Listen to me. There's only one possibility in which all of us make it out of this alive. One. Now that Aspen is willing to fight Teagan, we might have a chance."

"We need to keep him from getting out of Olympia." She set her hands over his. "If there's a chance that we can do that, we have to take it. We can't let him take Aspen. We can't let him take those fae."

Declan pointed out the window. "If this weather keeps up, he won't be able to leave."

"You forget," Paulo said, "he has fae at his disposal and water folk in his pocket. If he really wanted to leave Eleusia, a storm wouldn't be much of a deterrent."

Conley swept into the room, a soaked Diana behind him.

"I followed as far as I could," Diana said. "They're headed downriver, but keeping track of them in the storm is near impossible. There's something strange in the air. We may need to wait it out."

"We can't wait," Laurel and Paulo said at the same time.

Declan pushed himself out of the chair. "Then there's no time to waste." He headed for the door.

Paulo went right behind him. "I'll send for some of the guard to accompany us and tell Mater what's going on. She and Donnie will keep things running here."

The rest of the room followed him out.

"Conley," Laurel said.

He stopped at the door, letting Mare breeze past him. "Yes, Master."

Her eyes flicked to the door, and he closed it.

When she heard the lock click into place, she pulled her mask from inside her jacket and held it out to him. "There's something I need you to take care of."

The rain pelted Laurel's face like punches. She could barely see Paulo's horse in front of her as they galloped down the road. With the way the wind thrashed the water, it had seemed much safer to ride the horses through the storm rather than risk a boat on the river. Paulo knew the quickest way across the march to reach the harbor city to the south. Laurel had told him to give Declan the directions and have him lead with Conley so Paulo could focus on his magic when he needed to. Diana rode beside him, their cloaks flapping as the rain soaked them through, and three dozen of Iatrus Castle's finest followed behind them.

Captain Issac's loss was deeply felt. He would have led the charge without batting an eye at the rain. Laurel gritted her teeth to keep them from chattering. They would have to stop if this rain didn't let up. It was getting too dangerous and too dark to ride in. There was no sign of the sun that should have been rising to the east of them. No sign of the storm letting up.

Mare's horse came out of nowhere, the gelding's black coat slicked with water. She raised one of her hands, pointing to the southwest and counting two then steepling her hands.

Two buildings to the southwest.

It seemed Laurel wasn't the only one worried about the rain.

But she shook her head. They needed to push through. They needed to get to Aspen. To stop Teagan. They needed to—

Diana shouted ahead of them. She reached over, grabbing Paulo's reins and pulling his horse to a stop. Paulo slid to the side, and she snagged his arm before he toppled.

When Laurel caught up to them, she launched herself off her horse. Paulo was halfway out of his saddle and half in Diana's. Curses fell from Diana's lips as she tried to keep him from falling.

Laurel raced around to the opposite side and grabbed his leg. "Get him back up!"

Diana pushed his shoulders as Laurel pulled his leg down until he was more stable on his horse.

His colorful eyes were half-lidded as rain poured down his face.

"Paulo." She sighed and pulled herself up to sit on the horse's rump behind Paulo's saddle. Praise the Goddess the beast was a giant and could hold the two of them. She wrapped one arm around him and used her other to take the reins from where they hung over the stallion's neck.

Mare came up beside her, Laurel's horse following behind her. Declan and Conley trotted back to where they'd stopped.

"What happened?" Conley asked.

Laurel tightened her hold around Paulo's chest. "We're going to have to stop. Paulo can't keep going, and we're going to need him if we want to beat Teagan. Mare spotted some buildings ahead of us. We'll stop there and let the horses rest and see if we can wait out a bit of this storm."

Declan nodded, guiding his horse over to where Mare held Laurel's and offered to take it. He called out to the guard behind them, having half of them ride ahead to check out the buildings and the other half to act as protection so Paulo could ride at a slower pace. Mare took point and the rest of them followed behind them.

Paulo sagged further in her grip, and she tried to wrap his cloak more tightly around him. By the Goddess, he had to weigh as much as his blasted horse. They couldn't ride at much more than a trot, but the buildings ended up not being far.

A small stable and what looked like the shabby remains of a house sat a little way off the road. Someone had obviously come through and ransacked the place, the windows broken in and the front door hanging crooked on its hinges. Mare directed them toward the empty stable, dismounting at the door and leading her horse inside.

Laurel rode behind Paulo all the way into the building, sighing in relief when they passed through the doorway. She'd probably never feel dry again after all this rain.

The others tied their horses off on posts and circled her and Paulo.

"Watch his head," Diana said as she gently pulled Paulo toward her and Declan.

Laurel did her best to keep the horse steady as the others pulled him from the saddle. The horse only flicked his ears when Paulo fell into their arms, Declan holding his shoulders and Diana taking his legs.

"Sweet Gaia, have you been taking fourths at dessert?" Diana asked. "You're so cursed heavy."

Laurel dismounted, looking through the stalls to find a mostly clean one.

"In here," one of the guards said, holding a magelight so they could see into the dark stall. Declan and Diana brought Paulo to the guard. Conley followed them in, carrying Paulo's saddle blanket.

Laurel's nose burned as she watched all three of them settle Paulo on the ground, tucking the blanket under his head. They'd all grown so close over the last several months. The scholae trusted Paulo. They regarded him as one of their own. Diana too. They would be all right after this.

Diana stood back up. "He's too cold. I'm going to see what I can scrounge up from the house. It's warm in here, but we might need to strip him if he doesn't warm up fast enough."

Laurel nodded, crouching down beside him and brushing his wet hair from his face. "How long do you think he'll be out?"

"Can't say. The longest he's been unconscious has been a few hours. His brain can't take the headaches sometimes, especially if he's been using his magic for long periods of time. I'm sure he has some herbs in his saddlebag. I'll get him some tea for when he wakes."

Laurel fiddled with the lead weight hanging around her neck. "You saved him, Diana."

She winked. "I've got some wicked good twin sense. I knew something was off before he even started tilting." She disappeared out of the stall with Conley, and Declan turned to Laurel.

"I'd like to take Mare and see if we can't spot Teagan," Conley said. "It would be nice to know where he is."

Laurel nodded. "Let's give Paulo four hours before we move. I don't want to leave him here, but we can't lose Teagan."

Declan saluted, pressing his fingers to his eye, nose, and lips, before slipping out after Conley.

Once she knew the rest of them were far enough from the stall, she closed her eyes and let her tears fall. Her throat ached with the need to sob, but she swallowed it back, only allowing the tears to betray her.

She leaned down and pressed a kiss to Paulo's forehead.

"I'm sorry," she whispered against his hair. "I'm so sorry for what comes next."

But she couldn't be sorry for saving the fae. She couldn't be sorry for saving Aspen. And if she had to die to make it happen, she would.

59
AN UNEXPECTED WEIGHT

PAULO WAS NOT ON TOP OF A HORSE AS HE'D BEEN THE LAST TIME HE'D checked.

He stared up at the rafters of a wooden ceiling, the slats gray with age and weather.

He bolted upright, a blanket falling from his chest. He was shirtless. Why was he shirtless? He peeked under the blanket now pooled in his lap. Trousers kept him covered, but his socks and boots were gone.

Something shifted beside him, and he nearly went dizzy with how quickly he turned his head.

Laurel slowly pushed herself up, her brown eyes flicking over him. "How are you feeling?"

"Where are we?" They didn't have time to worry about how he was feeling. They should be on horses.

"We're in a stable about ten miles outside of Eleusia. We made better time than we thought."

He ran a hand through his hair. "What happened?"

She pulled her knees up and rested her arms atop them. "You nearly fell off your horse and got yourself trampled."

Had he? All he remembered was the magic swirling around him, tracking what Teagan would do next. The details were murky, but the last thing he saw had been Teagan hauling Aspen onto his ship and shoving her into his quarters before barring the door to keep her from escaping.

"I shouldn't have lost control like that."

"No, you shouldn't have." She chewed on the inside of her cheek. "I need you, Paulo."

Paulo's stomach did a funny little squirm, and he raised his eyebrows. "Oh? Are you just realizing this now?"

She rolled her eyes. "Don't get cheeky. I'm being serious. I don't know how we're going to stop Teagan if we don't have your magic with us."

Paulo scooted back until he was leaning back against the wall. "About that. I'm pretty sure the ship is spelled."

"What?" Laurel straightened. "Spelled how?"

"I think Teagan had it charmed to not let magic users use their gifts on the ship. It would make it impossible for the fae to escape with their magic even if they were able to get the iron off. Every time I looked at our fight on the ship, there was never any magic."

"So we won't have any fae to contend with," she said.

"So I won't have any magic either."

She deflated.

"Oh, don't look so dower. I can still hold my own in a fight. Conley's been running drills on me like a madman. I can tussle with the best of the assassins. What I'm most worried about is not being able to remember what paths we need to take Teagan out. There are too many pieces for me to keep track of. Too many possibilities for error."

She rocked up so she was on her knees. "Show me."

"What?"

Her hands settled on his shoulders. "If there's still that chance that you saw, the chance for all of us to get out, then show me. Use that fancy magic of yours and let me see."

He pushed himself up to his knees as well. "Laurel—"

"I've been thinking about it a lot," she said, cutting him off, "about how you said the magic works because there's a two-way connection between us. But it didn't make sense to me."

"What didn't make sense?"

"How that moment was the first time I felt the magic. You said it was love, but if that's all it was, I think I would have felt it before then."

His heart nearly stopped in his chest. "Are you saying you've been in love with me for a while now?"

She hiccupped, not quite a laugh but not quite a cry either as a single tear slipped over her cheek. "I think you might be the slowest acting poison I've ever taken. I didn't even know I was lost until Conley told me."

Paulo reached forward and caught the next tear before it could fall down her cheek. "Not sure being compared to a poison was the way I wanted you to tell me that you love me, but I'll take it."

She laughed, pressing a hand against his palm where he cradled her face. "Sorry. What I was trying to say was I don't think it's love that influences the magic." She set her other hand against his chest. "I think it's that I grew to trust you, Paulo. Not just with my life, but my heart. I realized I had already fallen in love with you, but it wasn't until I truly trusted you that the magic let me in. That I let you in. Love can fade, but trust? Trust would have to be broken for it to die between two people. It's stronger than love. It's hope in its greatest form, and I have hope for you Paulo MacGregor. I do love you, but more importantly, I *trust* you."

Paulo closed his eyes, the words washing over him. He set his forehead against hers. "You trust me."

She poked him in the chest. "And *you* trust me, or else this wouldn't work. The magic wouldn't work. So, I need you to trust me now. I need you to trust me with your visions so I can get us through this. I need you to trust that I'm going to do my best to fight for that one chance that we all have to make it out of there."

She pulled back. "Here, I even have a bargain for you."

He dropped his hands but settled them on her knees. He didn't want to stop touching her. "A bargain?"

Her hands reached around her neck, and she untied the leather string she always carried with her. "When we were interrogating Declan after his return, he talked about how assassins don't keep sentimentals. Well, he was wrong."

She laid the string so the lead bead sat in the middle of her palm.

"This is the only thing from my childhood I still have. It was my father's lucky fishing weight."

Paulo brought up his hand, gently brushing a finger over the little lead ball.

Laurel wiped her nose on her sleeve. "He died when I was seven. There was a fever that came in on one of the ships. The dockworkers got hit first. Many of them made it through, but for some reason, the Goddess decided my father wouldn't be one of them. He laid in bed for an entire week, barely able to speak because he couldn't get enough air into his lungs. It took him within ten days, no matter what we tried. When he finally passed, my mother sold everything in our house, but I sneaked this out of his tacklebox before she got her hands on it. I kept it in my sock, so worried she would sell my shoes when I slept. Instead, she sold me and Aspen, shoes and all, to Stellatus Hall. Once I was sure no one would steal it, I put it on a string. I learned the right length to make it so it wouldn't become a problem when I was in a fight if I wore it either on my wrist or around my neck. But I never went anywhere without it. I've had it with me since he died."

She reached around Paulo's neck.

The back of his throat grew tight. "Laurel, you don't need to do this."

Her fingers brushed against the back of his neck as she tied the leather in place. The weight fell to land right below his clavicle.

"Listen, Paulo MacGregor, and I'll make you a deal. This is a sign of my trust, that you will do everything in your power to get all of us out of this fight alive."

"Of course I will." He reached up to untie the knot. "I don't need this as a token of that."

She grabbed his arms and pulled them down. "I'm not finished. Wear this as a token of the trust I have in you and of the trust you have in me. As long as you wear this, you'll trust me to do the best I can to help us all get off that ship. That I'll use the magic you give me to give all of us our best chance."

She touched the bead. "You wear this so you have to return it to me. You hold on to it until all of us are on the other side of this fight and put it right back in my hand, because I need to know that you're going to do everything you can to make it happen."

He grabbed her hand. "I would make that promise without the weight."

"I know, but I also want you to know that I'm going to do everything I can to get that bead back. To make it out of this fight so I can let you give it back to me. I trust you, Paulo. I trust you with my life, my heart, and with the last piece of my father that I have left. Do you trust me?"

He used his thumbs to wipe away the tears that were still falling down the sides of her face, his own tears falling with hers. "I trust you, Laurel Flumen. I trust you to do everything you can to not die on that ship. To stop Teagan. To use my magic to give us that chance."

She smiled, a soft, sad thing. Leaning forward, she brushed her nose against his.

His eyes fell closed as a shiver ran down his spine.

"Then I need you to show me."

She pressed her lips against his.

He answered in kind.

Magic swirled behind his eyes, but he pushed it back, wrapping his arms around her back and pulling her closer to him.

This kiss wasn't one of passion or want or need.

Her lips were soft as he pressed his more firmly against hers. As he tried to pour every ounce of what he felt for her into that one kiss. That if he could prove how deeply he loved her, then she would really trust him. That she'd understand he didn't just want her trust, but all of her. He wanted to prove that it wasn't about the magic for him. It had always been her. She was what he wanted.

He brought up one hand, brushing it against her neck as he pushed her hair back and tilted her chin up. He nearly groaned when she deepened the kiss, taking everything he would give her.

And he would give her anything she wanted. He would tear apart fate itself if she asked it of him.

He pulled back, just enough so he could see when her eyes opened. Her irises were smattered with spots of honey and earth, orbiting the ring of dark brown around her pupil. His fingers twitched to sketch them, to draw this one moment in the present rather than the thousands of moments he could see of their future.

"I trust you, Laurel," he whispered.

Her eyes crinkled with her smile.

"I love you too."

He captured her lips with his again, sealing those words between them.

Then, he let his magic pour into her.

He let her see her death.

He let her see their one chance.

And he prayed with everything that he had, that it would be fate.

60

THE MASTERS

Laurel crept through the rain-soaked streets of Eleusia. The city was much changed from when she'd first arrived. Like the capital, there were holes where houses had once been. Painted compasses decorated walls. If it hadn't been raining so hard, Laurel likely would have smelled all the iron that had replaced windows and doors.

But there were distinct differences between this city and the capital the last time Laurel saw it. Strips of red lay in the mud, and Olympia's seal flapped in the wind from the windows of the buildings. Here there were plants everywhere. Large vines covered houses, some taking entire lengths of a street. Paulo had said to avoid the vines at all costs, saying they were a Barclay special and would have whoever touched them wishing they could tear their skin from their bones.

Laurel stepped over one of the vines as she darted into an alleyway.

She could practically feel the river.

She couldn't hear the water over the rain, but the air on her skin grew humid, the mud under her boots become more viscous. Her entire body was soaked, but she ignored the cold, focusing on the memories in her head.

Paulo's visions.

She flicked through them like recipe cards, picking one up to see if that was the best option before moving on to the next. He'd been right to say there were a thousand possibilities. It was difficult to choose which things to follow and which to ignore.

Luckily, Paulo had told her which sequence of events would give them their best chance. Which one would see all of them to the other side of this fight.

They would get to the docks.

A dozen castle guards would set to fighting those on the docks who were prepping *The Shining River* for launch and keep any of the other assassins on the other ships at the docks from coming to Teagan's aid.

Laurel would lead the rest of them onto the boat. The other assassins would be ready to meet them, but they wouldn't be prepared for a fighting force like theirs. They would fight as a single unit, moving carefully from the gangplank and working their way across the deck. When everyone was on the ship, they would split into two groups, one group taking the rear of the ship, where Aspen was and where more assassins waited below. Paulo would be the one to let Aspen out. Laurel would go with the scholae and push for the hold. Once they got there, Conley and Mare would set to releasing the fae.

However, the guards on the docks wouldn't be able to keep the ship at the harbor.

The ship would start toward the coast, and once that happened Laurel had twelve minutes to get off the ship. Twelve minutes until they broke away from Olympia's borders and the terms of her geas would activate. She tried to ignore the visions that showed that happening. Tried to stop watching herself die over and over again.

By the Goddess, how Paulo could stay sane was a miracle. How he'd been able to see these visions and still save her even though it felt so futile... she would never again doubt him.

The harbor opened up in front of her.

Half a dozen docks stretched out from the shore, boats of all colors and sizes bobbing in the water. People scuttled about, covering cargo to protect it from the rain and rushing into the buildings against the shore. The docks were made of solid wood planks, sun-bleached and slick with water. Laurel couldn't see the other side of the river from where she stood, but she did see where *The Shining River* rocked at the far side of the harbor.

Once they got the fae off the ship, they had to find Teagan. Depending on what choices he made, there were several places he could be. He would be in the cabin with Aspen, which Paulo would discover quickly. He would be at the rudder, screaming at the ship's captain to get them out of the harbor. Or he would be standing over the hold, making sure the fae were settled in for the trip.

All three would make things difficult, but the best option was if he was at the back of the ship, keeping him as far from everything else when it all began. But all they had to do was keep him from getting to Aspen. If they could do that, they could get her off the ship. After that, things got difficult.

But they weren't impossible.

Aspen would jump off the side of the ship with the fae.

Teagan would either jump after her, or he would fight to stay on the ship. And Laurel would kill him either way. Her job was to make sure Teagan didn't make it through this fight alive. He was the mark, and the reward would be the sweetest she'd ever taken.

The ships in the harbor bobbed with the wind pulling at their sides. It was certainly dangerous weather to be sailing in. The sky above them was thick with black clouds, lightning crackling within them.

Laurel sprinted for the ship on the farthest dock, the one with the red sails flapping in the wind.

She heard the pound of boots behind her. The drumbeat of death.

When they hit the wood planks of the dock, Paulo raised his sword and roared.

Laurel roared alongside the scholae at her heels and the three dozen guards behind them.

The men and women on the docks jumped, either abandoning their posts or frantically attempting to finish their duties before Laurel and Paulo descended on them.

Laurel swung her daggers, giving them the quick taste of blood before running past those on the dock.

Assassins jumped down the gangplank, half a dozen coming to meet them.

Paulo pushed in front of Laurel, taking on the first of the assassins— Meg, one of Conley's favorite weapon experts.

Laurel gritted her teeth and took on Ellis, who came second. She knew every one of these faces. Every one of the ugly souls standing between her and Teagan. The scholae swept past her, Mare taking down two— Alf and Landon— and leaving the last pair for Conley and Declan.

They sprinted up the gangplank.

Laurel saw when Paulo's magic left him. He gritted his teeth, his shoulders stiffening. He stabbed his sword into the chest of the closest assassin.

Laurel split off from him, her daggers flying. She just had to get to the hold.

Thunder vibrated across the deck as she raced forward, relying on Paulo's vision to guide her and praying Mare and Conley were right behind her. Her brain tuned out everything but the flex of her muscles and the one chance they had to take down Teagan. She punched one of the assassins square in the nose, making him reel back, then sank her blade into his chest.

Conley swept past her, engaging another of the assassins. He swung his sword, which the assassin dodged.

Mare was there to fill in Conley's movement.

The assassin fell and spun to take on an assassin that brought a dart tube up to his lips. Laurel threw one of the throwing knives from the bandolier at her chest. It sank into the assassin's shoulder, making him miss his shot. Conley finished him off.

Laurel reached the door to the hold first, allowing the dozen guards that had followed behind her to circle them.

Wide eyes in a multitude of bright, gemlike colors looked up at her through the iron grate making up the door. There were dozens of them, all crammed together, their arms linked by iron chains.

Mare slid to her knees next to Laurel, pulling the picks from her pockets. With the door well in hand, Laurel shot to her feet.

Teagan stood at the back of the ship, screaming down at the man on the rudder. His thin face twisted in that raging tyrant way of his. The one he only let out before he was about to kill someone.

Laurel turned back to the assassin with the blow dart. She dug through his pockets until she found an iron key.

The doors to the hold burst open.

"Hurry!" Laurel shouted. She tossed the key to Mare. "All of you need to get off this ship, quick as you can!"

The fae crowded around Mare, their eyes on her key, hungry for the freedom she promised them.

"*One at a time!*" Conley roared over them. He brandished another key and set to quickly unlocking the fae.

Laurel kept the doors open as they poured out. The magic suppressor of the ship kept them from exploding with magic, which would be helpful until they got off the ship.

The deck jerked under Laurel's feet, and she nearly fell into the hold.

Blast it. The ship was already moving.

Twelve minutes.

"Move!" she thundered. Pulling the closest fae out the door and into the rain. "You're going to have to jump."

The fae woman looked back at her and nodded. She took off toward the side of the ship, leaping over the side.

A bellow rang out over the ship.

Laurel looked up and saw Teagan, his face murderous as he met her gaze.

"*They're mine!*" he screeched. He pulled a blade from his side.

Laurel ducked to avoid becoming a pincushion, but he hadn't been aiming at her. The knife sank into the back of the male fae running for the side of the ship. He fell, hitting the deck face down.

The couple of fae behind him scattered.

Laurel fought off one of the assassins who tried to go after the fae, taking him down with a well-placed dagger. She saw a small head of brown hair dart toward the front of the ship.

The little fae boy. The one she'd seen all those months ago, lying on the cold street of Olympia at Luc's feet. The one whose magic had blasted apart the gates of Iatrus Castle.

By the Goddess, he was here. She was going to save him.

Eleven minutes.

One of the assassins broke through the guards and charged at her, an iron dagger in his hand. Laurel sidestepped his swipe at her face and kneed him in the stomach. He gasped as the air flew from his lungs. She stabbed him in the spine and kicked him away from her.

The fae were streaming out of the hold now, each face more desperate than the last. Light erupted in the water behind the ship, their magic bursting out of them as they freed themselves from the magical constraints.

Laurel took out another assassin trying to grab a fae cradling a child in her arms.

Ten minutes.

She looked up, watching for any sign of Paulo or Diana coming out of the cabin area.

An assassin across the deck raised his crossbow.

"Declan!" she shouted, pointing at the sharpshooter as she raced in that direction.

Declan's head of silver hair popped out of the mob of fighters collected at the stairs leading down to the cabins. With a roar, he pulled a hammer from the hand of one of the assassins and threw it.

The assassin got knocked in the chest, having turned to point his crossbow at Laurel when she'd yelled. No one went to her aid. The assassins had never learned to fight as a unit, and it would be their downfall.

Laurel raced across the deck, leaping up and landing a solid two-footed kick on the assassin, sending him sprawling.

She swept up the crossbow.

Someone screamed.

Laurel's head whipped around, and she found one of the fae pointing at the sky ahead of them. Above the storm, hundreds of bolts of red lightning struck the clouds, turning the sky red.

Just like Paulo had said there would be.

The assassin she'd kicked down pulled himself to his feet. She swung the crossbow around and aimed it as his chest, but he wasn't looking at her. He was watching the sky.

"Teagan's leading us all to our deaths." He met her gaze and without another word, he jumped from the side of the ship.

Laurel let the crossbow drop.

Praise the Goddess, something was going right.

Nine minutes.

More of the assassins followed the fae into the water, abandoning their master to his fate. They swore at the crack of red in the sky before them, the rattling thunder from the strikes of electricity high up in the sky.

What they didn't know was that red lightning never moved below the clouds.

Laurel grinned as she pushed back toward the hold, taking down any assassins that decided they wouldn't abandon the ship. When she reached the steps down to the hold, Mare's head popped out, her eyes blinking up at Laurel through the rain.

She brought up her fingers. *Six.*

There were six more fae.

Laurel glanced back up to where the guards were holding the assassins back from going down the stairs into the cabins.

Eight minutes.

She loaded the crossbow and shot one of the assassins that had taken down two of the guards. Without any more bolts, the crossbow was useless, so she threw it and hit another assassin in the head, knocking her sideways and allowing the guard fighting her to finish her off.

The air grew saltier, the impending coast wrapping its fingers around her throat.

There was still time.

She reached the stairs, plunging into the fray and avoiding getting her head chopped off before she could even reach the hallway.

Diana was at one end, her quiver empty. She used the bow as a staff, taking out the assassins and crewmates below deck as they tried to push down the hallway. Three guards helped her.

The door to Teagan's cabin was open, and Paulo carried Aspen out of the room.

Her eyes were bloodshot, and she couldn't seem to track anything with her eyes.

But she was alive.

Laurel sprang toward them, lifting Aspen's eyelids to widen them. She cursed. "She's drugged."

Paulo nodded, his breathing labored from whatever fighting he'd been doing as well as whatever it had taken to get the sealed door open. "We need to get her out of here, but she'll need help swimming."

Laurel drew her daggers. "Just get her off the boat and I'll clear the way for you."

He called for Diana to follow as Laurel raced toward the stairs. The guards at the bottom steps saw her and called for the others at the top to clear the way. By the time she got there, the guards had pushed the assassins back, creating a path for her to race through.

She ran up the steps, daggers swinging as hands scrambled for her and knives flashed past her face. It was a whir of blood and iron. She stopped at the end of the gap, past some of the assassins and gave Paulo an out.

Conley was there a moment later, grabbing Aspen from him.

"Make sure Laurel gets off the ship!" Conley yelled over the pouring rain.

Before Laurel could protest, Conley tucked Aspen close to his chest and ran for the side of the ship, disappearing over the edge. Mare trailed behind him, a fae woman's arm in hand. Mare twisted around, taking a hit from an assassin meant for the fae. A long line of blood opened up along her arm, and she bared her teeth at the assassin before sinking her thin dagger into his neck. Mare held onto the dagger, pulling the fae and the assassin over the side of the ship with her.

Six minutes.

"Laurel!" Paulo shouted, pointing to the front of the ship.

Teagan stood at the bow, a gleaming sword in his hand.

And a brown-haired little fae boy in his arms.

"We have to save him," she said.

Paulo tried to reach for her. "He wasn't in the visions! Laurel!"

But Laurel ignored Paulo's pleas, racing across the deck.

She had to take Teagan out.

Teagan's manic laugh rang out over the ship. "You just can't stop, can you?"

Laurel raced up the steps, slowing at the top step. "Give it up, Teagan. You've lost."

"Only because of *you*! Only because you had to be the masters' little pet. You just had to become Master Schola. And that wasn't even enough!"

Paulo crept up the other set of stairs. Laurel would have missed it if she wasn't expecting him. He tucked himself behind a crate.

Laurel licked the rain from her lips and tightened her grip around her daggers. "I never wanted to be Master Schola."

"Liar! You've been trying to usurp me for years, seducing the other masters and whispering ideas in their heads. How long until the lot of you were ready to kill me just so you could take over Stellatus Hall?"

"I don't know what you're talking about."

Teagan snorted, his face twisted up in rage. "Don't try to play ignorant. You convinced the other masters to name you head of Stellatus Hall. To take *my title*. That's why I had to summon the warlords."

The rain became a distance noise in Laurel's ears. "It was you. You had the hall attacked." Her and Paulo had talked about this possibility but hadn't known why. Had the other masters really been plotting a coup? She hadn't heard anything about it. At least, they'd never approached her about taking Teagan's place.

"I hope every one of those sniveling traitors died slowly." The little boy yowled as Teagan yanked on his matted hair, pulling him closer and setting his sword at his neck. "You've taken *every-thing* from me. I was going to have the world, *the world!* But you just had to keep ruining it all!"

Laurel's grip around her daggers tightened. "Let him go!"

"You want me to let him go?" Teagan asked. "Fine. Fetch."

He threw him.

Not toward the side of the ship.

But the front of it.

Laurel charged forward, what felt like miles between her and the boy as he sailed through the air toward the railing.

Declan appeared out of nowhere, diving for the boy and wrapping one arm around him while grabbing hold of the line hooked to the bow of the ship. He swung around slamming both him and the boy against the bow.

The boy grabbed hold of the bowsprit, wrapping both arms around it.

But Declan couldn't get a grip fast enough.

He disappeared.

Laurel roared, charging forward to look for Declan, but Teagan's sword flashed out of the corner of her eye, and she had to dive to the side to avoid getting skewered.

A streak of color hurtled toward them and Paulo tackled Teagan to the ground.

Laurel's breath stuck in her throat, but she raced for the front of the ship. She swung her legs over the railing, looking down at the water below.

Declan was nowhere to be seen.

She cursed, praying that mule of a man at least had enough stubbornness to outlive falling in front of a ship and getting swept underneath. She shuffled forward, placing both legs around the bowsprit and stretched her arm forward. She wrapped one hand around the boy's wrist.

Four minutes.

He stared at her with wide eyes.

"Let go! I've got you!"

The boy shuddered, but he let go.

Laurel hissed through gritted teeth as her shoulder nearly jerked from its socket. She pulled the young boy, yanking him up.

He met her gaze again, his limbs shaking as he clung to the wooden rail.

Laurel pushed him back onto the ship.

"Over there! Run down the stairs and jump for the side."

He didn't hesitate. He ran for the stairs.

Laurel turned her attention back to Paulo.

Teagan swung at Paulo's head, his sword arching as fast as the lightning above them. Paulo's sword came up to block. Blood ran down the front of his leg, a long slash in his pantleg exposing a slice he'd taken from Teagan's sword.

Laurel reached for her long daggers. Her right sheath was empty.

Shaking her head, she unsheathed her left and pulled her last throwing knife from the sheath at her chest.

Paulo shoved Teagan's sword away with a roar.

He didn't see Teagan's fist.

Paulo fell to the deck, his sword clattering a few steps away from him.

Teagan laughed, raising his sword above his head.

Fate be hanged.

Without even considering what this would bring to pass, Laurel smashed into him.

She miscalculated how far away he was from the edge of the balcony.

Teagan twisted, trying to get his sword up.

The railing broke away under the weight of them.

Teagan's eyes went wide.

Laurel slammed her dagger into his chest.

They landed together on the deck, and something in her leg cracked.

She screamed. By the Goddess, the pain seared through her leg, worse than a cursed stab wound. If her blasted geas didn't kill her, this would. With a groan, she turned her head to the side, blinking away tears. She'd seen a similar future to this.

Three minutes.

Teagan lay only an arm's length away, his icy stare empty as he looked up at the sky. Laurel's dagger stuck out of his chest.

She closed her eyes. He was gone. He wouldn't hurt Aspen ever again.

"Laurel!" Paulo shouted.

She opened her eyes and met his wide gaze. "I can't move!" she shouted back.

"I'm coming!" Paulo flew down the stairs. He skidded to a stop next to her, his gaze darting to the quickly arriving coastline. "We've got to move."

Laurel swallowed, trying to blink back her tears. "Paulo, my leg is useless."

"Up with you," he said, tucking his arms under her knees and waist.

Laurel screamed at the movement but wrapped her arms around him as he hauled her up. He nearly staggered, but she held onto him tighter. As if just wrapping herself around him would stop fate from coming.

"Everyone else is off the ship," he hollered over the rain. "We can make it."

Laurel pressed her cheek against his, her dark hair sticking to the sides of her face from rain and tears.

"It's all right, Paulo." She couldn't help the small smile. Even as her heart raced in her chest, her limbs went weak with relief. "We did it. We saved them. It's all right."

Paulo gritted his teeth, running for the side of the ship.

The land sped by them on either side, stretching farther and farther from one another. They widened toward the sea, as if spreading their arms to release the ship out into the open water. She could see the coast, the rocky shore.

One minute.

Laurel's arms wrapped tightly around his neck, tangling her fingers around the leather string hanging there. "It's going to be all right."

"Stop saying that!" he snapped. "I know it's going to be all right when I get you off this blasted ship and back home. We'll have a good long laugh about it around a pile of your *dolmades* and a full pot of piping-hot tea." He raced through the crates and bodies as fast as his feet could carry him.

Laurel tucked her nose under his jaw, wanting to see and feel nothing but him. "You're going to be all right."

He roared as the ship broke out into the sea.

61

AN UNEXPECTED FATE

Laurel will die. She was always meant to die.

Paulo nearly dropped Laurel as she went completely limp in his arms.

He held onto her and crashed onto his knees against the deck. A gasp cut through his lips as the splintered wood bit into his skin. He tried to push himself up, but the full weight of Laurel in his arms made him slip on the rain-soaked deck.

"Laurel?" He held her to him, her head lolling to the side. This couldn't be happening. It couldn't be happening. He shoved himself up, limping toward the railing a dozen feet away. They just had to jump.

Lightning skittered across the sky above them and thunder boomed only a few moments later.

"*Laurel?*" he demanded. Something in his chest cracked, and it sent him to his knees again. He cradled her head in his hand so he could look into her face.

"Look at me, love. We've got to move, and I can't do this on my own. Come on, just open those angry brown eyes of yours and look at me."

She didn't move. There was no flutter of her eyelids. No twitch of a smirk. No rise or fall of her chest.

"No. No no no no." He pressed her cheek to his chest and wrapped his arms around her again. His entire body shuddered as he pulled her closer, trying to push his warmth into her rapidly cooling skin.

The rain continued to pour down on them, but Paulo couldn't feel it.

He couldn't feel anything.

Not the rain.

Not the cold.

And not the beat of Laurel's heart against his chest.

By the Goddess, he couldn't even feel his own heart. It was a ragged thing trapped in his ribcage, slowly dying as he held Laurel's body against his on the deck of the ship.

The thunder rattled above him, and he turned his face up to the sky.

And he screamed.

He shoved himself to his feet. His throat raw as rain and tears and blood blurred his vision. He stumbled forward, not once stopping until he hit the side of the ship and fell into the churning waves below.

"Get him out of the water."

"Is he breathing?"

"Paulo! Wake up, you stupid idiot, and look at me before I shoot you."

Diana's voice was the thing that brought Paulo out of whatever haze he was in. He coughed, water spewing from his lips. Someone shifted him to the side, and he hacked the water from his lungs.

He was on a beach, rough sand biting into his skin.

A few feet away, a wave crashed into the sand.

His aching chest seized.

He flopped onto his back, trying to get air into his lungs.

"Laurel!" he croaked. "Where's Laurel?"

Diana's face cracked, her eyes filling with tears above him.

"We have her," she said. "We found her first. Paulo. Oh, Paulo, I'm so sorry."

That ache in his chest cracked something inside of him. Darkness crowded the edges of his sight. Goddess take him, it was too much. The gaping hole in his chest was too much. His body shuddered as a sob tore from his throat.

Diana pulled him up to her, wrapping her arms around him as she trembled.

"Diana!" a shout sounded from behind her. "You've got him?"

She lifted her head. "I've got him!" She wrapped her arms tighter around him.

"I've got you, Paulo. Whatever comes next, I've got you."

62

AN UNEXPECTED GRAVE

PAULO WALKED INTO THE CARPENTER'S SHED AT THE CORNER OF THE graveyard. The building had been one of few untouched during the siege. Of course it was. Who wanted a coffin during a war?

He pushed open the door, wincing as his leg smarted.

"Let me," Diana said from beside him. She held the door open as he strode through. The slash on his leg wasn't healing nearly as fast as he would have liked.

He stopped at the table against the wall and pulled the fabric from the coffin that had laid there for almost a year.

The thick canvas fell away.

He'd had it made of oak, but the carpenter had carved laurel leaves all the way around it. In between the leaves, he'd created swirls of filigree to peek out of it, the gold leaf bright against the wood. The carpenter had done a beautiful job, weaving the filigree through the branches of laurel. The lid was almost completely smooth except for a wreath of laurel surrounding the carving of her mask, matching Cal's coffin.

She would have liked that.

Diana grabbed one of the handles, those carved of creamy ivory instead of gold. "Are you sure I can't get someone else to help haul it out?" Paulo shook his head, and she gave a resigned sigh. She scooted the coffin down the table and Paulo grabbed the other end. They carefully walked it out of the shed.

Conley and Declan stood next to where Cal's headstone rested, a new hole dug only a few feet away. Mare set a bouquet of blooms on top of Serene's grave, her headstone not yet finished.

Aspen had flowers in her hand as well. Tears fell down her cheeks as she held them tightly to her stomach, Mater wrapping her arms around her shoulders, her own eyes wet.

At their feet, lay Laurel.

Diana stopped at Laurel's feet, turning as Paulo brought the top around to lay the coffin parallel to the pallet Laurel lay on top of.

Conley and Declan stepped forward, gently taking the corners of the blue blanket under Laurel and lifting her up. They gently set her inside the coffin, tucking the corners of the blanket around her.

When they finished settling her inside, Mater guided Aspen forward and they knelt beside Laurel, settling flowers around her. The bright blooms contrasted against the black of Laurel's long coat and the silver of the daggers against her thighs. Mare had found daggers to replace the ones Laurel had lost on the ship.

Mater got to her feet first, straightening her black skirt.

It wasn't until that day that Paulo truly understood why she continued to wear her mourning colors. He didn't think he'd ever wear another color again.

Aspen finished straightening the flowers, setting a long-stemmed lily in Laurel's hands.

Paulo grasped the knot at the back of his neck.

The lead weight still hung against his chest.

He hadn't taken it off. He'd sworn he would hold onto it until he could put it in her hand.

His magic surged forward.

Laurel, her brown eyes filled with tears as he placed the weight into her palm, a forest of oak trees around them.

He stopped, the breath catching in his throat.

"Paulo?" Diana asked, watching him across the coffin.

Slowly, Paulo dropped his hand from the back of his neck, leaving the knot in place. He looked to Conley. "Will you do the honors?"

Conley grabbed the bucket of nails and the hammer. As with

Cal's and Serene's, he closed the lid over the coffin and pounded eight nails into the rim of it.

Mater stepped out of the way as the rest of them placed the coffin into the freshly dug hole. Paulo grabbed one of the shovels first, driving it into the pile of soil at the head of the grave and spreading the soil over Laurel's coffin. Tears streamed down the sides of his face, but he didn't stop. The others joined him, helping him lay Laurel's body to rest, sealing her in the ground for the Goddess to accept into Her arms.

The hole filled faster than Paulo wanted. It felt like he'd been digging this grave for so long and now that it was filled, he had nothing left. There was nothing else he could do but stare at the mound of dirt that separated him from her.

He clasped the bead hanging underneath his shirt.

The scholae gathered at the foot of the grave, their faces somber as they stared down at the dirt.

Paulo set the shovel down on the ground and joined them. "I believe now is the time, Conley."

Every face turned in his direction, Mare and Declan's included.

Conley rubbed a hand over his bald head. "Before we left Iatrus Castle, Laurel tasked me with a few things, should her death happen."

Aspen covered her mouth with her hand, a sob ripping through her.

Reaching into the breast of his jacket, Conley pulled out Laurel's silver mask and held it out to Aspen. "She asked me to give this to you. She wanted you to know you had the makings of a schola, even if you weren't ready for the responsibility yet. She asked me, that if she wasn't here to do it herself, if I would train you in the oaths, so that when you were ready, you would be able to take them."

Aspen shook her head. "I can't. I don't deserve it."

"Not yet perhaps, but there will be many opportunities to prove yourself when we travel back to the Continent and take back our home. That is, if our master wishes it to be so." He turned to look at Declan.

Declan's face went slack with shock. "What? She named me Master Schola after her?"

Conley nodded. "She realized you were the next one after you revealed Xander as the traitor. She recognized you were the only one of us who would be able to guide us to take the hall back. That you were the only one who would be able to take all of us back to the Continent and rally the rest of the scholae that have fled. She believed in you, Declan."

A single tear dripped down the side of Declan's face, but he wiped it away as quickly as it came. He turned to face the grave and stared down at the mound of dirt he'd helped place there.

"If she thinks we can take back the hall, then that's what we'll do."

Aspen wiped her face with her sleeve. "When do we leave?"

He looked to Paulo.

Paulo did his best to give him a reassuring nod to tell him whatever he chose, Paulo would support him.

Decla turned back to the scholae. "We have some unfinished business here, but once it's done, we'll head for the Continent."

Paulo stood at the sitting room window as he watched the scholae, Aspen included, disappear down the road. He saw Mare turn back, her white hair glowing, and raise her hand in farewell.

They had come to him two weeks after they buried Laurel, letting him know they were ready to rally their order to take back their hall from the hands of warlords. They'd stayed long enough to make sure the fae prisoners had made it to the border and that Iatrus Castle was well on its way to recovery. They could have left if Declan had ordered it, but both Paulo and Aspen had needed the time to lay Laurel to rest. To find their own ways to say goodbye.

Paulo raised his as well, though he doubted Mare could see it.

He let his magic flood him, watching for what their futures held.

Aspen, a silver mask covered in filigree tucked under her hood as she follows Mare down a dark hallway. Declan and Conley, arguing as much as they laugh together. A gathering of scholae, the masks coming and going as quickly as Declan hands out orders. Stellatus Hall, shining with light once again.

Laurel had made the right choice making Declan master. He wouldn't let the scholae get away with anything under his reign and the hall would be far better than it had been before.

An arm slid over his shoulders, and Diana leaned into him. "Even though they nearly got us killed a hundred times over, I think I might miss them."

Paulo reached up to touch the lead weight under his shirt again. "I think I will too."

"Donnie said he's going to see what the kitchen's making for dinner. Do you want to join us?"

Magic pushed at the edges of his mind. It had been doing it since he'd stood at Laurel's grave, picking at him, driving him to insanity.

"No. I have a letter I need to write."

63

AN UNEXPECTED ENDING

SIX MONTHS LATER

PAULO PUSHED THE HEAVY STONE AS IT SWUNG FROM THE ROPES HELD UP
by the lift. "Just a bit more, Jenkins."

Jenkins used the crane out of the back of the cart to move the
hanging stone. Diana stood on the other side of the stone, making
sure it stayed level as the crane shifted. Her blue eyes were still
red-rimmed. They had been all morning, and he'd caught a few
stray tears fall from her chin on the short walk from the castle.

"Right there!" Paulo held the stone still, and Jenkins used the
crank to slowly lower the hunk of granite until it settled right
where the ground had been marked out.

Paulo wiped the sweat from his brow with his sleeve. The
scratch on his exposed forearm from the ropes burned slightly,
but it was worth it. He pulled the ropes from the hook of the crane
and yanked them out from under the rock.

Mater came up next to him, a couple of polishing rags in hand.
They set to rubbing down the stone, wiping away the dust that
had collected from travelling there from the stonemason's shop.
Paulo worked the front while Mater and Diana wiped down the
back. The gray stone glistened in the light, and Paulo made sure
to dig out the little bits of dust that had made its way into the
chiseled face. It had to be perfect. He wouldn't settle for anything
less.

But polishing didn't take long. Mater returned to the cart first, throwing down her rag and grabbing the bouquet of laurel leaves and forget-me-nots. She'd even had a vase crafted to sit in the small slot on the side of the stone. Paulo stood to give her room to put it all together.

It fit perfectly. She would likely make sure it was always full of fresh flowers, just as the stones on either side of it and the one across the graveyard always were.

Taking another full step back, he studied the curling script engraved into the stone.

Here lies
LAUREL FLUMEN
An imperfect sister, masterful cook, and honored hero.
She was watchful. She was focused. She was silent.
May the Goddess receive her with open arms.

Paulo laughed waving at the stone. "She would have thought it so impractical. Would have told us to use the blasted thing to help rebuild the wall." He felt a tear fall from his jaw and wiped it away. How he had any more tears left, he didn't know. He still woke up most mornings with them on his pillow. Waking up to a world without Laurel never truly felt like waking up. Maybe one day it would but not yet.

"I'll write to Aspen," Mater said, tucking her hand into the crook of his elbow. "She'll be happy to know Laurel finally got her headstone."

Aspen had opened communication with Mater two months ago, letting them all know they'd taken Stellatus Hall back from the hands of the warlords and were on their way to rebuilding the assassin order. She'd claimed Declan had become a tyrant, but it seemed to be working out much as Laurel had hoped. He was rebuilding one brick at a time, bringing back the assassins and doing away with Teagan's methods of running things.

Diana leaned her head on Paulo's shoulder. She stayed silent, simply dwelling with him in the moment. They did that often now, sitting in the silence of their thoughts in the same space. Neither of them had healed from the wounds of the war, but eventually, Paulo was hopeful they would. That they would both come to a place where they could flourish.

The three of them stayed in that fashion for what felt like hours but could have only been minutes. Time had ceased to make sense for the past six months. Paulo's magic was spotty at best, looking for reason in a whirlwind of calamity. It seemed everyone was simply living one moment at a time, just as he was.

Jenkins cleared his throat. "I believe the kitchen was planning to have luncheon prepared for your return."

Paulo gave him a faux glare. The valet had made it his sole duty to make sure Paulo ate food until he burst. If he hadn't taken up a regular sparring regimen with Diana, he would likely be busting out of his clothing. The shoulders in all his jackets had already needed to be let out. But he couldn't exactly be angry with the man. Not after all he'd done to make sure Paulo still got up every morning those first couple of weeks.

"Thank you, Jenkins," Mater said sincerely.

Diana lifted her head but didn't stray far from Paulo's side, as if that twin sense told her if she left, he might crumble.

She might be right.

With a deep breath, he allowed himself to turn from the headstone. Allowed himself to let go of that breath, even if it shuddered on its way through his chest. He allowed a few tears to fall. But he didn't crumble. Laurel would tell him to keep walking. He watched his feet, keeping one foot falling in front of the other.

They walked through the open fields separating the castle from the graveyard. Oliver had been right about the fava beans all those months ago. The ground around the castle was covered in them, the sheep happily munching on the beans on one side of the castle while the few farmhands Peter had hired for the spring picked them on the other.

When they reached the front courtyard of Iatrus Castle, Diana stopped. She probably wanted to do a quick run through the forest. There were still rebels running around, and she'd made it her personal mission to take each and every one of them to a magistrate. He looked up to watch her head out, but she still stood in the path, her eyes wide.

He followed her gaze to the front steps of the castle as a lady stepped out from the shadows of the doorway, the sun shining off her auburn hair.

Paulo froze as well, and Mater gasped.

Diana was the first to start running, Paulo just after.

She crashed into Penny hard enough to send them both to the ground.

Paulo reached them a moment later. A reprimand was forming on his lips, but the words died at the peeling laugh bubbling from Penny, who hugged Diana back just as fiercely.

Paulo went to his knees, wrapping his arms around the both of them.

"By the Goddess!" Penny gasped, the laughter slowing but not leaving her voice all the way. "The two of you are even more muscled than the last time I was here! What on Danu's green earth have you been eating?"

Diana laughed, the first boisterous sound out of her in weeks. "Ask Jenkins. The man has been practically force feeding all of us for weeks."

Penny looked past them at where the valet stood. "Perhaps you can send me their menu. I don't think I'd get pummeled near as much during my practices if I was built like an ox."

Paulo could feel the grin stretch across his cheeks. The strain of those muscles from disuse was entirely welcome.

"All right, you two, let Her Majesty stand up." Mater rolled her eyes in feigned exasperation. "You'd think I raised a pair of heathens."

"You did," Paulo and Diana quipped at the same time. They shared a smile as they hauled Penny to her feet.

The High Queen brushed the dust from her purple skirts.

Paulo and Diana folded into identical bows. "Your *Mage-esty,*" they said.

Penny pulled them both back up to standing. "You two are ridiculous."

Paulo straightened, but his eyes caught on a swirling black mass that appeared a few feet from the front door of Iatrus Castle.

Farrah stepped through, her dark eyes wide as she looked at Paulo. "Is that what you're wearing?"

Paulo frowned down at his work clothes. "Yes?"

Penny shook her head. "I haven't told him yet."

"What? You've been here for fifteen minutes and haven't even told him?"

Something in Paulo's heart roared to life as Penny turned back to him. Her emerald eyes glittered with glee.

"You..." He couldn't even form complete words. He couldn't put voice to the little spark of hope that turned into a blazing sun in his bones.

Penny reached into her pocket and pulled out a length of leather cord, the small, lead weight hanging from it. "I got your letter, Paulo. Just this morning, in fact. It's one of the reasons my mother will be raging mad when I show up late for the lunch, she insisted I be in attendance for this afternoon." She took his hand and placed the simple piece of jewelry in his palm.

Paulo couldn't even breathe as the small lead weight settled against his skin.

Penny looked up at him, a few tears gathered at the edges of her lashes. "She told me to tell you that you made a bargain with her, so if you want her to take it, you'd better come give it to her yourself."

Before she let go, he grabbed his arm with her free hand. "If you do this, Paulo, you won't be able to return. The High Council has reinstated Am Fear Liath Mòr to act as guardian over the border alongside those the Goddess has allowed to live within the forest there. But the magic of the Land won't allow you to leave once you arrive. Trust me, I asked when I finished your letter, but to remain with Laurel, there are things that will be required of you. One being that you're to remain in Faerie until the end of your days. I think the Land is testing you in this, as it tested me."

"I know. I know what this will cost and I'm willing to pay it."

She studied him. When she found whatever she'd been looking for in his gaze, she nodded, letting her hands drop.

Paulo exploded into motion. He burst into the castle, Mater calling after him.

He needed to go. He needed to go right now. But there were two things he needed to do first.

He nearly broke his door as it smacked against the wall of his bedroom. He didn't let go of the weight in his hand as he slid to his knees at the side of his bed and grabbed the box out from underneath. He'd saved all her favorite daggers that Conley had let him keep. Her favorite cooking apron from the kitchens. Her poison jacket.

He threw it into his slightly larger trunk along with a few pairs of trousers and his favorite jacket.

Diana skidded to a stop in his doorway. "What on Gaia's green earth, Paulo? You nearly gave Mater a heart attack!"

Paulo clicked his trunk shut and strode through the door, grabbing Diana's hand. "Come on."

She followed behind him, keeping pace with his harried steps. He shouldered open the door to his study and threw the trunk on his desk, sending papers flying in every direction.

"What's going on, Paulo? Why did Penny have Laurel's weight?"

Paulo grabbed the folio of papers hidden at the bottom of his desk drawer. He handed it to Diana. "Here. It's yours."

"What?" Diana opened the leather cover. When she reached about halfway down the first page, her head snapped up. "*What?*"

Paulo grabbed his trunk again. "It's yours. The title, the estate, the council seat, all of it. King Dion already approved it when I sent it to him a couple months ago. Peter will give you all the details. You are now the Marchioness of Delphine. I leave it all in your capable hands."

Diana looked down at the papers again as if they would vanish if she didn't keep staring at them.

But Paulo didn't have time to wait for her to come to her senses. He wrapped her in a one-armed hug. "I love you, Diana. I know you'll do all of us proud."

A sob broke from her chest as she returned his embrace. "I love you too."

Paulo released her and raced for the door.

He found Mater still at the front entrance, her eyes filled with tears. But a smile stretched across her face. Paulo's own tears fell as he dropped the trunk and pulled her into a full embrace.

Mater laughed, the sound filled with joy and sorrow. "Go, my son. Go and be happy."

He pressed a kiss to her cheek. "Thank you, Mater."

She let him go and he turned. Diana made it to the doorway just as Farrah summoned another doorway of shadow.

Penny's smile turned absolutely giddy. "I'll come visit you in six months, Paulo. I expect to find both of you in absolute bliss by the time I get there."

Paulo knelt at her feet, taking her hands in his and kissing them. "Thank you, my friend. I'll never be able to repay you."

Penny laughed, pulling him to his feet. "Oh, I'm sure I can think of something. Now go! Before my mother figures out where I am and rains down her wrath upon everyone for keeping me here."

He didn't need any more encouragement. He hugged Mater, which Diana immediately joined. Stepping away, he sent a nod to Jenkins, who gave him a nod in return. He gave Penny one last wink, and with a laugh that felt brighter than the sun above them, walked straight into the shadows.

When the darkness swallowed him, his chest seized. The light he'd felt vanished, swallowed up by the emptiness around him.

He would die in this darkness. He'd been a fool, and he would meet Laurel in the next life instead of in Faerie where Penny promised she'd be waiting for him.

But then the darkness parted.

He staggered out of the portal, his chest heaving. The black miasma blinked out of existence, leaving him completely alone.

Oak trees soared above his head, their skinny leaves reaching down toward him. Being early spring, the branches should barely be seeing their first leaves, yet these trees were full, as if it were the middle of summer. Light trickled in beams through the canopy, warming the ground beneath his boots. Chunks of gray gravel peppered the ground, though there was plenty of new grass shooting up between the roots of the trees.

Paulo set down his trunk and turned in a slow circle until his eyes were drawn to a certain tree.

A thick oak stood a few paces away. While it looked like the rest of the forest around him, the soil around the oak had been upturned, as if this tree had shot out of the ground and the dirt had been pushed aside to make room for its wide trunk.

Paulo's stomach did a slight flip, and his palm sweated around the lead weight in his hand. He took a step toward it.

Laurel stepped out of the trunk.

His lungs nearly burst as her keen brown eyes— eyes that nearly brought Paulo to his knees— met his. Golden skin with the faintest sheen of green glowed under the shining sun. Her dark hair was pulled back into a simple braid, but a few stray pieces framed her lovely face.

For all the times he'd seen this moment in his head, he could have never prepared himself for what seeing her alive again did to him.

It was like his heart could finally remember how to beat in his chest.

Like that hollow hole inside of him had merely been waiting for this very moment.

He ran to her and she to him, as if the strings of fate tethering them to one another couldn't take the distance anymore. They collided, his arms wrapping around her as hers encircled him. He buried his face in her neck, pulling her to him hard enough that he could feel the rapid beat of her heart against his chest. He couldn't keep his feet under him, and they sank to the ground, his arms still wrapped around her.

He didn't let her go, but he did pull away from her slightly. Her cheeks were wet with tears, and he used his thumb to brush a few from her jaw.

Slowly, he opened his fingers and held out the lead weight. "I believe you dropped this."

Laurel's laugh burst out, the sound as beautiful and carefree as Paulo had ever heard. It was sweeter than Donnie's best wine and brighter than the sun shining on Iatrus Castle.

Two more tears joined the others as Laurel smiled down at the little ball in his hand. She reached up and curled his fingers back over it. "Not mine," she said quietly. Her voice still carried that husky quality, that low tone that he recognized as only hers.

"Are you certain?" he asked. "I could have sworn it was yours."

She shook her head. *Stubborn woman.*

He pressed his forehead to hers. "It's my duty, as a gentleman, to make sure this gets back to its owner."

She shifted, pressing her nose next to his. "As I said, it's not mine. You see, I gave it away, along with my heart, to the most ridiculous man I've ever met. I fell in love with him, and I'm hoping he'll keep the two of them safe for me."

Paulo closed his eyes. "I will. I swear I will for however long you'll trust me to."

He captured her lips with his.

She kissed him back in kind.

Tears fell against both their cheeks, but Paulo couldn't tell if they were his tears or hers. He pulled back just enough to look at her again. To cradle her smiling face in his palms. To see that keen light in her beautiful eyes.

"I love you," he breathed, pressing his forehead to hers.

"I trust you too," she whispered back.

He kissed her again.

"Oh, by the goddess, I thought I wouldn't have to deal with this once I left Crann Mòr."

Paulo broke away and jumped to his feet, positioning himself between Laurel and where the voice came from. His hand strayed to the dagger at his belt.

Hart Carys leaned against a tree a few feet away, his eyes glittering with mirth as he stared down at them.

The press of Laurel's hand on Paulo's arm stopped him from pummeling the man.

"Who are you?" she asked, though Paulo could hear the touch of annoyance in her voice. At least he wasn't the only one put out by the man's appearance.

"Why, I'm Hart, the begrudging babysitters of these people that Queen Penelope has yet to figure out a name for." He pushed himself off the tree and sauntered toward them. "If either of you thought you'd be able to sneak away together and live the rest of your lives in romantic bliss, you've got another thing coming."

Paulo snaked his arm around Laurel's waist. "I think I've earned some romantic bliss."

Hart scoffed. "You think Olympia's great oracle and the Continent's most revered assassin are going to get a day off when there's still rebels to boot out of Faerie and a whole bunch of Aigeans to harass into releasing a prince? Think again."

Laurel straightened, wrapping her arms around Paulo. "What do you want us to do?"

Hart circled them, his eyes narrowing. "The war might be over, but there's work to be done. Are the two of you ready to be thrust into a world of magic? A world of mayhem? A world where the creatures of nightmares and dreams are reality? Where Danu's children walk the earth, and you don't know friend from foe? The land of Faerie is not for the faint of heart. There are challenges yet to come and only the most stalwart will survive."

Paulo leaned toward Laurel. "Do you think he practices that in the mirror every morning?"

Hart whirled on him. "You think this is a joke? You think life in Faerie is going to be easy?"

Paulo turned fully to Laurel. "What do you think?"

Laurel shrugged. "Magic, mayhem, and survival? Sounds like a normal day on this cursed isle to me."

Paulo's cheeks pulled up in a grin, and he turned back to the sputtering man in front of them.

"Well, I suppose we ought to see what fate has in store then." He took Laurel's hand and pressed the back of her fingers against his lips. "Shall we?"

AUTHOR'S NOTE

The tragedy of Apollo and Daphne hit me really hard when I was researching Paulo's character for The Cartographer's War books. There are many ways their story is told throughout history. In the telling by the poet Parthenius, Daphne spurns Apollo simply because she has other goals. Hyginus says it was the goddess Gaia that begged the river god for Daphne's rescue from Apollo. But it was Ovid's account that really sparked my story brain. Apollo, cursed by Cupid's arrow to love Daphne and Daphne cursed to flee from him. What if their love was truly cursed? What would Apollo have done if he'd known their fate from the beginning? Would he have let Daphne run from him, or would he have found a way to save her? And what of Daphne? Would she have spurned him because she had to, or would she have fled from him to save them both from the heartache of their curse?

I like to think that was what truly sparked Paulo and Laurel's story. It was envisioning a love so deep that it wouldn't matter what fate had decided, that love was worth having even if it was doomed. That if Apollo had known Daphne would become a tree, he would do everything to stop it from happening, and Daphne would still become a tree because she was doing it to save the both of them. Now, I'm not claiming to know what either of them really felt while under the influence of their curses, but the romantic in me hopes they would have tried to save each other.

That they would have cared about each other enough to see there was no other way. That tragedy was better for the both of them rather than the unrequited love they would have been cursed with for the rest of their existence.

That's what true love is, isn't it? It's not about the butterflies or the moments of bliss. It isn't only about how they make you happy or comfortable.

True love is about sacrificing your dream for a dream bigger than you could ever make on your own. A dream that transcends happiness. One that transcends death.

It's about finding that one person who you would walk through tragedy with.

Who you would fight for even when the battle rages around you.

Who you would rewrite fate for.

At least, that's what true love is for me.

ACKNOWLEDGMENTS

We're here. We're actually at the end of The Cartographer's War. I almost can't believe it.

Thank you. Yes, YOU! Thank you for reading this book. For going on this crazy journey with Paulo and Laurel. Thank you for letting a piece of them into your life. They changed mine, so I hope they changed yours.

There are several other people I need to thank for this book as well. A book is not the work of one person and so many people's fingerprints mark these pages.

First, Eric and my girls. Seriously, I've said it a million times before, but it only gets truer the more I write: I couldn't do any of this without you. Thank you for being part of my crazy world, for listening to me talk about people that live in my head and for going with me on this crazy adventure. Thank you for putting up with my insanity and the piles of laundry I keep saying I'll fold. Seriously, there are so many heavenly kudos waiting for you.

Thanks also go to my dad. Thank you for telling me to join your writing group five years ago. Can you believe it? It's been five years since we started on this crazy journey. Since I called you with that wacky dream I had, and you told me to write it. I wouldn't be here without that phone call.

I need to thank Tanya Anne Crosby and the team at Oliver-Heber Books. Thank you for making my dream a reality. Thank you, Kate Ward, for making my books better than I ever could on my own and thank you, Sally O'Keef, for making them look so good. I'm so excited for what we have planned next.

Thank you to all my author friends. Thank you, Jeff Wheeler, for your continued encouragement and for not running the other way screaming anytime you see me. Your friendship means the world to me. Thank you, Lindsay Hiller. You're my hero for reading this book before everyone else and telling me how to fix it. Thank you for loving it as much as I did. Thank you to my writing groups! Dad, Robbie, Ben, Tracy, Marci, Aimee, thank you for not kicking me out of the OSAWG group even though I've been so absent while trying to get this book done. Bonnie, Heidi, Natalie, Amber, Marci, Kayla, Lindsay, Tarry, Sally, and Kelsey, thank you for being in my corner. Thank you for cheering me on and not rolling your eyes at how bad I am at keeping up on our text thread. I seriously love each and every one of you and am so excited to read all the books now that this series is over.

Thanks need to go to Tyleah Merino, my shining star of an alpha reader. I'm so excited to snuggle your little girl when I see you next. Thank you for still taking my phone calls and talking me through growing these characters while you've been growing an entire human. Thank you for being my champion.

Thank you, Cauldron Press Designs, for this last cover. It really is a masterpiece. Thank you to the team at Podium for the audiobooks of this series and for bringing my characters to life.

Lastly, thanks go to my Heavenly Father. I wouldn't be on this path without Him and it's through Him and His Son that all things are made possible. They are the ultimate authors of fate and I'm so grateful to have Them writing my story.

ALSO BY ALLISON ANDERSON

Children of Ash

Children of Ash

Son of Steel

The Cartographer's War

The Spring Maiden

The Shadow Lord

The Unseen King

The Unwanted Queen

The Cartographer's War: A Necessary Tragedy

The Seer's Assassin

The Fated Mage

ABOUT THE AUTHOR

Allison Anderson lives her best life as a wife, a mom, a dedicated member of The Church of Jesus Christ of Latter-Day Saints, and a fantasy writer. As a lifelong fantasy nerd, she finds it natural to create stories of her own and you can often find her jotting down new story ideas or talking about dragons. She's spent most of her life across the southwestern United States.

https://www.allisonandersonauthor.com/